Imperfect Pairings

Imperfect Pairings

a novel

JACKIE TOWNSEND

For information about this title or to order other books, contact the publisher at info@ripettapress.com. Download the press kit and/or Book Club Guide at jackietownsend.com.

Library of Congress Control Number: 20139022820
ISBN: 978-0-9837915-2-2
Printed in the United States of America
Cover and Interior design: 1106 Design

Ripetta Press
New York, NY

For our Italian family

"It is fate that I am here," George persisted, "but you can call it Italy if it makes you less unhappy."

—E.M. FORSTER, *A ROOM WITH A VIEW*

"Nothing can be compared to the new life that the discovery of another country provides for a thoughtful person. Although I am still the same I believe to have changed to the bones."

—JOHANN WOLFGANG VON GOETHE, *ITALIAN JOURNEY*

Imperfect Pairings

CHAPTER I

La Mamma

*T*HE WHEELS LIFT OFF the tarmac and suddenly his name is not one syllable but three: Jack, now a melodic Giovanni, as it might be sung in an Italian opera. This is somewhat baffling for Jamie, who until this moment had known him as a man who kept his heritage secured in the vault of his boot-shaped soul. He unleashed a primal craving for pasta every so often, an undecipherable curse word, but otherwise, if Jamie mentioned an Italian restaurant for dinner, he'd redirect the discussion to Chinese or Thai. If an Italian tourist asked him in struggling English for directions on the street, he'd answer in struggling English. He has American friends, at work at least. In fact, when she first met him she'd thought he was American. On his voice mail he sounds American. No Rs are rolled.

Jack is short for John, he tells people. True, but John is Gian in Italian, short for Giovanni, the name she'd discovered

1

on his passport only this evening. This was just before they boarded their Alitalia flight, when the stewardess greeted the Italian couple before them with a "*buona sera e buon viaggio*," and then proceeded to greet Jack with a "Good evening and welcome." *Vaffanculo brutta stronza non vedi che sono italiano pure io* came rumbling through Jamie's inner ear. "*Buona sera signorina*," is what the stewardess then heard, in Giovanni's very polite but make-no-mistake-about-my-identity voice. "*Scusi, scusi, mi scusi*," the goddess clamored. "*Nessun problema*," he assured her, and the two fell into a melodic exchange while Jamie stood there staring because she never heard Jack's voice so natural, so content before.

After the plane levels off and they finish their first glass of business class prosecco (upgrades via Jamie's unused, ever-growing stock of American Express points), the little fight they'd gotten into in the terminal, perhaps their first, is long forgotten. (He had insisted on holding her ticket and passport. "This may be my first trip to Italy, she'd scoffed, "but it's not as if I've never flown before." The weird thing she still can't get over is that she'd given in and handed them to him.) Now their seats are extended far back and Jack/Giovanni is talking more than she's ever known him to, perhaps more than she ever wanted him to, because something about the word great-grandfather makes her sleepy. *Bisnonno* is how they say it in Italian. "Bisnonno made a fortune in steel."

Apparently her affliction crosses languages: she immediately yawns and her eyes fill with water—"must be that all-nighter at work," she says, but Giovanni continues, "He bought Villa Ruffoli in the 1920s as a summer home for his extended family, a way for everyone to convene and escape the city's suffocating heat." *In fact, I should get out my briefcase and start drafting those e-mails.*

"…Bisnonno had four sons…" Something in the fervent rise and fall of his voice, more so than his words, is absorbing her subconscious. Like a dream, snippets are getting through. "…Federico ran sales out of Milan, Peter went to the war, another took over operations in Asti, and my grandfather, Nonno Giacomo, became CEO with headquarters in Torino. There were uncles and second cousins in Milano and Abruzzi, Godparents in Rome…" At one point Jamie has to tell him to go back a couple of generations, because she's lost.

"And this is just my mother's side…" he turns at her and smiles that taunting, alluring smile, and just like that, it's as if he's reached in and touched her heart. "Go on," she tells him.

"I'm boring you."

"Please."

Gazing at their entwined hands, he continues. "There were never less than twenty people at the dinner table. Nonno Giacomo sat at the head, me, the oldest grandchild, to his right, always. It was my job to taste the wine in case it tasted like vinegar." He looks pointedly at Jamie here. "It often tasted like vinegar."

"The meal was chaos, always a plethora of debates going on at once: which cow produced the best cheese, politics I didn't understand, why the farmer screwed up the wine or the cook ruined the chicken; the latest scandals at the company, who was sleeping with whom. Meanwhile, Nonno Giacomo, bored by all this nonsense, entertained himself by doodling on paper napkins that he would pass to me under the table. I'd have to use all my strength not to burst out laughing at some of those sketches of Zia Maddalena's breasts. When the meal was over, my cousin Luca would run around drinking up the dregs of wine left in glasses."

Jack relaxes back in his seat and smiles at a thought.

Or is he frowning? She can never tell.

She orders more prosecco.

Their heads fall together.

"You've never tasted real milk, Jamie. There was no need to leave the property. We had cows and cattle sheds and made our own butter. Live chickens and pigs, too," and when her eyes don't scream with envy, "You've never tasted real pork, Jamie."

"Do I want to?"

"We ate fruit right off the trees: apples, plums, cherries, hazelnuts…"

"Peaches? I love peaches."

"You've never sucked on a real peach, Jamie." And from his eyes she can see that she hasn't.

"We had our own vineyards and made our own wine."

They fall quiet for a time; he remembering it all, Jamie imagining him remembering it all.

"Ah, well," he sighs, and then reaches for his *La Stampa* in the seat back pocket in front of him.

"Ah well what?"

He is closing back up, as he can do. "Jack?"

"It's all gone," he shrugs.

"Gone?"

"Everything."

She clears her throat. "Everything?"

"I still can't believe it."

"Even the cows and the milk?"

"Gone."

"The peach trees?"

"Gone."

"Chickens?"

"Jamie, *basta*, enough."

"What happened?"

"It was a long time ago. I was away in the States at MIT."

"You must know something."

"We're Italian."

"That's not an answer."

His eyebrow goes up. "Have you ever been to Italy?"

"Really Jack, what happened?"

"There was finger pointing…accusations…the war made them rich, and when the war was over, when they had to really manage things, well, the truth came out—they were mis-managing everything. Nonno's brothers blamed him, as CEO. Nonno blamed his sons-in-law—my father and Zio Marco—who then blamed each other. To tell you the truth, I didn't want to know. I didn't really care. I only felt sorry for Nonno Giacomo because he died with nothing. The vast empire of Ruffoli property was sold, and all he had left were some vines, a crumbling villa, and my mother to look after him; the villa's surrounding land had been redeveloped into apartments, and those that weren't sold were piece-mealed off to family members as some paltry kind of inheritance."

He falls silent.

"And your father?"

"Napoli," he says, after a dark moment. "He went back to Napoli."

"So they're divorced?"

"Nonno wrote me a poem the day I left for MIT…" he says, not so much ignoring her question as refusing to acknowledge it. His parents are Catholic, of course they're not divorced. "…It never occurred to me until years later, after the dust had settled and I re-read the poem, how talented he was." He pauses, as if reciting the verse in his mind, and it occurs to Jamie that Jack may have left the wedding invitation, the impulse for this trip, out for her to see on purpose.

He clears his throat of whatever emotion got caught there, and then the plane suddenly roars from below for no apparent reason. They catch and hold eyes in the moment of uncertainty. A flicker of something, fear, could he be afraid, she wonders, and in a gesture that feels apart from her, she reaches out and touches his cheek. Her fingers follow the curve of his jaw and settle on his chin. There is a tiny crevice there, a small crack or fissure, and she spends an abstract moment contemplating this little part of him. Then the roaring subsides, and her hand moves back. She stares at it a moment wondering what just happened, then clambers out of her seat to get her briefcase from the overhead compartment.

"You know what to do?" he says, at last handing her her passport when they arrive in Italy. Without bothering to respond, Jamie takes it and steps into the line for aliens while Giovanni proudly heads off to the line for nationals. This feels odd, because he is the alien, isn't he? It doesn't occur to her until they meet up on the other side again that no, in fact it is she, the frequent flyer who's never traveled outside the States except to Mexico that one time, who is the alien now. The *americana*.

Jack, for his part, is no longer Jack but Giovanni. Jamie must keep reminding herself, as it says so on his passport, and now in his demeanor as well. If he's not at ease in the hapless, chaotic disorder of his native land then he's certainly resigned to it, methodical in his step, knowing exactly what to do and where to go.

Jamie drank too much prosecco on the plane. Is it just her, or are the people here smaller? She actually asks him this in an attempt at humor, for he seems nervous and it's making her nervous. Why is she nervous? She's never had problems meeting the proverbial mother before. Sure, there's going to be a language barrier, but no doubt there's already going to be a language barrier, the one inherent in the relations between any mother and the woman her son brings home, and these thoughts aren't helping Jamie stay calm. By the time she follows Jack out the sliding custom doors, her heart is beating wildly.

A blinding moment, her first in Italy, one in which there are flashing bulbs and wild applause, stylish crowds and sleek architecture. They are in Milan, after all, fashion capital of the world; but the world that then comes to life is in the form of a dreary terminal stinking of burnt coffee and toasted cheese. No crowds, just a few clusters of young Italians wandering around in dark leather and piercings, aimless and self absorbed. They make Jack's mother easy to spot—no, Giovanni's mother—though Giovanni seems to be, for the moment, pretending it is not his mother, this tear-stricken woman leaning so anxiously against the low gate that Jamie fears it might toppled over.

She is pretty, Jamie notices right off, despite the wrinkles and the roundness. Heirlooms cling to her neck and fingers; her skin is golden, her hair a pearlish-gray. Her light features are a northern quality, Jack had informed Jamie with pride on the plane. When Jamie had inquired about his own features—a darker bronze—he'd responded with some foreboding, "My father's from the South."

Cheeks are kissed over and over.

"*Mamma, ma dai, mamma,*" in a tone part revel, part pity, Giovanni at last extracts himself from La Mamma's embrace and motions for Jamie, who steps in. "*La mia fidanzata,*" he says.

Jamie, with a "*Ciao*" stuck in her throat says, "Hello," idiotically.

La Mamma glances at Jack as if for translation, then leans in for those kisses Jamie finds so awkward—which side comes first, how many, exactly. By the time La Mamma steps back to examine this tall ginger woman from head to toe, toe to head, Jamie is blushing in all directions. Some conclusion is made, seemingly, because at once La Mamma takes Jack's arm and the two walk rapidly on, she in her rubber shoes and thick stockings, Jamie trailing in new sandals that keep slipping off her feet.

At one point they turn and ask if she would like to *prendere un caffè* at the airport bar. "I would love to," is her gracious response, hidden beneath a caffeine-desperate smile. And they weren't kidding about the "*prendere*" (to take), because that's essentially what drinking coffee is here. Jack pays at the register, hands his ticket to the barista, and one minute later three tiny cups are sliding along the counter at them. Jack "takes" his, loads sugar into it, and drinks it in one gulp. "*Ancora?*" La Mamma says, also done.

Jamie looks at her thimbleful, thinking, *this will not be enough caffeine.*

"*Sta male?*" La Mamma asks. Is something wrong with her? Yes, there will be, when Jamie soon discovers that there is no lingering or dawdling over coffee in this country.

They move on through the terminal that seems both empty and yet chaotic at the same time. The few present are crowded with their overflowing luggage carts at the elevator bank because one of the lifts is broken, while others seem lost. Jack leads them on a search for the stairs that have gone mysteriously missing. Circling back to the lifts just in time for the doors to magically slide open, they shove on. The ride down is slow and harrowing, what with Jamie's mind still ruminating on Jack's *fidanzata* reference. It sounds perilously close to fiancé, and an alarm has sounded in her head. She and Jack are in no way engaged. In fact, they have been together only two months and she has yet to call them a couple, let alone act like they are headed down some path of commitment.

He had overwhelmed her, certainly. Jamie hadn't expected to fall in love so definitively, to love someone so completely as to make even the word *love* sound ridiculous, and utterly redundant. The only hope now is to keep reminding herself that this is not the first time she's fallen in love. She'd been overwhelmed those other times, too, hadn't she? Love does not give him claim to her soul, after all, and anyway, she has a Partnership to achieve at the firm, money to accumulate, goals and milestones to reach.

Dai, muoversi. Come on, let's go.

It is a tiny Fiat Panda in which Jamie sits squeezed in back with the luggage that won't fit in the trunk. "*Che cosa fai mamma?*" he says after his mother, who has jumped from the car because she forgot to pay the parking ticket.

"*Fidanzata?*" Jamie leans in and whispers in his ear.

"Girlfriend," he responds, pensively looking out for his mother.

"Just checking."

"In Italian it means girlfriend."

"I heard you the first time." She sits back, unsatisfied. Girlfriend doesn't sound right either, but she is too tired to think or talk rationally. The morning haze is like a drug. She is asleep before they exit the parking structure.

A convulsive verbal exchange floats into Jamie's subconscious, intermixed with loud, abrupt silences. The Alps soar past the Fiat window in a gray, misty blur, however faintly. She is awake now, and they are practically hydroplaning on the Autostrada toward Torino, a straight shot of dreary farmland, factories, and lime green gas stations. At A26 they turn off and head toward Alessandria, where the land is at first flat and wet, then jade and undulating. The fog begins to lift, a pink sun overtakes the sky, and the hills grow wavier, a richer green. Clusters of terra cotta emerge on distant hills along with castles and *campanili* that don't seem entirely real, until they get closer, and then they still don't seem real.

La Morra, Barolo, Verduno, Cherasco, Roddi, Grinzane… Signs point crooked arrows in all directions. "Barolo, like the wine?"

"Yes, Jamie."

"I'd said it was orange," she muses.

"Brown."

"Whatever. You fed it to the lamb. I remember that."

He smiles somewhat deliciously at her in the rearview.

"*Che cosa?*" La Mamma wants to know what they are saying to each other.

He'd been braising a lamb shank one night, Jamie thinks back. A few hours in the oven and counting, her entire apartment radiating in its tender, juicy fumes, suddenly Jack grabbed his keys and rushed out the front door. "Now this is a wine," he said twenty minutes later upon his return with a bottle of Barolo. "*Moncrespi*," she said, reading the label.

"*Mon-crrrrrrresss-pi!*" he'd corrected with a vehemence that startled her. She'd asked him if the embellishment was necessary. It's not embellishment, he'd said, it's correct pronunciation, and yes, it's necessary. She'd handed him the bottle opener without further comment, for she'd already had a flogging that day by her client and needed a drink. He opened the bottle while she got out glasses, but instead of pouring her a glass, he'd opened the blazing oven and poured the lamb a glass before setting the bottle aside and insisting she wait for the wine to open up. She studied him, then the wine-soaked lamb, considering a martini. When Jamie wanted something, she often wanted it now; but this man had a way of making her wait, and if he could wait she could wait. An hour later, the lamb done, she'd taken her first real sip, making a conscious effort to understand what she was drinking. She was thirty-two. Maybe it was time.

"It's dry," she'd said.

"Look at the color."

"Brown?"

"Amber," he'd said, gazing into the glass with eyes just as brown, just as amber. It was a haunting look, the one he had turned and given her, the same look exuding from him now, she imagines, as he speeds intently into the distance before him. That look sends her stomach into turmoil, or perhaps it's the road, which has grown narrower and windier. She rolls down the window. The air smells of earth and tar, the sun has gone missing again, and grape vines are everywhere, clinging to the hillsides sweeping up and down all around them. Uninspiring yet pleasant farmhouses and villas are sprinkled among those hills, and Jack is announcing their names, friends or foes, the Crespi Vineyard one of them, as in *Mon-crrrrrrresss-pi!* There don't seem to be any visible markings or signs, no elaborate Napa Valley-styled entrances. Their families go way back, Jack is telling her now, as if she'd understood what he and his mother had been saying. Whose families?

The light dims suddenly; the road levels off with a vibration so jarring Jamie braces her breasts with her forearm as their car bounces over the cobblestones, and Jack is pointing out some-thing seemingly critical. She looks up and around for a castle or a *campanile*—instead it's a newspaper kiosk where he buys his *Gazzetta Dello Sport*. This is the main town, he explains, a curved incline of shops tucked inside stone where the sun apparently can't reach. Only a few locals in coats trudge up the road. Otherwise the place feels barren, cold even though it is June, the beginning of the warm season.

"Bar," she says unconsciously at a lonely shop sign, thinking about a pre-dinner cocktail, but then remembering the airport. Not that kind of bar.

They are winding again, ascending. The road is narrowing farther, as if that were possible, and is generously lined with trees and hedges. Jack pulls over to let a car coming from the opposite direction pass. A few more turns and they are confronted by an iron gate with a rusted Villa Ruffoli emblem dangling off the front. Jack gets out of the car to straighten the emblem and type in the code, then hops back in, grips the steering wheel and mumbles in Italian while the gate swings too slowly open.

Jamie can't help thinking back to how little she knows Jack, or Giovanni, or whatever his name is, and this place he calls home. Back in San Francisco, outside of their time together, their lives remain distinct and separate. They don't probe into each other's pasts or origins and make it a point not to cross paths at work. He is a senior engineer at L-3, and she is a consultant for Norwest Aerospace, which is in the process of acquiring L-3. Jamie is in charge of the financial integration of the two entities, and although the merging of the engineering operations, which includes Jack's group, is her peer's responsibility, her relationship with Jack is still a serious no-no.

She's not sure how she let it happen. They'd met at a bar where both firms were celebrating the project kickoff, a get-to-know-each-other kind of event. She'd spotted him the same moment he'd spotted her, in what became an other-worldly sensation, as if some foreign, intoxicating gas had filled the air. That's what it was, she'd had to stop and check herself, a purely chemical sensation. It had attacked all organs save her mind, which was still intact apparently, because she could read right through his unreadable expression; the frown that wasn't a frown at all, but a smile, one that seemed, if she wasn't mistaken, to be meant only for her. He was tall, the supple leather of his jacket seamless with the skin on his neck and face, as if his features had been carved from some rare, precious stone.

Walk away. The rejection will hurt. (In her experience with handsome men, they tended to stay clear of light freckles and red hair.) Anyway, none of this mattered, because it was against firm policy to date a client, and Jamie was a play-by-the-rules gal; but after a couple of drinks, lo and behold, there she was letting her arm brush softly against his, accidentally. When they finally did get a conversation going he didn't laugh at her sarcasm; he could only stare at her with an odd sort of wonder as she nervously rambled on. Her belligerent American co-workers thought him snobbish and aloof, but she didn't know what to think of him. He was quiet and intense, had no trace of an accent, and it didn't occur to her that he was a foreigner. Not until a week later, that is, when he'd invited people over to his apartment for the European Champions League game. Jamie was the only guest without an H-1 visa or second language; not to mention that her passport had only one stamp on it. She'd sat and watched, but didn't understand the game's nuances. The wild adrenaline rush of everyone standing up after sixty-five minutes and screaming, "Gooooaaaaallllll!!" at one p.m. on a workday, had been a complete and utter revelation.

Theirs is an unspoken agreement, she reminds herself now, as Jack…Giovanni squeezes the car through the narrow roadway, to lay no claims upon each other. And anyway, apparently there's no longer anything to claim, as he had explained to Jamie on the plane, though he never did elaborate on the bankruptcy, and his manner in that moment had been so intense that Jamie isn't sure she ever wants him to. All he could say was that Villa Ruffoli is not in any way what it once was, and that is the reason why he has not, in the decade since, returned to the place he once called home.

CHAPTER 2

Villa Ruffoli

A SUBDIVISION OF UNAESTHETIC, water soiled apartment complexes cascade up what once might have been a luscious hill. Telephone wires and hanging laundry further entangle the view. La Mamma is pointing out where respective family members have settled now, post bankruptcy, and Giovanni is growing tenser with each passing complex. At last the road dead ends into a fence overgrown with capricious foliage. Jamie extracts herself from the car and proceeds to balance herself on the steep driveway. When she does get hold of her stance, a bell clamors so loud, it almost knocks her over.

"La Mamma was married there," Giovanni says, looking up.

Jamie thought they were already up as far as one could go, but no, she follows Jack's gaze to a tranquil little church looming just above their heads.

"It used to be the Chiesa Ruffoli," he says, though it is La Mamma who is speaking; Giovanni is translating. "Her parents and brothers were married there too." He speaks absently, his gaze having moved to the dilapidated field beside the church.

"And there's where you played soccer?"

"Football," he corrects her.

"Next to God."

"Absolutely."

Two setters come charging up at them from behind the gate. Giovanni yells at the dogs in Italian and someone yells back. It is Luca, coming after the dogs. Jack and he are both yelling at the dogs now, as well as at each other, as Luca grabs their collars, pulls them off the gate, and squeezes through. He makes to give Giovanni a hug, but then turns at the last moment and hugs Jamie instead. "*La rossa,*" (Red) he beams, and she has no chance to prepare for his kisses, both checks, always both, when she can barely manage the one. "My cousin hides you," he adds in a thick accent with piercing eyes.

Luca is Jack's cousin, his wedding the occasion for this visit. "This guy here…" he pinches Jack's cheek with his knuckles. "He's so stubborn."

Jack jerks his head back, "*Non rompere le palle,*" Don't be such a pain, he says, fighting a smile.

"You speak English," Jamie tells Luca, as if he might not know.

"I have many talents," he assures her.

For Giovanni, however, the English language no longer exists. He and Luca fall into a gesticulating verbal exchange. It takes Jamie a good minute to settle into the idea that she doesn't understand what they are saying, that all she can offer are ignorant smiles, the equivalent of a one-year-old. There is a sensory understanding, though, like the deep warmth and affection flowing between these men; they share their dark eyes, but otherwise look and act nothing like each other. Luca's body is sturdy and muscular, his hair golden from the sun and tied in a ponytail, while Jack is almost absurdly tall for this country, dark haired, and, according to his mother, far too thin!

Luca's arm is draped around La Mamma's shoulders now, and while his gaze on Jack remains amused and playful, hers remains proud and tragic. "A son must see his mother," Luca admonishes Jamie, as if Jack's absence were all her fault; as if she had some control over him, as if she wanted some control over him. "He has abandoned us," Luca goes on, and Jamie wonders if he has spoken correctly. She searches Giovanni's eyes to find out, but his gaze has moved off fleetingly, as has La Mamma's.

The conversation among the three of them grows heated now. A curt and low *vaffanculo* emits here or there, which La Mamma is quick to chastise. Jamie recognizes the expletive from the Sunday morning football games Jack watches religiously on RAI TV, usually while she is working in the other room. The tumbling succession of words make her dizzy suddenly, or perhaps it's the angled road she has been bracing herself on while proceeding to listen as if she understands. She wants to understand, she is all about understanding. In fact, there is some mild assumption that she is understanding, until Jack finally makes a translation for her, one word: "lunch," which is not at all what she'd expected him to say. It's all she can do to smile, sort of, because she'd thought they'd been discussing global warming or the war on terror or some other global crisis, what with all the hand waving going on.

Her stomach growls then, and she thinks, well…anyway… above all else, I am starving. At least hunger crosses borders, and it's this precise moment that Jack reaches up and picks something from the tree above their heads. He holds it out for her in his cupped hands as if in it he is offering her a taste of his secrets. She examines it tentatively, then looks up at him, helpless—some kind of rotting nut? "Fig," he says, breaking it open with his thumbs.

The original structure of Villa Ruffoli still exists, Giovanni explains to her as they enter through the gate and maneuver down the steep gravel driveway with La Mamma and Luca holding the dogs by their collars. A faded pink dome pokes out behind an overgrown magnolia tree, but otherwise the structure is masked by thick ivy, half dead vines, and overgrown bougainvillea.

"So it's not all gone," Jamie says.

"It may as well be."

They duck through a thick wooden door that hangs open at an angle. "You're sure it won't fall down?"

"I hope not," he says, leading her through an archway that opens up into a large courtyard. The courtyard foundation is a pattern of swirling pebbles, its frame an aged balustrade adorned with statues whose heads or arms are missing. Luca goes and chains the dogs up to an old, unused well. Behind them stands the villa's backside; faded pink with trimmings that were presumably once white, green shutters closed over the windows, façade balconies. The view before them opens up to the dropping hillside, a dilapidated tennis court, a verdant forest speckled with more of those ugly apartments.

"Wasn't that Zio Marco's apartment?" Jack, dazed and confused, is pointing down the hill.

inside

elsew
strai
whe

then
The
for

They maneuver around the dogs
neath another stone archway. "Thi
Giovanni says. Jamie is careful
floors as she follows them th
They pass little alcoves, n
high-ceilinged rooms
niture. "Only a few
damage to the r
says, "and th
the retaini
La Ma
kin

"And the Romanians."

"*Teste di cazzo.*"

She glances around, finding it difficult to believe that this quiet spot under that tranquil church could be dangerous.

"The villa itself is a historic landmark…"

"*Grazie a zio,*" says Luca, lifting his eyes to the heavens, and Jack explains to Jamie that it was Zio Marco who got them the landmark status, though no one ever asked how he'd actually done it.

"In Italy there are some things better not to know."

Jamie is still confused on who Zio Marco is, exactly.

"The husband of my mother's sister," Jack clarifies. "*Zio* means uncle. And what the status means is that no one can ever tear the Villa down. If only Zio Marco had not hired those incompetent developers, *che cazzo*, they really did a job on this land, eh Luca?"

"*Mah,*" Luca flips a hand in the air. "What's done is done."

and pass inside, under-
was the service entrance,"
not to trip on the undulating
rough a series of dark corridors.
oks, crannies, and then some larger,
stuffed with heavy, cloth-covered fur-
rooms are livable now because of the hail
of that no one has the money to fix," Luca
roots of the magnolia tree have grown through
g wall." He shrugs. "But I make the stove burn for
mma, and keep the water running because this is the
of godchild I am. I must do all Giovanni's work because
e is not here."

The chandeliers have cobwebs. Cracks run through the
stucco. Dark, tragic oil paintings cover the walls in ornate,
gilded frames. In one hall near the kitchen there is a series of
watercolors Giovanni pauses to examine. "Nonno Giacomo
painted these." He tells her that they represent what this place
once looked like. Color, light, life—they don't match the reality that surrounds Jamie now, as she moves closer to examine
them herself. As she does, her hair falls against Jack's shoulder,
sending a tingling sensation up her neck, and down his, apparently, for he turns and searches her eyes; their lips brush. "You
smell like that fig," she whispers.

He reaches in to his pocket. "Don't tell anyone," he whispers
back, showing her the handful he's got there.

Luca leads Jamie and Jack up a staircase to an expansive,
square floor framed by an inner balcony. This used to be the
children's quarters, Jack tells Jamie, but it's where La Mamma
stays now. "She is happy here," Luca assures Jack, eyeing his
cousin intently as they pass her room to enter his, next door.
Jack's boyhood room, Jamie gathers, by the boyhood looks of it.

Luca deposits Jack's bag and then retreats back by the doorway.

Giovanni is looking around the room.

"She keeps it ready for you," Luca adds.

Jack's back is to them now and though Jamie can't see his expression, it occurs to her that his possessions might be just as he'd left them ten years ago. Jamie is stunned. The room she grew up in was repurposed the day after she left for college. She has no idea what has happened to her childhood things, let alone her childhood bed. By the looks of this one, it must have been Jack's.

Luca disappears with a "*Ci vediamo all'una*," See you at one o'clock, and Jamie goes over to test the mattress. Her butt has barely brushed the surface of it when La Mamma rushes in, picks up Jamie's suitcase, and instructs her to follow. They ascend another, narrower flight of stairs to a tiny, after-thought of a room with a low, angled ceiling where she can hear water trickling from somewhere. The wet nurse slept here, Jack tells her, taking Jamie's suitcase from La Mamma and laying it in a corner. It is Giorgio's room now. Giorgio, Jack's father, will be returning to live at the villa soon. La Mamma implores Jack to explain this to Jamie, which he does with a few cryptic, ambiguous words, for it's a subject he will not elaborate on, ever, his tone says.

Giorgio must be small is Jamie's only thought after they leave her with some time to freshen up before lunch. She has to crouch to move around. The furniture appears doll-sized; a child-sized bed, a tiny stool before the tiny vanity that holds two tiny linen towels. Even the window is tiny, cut out of the ceiling to provide the only light. She is cracking it open to let the must out and the air in when it finally hits her that she and Jack will be sleeping in separate rooms on separate floors. He'd not mentioned this part of the arrangement, a disparity that is dwarfed by the sudden reappearance of that church bell tower in her vision, its position from this window an ominous leaping distance away.

She goes to her suitcase and searches for something to wear amongst the blacks, browns, and muted colors that make up the bulk of her wardrobe. Slipping on jeans and a gray sweater, she grabs her toiletries and heads back down to the second level where there is a bathroom whose door locks with an ancient key. The tub is curtainless, a nozzle hangs over a low bar, and it is unclear how to bathe without soaking the room. Jamie decides to wash her face in scalding water at the sink instead (she'll learn quickly that "c" stands for *calda*—hot, not cold). After brushing her teeth and putting on just enough makeup to make it look like she's not wearing makeup, she sneaks into Jack's room across the hall. "Do you guys really use that thing?"

He has not changed or freshened up or unpacked.

"You know," she stammers. "That bowl…"

"It's called a bidet."

"You really use it?"

"Yes, Jamie. We use it," he says in that toying monotone; he is preoccupied with a large book he's got open on his lap.

Jamie crawls in behind him on the thin mattress.

The 1982 World Cup Champions, he shows her the hard cover.

"The beds are so tiny."

"Welcome to Italy."

Her feet dangle over the foot board and she can't imagine how Jack, at six-foot-two, will manage to sleep unless he's at an angle. It's three a.m. in San Francisco; her body feels like lead and the urge to sleep is overwhelming. "At least you can stand upright," she yawns, as he does just that to go peruse more of his childhood belongings. She watches him for a while, intent, contemplative.

He extracts a poster from a tube, unrolls it, and comes over and sits gently back down beside her on the bed, examining it. "My Saint's Day," he announces, frowning, smiling, and then frowning again. He holds it out for her to see. It looks like an ad for that Fellini movie he'd insisted she watch with him, and she sits up and sighs her head onto his shoulder.

"You have a whole saint's day, with a parade and everything?"

His face softens, and she examines not so much the poster but his boy-like expression.

"Everybody does," he whispers, tracing a scent on her neck, if only to hide the depth of his nostalgia. He knows it will confuse her, even scare her, for she has always laid claim upon her own lack of such an emotion, what for her holds no purpose. His caress begins to tickle, and she can't help but giggle and squirm. But he won't stop. He won't let her see his face. *Look at me,* she wants to say, struggling to free herself. *I want to see if this boy is really you.* But no words come from her, and at last he does stop, and she nestles her face into his chest with a need to dissolve underneath his skin with those unsaid words, and hide there forever.

There is a noise in the hall and Jack abruptly stands, leaving her to fall over. He seems out of sorts, uncomfortable with her in his childhood room, lying on his childhood bed, and she wonders if he's ever even had a girl in here before. Which reminds her, they are not kids. "Separate rooms?" She props herself up on one elbow and asks at last. She and Jack have slept in the same bed every night since that Champions League game, and the thought of them not entangled in the same sheets is well, well…something she refuses to admit. "We're over thirty, Jack. What's the big deal if we sleep in the same room?"

Jack rolls the poster back up, inserts it carefully inside its tube, and then sets the tube in the corner.

"This is the twentieth century, after all. I get the religion thing, but…"

"No," he says pointedly. "You don't."

There is a pause. "Don't what?"

"Get the religion thing."

She refrains from saying, what's to get? "Then explain it to me."

He doesn't.

"Can't we just be who we are?" Of course they can't. It was just something to say, to make him react, but then she sees that he's long gone from her now. He's kneeling over an antique chest he's just broken open, and she must cover her mouth as the stench of mothballs compounds in the air with each wool sweater he extracts. Each sweater is thicker than the last, each one more cherished—Jack detailing the history of to whom it originally belonged centuries ago, who knitted it or from which store it was purchased, how it came to be in his possession.

He stands up and slips one on—thick, fuzzy, hazel. "It was Nonno Giacomo's," he says, holding out his arms to examine the sleeves. He looks at her. "What do you think?"

She bites her lip.

"You don't like it?"

"I didn't say that."

"How could you not like it?"

"I like it," she lies.

He takes off the sweater, folds it carefully, and sets it back in the chest. Watching him, she gets this foreboding sense. Was coming a mistake? It had been her idea. What had possessed her to think so optimistically? She drops her head back on the pillow whose skeletal feathers poke at her skull, and tries to remember. She had suggested it rather flippantly, but only because she'd expected him to reject the idea outright, as she would have done had he suggested coming home to meet her family with her.

It was a month ago that Jack had received Luca's wedding invitation in the mail, a simple, folded card printed with elegant cursive writing, distinctly foreign, not because it was in Italian, but because the writing crossed over the fold. Jack had left it lying on his kitchen table and she'd felt, she wasn't sure really, vulnerable that day maybe.

That morning, Donald, the Managing Partner of her group, had called Jamie into his office to announce that she was being groomed for partner. This was no surprise, it's what she had worked very hard for, and they immediately started mapping out a strategy. Ultimately Donald would have to sell her to the Board, and he wanted no uncertainty. Revenues, client references, and peer reviews would all be critical. By next year she must be ready to present her case.

Thirty-two was relatively young, but the firm needed women partners, Donald wasn't shy to say. Jamie wasn't shy to accept. If being a woman was what it took, then so be it. This is why instead of relationships, she had an MBA and a CFA. She descended from generations of career women; her great-grandmother had been a nurse, her grandmother a teacher, her mother a prominent businesswoman, and her older sister is a lawyer for the Fed. Self-sufficiency is in Jamie's DNA.

So then why had she stood staring at that wedding invitation with her heart in her throat and fear running through her veins? Why had tears stung her eyes so uncontrollably?

"I'm glad you came," he says, as if hearing her thoughts and bringing her back to the present.

"Are you?" she asks, just as the church bells clamor, which sets the dogs off howling. "Oh my God."

The door slams open. Jamie bolts upright on the bed, feeling childishly caught as La Mamma enters spewing Italian. She goes directly over to Giovanni, where he's been moving clothes from his suitcase into a dresser drawer, and stands there expectantly. Her words sound garbled and rambling, until Jack hands her a plastic bag and she goes quiet examining its contents—some underwear, a t-shirt, a dress shirt. She puts them back in the bag, not entirely satisfied, until Jack turns to Jamie and says, "She wants to know if you have anything for her to wash or sew."

Seriously? Is Jamie's only thought as she glances from him to La Mamma back to him and discovers that yes, they are serious. "I just got here."

His face says that that is not an answer.

"Tell her that's very kind, but I'm thirty-two. I've been doing my own laundry since I was eight. If she can just show me the machine…"

"Jamie," he stops her. "It doesn't work like that here."

CHAPTER 3

Il Primo Piatto

THE KITCHEN IS TUCKED INSIDE a brick archway in some corner off the villa's first floor, a place Jamie probably couldn't find again by herself. It is too small for the number of bodies and the flurry of activity taking place there. Wood burns in an open fireplace in one corner. There is no counter space, just a rickety wood table, an ancient stove with only two burners, and a tiny icebox.

Giovanni introduces Jamie to the plethora of women, and in all the kissing and examination of her apparel Jamie can't remember which name belongs to whom, except the one they have for her, courtesy of Luca; "*La rossa,*" Zia Claudia calls her in a raspy, frog-like voice. Zia Claudia is the mother of Luca and she is gazing intently at Jamie's red mane.

"You like Villa Ruffoli?" Zia Maddalena steps in, the wife of Zio Marco and the daughter of Federico, Giovanni reminds

Jamie. But Jamie has forgotten who Federico is, or was, and the strain must show on her face. "He is tired, no?" Zia Claudia asks Giovanni.

"*She* is tired," Zia Maddalena admonishes Zia Claudia, who giggles.

"Do you like Italy?" "We hope you will like Italy very much," the women take turns saying.

"The *zie* (aunts) want to know if you like Italy," Giovanni repeats after Jamie still hasn't responded. *I just got here* is all she can think, nodding and smiling.

La Mamma, working at the counter, insists Giovanni help her roll the *arrosto farcito* as if she were helpless without him, but the stolid, determined woman seems anything but helpless. The sleeves of her dress are pushed up to reveal strong arms and hardened hands. Though her hair is falling out of her bun, she wears her entitlement proudly, if not by her unflinching demeanor then by her jewelry; she might be wearing every stone she owns, the matriarch of this brood now complete, or almost complete, with Giovanni's presence.

After scouring his hands at the sink Giovanni is now before the *arrosto,* looking like a doctor about to perform surgery. He is going over the ingredients his mother has layered over the thin slab of meat— "...pancetta, garlic, oregano, parmigiano, rosemary...*perche' senza salame mamma?*" Jack cries out suddenly, as if everything is at once ruined. "*Dove' il salame?*"

La Mamma makes an imploring, defensive response.

Jack sighs and they proceed, their four hands working in unison, she holding the rolled up meat closed while Jack ties it with string. Their expressions are easy; relaxed in the familiarity of this cooking process that they have shared a thousand times, as if Giovanni had never left, as if he'd never for one day or one moment been anything but hers.

Luca pulls a wide-bodied, Medusa-haired Antonia into his arms. She's been at the table making pasta by hand and is covered in flour. *"Antonia, carissima,"* he sings, palming both hands to his heart. The women moan and roll their eyes. *Ma dai, Luca.* Jamie and Antonia exchange kisses and surrendering looks. Like La Mamma, Antonia speaks not a word of English, so they can't even pretend to communicate except for one mutually relieved expression, Thank God. It's almost easier this way.

"Agnolotti!" Giovanni roars upon discovery of *il primo piatto.* He picks up a perfectly imperfect little square of pasta and holds it to his nose, then to Jamie's. His eyes are begging her to guess what spice is inside, a response he doesn't wait for. "Nutmeg." He is practically giddy.

"Antonia wanted to make polenta, but I say no!" Luca beams. "We make the *agnolotti* in honor of my famous cousin from America!"

"I love ravioli," Jamie offers, which sends the room into silence.

Giovanni squares himself to her. "Let's be clear, Jamie," he says, waving his hands together in prayer. "These are NOT ravioli. These are *a-gno-lo-tti,"* he enunciates each syllable, "a specialty of *Piemonte*—veal, pork sausage, egg, parmigiano cheese, nutmeg, parsley, the filling is always the same." The muscle in his jaw is pulsating. "Repeat after me, Jamie; these are not ravioli."

Now everyone is talking again and Jamie doesn't know who to listen to. A young woman appears in the doorway, out of breath, cradling something in her long, kimono-like blouse. *"Dove vai?"* Where have you been? Zia Maddalena cries. Her name is Simona, Zia Maddalena's daughter, and she's been in the garden picking plums, which she proceeds to dump onto the wood table. One tumbles onto the floor.

"*Via Simona, fuori,*" Go on Simona, out, Giovanni jokingly deplores, and everyone seems to be in agreement.

"Simona is not allowed in the kitchen," Luca tells Jamie. "She is dangerous with sharp objects."

"*Non e' vero!*" Simona cries. That's not true!

"Which is ironic because she's a sculptor," Giovanni adds.

"Perhaps not so good a sculptor is my cousin," Luca says. "You must see the statues of the four seasons!"

Simona shoves Luca playfully. She has emerald eyes, bronze curls, and a rapturous smile immune to her cousins' abuse. She wears that kimono over jeans and a cascade of eclectic beads with a tiny, gold cross dangling among them. Jamie puts her hands to her own neck, conscious of its bareness. The muted color of her clothes and her lack of accessories suddenly make her feel plain and dull. She hadn't expected the casual elegance of these Italian women, their petite, stunning features and gorgeous, if not always naturally, golden skin. She admires their colorful nature and stylish dress, but it's the warmth they embody that's overwhelming. Individually, collectively, they are beaming with inner warmth.

The only exception is La Mamma, who is presently demanding that Jamie do something about the tray cart on wheels stacked with antique china, polished silver, ancient linen, pitchers of water and oil, and tiny crystal glasses. Simona and Jamie must stop idle chatter and get to the task of setting the table, which means rolling the wobbly cart through and around the villa's corridors, nooks, and crannies, over undulating stone floors, to the outside veranda overgrown with weeds and wildflowers. Jamie looks with desperation at Giovanni. *Do not leave me,* her eyes plead. *You're alright,* his eyes muse back, and then he and Luca are off to find their uncle in the garden, smoking a Toscano.

The rattling is unbearable. For sure one of these precious crystal heirlooms will break, especially with Simona giggling the entire way at Jamie's petrified expression. The girl is paying no attention at all to the protruding doorway crevices, but at last they arrive, everything intact. The windows of the veranda have been cast open, exposing a room full of warmth and sun. Ferns and flowers hang from the ceiling; a cactus spreads up one wall and down another. "Are these them?" Jamie asks about the statues adorning each corner.

Simona frowns at them. "They are not very good I am afraid. They are the joke of my family." She begins to set the table, putting out dishes and utensils. Jamie watches her, unsure about what goes where—the knives right, the forks left, the tiny spoon up top, water glass, grissini, chunks of bread, personalized napkins identified by oddly shaped holders. This way the linen cloths can stay with their owners for more than one meal before washing and ironing is required. Simona hands Jamie her napkin for the week. It's holder is goat shaped, and used to be Giorgio's. Jamie examines its curled horns, then sets it down. She has yet in her life to set a table with real thought of proper etiquette. Sensing Jamie's angst, Simona starts placing forks on the wrong sides of plates and strewing the napkins about haphazardly. Her mind is on other things, her whimsical gestures say, like this American woman before her. She wants to know all about what Jamie does and how she lives and what the great city of San Francisco is like.

"Foggy," Jamie replies.

"*Ah, si, e' vero!*" Simona gasps. "*La nebbia, si.* Here we are not so different."

Jamie pretends to understand. "I am only rarely in San Francisco. I am mostly on a plane, traveling somewhere else."

With this confession Simona takes Jamie's arm and leads her out a glass door into the garden that is unkempt. They walk far off to one side, under a trellis tangled with dead vines.

"You are very smart?" Simona asks, lighting a cigarette.

"I work hard," Jamie offers, trying not to notice the old woman staring down at them from a balcony. "There's a difference."

"You are modest, I think."

"And you? Are you a good artist?" It feels odd to ask the question. In America, if there is a good or bad, a beautiful or ugly, certainly we don't talk about it directly. Jamie would never tell Simona that her statues were *brutte,* as Luca had.

"I will go to art school in Paris for the summer."

"That's wonderful."

"I want to travel the world," Simona explains. "Like you."

"Not like me, I hope. I only travel to places like Arizona, Seattle, and Los Angeles. Where the aerospace industry is, I go."

"Ah, but Arizona! The Grand Canyon. *E' bellissimo, no?*"

"So they say."

"You've not seen this place?"

"Anyway, I would prefer Hong Kong."

"I'd like to go to Bangkok. Someday you and I will meet in Bangkok!"

Jamie laughs. This is hard to imagine.

"'*Matta da legare.*' It is the saying of my parents. 'She is so crazy, we have to tie her up.'"

"My family couldn't wait for me to leave," Jamie finds herself confiding, much to her surprise. Simona is so comfortable with herself, so free about sharing her dreams, she puts Jamie strangely at ease.

"Nobody leaves Italy," Simona says, a hint of mockery in her tone. "Italians love Italy. You are crazy to leave Italy."

"And Jack?"

Simona smiles at the sound of her cousin's American name.

"Giovanni, I should say."

"Ah yes, Jack, The Chosen One!" Simona takes a drag off her cigarette. "The rest of us cousins are but his poor servants."

Jamie tries to read her sarcasm, if that's what it is. "Luca says Giovanni abandoned you?"

Simona exhales, "Poor Luca. He has no understanding. I understand. Why should Giovanni come back?"

"Understand?"

"Giovanni has not told you?"

"He's told me about the orchards and the vineyards and the fresh milk I will never know."

"But he does not tell you about why we call him The Chosen One?" Simona seems genuinely shocked.

Jamie looks at her strangely.

"Oh, it is a very tragic story." Her eyes have a gleam. Jamie can't tell if she is serious.

Caterina, Luca's thirteen-year old sister, suddenly comes out to the garden and joins them. She is taller than Simona, with big bones and Luca's blond curls.

"Say something in English," Simona demands, linking the girl's arm in hers.

"Hi," Caterina says.

"*Ho detto a Jamie quant' e' brutto Giovanni,*" Simona informs her, and Caterina laughs, some inside joke, "*E anche cattivo.*"

"You speak of the great cousin in America!" Luca appears from behind a bush, in hunt for one of Simona's cigarettes. She gives him her pack from which he takes two, and then he turns so Jamie can examine his profile. "I was always the handsome one."

"Giovanni says you were the wild one," Jamie offers.

"Many, many girls," he says, smiling widely.

"Lots of trouble with Luca before Giovanni left," Simona adds.

"What trouble?" Luca demands. "I make wine. How is this trouble?"

Caterina grabs his ponytail and pretends to cut it off. "*Sei un cane,*" she says. Everyone keeps saying this about Luca, *sei un cane.* He looks like a dog, apparently. He must cut his hair before the wedding next weekend or Antonia won't marry him.

"Ah, but my Antonia is a real girl," Luca purrs. "I will do anything for Antonia."

"Antonia is good for Luca," Simona agrees.

"For Antonia I will give up my vines and sell tires." There is a hint of resignation in his voice that Caterina doesn't seem to like. She speaks scoldingly, and Simona translates for Jamie. "She asks Luca how he plans to sell tires when he won't even sell Barolo to someone he doesn't like."

"America is good for Giovanni, no?" Luca asks Jamie, who is thrown by the question. She averts her gaze to the ash burning down his cigarette, wondering if they realize how little she knows this Giovanni person. To her he is Jack: stoic, pointed; a talented, passionate design engineer with a strong future at Norwest post-merger with L-3.

There have been times, though, she recognizes now, that he has been Giovanni…like that Saturday he spent all day in her kitchen preserving tomatoes; or the time she cut her spaghetti with her fork and he stood up and walked out. Then there was that time she'd been at his place and he kicked the trash can across the room. She'd asked him what was wrong, and he couldn't even tell her.

"Is it?" she responds to Luca finally. "Is America good for him?"

"You will be lucky for him," Simona says.

Jamie ponders the word lucky. It is an odd choice of word, she thinks, because love, by its very nature, is doomed and unlucky.

"With you I can tell something," Luca says.

You can tell nothing.

"I know you," he says.

She smiles and steps back.

"You believe in *destino*, Jamie?" Simona says.

"Destiny," Luca says, stepping in closer.

"God no," Jamie responds, and their faces grow wide with disbelief. "I believe in choices and the consequences of those choices."

Simona and Luca nod at Jamie gravely. Then they turn and giggle at each other.

Jamie has no idea what is so funny. Perhaps the word "choices" got lost in translation. "How have you become so fluent," she asks Simona, changing the subject.

"My French is better."

"Of course." Jamie says, self mockery lacing her tone for remembering only ten words of the Spanish she'd taken all through school.

"I also spent a year on exchange with a family in Wisconsin," Simona laughs at the expression on Jamie's face when she says Wisconsin, then goes on describing with a gracious kind of wonder the family she'd lived with, large not in numbers, but in volume. She goes into great detail about the tubs of ice cream eaten on the couch in front of the TV, the frozen fish sticks and cereal boxes and bricks of orange cheese. "They were the nicest people on the face of the earth, but *mamma mia*, the food. I gained ten kilos!"

"I grew up in L.A. They don't allow you to be fat. Food functions pretty much the same as in the Midwest, though;

basically, everyone feeds themselves. I was microwaving my own frozen pizzas by the time I was eight."

"Ah, I see." Simona nods, though it is unclear if she understands what Jamie has said, if an Italian could possibly understand.

"And as far as eating together," Jamie points her head in the direction of the table they'd just set. "Nobody in my family even lives in the same state."

Simona's eyes are practically popping out of her head, which is shaking in disbelief. This goes on for a minute, until at last she can find the words to express what she feels. "*Grande* America!" is what these words are, and they make no sense.

There are twelve of them at a table that seems fit for eight, women trending on one side, men the other. La Mamma is seated proudly at the head, instructing Giovanni to take the other head, a seat normally reserved for Zio Marco when he is up from Torino, where he lives and works during the week as a bank manager. Zio Marco bows dutifully and steps aside, taking the seat just to the right of Jack. Jamie has yet to hear the man actually speak—when she'd been introduced to him his ears turned red and his eyes flitted about. He does not kiss cheeks, she'd been pre-warned, a sure sign that he and Jamie should get along, if only she could pierce those beady eyes of his, or set off his alarm in some way. The man seems wound like a clock, ready to dart or shift at any moment.

Cin cin, salute everybody clinks glasses. Jamie tries to relax inside the close proximity of bodies. She is not used to all the knocking of elbows and brushing of legs, everyone eating and talking at once. Unmarked bottles of red that Luca has brought up from some crevice in the earth are being passed around with the antipasti. *"Acciughe con pomodoro, peperoncino e aceto,"* Zia Claudia explains as Jamie scoops tomato sauce onto her plate, surprised to discover an anchovy buried there. La Mamma passes her the *peperoni arrosto,* and as Jamie helps herself to what looks like a bell pepper, a drop of olive oil falls from the serving spoon onto the lace tablecloth, somebody's great-grandmother's tablecloth. La Mamma at once wets her napkin and dabs at the lace, assuring Jamie *non ti preoccupare* when the woman looks completely distraught, and yet seemingly pleased at having to make this little fuss over Jamie's mess.

"How do you like the food so far?" Zia Maddalena leans in and asks her, taking a break from her argument with Zia Claudia about the spices in the *tumin,* a marinated cow cheese; but Jamie can't answer because Luca is calling out for her to try the pickled, hand-picked porcini mushrooms.

"Non mangia?" La Mamma cries, when the anchovies come back around and Jamie still hasn't eaten the one on her plate. She quickly grabs a *grissino* off the table and uses it to help her slip the anchovy onto her fork as she'd just watched Jack do across the table. *"Ancora?"* More? La Mamma wants to know. She is holding out the serving dish for Jamie to take after having spooned a heaping portion of the slimy creatures onto a piece of bread for herself. Jamie takes the plate, and La Mamma gobbles down the sopped bread in one bite. When she can speak again her eyes tear reminiscing about the gluttonous child she bore, *il goloso,* the baby who would eat until he was sick. La Mamma smiles across the table at her son, who is ignoring her, then she pushes the bowl of *peperoni arrosto* in front of Jamie. *"Mangia, Jamie."*

"I'm fine, thank you," Jamie says.

Wrong answer. With a bitter quiet, La Mamma turns from Jamie and passes the plate to someone else. *But...*is the only apologetic word Jamie can muster, and even then it's only in her mind. It isn't that she doesn't like the *peperoni*. But she knows there is a *primo* and a *secondo* coming, and Jamie has a strategy to get through this meal and all the subsequent others on this trip. She'd dropped the last pound of her college twenty some time ago—the ugly, heartbreak years—and she has no intention of ever gaining it back.

"Does there always need to be a strategy?" Jack had asked her once, back in San Francisco when she'd decided to forego lunch because they were going out for a fancy dinner. She'd looked at him oddly—of course.

Antonia sets a gigantic bowl of *agnolotti* on the table before Jamie, who keeps repeating to herself this is not ravioli, and then delicately extracts three pieces.

"Make sure you scoop out the sage and butter," Giovanni commands from across the table. Someone hands her a hunk of *parmigiano* cheese in a plastic toy-looking grater that takes a while to get working. "*Mangia*," La Mamma insists while filling her own plate. "*Mangia mentre sono caldi.*"

Jamie watches the bowl being passed around the table, the pieces extracted as if made of solid gold. Giovanni is panicked by the time it reaches him, the last one, as if there might be none left. He stares into the bowl for a long, soulful moment. When at last he serves himself, Luca counts out the pieces Jack takes to make sure things remain even.

"*Buoni, molto buoni,*" Jack drops his fork and moans to Antonia. Then he gazes at Jamie, who's forgotten to eat; it's satiating enough to watch him eat. Now everyone at the table is waiting for her to say something, anything, about the food, particularly Antonia—until Luca reaches for the saltshaker and all hell breaks loose. Antonia sits back, folds her arms, and glares at him; spicing food is an insult, apparently. Luca cries in defense and a loud argument ensues over whether anyone, anywhere, at any time, can make *agnolotti* better than Nonna. All eyes get cast to the sky, and feeling sorry for Antonia at this point, Jamie takes her bite. There are many words for this bite. She looks at Antonia, wondering how she can express these words to her. *Buona,* she offers finally. It sounds terribly insufficient, ridiculous next to the bemoaning from Jack, but it doesn't matter. By now no one is listening.

The men are arguing about the food and wine that will be served at Luca's wedding, more important than the wedding itself. Antonia's family is from near Bra, and families from near Bra are known for being stingy. Certainly there will not be enough food, and why should good Ruffoli vintages be wasted on these people who are too stingy to spend money on enough food?

Meanwhile the women are belaboring about Antonia's massive dress. It has been a tragedy for La Mamma to sew, apparently. Zia Claudia explains to Jamie in a raspy voice that seems to go with the thick scar running along her collarbone, the one that goes with the scar running across Luca's chin and down La Mamma's leg. They were all in a car accident, Jack had mentioned to Jamie before arriving. Jack and Luca were fourteen, Zia Claudia was pregnant with Caterina, and Luca's father, Dino, was killed. Jack was the only one who crawled out unscathed, and his mother has not stopped praying since.

She may be praying even now, just before serving her infamous *arrosto farcito*. It's infamous because La Mamma always overcooks the *arrosto farcito,* everyone is sure to tell Jamie. One of the bottles they'd opened earlier is being passed around. Giovanni examines the cryptic 1996 scribbled in chalk on the dark green glass, pours, swirls, smells, and sips. There is a moment of utter silence. Then he nods at Luca. "Not bad, cousin!"

"I told you, cousin."

"Not bad for seven years, cousin." Giovanni is still staring into the bottle. "So this is what you've been doing since I've been gone?"

"I not go to the famous MIT, but I make beautiful Barolo."

Zio Marco raises his glass. "*Al contadino*," he says. These are the first words out of his mouth, and the way people react, it doesn't seem to be a compliment. *Cin cin*.

It means farmer.

"You're not a farmer, you're a genius," Giovanni says. "This is the best wine I've ever tasted." He passes the bottle on, finally. "Bisnonno would be proud."

"Tomorrow I pour you the '89."

"You still have the cases?"

"Or would you prefer the '82?" Luca smiles, a gleam in his eye. "It is beautiful, the vineyard. Not as many hectares, but better grapes. Tomorrow you will see all that I have done." Then reality hits; Luca remembers his future at the tire company, and sinks back into his chair while Jack gazes quietly into his wine glass.

Sometime later, the bottle is empty. They are all still at the table; no one seems to have anywhere else to go. Even Jamie has momentarily forgotten that she'd promised her client a phone call; the thought of work drifting lazily to the back of her wine-soaked mind. Various cheeses have been consumed—fontina, gorgonzola, mascarpone. A bowl of walnuts is being passed around with *ribes* and some *gianduiotti* that Zio Marco brought from Torino. If Jamie has lost track of the conversation, she no longer cares. She is relaxing to the rhythm of their melodic verse, exploring the concept of eating this pear with a knife and fork.

She hears the women giggling about something and looks up to see Simona and Caterina linking arms again; Zia Claudia and Antonia are doing the same. Jamie slides her own hands between her knees, imagining linking arms with her mother or Jill. Hers are not physical people, and there is no scene with her family even remotely like this one. There is no table in her memories, only a kitchen counter where Jamie and her mother, or Jamie and Jill, or on rare occasions all three of them stood eating finger foods before hurrying on their way somewhere else. She looks at Giovanni now, and then takes the last sip of her wine that had been poured from the bottle with no label.

Toscano cigars are passed around to the men as the women get up to start clearing dishes. For Jamie, this means restacking the plates, glasses and utensils back onto that wobbly cart, then wheeling it back to the kitchen. When she returns, sweating, the room is clouded in smoke, and La Mamma is in tears before the men, who are arguing. Or it seems like they are arguing. It's hard to tell the difference between arguing and conversation. Zio Marco is suddenly full of things to say, puffing on his cigar and going on about something to Jack, something that is infuriating Luca, apparently. Even Jack can only listen abstractly, his eyes narrowed against the smoke falling from his mouth, until Luca can't take it anymore. He slams his hand on the table, pushes his chair back, and stomps off.

"*Ma dai, Luca,*" La Mamma cries after him, and then looks to Giovanni to do something.

"We are talking about the Crespi," Jack explains to Jamie, motioning for her to come take Luca's seat. "Bisnonno and Signor Crespi were great friends." He pauses to say something to Zio Marco in Italian. "The Crespi must come to Luca's wedding,"

Jack continues to Jamie, as if she were an important part of this conversation, as if she had any idea what they were talking about. "Luca is just being a pain in the ass."

"I'm a pain in the ass that makes good grappa!" Luca has reappeared with three odd shaped bottles of clear liquid. Tiny glasses are passed out and Luca begins explaining to Jamie how he uses the residual skin, stems, and seeds from his grapes plus the rose petals from his mother's garden to make the family grappa recipe that's been handed down over generations. Meanwhile, Zio Marco does the honors, pouring glasses for the men as if there had never been any disagreement between them, plus one for Jamie.

The other women have trickled back into the room, but apparently they don't drink grappa. Jamie wonders why Zio Marco assumed that she did, if this is a compliment or a criticism: *Americans drink*. Anyway, she is relieved to be included because however warm and sumptuous and other-worldly lunch was, it was ultimately stressful under La Mamma's discerning eye, not to mention these frequent, sudden outbursts between the men. She'll have to ask Jack about the Crespi later; right now she can't focus. Zio Marco is pouring her another glass from another bottle, inching in closer. She sips the grappa, masking the burn. He inches closer still, examining her through the smoke of his cigar as if perhaps he is not so shy after all. Perhaps she is sleeping with her eyes open; or she's just drunk. She has no idea what is going on.

"*Ti piace la grappa?*"

Yes, she says, she likes it very much.

CHAPTER 4

Roots

*T*HE NEXT MORNING Jamie is wide awake at four a.m. The eyes of the Virgin Mary stare at her from across the room; stars fade in and out through the skylight; everything is still but for the church bell that rings every half hour, which sends the setters off on a startling and creepy barking tirade each time. She turns on the table light, figuring it a good time to get some work out of the way. E-mail is going to be a problem, she senses, but her cell reception is surprisingly good. Perhaps being so close to God has perks after all.

Still tucked under thin covers she makes some calls to San Francisco, is informed by an associate that the updated proposal is waiting for her in e-mail—she'll need to download it somehow—and that Jim, her peer on the merger project, can't seem to understand the updated financials she sent him before leaving. They spend a while on the phone about that.

She's worked with Jim for years, though she wouldn't call him a friend. Jamie doesn't have co-workers who are personal friends, those involved in her life outside the office. Anyway, Jim has no idea she's in Italy. He thinks she's visiting her sister, Jill, who recently gave birth to twins, in Virginia. "The twins are great," Jamie cuts him off, quickly ending the call because her door is creaking open. She goes still with the weird feeling it's La Mamma, and sighs with relief when she sees that it's Jack.

He shuts the door, careful not to make noise, and comes at her with that intent look in his eyes. With a quiet force he folds her into his arms, and they fall naturally into that sweet spot of entanglement. "I couldn't sleep without you," he whispers.

"Me either," she says.

But the ache feels too close, too much, and they pull away from each other, for the villa is too quiet to make love, especially with La Mamma next door. Jamie turns onto her stomach, props up on her elbows, "I shouldn't be telling you this."

He eyes the phone on the nightstand, the papers he might not have noticed before.

"Jim said your group is going to come out on top of the merger. There's going to be a lot of advancement opportunities. You know you deserve to be managing that group."

He stays quiet.

Jamie has always valued the fact that she can talk to Jack about work; that she can come home at night and bring up a conflict she might have had with a client that day, and Jack, with his industry background and insider's perspective, might offer an intelligent solution or honest, helpful suggestions. "What do you think?"

"Jamie," he says curtly. "I'm on vacation."

"Yeah but…"

"I have no interest in talking about work. I don't want to think about work."

After a pause. "Seriously?"

"I need to turn off."

Right, she thinks abstractly. Turn off. She wishes she could turn off. But once she turns off she's done. If she lets down her guard it's over. She'd prefer to work like the devil now in order to remain cool and calm then, when she's back in front the client. "I envy you," she says. She knows that something is wrong with her. "How do you let it all go?"

"I just can."

"I'm sorry," she says, unsure if in fact she is sorry, because she wonders if there is something wrong with him, too.

"It's okay, Jamie. Do what you need to do. Just don't expect me to do it, too."

At this point she just wants the moment to dissolve, to go away. Slowly it does, as his jaw releases and his shoulders relax. They crawl under the covers and resettle into the warmth of each other, however altered that warmth is now, and stay like that waiting for sleep or dawn, whichever comes first.

Six chimes of the bell and they give up on both. They get dressed and meet downstairs in the kitchen for coffee that he makes in a tiny, ancient looking espresso maker. She has her thimble full, not enough, she groans, so he makes another, which doesn't help. At least daylight is breaking; a walk will help. He grabs a flashlight, but once outside, she's freezing. In fact, she's been cold since they arrived, having brought no warm clothes, not thinking she'd need them in June, what with all those visions of herself lingering sleeveless in outdoor cafés. And these flats with no traction were another packing mistake. Jack leads her through the courtyard and down the foggy hillside until he finds what he's looking for, a doorway carved into the hedge, which they proceed through.

"Watch your step," he warns her, as they make their way down a path of stone steps overgrown with grass and weeds. It snakes between two darkened apartments connected by a laundry line, where Jack decides to stop and search the sky for the *campanile* that has a big morning star floating right next to it. "Ah," he says.

Then he points at their feet and announces that this was the chicken coop. And way down there, where Zia Claudia, Luca, and Caterina live in that apartment, that was once the apple and cherry orchard. And over there, where Zio Marco, Zia Maddalena and Simona live on weekends, used to be walnut and fig trees, not the barn. The barn was over where that ugly apartment sits now, where he and Luca would watch the farmer kill rabbits with a mallet. Jamie shudders at the thought.

What used to be the villa's grand entrance is now boarded up by a cement wall, spoiled by graffiti. It butts up against the main road that leads into the town they passed on the way in, where old tires have gathered. There used to be a gravely road lined by cypress trees that weaved up and around from the entrance to the villa. The cypresses are gone now and the path is weeded over, stunted by the tennis court they'd installed as part of the redevelopment effort, but it was never kept up; its net is sagging and tattered.

He leads her down another steep patch of grass until the ground levels off at an old storage shed. "This used to be the gardener's workshop," he says, looking inside a dirty window.

"Simona must use it for her sculpting now."

Jamie peeks in. The place is cluttered and stacked with unfinished versions of the infamous four seasons. "They're not so bad," she says, looking at him. "Do you really think they're bad?"

"They're bad."

His back is to her now. "That used to be the *bocce* court, I think." He turns to look at her. "You know what a *bocce* court is, don't you?"

She's embarrassed to say that she doesn't. "What do you think, I'm an idiot?"

He flashes her a sardonic look, then turns and hunts around for a door in the wall of earth that "used to be right around here somewhere." He gives up and opts for another muddy incline. Her flats are a disaster. It is not long before they are wandering through rows of early season vines. Pockets of mist are tucked here and there, so thick she can scoop them up in her hand.

Jack has crouched down to examine some bulbs. "Bisnonno planted these vines almost eighty years ago." He digs his fingers into the crusty, hard dirt, then lets the chunks fall through his fingers.

"Nebbiolo is the toughest grape to grow…" It's as if he's speaking from someplace else. "… and yet it thrives in this region because of our tough, chalky soil. It grows deep, through layers of clay and sediment, into this slanting earth. This is how they become rich. It takes decades to achieve this." He pauses as if he's lost his thought, and a minute passes before he speaks again. "I knew Luca had been keeping the vines going, but I never realized…" He looks behind him as if he just felt something, or someone, there. "That '96 we had last night… it's like they're still living and breathing."

Jamie looks around, too.

"The vines were Bisnonno's passion."

"I thought your great-grandfather was a steel guy."

He stands up and they continue walking. "In Italy we work so that we can pursue our passions. The vines were the reason Bisnonno bought Villa Ruffoli in the first place. He passed his passion for wine on to Peter, his third son, Luca's grandfather, and while Nonno Giacomo and his brothers ran the business, Peter made an art out of those vineyards; and believe me, Jamie, this wasn't easy. Piemonte is no Tuscany, where back in the day aristocratic families continued the grand tradition of wine making. Piemonte was made up mostly of farmers who grew grapes as a way to survive. They sold them at auction in Bra for nothing and all the wine tasted the same. But Bisnonno didn't need the money. He made wine for his family's personal consumption, and to give away as gifts to the workers in the factory, or to clients." His eyes find hers. "Ferrero, Olivetti, Fiat—Italian institutions." Names he says proudly, though Jamie can hear a trace of longing, regret.

"When Peter died in the war, Bisnonno lost the heart and hired a farmer to take over the vineyard; but the wine was never as good as when Bisnonno and Peter were producing."

"Hence the vinegar."

"Either the cellar was too hot or too cold, or the barrels were not cleaned properly." He smiles. "I remember when I was a kid, Luca and I would help the farmer crush the grapes with our feet."

Jamie, smiling at a vision of an *I Love Lucy* episode, does not know whether to turn up the slope or down. They have come to the end of the row; the world smells like earth and she is all turned around. It's hard to make anything out in the thickets of vine and light of dawn. For a moment she has lost him, but then sees that he has wandered over to a plateau where there is a viewing point over the valley. She goes over and takes his hand and they look out together. The low mist looks like whitewash, the land a series of waves that remind her, oddly enough, of home.

"This whole region was once an ocean."

"Where are we, exactly?"

"The Langhe."

It sounds like a dream.

"Our land stops there," he points far off down the hill to a fence. "We used to have six hectares, but the Crespi got three as a settlement during the bankruptcy. We owed a lot of people money. There were many law suits."

"It's that Barolo we drank in San Francisco, right?"

"Those were our grapes, or some of them anyway." He turns around and they start walking back. "The Crespi were willing to buy all of our hectares. I should have taken their offer."

"Was it your decision to make?"

"Unfortunately, yes. The villa, the vineyard, Nonno left them to me."

She pauses mid step. He continues walking.

"The Chosen One," she says.

He stops and turns.

"Simona," she explains.

"What did she tell you?" His voice is low and uneasy.

"Nothing. Just that you should tell me why they call you that."

He turns away. "It's become a joke."

"I imagine it's not very funny."

"Oh, it's funny." He turns back, his eyes devilish and strange. "You want to know why it's funny?" He doesn't wait for her response. "Ever since I was born, Nonno Giacomo groomed me to take over the business. He didn't trust his sons-in-law, my father included, and God forbid he'd leave the business in the hands of his daughters, who didn't even finish high school." Anticipating her alarm, he adds. "We were the elite, they were women, what was the point?"

A moment of silence.

"I know it's crazy. I'm just telling you how it was, Jamie."

She remains quiet.

"But with me it was boarding school in Torino, then Milano, then to the States and the great MIT so I could bring back all this knowledge."

"…and then there was no business to bring the knowledge back to."

"There's your joke."

The man hides his disappointment well.

"Why didn't you take the Crespi's offer at the time?"

"Luca," he sighs. "He was always such a crazy fuckup back then. The one thing he never fucked up was those vines. They gave him his life."

"And now?"

"Now Antonia will be his life. He's going to sell tires for his father-in-law, and I am going to sell the remaining vines to the Crespi once and for all."

"Why can't he continue working the vines?"

"Zio Marco manages the estate's accounts, what's left of them, and he says that the vineyard is a money pit, that Luca barely breaks even each month. Anyway, it's all been decided, Jamie. It's the reason I'm here." The muscle in his cheek is pulsating. "The Crespi have made Zio Marco a new offer, and this time I'm going to take it." His head smacks into an errant tree branch, and he kicks the trunk. "*Cazzo* Luca."

"You speak of me?" A voice bellows, and Jamie gasps as the mist parts, and out comes Luca with a big pair of sheers. "Why you hurt my tree?" He's wearing jeans, cowboy boots, and an AC/DC t-shirt.

"Because it's right here, in the way."

"It is here to flavor my vines." Luca picks a peach and hands it to Jamie. "It is not yet ripe, but good for preserving."

Giovanni, rubbing his head, grumbles in Italian.

"I am always here," Luca responds, bending over to prune a vine. "Did you tell her about the roots?"

"*Si*, I told her about the roots."

"Then *vieni*, come, I will show you the cellar."

Luca leads them back down the sloping earth to where the *bocce* court once was, and to the door in the wall of earth Giovanni could not find earlier. It is rusty and overgrown with shrubs and ivy; Luca has to give it a good shove before it opens. They follow him down a stone staircase with no rail, through a narrow corridor and into a large, vaulted room. The room has brick ceilings supported by wood beams; it's lined with humongous wood barrels that seem to transport Jack into another world. His eyes have glossed over and yet his body is fully alert down to the last hair on his neck, as if every sense has been awakened. "Smell that, Jamie," he presses a hand against a barrel, breathes in deeply. "Oak, must, wine, I love the smell of this cellar." He leans in, listens, and then steps back suddenly. Triggered by what, Jamie wonders. Jack is deftly scanning the room now, his face flashing of curiosity, disbelief. Pride. "It's just as I remember it."

"*Esatto*," Luca says, watching him intently. "Everybody else change everything. I change nothing."

"This is your strategy?"

"I make Barolo that tastes of Bisnonno and Peter and Villa Ruffoli. No Barolo tastes like my Barolo." He bounds up a rickety old ladder leaning against one of the barrels and sucks out some wine with a siphon, releases it into a thin plastic cup, which he hands down to Giovanni who is perched on a low, sagging rung. Jamie cringes, certain that that ladder will topple over with the two of them on it. Giovanni sips the wine and then steps off the ladder to hand Jamie the cup. She sips, unsure what to think let alone say about wine drunk at eight a.m.

"2000 will not be one of my best," Luca says bounding down, "but still excellent." He jumps off the ladder. "The summer was dry, autumn wet, and we suffered a hailstorm. So I only use half the grapes, because I refuse to make Barolo that is not excellent."

Jack puts his nose to the cup again.

"Everyone else is using chemicals, yeasts, and smaller barrels, or mixing their grapes with other grapes to produce more wine in less time. I don't trust these people. I have always done the work myself, with the help of Caterina."

"How much do you sell to the Cooperative these days?" Jack wants to know.

"Jugs of Nebbiolo are still the bulk of my business," Luca explains. "Most Italians aren't going to buy cases of Barolo. My Barolo I sell to people who appreciate wine, and some select restaurants in Torino. More and more people find out about my Barolo though, and they want it."

"Have you tried selling in the States?" Jamie's mind is churning. "If the Crespi can sell their wine, then…"

"*Teste di cazzo* that's not wine, that's shit."

"That shit sells for a hundred bucks a bottle," Jamie says, and Luca looks at her, stunned.

"I'm afraid she is right, cousin."

"I would rather have those vines shrivel up and die than sell them to the Crespi." Luca is seething. "Do you know they use *Barrique!*" He paces over to a large open chimney, lights a cigarette, and takes a long drag.

"We've already talked about this, Luca, we've agreed."

"*Mah,*" Luca exhales. "In two days I will be married. In two days I will sell tires for Antonia's father."

When he has finished his cigarette they move down another corridor lined with jugs and wood crates full of bottles.

They pass through a hole in the wall into a smaller, cave-like room. Hundreds of dusted over bottles lie stacked on shelves carved deep into the stone—no labels, just chalk scribbles on the dark green glass.

It's a minute before Giovanni can speak. "This is still here?"

Luca smiles mischievously back. He then apologizes to Jamie, for what he must say next must be said in Italian, and this keeps Giovanni captivated for a time. When Luca's finished, Giovanni goes to a wall opposite from where they entered and begins pulling out stones, one by one. "You see how this door seals off?" he says to Jamie. "Bisnonno modified the cellar this way so that the Germans wouldn't find the wine during the war. What Luca just told me is that he sealed it off again during the bankruptcy proceedings. No one knew it was here."

She clears some dust from a bottle. "Does that say 1925?"

They come and hover around her.

"Will this be drinkable?"

Luca with a gleam in his eye, "We must find out."

CHAPTER 5

La Maledizione

"*POVERETTA, NON VEDI CHE HA FREDDO?*" Can't you see that she is cold? Luca admonishes Jack, who didn't know Jamie was shivering. "My American coffee will warm you up."

"Thank God," she mouths, as Luca leads them out of the secret cellar via that hidden door, then in a different direction from before, through a corridor in which they must crouch, one that grows alarmingly darker and narrower. There are a series of these passageways down here, presumably some that they've never explored, Jack tells her, joking that hopefully they are not lost. Jamie starts to panic as she does in confined spaces, just as they reach yet another set of stone stairs that circle up to a small door, a crawl space that puts them in a broom closet, pantry, then finally back in the kitchen where they had all crowded yesterday making lunch.

"Please don't make me do that again," she says, evening her breath.

Luca puts some wood in the fire and Giovanni sets up the espresso maker. *Un caffè americano* is an espresso served in a coffee cup with a shot of hot water on the side. A start, Jamie thinks, as Luca's cell phone rings some brassy Italian song that feels incongruous with these rustic surroundings. "Claudia," he resigns, seeing the number.

"He talks to his mother ten times a day," Giovanni informs Jamie.

"If I don't talk to my mother, I get sad," Luca defends himself before picking up. "I worry, she worries." He answers, their exchange lasts thirty seconds, at which point he tells Jack with childish foreboding that Jack's mother has told Luca's mother to tell Luca to tell Jack that she is looking for him, which is exactly the moment La Mamma enters the kitchen, same hair, same dress, same jewels as if she'd slept that way, carrying a large suit jacket which she immediately slips Luca into—Nonno Giacomo's *tight*—Luca will be wearing it for the wedding. "A tux for the Italian…" Jack makes quotes with his hands, "upper classes."

Nonno Giacomo was a wide man in girth. Luca swims in the jacket and adjustments seem preposterous, but La Mamma remains undeterred, digging around in her sewing kit because do not be mistaken, someone in her family is going to wear this damned *tight* at their wedding before her death; and this is not the only burden she must bear. After living her life under the care of maids and servants, La Mamma is now the resident seamstress. After she takes Luca's measurements she will go to Zia Maddalena's to work on Antonia's wedding dress, and Jamie will come with her.

Jamie looks up here, having heard her name referenced. She tells Giovanni to tell La Mamma that she is so sorry, but she is expected on a conference call and needs to do some work. "I'll need access to e-mail," she takes this opportunity to remind Jack, and when he hesitates she adds, "Maybe we could take a drive into Turin and find an Internet café…"

"We have access to the Internet, Jamie. We're not Neanderthals." He exchanges words with La Mamma. Meanwhile, Jamie is envisioning sitting with Jack at a café in Italy's "Little Paris," wandering around that Egyptian museum she'd read about in the guidebook, a dinner reservation maybe, or a late night stroll along the Po River. Perhaps tomorrow, she thinks…

"La Mamma will take you to Zia Claudia's now, where Caterina can show you how to dial in."

"Dial in?" She'd almost forgotten about the report.

"I'll be with Luca in the cellar, examining the fermentation tanks."

La Mamma waits by the door with her sewing kit while Jamie goes upstairs to change her shoes so she can keep up with La Mamma's determined pace. Their walk is brisk, awkward. La Mamma makes an attempt at small talk, though she could also be trying to relay something pressing. Jamie can't tell. So she just keeps nodding intently, and smiling so hard her face hurts.

Two minutes later Zia Claudia welcomes them into her kitchen, the only way one enters the narrow, dark, poorly constructed apartment allotted to her from the redevelopment. Dino, Luca's father, was a philosophy professor in Milan, and so their walls are lined with shelves of his books, tomes that look like they might disintegrate if opened. Antique maps were his passion, Zia Claudia explains to Jamie, and no wall is without one. They are in the living room and Zia Claudia is explaining the origins of a map they stand before now, amused by her need to honor her husband in this way. Far from the tragic widow, her dress a happy pink, she seems amused by almost everything. Even now, back in the kitchen, watching Caterina attempt to dial in on Jamie's laptop, the woman is full of curiosity and smiles.

"*E' intelligente come suo papá*," she says about her daughter's intellect even though Caterina can't seem to master the phone line, which keeps dropping. La Mamma calls Zia Maddalena because Zio Marco and Zia Maddalena have all the modern things and they all go traipsing over there. Their apartment is a carbon copy of Zia Claudia's except the kitchen has a skylight and terrace, with cabinets and appliances all new and sleek. Zia Maddalena is at the table, sifting through a pile of raspberries picked from her garden for the *torta* that will be Luca and Antonia's wedding cake.

"Ah," she says, standing up to greet them, "*Vieni a vedere.*" Come and look. She leads them into the living room, where walled windows look out onto another, larger terrace, and where Antonia stands on a step stool in her wedding dress, bathed in a pool of sunlight.

They all stare at her for a moment.

An older, bigger version of Antonia, her mother, Jamie presumes, stands holding up Antonia's hair. She is distraught, like everyone else, about that dress. They are right; it is massive. La Mamma immediately goes over and fusses with the lace collar strangling Antonia's neck.

"She is a house. They all say she is a house in that dress." This from Simona, suddenly there at Jamie's side, just in from her sculpting studio presumably, as her clothes are covered in clay. She's popping raspberries into her mouth.

La Mamma puffs out her cheeks, as if to confirm Simona's point.

Jamie glances at Antonia for her reaction, expecting her to say *vaffanculo* and stomp out (as Jamie would do if someone referred to her as a house), but Antonia just stands there getting stuck with pins. It's painful to watch, and Jamie goes back to check on Caterina's progress.

The line seems to be holding this time; her document is sending. Simona comes over to watch, so does Zia Claudia, then Antonia's mother and Zia Maddalena. "It's going to take some time," Jamie tells them, hoping they'll step back, and when they don't she turns to face Antonia again, still standing there with her arms out and La Mamma crouched by her feet attacking a piece of her trellis. "It was Antonia's mother's dress," Simona says, and La Mamma shrugs as if to say, so there is not much we can do.

"This wedding is a great tragedy for the family," Simona goes on to explain. "Because Luca will live with Antonia's family in Moncalieri after they are married, and Zia Claudia is worried for his health."

Jamie looks over at Zia Claudia, who is still frowning curiously at the message on Jamie's computer. "Moncalieri is very far then?" Jamie asks, thinking that by the way they are acting it must be on the other side of Italy, maybe even in another country. But then someone tells her that it's only a forty minute drive from Alba, and Jamie can't hide her bemusement. "Forty minutes? I must take a plane to see my mother."

The room goes silent after Simona translates what Jamie has said. Zia Claudia, with the direst of expressions, comes over and puts an arm around her. "You miss your mother very much."

Jamie smiles and nods as best she can.

La Mamma, wanting to curtail this tender moment, announces, via Simona, that Luca will be the first Ruffoli not married in the *Chiesa* Ruffoli. This sets everyone off talking at once. Antonia must be married in Moncalieri, in the church in which she was baptized, her mother insists. It has always been this way with their family. Luca will be happy in Moncalieri, she assures them. No, Luca will be miserable in Moncalieri, someone else assures, and Luca will miss his vines very much. Not to mention *la maledizione* (the curse).

Curse?

Simona explains to Jamie that because Zia Claudia's father Peter died when she was in her mother's womb, and then her husband Dino died when Caterina was in her womb, she is afraid of Luca dying when Antonia has a baby in her womb, especially if the baby is a girl. Every night Zia Claudia prays that when they have a baby it will be a boy.

A discussion on the various tragedies ensues back and forth. Jamie's eyes retreat to the wall prints that she's just now noticed: hunters on snow capped mountains, hikers, birds, all kinds of animals eating other animals—suddenly she is ready to crawl out of her skin. Luca and Antonia are happy together, this is obvious, so what is the tragedy?

In fact, it is all very clear to Jamie. The vines and villa should be sold, Giovanni should reinvest the sales proceeds in a livable apartment for La Mamma and a proper living trust, and Luca should move away from his mother, this place, and sell tires for God's sake. He's thirty-two after all. Who lives with their mother at thirty-two!?

Jamie is waiting for a break in the antics to make some version of her point known, until it occurs to her that the topic is no longer Luca and Antonia; the conversation has moved on to the topic of lunch. Ten a.m. on a Friday—doesn't anybody work around here? She is finding it hard to breathe again. Luckily, she hears Zia Claudia clap and cheer from the hallway. Jamie hurries over.

"Document sent." She snaps her laptop shut and flees, but just before leaving she stops, turns, and says to Antonia, "The dress is really beautiful," because no one else will. She hurries back to the villa, up to her tiny room and tiny bed so that she can stare through that tiny hole in the cracked roof, starving. In fact she's been persistently starving ever since she got here, which makes no sense.

❧

For the next five days, when they aren't preparing meals, at meals, or discussing what to eat at the next meal, Giovanni is either in the vineyard with Luca or in the cellar with Zio Marco going over finances, performing due diligence in preparation for their negotiations with the Crespi over the hectares.

"Luca's got this ridiculous idea that he can work in Moncalieri and still take care of the vines." It's not the first time Jack has returned from a day at the vineyard lamenting like this.

"I thought you said this was all decided."

"It is."

"So then why are we still discussing it?"

"Luca's crazy. He's nuts. The sale will be better for everyone."

"You don't need to convince me, Jack," she reminds him from her room where she's been spending the afternoons 'catching up on work.'

"Are you going to hide in here all day?"

"I was hoping you would hide in here with me."

He falls down on the edge of the bed beside her, slides his hand into hers. "Tomorrow, I promise, we'll go into Torino, ALONE. *Facciamo una passeggiata!*"

"*Passeggiata?*"

He laughs at her pronunciation. Then explains, with an accompanying hand gesture, that *passeggiata* means *little stroll*.

"Ah yes, you said that yesterday."

"I did?"

She smiles. "And the day before that."

"Yes, I probably did." He sighs.

She sighs back.

"I'm sorry I'm so distracted."

"Of all people, Jack, you know that I understand. You came here to sell the hectares. Sell them."

"If it were that easy."

"But why isn't it easy, Jack? What's going on?"

"It's complicated." He frowns.

"I'm listening."

"I haven't been here in ten years, Jamie. You don't understand what those vines once meant. This would be the end. Of my grandfather. Of Luca…"

"That seems rather dramatic."

"Of us."

She goes still, unable to fathom what to say. To speak her mind or her heart. "You have good judgment, Jack, a keen sense. I've always said this. Go with your gut. If you're not ready, don't sell the hectares. But I'm worried about your mother, this place. Can she sustain herself here?"

"No," he says.

"Then you need to do what's right, Jack."

He pulls his head back and studies her.

"What?"

"I don't know."

"What?"

He can't seem to figure it out. "You're different."

She closes her eyes, rubs her brow. "I know. I'm sorry."

"Don't be sorry."

She looks around at the work papers spread around her. "I'm not sure, exactly, how I got this way."

He touches her cheek. "I love you this way."

She rests her face in his palm. "Do what you think is right Jack. Don't listen to me. I have a skewed vision of things." Her eyes meet his.

"No, you're right. I should stick the course."

"Yes, the course." She flashes him a facetious look. "And what, exactly, is the course?"

"Therein lies the question," he says, rising to go, reluctantly, and she rises with him, her heart lurching from her chest.

"Maybe you could go down and help my mother," he suggests ever so gently just before opening the door. "She keeps asking where you are, if you're okay, if you're not sick."

What had been an unusually dreamy expression on Jamie now explodes into alarm, and he laughs; at least she can still make him laugh. At least they've still got that going for them, because sex has been impossible, and now he is gone again. She wants to slip on her shoes and go with him. Wherever it is he keeps going that leaves him smelling of earth and berries, she wants to go there too.

A little while later, Jamie creeps down to the kitchen where La Mamma is seated at the table before a basket of white candied almonds and a pile of mesh and ribbon. "*Confetti,*" she says, coming alive at the sight of Jamie slipping into the chair opposite her. "*Si fa cosi*," Like this, La Mamma slips some almonds into a tiny bag and ties it closed with a ribbon.

Jamie takes a bag, some almonds, and does the same.

La Mamma frowns at Jamie's finished product, extracting an almond from the bag. She adds an almond to the next one Jamie makes, and after a few attempts at communicating, they work together in silence until Jack comes bursting through the door. "Ah, *confetti*," he says, snatching up an almond and throwing it into his mouth. In an instant, La Mamma is up and at the stove, preparing his coffee, and Jack has taken her seat.

"Please, Jack, explain to me what I'm doing," Jamie says with a desperate smile. "There's something I'm not doing right."

He holds up one of the bags. "It's a symbol of bittersweet union." His tone is facetious. "Mamma says you need to make seventy-five for the wedding, one for each guest."

Her eyes widen.

"The number of almonds is very important." He counts out some with his fingers. "Even numbers are bad luck. Odd numbers represent fertility." He is speaking with that mocking Italian accent he likes to use for her entertainment. "You can put in three or five, but never four or two." He slips five in a bag, binds it with the ribbon, and drops it into the completed pile.

"Come on, you're the math major, you should be good at this." He goes to the counter and loads his coffee with sugar while Jamie sits there, giving him a dead stare.

"Maybe you should stay and help."

"You're doing fine." He downs his coffee.

"How are things with Luca?"

"Still nuts." He shakes his head. "But he's got some interesting ideas."

"*Luca si e' calmato,*" La Mamma assures Giovanni, who shrugs.

"What did she say?"

"That Luca's changed, that he's grown up."

"Changed?"

"He was always getting into trouble when we were kids."

"And you? Did you get into trouble when you were a kid?"

Giovanni puts his hands together in prayer and lifts his eyes to the heavens. "*Un santo,*" he says, and La Mamma squeezes his cheek, which he tolerates, barely.

Santo? Saint? The kind of guy who doesn't cross the street unless the sign says "walk," Jamie is inclined to believe him. She's also inclined to believe that *Santo* here, via that beguiled expression of his, is trying to send her a message. Something's been transpiring down in that cellar these past few days, a festering going on deep down in the roots of those eighty-year-old vines. Things have changed. Fine, she tells herself. It's no difference to her what he does with the vines, and she must not succumb. These peoples' lives are not her business. She and Giovanni will return to San Francisco the day after tomorrow. They'll pass back through immigration, this time Jamie as the National and Giovanni as the alien. She'll meet Jack on the other side, and things will go back to normal.

CHAPTER 6

Armageddon

THE WEDDING IS HERE. The seventy-five *confetti* are done. Jamie's got her new dress on: a black silk, sleeveless number. She rarely wears dresses, let alone something this sexy. At work it's pantsuits, at home it's usually jeans; but she had seen this dress at Nordstrom and thought, why not? She could be pretty; she could be beautiful.

Jack has this effect on her, and she was right to buy the dress, given the way he is now looking at her. *He could absorb the Atlantic with that look,* and now she is walking from her continent over to his in heels that are too high, she warns, stumbling into his arms. "Don't worry, I'll take care of you," he whispers into her ear as they embrace to help steady her. A strangled laugh escapes her for feeling, in that one heart pounding moment, as if she could let him.

It is two flights down uneven steps into the living room, where La Mamma is waiting in gray flannel and fur. She's had her hair done and is wearing mascara, and all those jewels. She is literally sparkling.

"*Che bella,*" Jamie says, a phrase she practiced with Jack, but La Mamma looks confused, as if compliments are an American extravagance. The older woman goes over and fixes her son's hair, then straightens his tie, which he tolerates in a way he wouldn't with Jamie. Then again, Jamie's never tried to fix his hair or straighten his tie.

At the bureau now hunting through a drawer, La Mamma brings back two plastic wrapped pieces of dark cloth, which, when she pulls them out, emit smells from the dark ages, presumably. Giovanni and she examine the cloths in a low exchange of words, and Jamie wants to remind them: You don't need to whisper, I can't understand anyway.

Giovanni then suggests very delicately to Jamie that she might want to wear a shawl.

"It's eighty degrees outside," she says. "Thank you, but I'll be fine."

La Mamma murmurs something to Jack, who holds out the thick wool shawl for Jamie to take. "Just wear the shawl."

Jamie, who has already had a talk with herself about being more open, knows that she should take the shawl out of politeness, but her arms won't budge from her sides, and he gives up. He can tell she is not to be battled with, that she will throw an empowerment fit.

Maybe she is tired. Certainly she is hungry. Her dress is loose, and it occurs to her that she's lost weight since she's been here, unimaginably. This, she decides, is unquestionably the problem. She's been so overwhelmed at meals, fearful about reaching for the fruit before the salad, using her fingers with the prosciutto, switching her fork to the right hand after cutting her meat, that she forgets to eat. Then there's that, "*mangia, Jamie, mangia…finisci la pasta,*" which only fuels her to do the opposite and leads to the problem at hand. It is now four p.m. and her stomach is growling.

If she were at home, she'd stand before the food pantry examining its contents until something struck her, but in Italy there is no snacking. There is no wandering into that tiny kitchen and hunting for some crackers or chips to tide her over. Certainly there are no leftovers, but Jamie knows she will not survive the drive down that winding hill without something in her stomach. Clandestinely, she asks Jack to steal her a piece of bread from the kitchen without La Mamma noticing, to which he responds by turning directly to his mother and asking, "*C'e' del pane?*" Is there bread?

Apparently, Jamie and Giovanni don't speak the same English.

"*Sta male?*" As predicted, is Jamie sick? Is she ill? They ramble back and forth, then turn to Jamie, waiting for a response, though Jack seems to be merely entertaining himself. Jamie is not amused; she is looking past him now, out the kitchen window to the unkempt garden, adjusting to the sight of her thong underwear tangled amongst the vines, blowing in the breeze for all the neighbors to see. All of her underwear, in fact, is on a laundry line next to Giovanni's boxers and La Mamma's brassieres. Jamie looks back at Giovanni. "Forget it," she says.

La Mamma leaves for the church an hour early with the still unfinished wedding dress—a tradition, apparently. The dress is the only thing that will fit into her little Fiat, so Jamie and Jack will drive with Luca in his pickup truck that someone's decorated with ribbons and bows. It is almost time to go, but Luca is nowhere to be found. Jack goes hunting for him in the cellar, meanwhile Jamie meanders through a maze of hallways and corridors she's not meandered through before. The doors to the rooms are all closed. Old pieces of furniture lay cluttered about or stacked in vestibules.

A blue shaft of light draws her down a long hall, at the end of which stretches an arched, stained window with a big crack down the center. Below it sits a footstool before an altar littered with burned down candles and a gold-rimmed bible open on a stand. Frames of all shapes and sizes, some no larger than a thumbnail, are set all around. Jamie moves closer to examine the black and white photos. An elderly couple, another elderly couple, a young man wearing a military vest that might be Jack's father (based on a photo Jamie had once seen). A large, elaborate silver frame with a rosary draped over it holds a picture of a toddler-aged boy; Giovanni, Jamie assumes, recognizing the scowl where a smile should be. On the wall hangs a picture of the Virgin Mary above a cross of Jesus. Jamie steps back suddenly, disturbed by what she is seeing. The feeling festers, and then she hears someone and spins around.

No one is there, just the wind.

A door slams somewhere and she gasps, then bolts, retracing her steps back to the living room where she finds Luca at the liquor cabinet pouring pear brandy into a flask. Jack is pacing the floor, pissed off about having just spent thirty minutes looking for the groom.

"No way are you wearing those cowboy boots with Nonno's *tight*," Jack is barking, "not to mention your hair, you've not even cut your hair!" Luca pulls at the collar of his shirt. The *tight* is made of wool, but it's Jack who is sweating. "*Dai, andiamo,* Luca, we're late!"

After Luca changes out of his boots and they make a quick stop at the town market so Jamie can grab the Pringles and Coke that, thankfully, never fail to make their way into the farthest reaches of the world, they are officially late. The truck has no air conditioning and they have the windows down, Jamie's still-wet hair blowing dry in the hot wind. She'd almost blown up the house when she turned on her American blow dryer.

A hairpin turn at top speed and Luca glances over at Giovanni, whose foot is rammed against the floorboard. "Don't worry, cousin."

"It's you who should be worried."

"I am not stupid, cousin."

"I never said you were."

"You make me very happy, cousin."

They exchange a deep long look that Jamie reads to mean only one thing, one very special and intimate thing that might bind the two of them forever. Then Luca beams into the distance, for they are down the mountain now. The road has straightened, and at last he can accelerate full throttle. Jamie releases a squeal as she falls back laughing. Jack grabs her hand; they are whizzing through fields of corn now, and it's rather beautiful.

The church is in an old village near Moncalieri that does not accommodate parking, so the streets are lined with cars, making it difficult to pass. Luca maneuvers the tight twists and turns randomly, it seems, until he finally just stops, turns off the engine, and gets out. Jamie and Giovanni slide out on Luca's side because the passenger side is jammed against a stone wall. Her shoes get caught in the cobbled streets but at least finding the church ends up being easy. The bells of the *campanile* ring, and they simply follow the sound.

The sun is blazing. Everyone seems to be late and yet in no hurry. There is a big white bow above the double doors under which Giovanni and Luca embrace before Luca runs off to enter through a side door. Jamie and Giovanni climb the wide steps together. She doesn't remember the last time she was in a Catholic church. It's stunning, or it stuns her, anyway; not the fact that it's domed and frescoed and guidebook worthy, but the fact that every woman, every single one of them—ancient, middle aged, and young—is wearing a shawl.

"Why didn't you tell me!?" she grabs his hand and whisper-shouts.

"I tried to tell you."

"You tried to tell me nothing."

Someone is waving at them from a pew near the front. Jamie was hoping to hide her bare shoulders here in back, but now they must parade down the center aisle. They squeeze in next to Simona and Zia Maddalena, both appropriately covered with shawls. La Mamma is situated in the first pew kneeling in prayer, eyes squeezed shut, thumbing through the beads on her rosary. Jamie thinks about the shrine she stumbled upon before leaving, wondering what one could possibly want so desperately, and then leave up to God.

The organ blares with a force so shocking and ominous that it almost knocks Jamie over. She's not prepared for it. Nor is she prepared for the emotion that rushes to her eyes as she rises along with everyone else to face the blinding light streaming through the church doors where the bride, a big shadow, has begun her slow, tentative ascent toward the altar. As Antonia's face comes closer and into focus, Jamie can see that the poor girl is petrified. "Jesus," Jamie whispers to Jack. "Is this a wedding or a funeral?"

He squeezes her hand until it hurts.

It's the music she really can't get over. It's like Armageddon.

The crowd takes their seats in one big, loud whoosh. Luca and Antonia are at the altar. The women get out their toy, plastic fans, and the ceremony commences its droning pace.

Jamie does not know the procedure, the prayers, or the hymns and kneeling, all of which Giovanni takes part in with a possessed absence. "I went to Jesuit school," he reminds her. "You don't forget these things." His palm is sweating, or maybe it's hers. She looks up at the ceiling, where two hands are trying impossibly to touch.

There are long, unorganized lines to take communion. La Mamma is one of the first, after the bride and groom. She closes her eyes and opens her mouth, and for that one moment when the priest places the wafer on her tongue, she seems at peace; a peace like no other, and Jamie can't take her eyes off her, even as she leans in and asks Jack, the two of them left conspicuously alone in their pew, why he does not go up for communion. He says that he has not been to confession. You can't take communion if you don't confess.

"If you were going to confess, what would you confess?"

"Nothing," he says, "just like everybody else. And that is why I do not go to confession."

"Is that why your mother is praying so hard? Is she praying for you, Jack?"

"She prays for my success, my health, my happiness."

"What about your father, Jack. Does she pray for him?"

He doesn't respond.

"I saw his picture in the shrine."

He looks at her, alarmed. "What were you doing back there?"

"I was looking for my underwear."

He's got no response for that.

"You look like him," she says.

"That's not my father," he says.

"But…"

"A shrine, Jamie, is for the dead."

CHAPTER 7

Per cent' anni

ONCE OUTSIDE THE CHURCH, to Jamie's great relief, the women throw off their shawls and bare skin in much more voluptuous ways than she. Their cigarettes are lit and their sunglasses are on. Rice is passed out, and when Luca and Antonia exit they are barraged with it, but Jamie hesitates throwing hers. "You must throw the rice," someone says. "It's bad luck if you don't, or good luck if you do." Jamie, no longer sure, lets the rice fall through her fingers. It looks like it hurts.

The bride and groom lead the parade of wedding guests through the medieval village to the villa where the reception is being held. La Mamma takes Giovanni's arm as they walk, and Jamie strolls some distance behind them, enjoying the peace, serenity, and vast silence you'd imagine after the end of the world. It's just before dusk and the village is quiet, just the old ladies staring at them from stoops and balconies. The air is cool, and she starts to relax in her dress, in her skin.

There is a young man keeping pace beside Jamie now, scrawny but handsome, with blond curls. He is staring at her so blatantly that Jamie wonders if he knows her. She smiles fleetingly into his big brown eyes, then walks a little faster.

He walks faster too, his head cocked forward so he can look at her. "I am Silvestro," he says.

Giovanni glances back. "Ah, the great cousin from Rome." He waves pinched fingers before his chin, "What a surprise that you are late again!"

"*Sto sempre all'ora di Roma!*" Silvestro says. He is on Roman time.

They all stop to embrace.

"Silvestro is the son of Zio Lorenzo," Giovanni explains. "La Mamma's brother, my Godfather. They live in Rome."

"*La rossa,*" Silvestro says to Giovanni, followed by something else Jamie doesn't understand and Jack doesn't translate.

"*Ma cosa ti sei messo? E' il mio vestito?*" Jack demands to know, staring at Silvestro's jacket. "Is that my confirmation suit?"

Silvestro clears his throat and poses for them. "*Quanto sono bello.*" How good looking I am.

"*Si, che bello,*" La Mamma agrees, plucking an errant thread off the hem of his sleeve. She'd taken the suit in for Silvestro years ago. It wasn't easy. He's as thin as a rail.

They continue walking, though apparently the introduction didn't help, because Silvestro can't stop staring at Jamie.

"You'll have to excuse my cousin," Giovanni tells her. "You are the first American girl he has met."

"I'm sorry," she says, pushing her hand through her hair. "I imagine he wanted a blond."

Silvestro puts a hand through his own hair, which is thinning.

✒

The villa has layers of terraces that look out onto violet fields. It belongs to Antonia's great-aunt. With her mother and sister, Antonia has worked for weeks clearing debris, washing the stones, stringing lights, and hanging lanterns. Small tables are spread out on the different levels, decorated with flowers and fragrant herbs to keep away evil spirits. Caterina is wandering around with a basket of *confetti* that Jamie feels rather proud about, though she won't be able to eat another candied almond for as long as she lives.

Jack and Silvestro waste no time hitting the antipasti table, Jamie the prosecco table. She grabs two glasses and joins Jack, who immediately slips something into her mouth. "*Salsiccia di Bra,*" he says. "A specialty of the region. Fatty pig's meat and veal."

She has no choice but to swallow it whole.

The *pomodori alla novarese* she doesn't like, but she loves the deviled eggs, she tells him, the *uova ripiene*. "They're not deviled eggs, Jamie."

"They look like deviled eggs."

"These have REAL mayonnaise, Jamie."

"And I suppose that's not tuna fish, she says, about the sauce on the *vitello tonnato*."

"It's tuna fish."

She'd been kidding.

He dips a piece of celery into a pot of spicy, hot oil. "Umm, *bagna cauda,* I haven't had this in forever."

She tries it.

"You don't like it?"

"I didn't say I didn't like it."

"How could you not like it?"

"I love it!"

By now they've lost Silvestro.

"Try this." Once again, in her mouth with no forewarning, a texture that confuses her. "*Bruschettine con lardo*," he tells her and she covers her mouth, which is still chewing. "Did you say lard?"

"Cured pork fat."

"It tastes like lard."

They find Silvestro at the cheese table, slowly backing up against a gorgeous brunette. He is like Waldo, hard to find but always there, popping up right next to some *bella donna*… *caprini, paglierina*, various kinds of *robiola, sola, toma from Biella*, Giovanni is streaming off the names, if only to taste their melody on his tongue. "*Coppa di testa!*" He gasps, swallows, and grabs a fresh plate. "Head cheese," he explains a minute later, holding up a gelatinous slice.

She stares at it.

He stares at her.

The Po River—the longest and most important river in Italy, she has been told—has its source in the Alps, near here. She can't see it, but she can feel it streaming beneath and around them via a sudden swarm of mosquitoes. Jamie is standing there pretending to listen to Giovanni and Zio Marco's conversation when she feels a bite on her leg. She scratches it into a lump, which morphs into another lump, on her arm this time. She tries to remain calm because Jack and Zio Marco don't seem bothered by the sudden attack, though she sees other guests flailing around. The din grows to a buzzing level. Could this really be happening? At one point she swats a huge creature off Zio Marco's face. One has actually bitten Jack through his trouser leg, he finally admits to her.

La Mamma, unaffected, is on her way over again. For some reason she feels the need to introduce Jamie to every person over eighty years of age. She's got two of them with her this time. "Ah, the Crespi," Jack says, smacking Jamie on her bare back.

"Ouch," she glares at him.

He shows her the dead, bloody bug.

"That's it."

"Stay calm."

"I'm going inside."

He is trying not to laugh.

"I can't take it." She scratches her nose.

He assures her that the mosquitoes will leave at darkness, but it doesn't matter. She is already fleeing, passing Luca and Antonia on their way over after welcoming all the guests. Glasses clink behind her. Someone cheers, "*bacio bacio,*" and Jamie glances back just in time to see the bride and groom entwined in a languorous kiss.

Inside, the hired help are handing out bottles of mosquito repellant to desperate guests. "See," Jamie says to no one in particular. "It's not just me." She covers her legs and arms and neck with the spray that goes everywhere. She's got five bites and counting, not to mention the one on her nose. She heads toward the first room she can find, an empty parlor or library, and takes refuge on a gilded couch with clawed feet that exhales the dust of past lives when she sits down on it.

If she moves she'll itch, so she sits utterly still.

A clock ticks somewhere. Time is passing; a good thing, because Jack said the mosquitoes would leave at darkness. Of course she in no way believes him, she reminds herself, glancing out the window to see if it has grown darker—not dark enough. An elderly woman shuffles in and sits down on the couch opposite Jamie. "I'm never going out there again," Jamie assures the woman, who gets out her fan and waves it at her face.

More time passes. There are loud, boisterous noises every so often. Jamie is missing the party, certainly she could use a drink. She starts to wonder why Jack hasn't come looking for her just as La Mamma comes rushing into the room. She stops short, surprised and disconcerted to find Jamie sitting there.

"*Stai male?*" Are you ill?

Jamie smiles and nods, no way in hell is she going outside until dark.

"*Hai visto Giovanni?*" Have you seen Giovanni?

"I think he's still outside," Jamie responds, with no idea how she'd understood.

"*Perche' sei qui?*"

All Jamie took away was why. "Why? Because your son is a lunatic, that's why."

La Mamma blinks at her.

Jamie has to pee, but decides it's best not to move until La Mamma leaves; otherwise she might follow Jamie into the bathroom. Finally La Mamma does leave, even if reluctantly, and Jamie goes in search of *un bagno*. "Up the stairs at the end of the hall," is her interpretation of someone's directions, which leads her to a closet. This is where she finds Simona, Caterina, and some other women hovering outside a closed door behind which Antonia is crying on the sleeves of her mother and aunt. "The wedding is ruined," Simona tells Jamie.

"I know," Jamie gasps. "The mosquitoes, they're dreadful!"

Simona looks at Jamie, confused. "Luca fought with the Crespi," she says, lighting a cigarette, more amused than concerned. "Antonia's dress has blood on it. She refuses to come outside."

Now Jamie is confused. She steps out onto the balcony and stands at the balustrade, searching through the bodies below for Giovanni or Luca, but quickly forgets them, for the air has cooled significantly and a faint breeze is rustling the leaves. The trees have also come to life with thousands of tiny white lights. Verdi is playing; the crowd seems almost entranced. Candles flutter on long tables set with various platters of pastas, meats, and other regional specialties. The red wine has been poured—Ruffoli '97 Barolo—they'd finally decided after a week's debate. Jamie can smell the tannins from here. Her gaze lifts upward. Can a sky really be lavender, she wonders, noticing for the first time that the mosquitoes are gone, just as Jack had promised.

She is back outside now, listening to Giovanni and Antonia's brothers-in-law discuss some person called *maiale*. Not a person, a pig—it finally dawns on her when she notices the smile glowing on Giovanni's face, the way he gets whenever he talks about this particular animal. "You know that Antonia is up there crying," Jamie feels the need to inform them.

"*E' Luca*," a brother-in-law says. "*e'cosi'*."

"She'll get used to it," Giovanni says.

"Where is Luca?" she asks, and someone snickers.

Jack explains that Luca emptied his wine glass on the Crespi kid's head, and the Crespi grandfather, the old geezer, punched Luca in the nose. "The old man packs a punch," he assures her. "Luca's got a big bloody one going. Zia Maddalena and Zia Claudia are putting ice on it now."

"Luca must have been provoked. What did the kid say to him?"

"We were having a friendly discussion, and then the kid, that *coglione* (jerk), said something about mixing our grapes with other grapes so they can market a wine that sells."

The brothers-in-law wince and shake their heads.

"The Crespi say that they are not in the business of vines. They are in the business of wines."

More snickering, and then they go back to their *maiale* discussion that Jack feels the need to translate for her, like how the pig is fed, slaughtered, sliced open, hung, drained, what pig parts are used to make what meats. "Every piece is used; it's the most efficient animal, Jamie," he says, looking sternly into her eyes. He seems to have a primal need to convince her of this animal's particular worth, the worth of all the food that has touched her lips since her arrival, for that matter. "Being in the business of wines instead of vines isn't necessarily a bad strategy, Jack."

He pretends not to have heard her. "It's important that you remember to eliminate the eyes, the cartilage, the nose parts, and the lips," Jack is saying, referring to the head cheese. "Then you take the pig's head, tail, feet, bones, tongue, heart and throat, boil it, skim it, kneed it together into a big ball of fat, and then stuff it in a sausage casing." His eyes are wild, not to mention amused by her reaction, which is to stare at him, horrified. In reality, she's less horrified than mesmerized, and trying to hold on to her senses, to not fall even harder for this man who might desire a pig more than he does her.

Luca, no worse for the wear, hops up onto a table and announces to everyone that the wedding feast is being served. Jamie can't imagine eating at this moment. Perhaps it's the head cheese discussion, but something does not feel right in her stomach. Silvestro, who hasn't really been listening to the *maiale* discussion because he's been fawning over another *bella donna,* hoists Antonia up suddenly onto the table with Luca. Groom with busted nose, bride with bloody dress. "*Viva gli sposi!*" everyone cheers. Long live the bride and groom! And then all the guests make a mad rush for the buffet.

The line is haphazard and long and people complain passionately about this. Zio Marco pulls Giovanni aside to confer about Luca's behavior with the Crespi, who have left. Jamie stands idly by, anticipating what Jack will say next, which is that he has decided not sell the remaining hectares. Apparently, this is exactly what he does say, for Zio Marco is now flashing her a scrutinizing look, as if this might be her doing. *This is in no way my doing,* her eyes say playfully back. A moment passes like that, and then Zio puts on a congratulatory face and slaps Jack on the back. Fear? Is that what Jamie senses shifting behind Zio's beady eyes. Or is it simply paternal concern, as well it should be.

Jack turns his attention back to the feast, which is eaten, discussed, dissected, criticized, analyzed, adored, disdained, and devoured. He seems almost giddy, as if a weight has been lifted from his shoulders. And he wasn't kidding about that pig. Every part of it is everywhere. It keeps waving its little butt around; in the *fritto misto*—a mixture of fried anything; in the *bollito*—boiled meats you dip in parsley sauce; in the *agnolotti*.

The raspberry tart is the size of a hot tub. It is served with *spumante* and a toast: "*Per cent'anni.*" For one hundred years!

A hundred years, really?

It's just a traditional saying, he tells her.

It's also tradition for the old people to go home and the young people to go wild as the party transforms itself. Disco music blares, dancing takes over, Luca flips Antonia over his shoulder at one point and her trellis rips off. "*Buona fortuna!*" someone yells. It means good luck. Luca rips open his shirt. "Is that good luck?" No, that's just Luca.

The party will go on into the night, she is told. These Italians are going to go wild, she is told. She should be happy, ready to let loose because as an American she can party with the best of them—and yet Giovanni won't dance; he simply refuses to dance. So they stand there with their sweet liquors and watch the antics. Luca and Antonia have disappeared, but Zia Claudia is out there, having a ball.

"You don't believe it, do you?" Jamie asks him.

"Believe what?"

"The hundred years, that people can be married forever."

"Like I said. It's just a saying."

She turns and examines him. He couldn't possibly. She sets her eyes back on the dance floor. "Well, I don't believe it. Not for one second." When he still doesn't respond, she adds, "So what happened to what was right, Jack?"

"What do you mean?"

"I mean your mother, this place?"

"I'm going to make it right," he says.

There it is again. That heartfelt intensity; it disembodies her. Throws her off balance, and she must collect herself for a moment. "I just keep thinking prudence, Jack," she offers finally. "Are you sure you're not letting emotion drive your decision? You're an engineer, after all. It's ironic…"

"I will tell you what's ironic, Jamie." He turns and looks directly at her. "Nonno Giacomo sent me to the States so that I could bring back fresh perspective and new ideas. Instead, Luca's kept this place alive by doing exactly the opposite." He glances at his watch. "That's what's ironic."

He's staring at her now.

She is staring at the dance floor. "I don't think our relationship can work if you don't dance."

He takes her hand and leads her onto the dance floor, through the throng of sweaty bodies, and out the other side. Across the terrace, inside the villa, through the kitchen is a laundry room. She wonders if perhaps they are finally going to make love, but then she'd thought he was taking her for a dance back there, too. She'd thought he was going to sell the vines. She'd thought she wasn't going to care one way or another.

"What's that rancid smell?" she stops short at the doorway and says too loud, for the cousins are all staring at her now. They sit crammed inside the tiny space—Luca, Silvestro, Simona, Caterina, and Antonia—before an open magnum of wine. 1925 is scribbled on the glass, the Barolo she'd seen in the cellar the other day. She lets out a little gasp. The first eyes she finds are Antonia's, which are resigned and a little desperate and suddenly Jamie wishes they could communicate. Things are not as expected. Luca is not going to work for her father's tire company, Jamie is guessing, and Antonia, at thirty, will leave her parents home tonight for the first time, for good.

Luca pours the wine into tiny glasses. The Chosen One is holding the groups' attention in some pontification about his decision to keep the vines, his decision to help Luca make this vineyard a sustainable business, something they can leave behind for future generations. He takes a glass and breathes in the fumes like he's not just breathing in his past, but his future. *"Ai nostri avi,"* he says. No need for him to translate. It's the hope in his eyes that's unbearable, and she edges herself backward. She can't be part of this family drama, this little circle of trust. She can't be because she doesn't know how to be.

Luca pushes a glass into her hand. They must all drink simultaneously, he says.

There is, of course, the chance that it will taste like vinegar, or worse, someone says.

"*Salute.*"

They raise glasses.

"*Cin, cin.*"

CHAPTER 8

Risotto con Barolo

JAMIE HADN'T ASKED JACK what it meant to keep the vineyard, how it would change things. She knew this wasn't a rational decision of his. But then she'd not been rational, either. She should have tried to dissuade him more. But alas, Italy had gotten the better of her, too. Especially after they'd polished off that 1925, and then gone on to party all night with his cousins. She couldn't remember experiencing a more spectacular evening.

But now, back in San Francisco, she assumed the reality would hit Jack of why he'd been sent to America in the first place. America is prudent. America is real. Jack has been designated to run Norwest's design group, post-merger with L-3. That is real whereas Italy is a dream, and since Jamie's return, in the back of her mind she's been hoping it will go away, or at least keep itself contained on the other side of the Atlantic.

At home she falls back into the throws of post-merger reporting. For the most part, their personal lives return to the way they'd been before Italy—Jack spending most nights at Jamie's place, their relationship enjoying its solitude and anonymity. Her post-merger obligations will be finished in a month, and for all Jamie knows, her and Jack's relationship will be finished too. Her safety net, a trick she plays with her mind to counterbalance the effects of a love that seems to only want to deepen, driven by some force stronger than nature, stronger than her.

She is pursuing another client in Seattle now and has just flown home from a pitch meeting there. It's only four in the afternoon, but she decides not to go into the office. She heads home to work instead, where she's surprised to find Jack in her kitchen, hacking apart a farmer's market chicken. Since returning from Italy he's been cooking with a new fervor. Her apartment is on the second floor of a Victorian on Russian Hill, with sweeping views of the Bay Bridge. The ceilings are high and the rooms are spacious, but the kitchen is a tiny afterthought. Jack, or perhaps better to say Giovanni, has always seemed at home in it. So it's no surprise to find him there cooking now, but at four p.m.? And with that chicken bleeding all over the place? "I think I was a butcher in a past life," he says. This is his hello, and she sits down on a stool right there, without the energy to even pull her briefcase from her shoulder.

It's Thursday. Normally they go to the wine bar on Thursday, but clearly he's got something else in mind, she thinks, watching him separate a leg from a thigh. "You're home early," she points out.

"I went to talk to Jim today about my green card application."

"You're applying for a green card?"

He looks at her like this is a stupid question.

She starts to feel stupid as he continues, "I'm coming up on my H-1 limit, five years. I was in the midst of the green card process with L-3 when the Norwest merger happened. Jim informed me yesterday that I'd have to start the process over because Norwest's policies are all different." He goes back to what he's doing. "So fuck it, I took the package."

Her briefcase falls to the floor. "The severance package? You took the severance package?"

"Norwest requires a three year commitment, Jamie." He waves his knife in the air. "*Vaffanculo,* I told him. At L-3 the commitment was six months."

"What's wrong with three years?"

"Three years is like death."

"But Jim had you pegged to run the group!"

"I don't want to run the group!" Thwack. He just split the chest. "Don't you get it?"

Her face flushes uncontrollably.

"I'm sorry," he says, about his tone, and works silently for a minute.

"I guess I'm just catching up here, Jack. I mean...I just assumed," she pauses to gather her thoughts. "I don't know... that you already had a green card? You've been here for what, a decade? How the hell have you been staying here without a green card?"

He sets down the knife. "Listen," he says. "This is how it works, Jamie." A big, rather ceremonious breath. "I had a student visa for four years when I was at MIT, then again for two years of graduate school at Cornell, plus one year on an F-1 that allows you to work for a year without an H-1, which I did at Ambient in Chicago. So that's seven years." He is using his fingers to keep track. "Plus the four I've been working with the H-1: one year with Parsons in Texas, the next year with

Hughes in L.A., and the last two with L-3 in Redwood City."
He picks up the knife again.

There is some silence.

"That bankruptcy really did a number on you."

Back at the chicken.

"So you've been working the system then."

"Yes, I have."

"Maybe you should get a PhD."

"Don't kid yourself. That's what a lot of foreigners do."

She's lost the thread, the bottom line. "Is this your way of
telling me you're going back?"

"You don't understand."

"You're right," Jamie says. "I don't."

"The severance package will give me six months pay, plus
my bonus. That money will give me flexibility to make some
investments in the vineyard. Meanwhile, I'll find another job,
another sponsor, one without a three year prison sentence."

The vineyard, she mumbles.

"If Luca's going to up his production capacity, he needs to
invest in new fermentation technology. He's got this crazy idea for
a new rotation device, only the modern tanks won't accommodate
his design and custom tanks are too expensive. I've started to do
some research, put together some designs of my own."

He pours water into the pot sizzling with vegetables,
dumps in the chicken parts. It occurs to her that she doesn't
have a drink. She gets out the martini shaker, shakes up some
vodka and vermouth, retrieves the glasses from the freezer,
two olives for him, one for her.

"Cheers," he says, taking his sip.

The vodka does its work. Another sip, just to be sure.
"How long do you have to find another sponsor?"

"Six weeks."

She swallows, hard. "Can you find a job in six weeks?"

He shrugs. "There's always the lottery."

"Lottery?"

"The INS hands out so many green cards per year on a random basis. You apply. It's like throwing your name in a hat."

"This is a viable plan?"

"It can't hurt."

"What if you apply for a different visa? A Tourist visa."

"I'll still have to leave, apply for it in Italy, and then come back; and when I do, no doubt the immigration asshole will look at my passport and say, dude, like, you've been in the states for over a decade. Go back and live in your own country."

This is all happening too fast. Jamie's mind is swirling. "You'll be totally fine, of course," she says, focusing on the chicken feet sticking up out of the pot. "You have an engineering degree from MIT and a Masters in Applied Sciences from Cornell."

He's disinfecting the cutting board.

"You'll have no problem finding another sponsor."

Salmonella, the guy doesn't mess around.

The idea of calling her sister for help comes unpleasantly to mind. She just spoke with Jill this morning.

"How was Italy?" her sister had asked, though Jamie could tell by her tone that Jill didn't want to hear about Italy as much as she was bracing herself for the drama that lay beneath it. To date, Jamie's career didn't leave time for spur of the moment trips to romantic locations. Jamie's travel was all about work, and she rarely returned with very interesting stories. Now, suddenly, Jamie was off to Italy with someone she'd been dating only two months? Jamie had only called and told her sister this little piece of information as she and Jack were on their way to the airport.

"Do we even know this guy?" Her sister would have done a background check if she knew how.

So when this morning Jill asked Jamie how her trip to Italy had been, Jamie remained blasé, keeping her emotions in check, as she always did with Jill. "I worked a lot, and his mother didn't like that. I won't be invited back any time soon, I'm sure."

There seemed to be relief on the other end. "Did you see Venice?"

"No."

"Bellagio is amazing. You were right near there, no?"

"I think."

"Aren't the Winter Olympics in Turin?"

Jamie had no idea how to explain to her sister why she had not seen these places. "Time was short."

Now, as Jack stood watch over a simmering chicken, Jamie sat resigning herself to calling Jill back. "Why did he resign again?" might be her sister's first reply. Still, if Jamie asked for help, Jill would be the first to give it. Problem resolution is Jill's MO. For Jamie, she'd give Jack the benefit of the doubt, plow through her contact list and have five interviews set up for him by next week. Then she'd call their equally well connected mother and instruct her to do the same. Yes, Jamie could resort to these driven, take-no-prisoners women if necessary. She could offer this to Jack.

So why doesn't she? Why does she let time pass until it's too late? It is another night, a different cooking fest three weeks later. Jack is waiting to hear back from an interview he'd had for a job in Denver.

"Risotto with Barolo," he says, popping open the bottle.

"Jack," she says, staring at the bottle. She's presenting her pipeline report to the Managing Partner tomorrow, after flying back and forth between Seattle and L.A. for the Boeing-Kline proposal. She is exhausted, stressed out, and gaining weight for the first time since college. "Let's be pragmatic."

She wonders if he already knows that this must happen but can't get himself to speak about it. He can't ask anything of her. He isn't ready for marriage, certainly.

"Let's just go down to the Justice of the Peace and not think about it." It comes out quick, no time for second thoughts.

He may have gone still, for a millisecond, she's not sure.

"Marriage," she says.

He ladles stock from one pot to another.

"If we get married, you can take your time finding a job."

He takes the open bottle of Barolo, pours a glass, takes a sip, and then pours it into the stock pot of rice that he has not stopped vigorously stirring.

"Jack…"

"I'm not going to marry you for my green card, Jamie." He doesn't bother turning around.

"Then what do you intend to do Jack, Giovanni, or whatever the hell your name is? You're going to move to Denver?"

She can't see his face. The stirring must not stop.

"Marriage is just a piece of paper, like your green card. It's a means to an end, not an ideal. I don't expect us to live happily ever after."

He adds more stock, continues stirring.

"In fact, if you think about it logically, it's the perfect revenge." She pauses. "Don't you see?"

"I don't have any idea what you're talking about."

She's getting animated now. Suddenly it's all so clear. "My parents wasted twenty years of their lives trying to make their marriage work—counseling, retreats, hypnosis—they even considered joining a commune, for God's sake. All the fighting, all the tears and betrayal—for what? My father eventually met a woman he truly loved, and walked out. He's still with her now; kids, the whole bit, after so many years of my parents' lives wasted."

Jack is still stirring, with purpose.

Jamie leans forward, on the edge of her seat. "Don't you see? It's not their fault. It is the institution of marriage's fault. Marriage has used mankind since its inception, destroying couple after couple, and now we can use it."

"Maybe it's not the institution that's destroyed the couple, but the couple that's destroyed the institution."

"Oh please, next you're going to tell me the reason you want a green card is because of your belief in the great, wonderful, U.S. of A."

"I'm not going to bother responding to that."

"And don't even get me started on your parents."

"That's different," he says, turning and glaring. "That's about religion."

"Marriage, religion, same damn thing. They're crutches, ways for people to believe they can control things and put off death."

"You're crazy," he says.

Maybe she is. But is he any less? The stirring is endless. Jamie wonders if his arm will fall off.

"I've done the research, Jack. We've only got to stay married two years for the green card to become permanent."

He puts down the spoon, serves their plates with a ladle, grates on *parmigiano*, and sits down across from her. She is still waiting for his eyes to find hers. She won't pick up her fork, which she knows unnerves him, because it is critical to eat the risotto while the consistency is just right. Jack is flattening his into a pancake, the way he does, so that he can eat from the outer, cooler edges, working his way inward.

"In two years you are legal for life, even if we divorce."

He throws his fork down, pushes his plate back, and walks out.

Her heart stops; then it pounds. It's all she hears for long, aching minutes, or hours, she's not sure. She thinks maybe time has stopped.

Then he walks back in again. "For the last time, Jamie, I'm not going to marry you for my green card!"

She looks down at her plate. What she sees there is as perplexing and unexpected as what she's just offered him. The risotto is purple. It looks like brain.

He takes her shoulders, turns her to face him, and calmly and sternly says, "I'm going to marry you because I love you."

She might be shaking, she's not sure, for she'd been afraid he would say something like that, and ruin everything.

He sits back down across from her. She averts her gaze to her plate until it's no longer brain there but her heart, coagulating now because she's waited too long. Why is it so hard for her to look into his eyes and admit the same thing? There is no uncertainty; some things are just known, but all she can do is pick up her fork and take a bite of what he has so lovingly prepared for her. She swallows this little piece of herself, feeling the weight of his eyes upon her and his desire to hear nothing of what she thinks. He knows what she thinks. It takes a minute for the raw, earthy flavors to reach down into her soul. It takes another minute for her to fully realize that this has happened.

CHAPTER 9

The Birds

*S*HE IS WAITING FOR THEM on the steps of City Hall, wearing a beige pantsuit and holding a bouquet of street-vendor tulips. It is windy and cold, and it occurs to her that she hates this city. San Francisco has always felt damp and vacant to Jamie, and yet, *it is the most beautiful city in the world*—this is what everyone says. It is what Jill said when Jamie was first applying to business schools. Jill had just finished her law degree at Stanford, and upon moving here Jamie had agreed with her, with them; but now a homeless man has just walked up and spit on her shoe, and Jamie thinks that perhaps she never really agreed with them at all.

She moves to the other side of the portico and checks her watch. Their appointment with the Justice of the Peace is for ten-thirty a.m. and her flight to L.A. is at two p.m. She had to finagle her schedule in order to be in town the past two days and get everything arranged: blood tests, marriage license, rings. No pomp and circumstance, this marriage is simply a prudent transaction. She feels for the gold wedding bands in one pocket, the instant camera in the other. They will need pictures for the green card interview, Jack has told her; proof that they are in love.

Jack's never late. She calls him on his cell but gets his voice mail, once again thrown off guard at the sound of Giovanni's voice, not Jack's. When, exactly, had he changed the message? She hangs up and he calls right back. They are exiting highway 101 and she can hear Silvestro's thick Italian voice in the background as it starts to drizzle. Coatless, she backs up underneath the white and gold leaf awning, along with the other loitering homeless.

Silvestro is here for the summer, having just finished his fourth year at Rome's La Sapienza University with no sights on graduating any time soon. His grades are poor, he's uninspired, and his father, Zio Lorenzo, Giovanni's uncle and Godfather, is worried his son will never finish. He has sent Silvestro to the States for the summer break, to learn English and perhaps be inspired by how the Chosen One lives. Jamie is still getting used to this little fact that Jack had withheld from her until only a week ago. Surely he'd known since Luca's wedding that Silvestro was coming, and probably even before that.

"Why didn't you tell me?" she'd demanded in a burst of anxiety. Not only was Jack moving in, but now Silvestro was too?

"I don't know," he'd responded blankly, amused by her reaction. "I didn't think about it." A minute or so went by.

"I'm in the final stages of my Partner Book, Jack. I'm traveling. I won't have time to take care of him, or be a good hostess."

"I'm not asking you to."

She spots them now, running up the stately, manicured lawn. "*Dai, sbrigati,*" Giovanni is yelling to Silvestro who is three paces behind. Once they reach her Silvestro falls over on his knees to catch his breath, raising a hand to indicate that she must wait a minute before he can speak. She smiles at the sweat spotting his golden forehead. He is exactly as she remembers him; striking nose, boyish eyes, and too young to be going bald. Quick kisses hello, then they drag him to the designated spot under the rotunda where the service will be performed.

"It's not the Duomo, but eh," Giovanni says, opening up his arms to the grand, baroque space. When he stops, Silvestro bumps into him. He'd been looking up at the frescoed ceilings, slightly amused, slightly awed, and certainly nervous. A woman in a tight skirt passes by in the opposite direction, causing Silvestro to spin around on one foot and follow her.

"*Dai* Silvestro," Giovanni calls after him.

Silvestro runs back. "*Bella* San Francisco," he says.

"You've explained to him that he's not here to see the sights?" Jamie says to Giovanni, handing Silvestro the camera.

"I am honored," Silvestro takes the camera and stands to attention. She can tell he practiced this phrase in the car with Giovanni, and imagines he must be shocked. He has just flown halfway around the world, has not even had the chance to change or unpack, and now he's been kidnapped as a witness to their hasty nuptials. His demeanor has turned serious now, torn, she believes, between his adoration for his cousin and his beliefs about the church and its absence from this proceeding. He keeps mumbling in Italian to Giovanni. *God should be your witness,* Jamie imagines him saying. Certainly, he must not approve.

"It's no big deal," she says, feeling the need to reassure Silvestro. "In America marriage is not taken so seriously." She says this quickly, and Giovanni doesn't translate. A family of pigeons flutters over their heads, making her gasp and duck before watching them settle on various high landings. "*Pezzi di merda*," Giovanni says about the pigeons, just as the Justice comes down the stairs with his aide.

There is something odd about the man in his robe, a thought that Jamie distracts herself with during what she keeps telling herself are banal, routine proceedings. Vows, rings, a kiss that feels silly with everyone's eyes now upon them. Silvestro snaps the photo. The judge shakes their hands and waddles back up the stairs. He looks like Alfred Hitchcock, Jack says to her. "And is it just me, or is there pigeon shit everywhere?" It's the first time she's felt at ease that day, not because the service is over, not because their journey together has just begun, but because, once again, their minds have settled on the same orthogonal thought. In this case Hitchcock.

It's a strange and slightly terrifying notion, one that leaves her feeling torn as she rushes off to catch her plane to L.A. for the Boeing project kickoff. For the first ten minutes of her flight she sits contemplating the seat back in front of her. Then the flight attendant brings her a glass of first class champagne. After a few sips her senses awaken, and Jamie reminds herself that the idea of Jack reading her thoughts and vice versa is a romantic notion. So is the part about two people becoming one. More sips, more sense. Screw the honeymoon, the heart shaped bed. She raises her glass; here's what she has to say about the institution of marriage: if and when the inevitable happens, when Giovanni decides to leave her, Jamie will let him. It will be painful, certainly, but their parting will be clean and brisk. Jamie's eyes are open on this one, she tells herself, finishing off her champagne, resting her head back, and falling asleep.

She brings a pile of work home that weekend. The merger did not begin well. There are factions and fiefdoms, way too much posturing. She suspects this client will cause her many all-nighters. Plus, she's working with a tax partner from the Chicago office who doesn't have a concept of time. He'll ask for something at five p.m. and expect it delivered by eight a.m. the next morning. On top of that, she's been designated to head an internal committee to redesign her firm's review process and bonus system—but she wants to forget all that for now. It's Friday night, and all she cares about is being in Jack's presence. Their weekends together are like entering a distress chamber. She's envisioning martinis at Red Roof and dinner at Little Thai, suddenly with a serious craving for fish cakes. She throws open her apartment door...

"*Ciao!*"

"*Ciao!*"

She freezes at the second *ciao*. While Jack had kept her updated about Silvestro on the phone this past week, she'd not considered the reality of him being a living breathing witness to the intimacy of their daily lives until this very moment. Jamie's feelings for Jack are so intensely private, she doesn't trust that they can survive exposure to human contact, like the supplest skin before a blazing sun. She'll be exposed, laid bare, he'll see her crying at commercials, the way she looks at Jack or lays her head on his shoulder, the way he makes her giggle and laugh. This is why she made Jack agree to keep their vows between them only, and Silvestro now, until they see how things go.

Is that fried bacon?

She lugs her things down the hall, maneuvering her suitcase around the framed Italian prints Jack's got stacked along the floor in preparation for hanging. "You can't leave the walls blank forever," he told her last week when they moved his things in. The Saints Day poster he'd brought back from Italy is now framed and propped against the dining room wall, where she drops her briefcase to the floor because the table is piled with his blueprints. She takes a moment to gather herself, then slaps on a grin and pokes her head through the kitchen doorway, only to be instantly alarmed by what she sees. "Is that a Budweiser?"

Silvestro leaps up from his stool. "Hi!" He waves and steps back into Jack at the stove.

"*E fa attenzione,* Silvestro."

"There's Corona, Jack," Jamie says, "or Heineken."

"I am in America!" Silvestro says. "I must drink the Bud Weiser."

When it occurs to her that he's not kidding, she glances at the pan Jack's got going on the stove.

"*Pasta carbonara!*" Jack announces, as if it were the answer to everything.

"It's Friday night, Jack. I'm sure Silvestro wants to go out."

"It's okay," Silvestro says. Okay is the one word with the same meaning in both languages; only it sounds funny when he says it.

"It's okay to go out? Or okay to stay here?"

"We eat in," Giovanni says, "like a good Italian family."

"*Non ti piace la pasta carbonara?*" Silvestro asks and Jack translates, "You don't like pasta carbonara?"

"Have I had it?"

"*Eehhh, la pasta carbonara…mamma che bbuona.*" Silvestro has his hands together, praying. The signature dish of Rome, his city, he's practically salivating. Jamie stares at him, then Jack, back at Silvestro, and then goes to change.

The walk-in closet smells of wool, cashmere, and fine leather that he's organized neatly and unobtrusively while she's been gone. His suits are hung, his shoes lined up on the floor, a shoe horn—not one pair of sneakers, certainly no sweats. She opens a drawer. His underwear is folded next to white cotton undershirts; his belts are coiled. When she sees the stack of hand-sewn handkerchiefs, she closes the drawer quickly.

Her clothes she changes ever so slowly, lingering in the smell of his things in the room, but also enjoying one last moment, of what she is not sure, just the sense that soon it will be gone.

"Are you hiding in here?"

Is gone. She jumps and gasps and falls back into the shoe rack.

He looks alarmed, then amused. "Are you Okay?"

Her heart beats wildly. "You scared the shit out of me."

"I missed you," he says, and she sighs as he moves in and they hold each other, awkwardly, clandestinely, the shoe rack digging into Jamie's lower back, but no matter, it's as if the tighter they hold on the more of last week's absence will be erased. Jack pulls back finally. "You're not going to hide in the closet for the next three months are you?"

"Are you trying to be funny?"

He pinches her cheek with his knuckles, hard and long, as if he can't help himself.

"Ouch," she says, rubbing her face. She'd seen his family do it, but never Jack, and certainly not to her. "What was that for?"

"I'm sorry," he says, not sorry at all. In fact he's beaming, and she wonders what it is he's got to be so happy about. "How was the Lockheed interview?" she asks, following him back to the kitchen.

"Good," he says.

"And you've got Bechtel Monday?"

"Thursday."

"What's with the flag over the toilet?"

"Juve," is all he says, and she remembers. Juve is short for Juventus, his soccer team; they're not doing well this year.

She pauses at the kitchen doorway because only two people can fit inside the space comfortably, or so she'd always thought. She suggests they clear the table in the dining room, but Silvestro insists that he is happy here, that the dining room table is much too big. So the wood block kitchen table that barely fits two now miraculously fits three. Jamie gets the martini shaker which takes a minute to find because Jack has rearranged her cupboards to accommodate his prime possessions: a wooden spoon, stock pot, frying pan, sauce pan, strainer, and razor-sharp knives.

A martini in Italy is essentially vermouth, Jack warns her.

"Yes, well, we're in America now," she says, retrieving the vodka from the freezer.

She mixes their drinks, hands one to Silvestro.

His eyes pop open. "Wow!"

"Not bad, huh."

"*Mamma mia.*"

"How's the English class?"

His eyes go dull.

"He's already dying of boredom," Jack says.

"*Forse un po'…*"

"Speak in English!"

"Maybe just a little boring."

"*E' pigro,*" Jack says. "He's so lazy."

"*Ma no!*" Silvestro appeals to Jamie. "*Ma tutto il giorno, otto ore…*"

"Speak in English!"

"We speak such boring things," he struggles to say. "What did you 'ave for breakfast? At what time did you wake up? *Ma che…*"

They revert to Italian. (Giovanni wants to speak in English about as much as Silvestro does.) When they are done, Jack informs Jamie that Silvestro is studying architecture at University in Rome.

"I love architecture," Jamie says with a burst of encouragement, not to mention nostalgia, for it was one of the many careers she'd considered while growing up; no closed doors where she came from.

"He hates architecture."

"Oh." Her shoulders drop. "Then why are you studying it?"

"His father is an architect in Rome, and everyone in his mother's family is an architect. They own a firm and someday Silvestro will work there. It's in his DNA."

"*Mah,* Papá wants me to be happy, to find something I like…"

"Then switch majors," Jamie suggests, thinking she's stating the obvious.

"It's too late to switch now. University in Italy is subdivided into smaller schools, each devoted to one major. He's in the architecture school, and has been going to architecture classes since day one. He'd have to apply to a different department, and start completely over. That could mean another four to five years."

"Oh dear."

Silvestro, shaking his head, "I think I will never finish."

"You must finish," Jamie says definitively, reflexively, for the alternative is unimaginable.

"But what is the point of school?"

Jamie glances at Jack. "To get a job, of course."

"In Italy it's different," Jack sets her straight. "University doesn't necessarily improve your chances of getting a job like it does in the States. Most students take six years to get their degree. You take classes with thousands of others, live at home, learn little from the experience, and then you still can't get a job unless you know someone."

"What about career centers, recruiters, job counselors?"

Jack explains the concept to Silvestro, who proceeds to look at Jamie like she's nuts.

"What do you really want to be?" Jamie asks.

"This is the problem," Silvestro responds. "I 'ave no idea."

"Tomorrow," Giovanni raises a finger in the air like Mussolini, "We go to San Carlos!"

"San Carlos?" she frowns. "That's not very exciting."

"I'm meeting with some tank manufacturers, and Silvestro will come with me."

"He'll be bored," Jamie says.

"He is here to learn."

"I want to learn," Silvestro agrees, though his eyes say something else as he suddenly leans in toward Jamie. "And now, Jamie, you must 'elp me."

Jamie leans back. "Help you with what?"

"*La professoressa…*" he says, looking at Jamie with those big, pleading eyes. He has fallen in love with his English teacher, Giovanni explains as if he has already spent the week listening to Silvestro go on about this blond haired, blue eyed, American girl of his dreams.

"Tell me, Jamie. How must I talk to the American girl?"

He gives up on English and has Jack translate the rest. "But how can I impress this girl with my charm if I cannot speak from the heart? How will she agree to go with me if I am not able to communicate the true Silvestro?"

"For real?" Jamie says.

Yes, for real.

"Play it cool," she tells Silvestro, suddenly concerned.

"Kool," he repeats the word.

"American girls don't go in for ogling and fawning."

"I must be Kool."

"Cool. This isn't Italy. We do things differently here."

"Kool."

Jamie sips her drink.

"Once she knows me she cannot resist me." He shows Jamie his profile. "*Guarda che figo.*"

She turns to Jack. "He's not getting it, is he?"

CHAPTER 10

Wine Buyers Guide

AFTER A DAY SPENT interviewing peers and colleagues for feedback on the firm's bonus system, which basically involved sitting around listening to everyone complain, Jamie returns home to find two bottles of wine open on the kitchen table. She follows the trail to the balcony to find Jack and Silvestro with their wine glasses, smoking, Silvestro his cigarette, Jack his Toscano. They stopped at a few wine shops on their way back from San Carlos, for research purposes, they tell her. There's not much of a selection from Piemonte, but they managed to find some overpriced bottles of Barbaresco and Nebbiolo. "In Italy you could buy that bottle for three Euros, the equivalent of five dollars." They bought it for twenty. Silvestro is still astounded.

They return to the kitchen to refill their glasses, and Jack slaps down a thick paperback text on the table, *Thompson's Wine Buyer's Guide*. He bought it at The Wine Club on Market Street.

She flips it open. "Soon your wine will be in this guide, no?"

"Jamie, this guy's an idiot."

"I thought he was the holy grail of wine."

"1,500 pages in here, 800 are devoted to France and only 100 to Italy. Even California has 300 pages. That's just wrong. *Testa di cazzo* Jamie, listen to this." He turns to an earmarked page. "This tannic, well-structured, muscular 1996 Barolo offers an intriguing nose as well as flavors of melted asphalt, tomato skin, jammy strawberry and cherry fruit…"

"Tomato skin?" She reads more over his shoulder. "Leather?"

His jaw clenches.

"Cigar box?"

Another random page, "Can a wine be lusty?"

"*Basta!*" Enough. Jack grabs the book from her and rips out the Italian section. Then he marches into the living room and throws what remains, almost the entire book, into the fireplace. Jamie turns to Silvestro, "So how was San Carlos?" His eyes cross at the thought of San Carlos.

"Why am I in California?" Jack says, throwing a lit match into the fire. "Nobody here has any idea what I'm talking about." He returns to the dining table, where he's got designs spread out and starts making notes with a mechanical pencil.

"But why you not buy the tank?" Silvestro, following him, asks.

Jamie says, "Good question," then repeats it, "Why must you make your own tank, Jack?"

"Because I can." He doesn't look up. "The price point is still too high, though. I've got to find a way to make it cost less."

Silvestro says, "Does it matter if the tank is wide or narrow, tall or short, oak or steel? People buy your wine because they like you."

"No, they buy my wine because Peter Thompson tells them to buy it."

"I like you, you like me, we become friends, you buy my wine."

"What Silvestro is saying, Jack, is that it's about relationships."

"This is what I say."

"He's asking if people really care so much about how a wine is made, as long as they like it."

"If you don't care now," Jack says, "...soon you will."

"All I know is that I like what I like and don't want to pay much money."

"Well, it's different now, Silvestro. Thompson's changing things. Even in Italy, you'll see."

"Sad but true," Jamie resigns. "When I buy wine, I'm embarrassed to admit that it's the price that guides me. If the price is high, then certainly the wine is better quality than one that costs less."

Jack flashes her a blatantly dumb, exasperated look. "That's ridiculous, Jamie."

"I'm a product of American consumerism. What do you want me to say?"

He throws down his pencil. "*Porca miseria,* I have to get out of California." He heads to the bedroom.

"What's wrong with California?"

He stops, turns. "Two words, Jamie." He waits to see if she can guess them.

She doesn't.

"Napa. Valley."

Silvestro grabs a cigarette and disappears. Jamie watches him slip out onto the balcony with an urge to join him, to hear more about his thoughts and dreams, to help guide him if she can. She's never had a younger sibling or a younger living anything in her life for that matter, someone who looks up to her not down, someone to worry about, and it feels kind of nice… She closes her eyes as reality cuts into her straying thoughts. After fifteen years she still can't immediately acknowledge the fact that she does, in fact, have younger siblings. Half-siblings that is, those who barely know her, let alone respect or admire her… Her thoughts stray to the house her father and his alternative family have settled into in Big Bear. Her father had always wanted to live in the mountains; he loved hiking, biking, all those outdoorsy, thin-aired activities. Jamie and Jill make the obligatory trip every so often. Their father is always inviting them to his home, but that's what it is, his home. Jamie never feels quite right there, just as her father never felt quite right in the home he once shared with his first wife and daughters.

"By the way," Jack adds casually. "Your sister called. She's in town next month for business and wants to do dinner."

Her mind jolts back to the present… "You spoke to her?"

"She says she wants to meet me."

Jamie sighs, inwardly. Jack recorded a new message on the answering machine when he moved in, with both their names in case the INS calls during his green card application process. Jamie had resigned to this, and the fact that when her sister or mother called they'd figure out that Jack and she were living together. If this was all they knew, Jamie could live with it.

Jack's family is not as liberal, however. He told them that he'd moved into a new apartment, not in with Jamie. "But what if they call, get the machine, and hear my name?" He assured her that his family would never call.

"No, seriously," he'd quickly added upon seeing her skepticism, "no member of my family will ever make an overseas call. Even if they were out of their minds with worry, they'd assume me dead before spending that kind of money."

"So do I get to meet her?" Jack wants to know, jarring Jamie from thought.

She pretends not to recall what they were talking about. Only when he sighs does she tell him that she's not ready yet to deal with Jack meeting her sister. "Let me see Jill alone."

He's seated on the bed, searching through a pile of wine magazines he's got stacked on the floor.

She stretches out on her stomach next to him. "Trust me. It's better this way."

He finds the one he's looking for and flips through it, looking hurt, Jamie notices, examining him. How can he be hurt? She turns on her back and stares out the big bay window at the fog rolling over the famous bridge. When Jack moved in they'd repositioned the bed in the center of the room, so they could see the Golden Gate without lifting their heads. The bed had been the only furniture in this room then; no pictures, trinkets, or side tables. Now on the mantle of the façade fireplace stand two tiny picture frames—Jack's grandfathers—and she is still trying to get used to them being there, the concept of a grandfather, or a grandmother for that matter, being as foreign to Jamie as her marriage to Jack.

"Do you really want to go?" she asks him.

"It doesn't matter," he answers.

She dulls her eyes, then frowns, then grimaces, waiting for him to look at her, to say more, for she can't tell if it really matters to him or not, which is when she notices for the first time that he's wearing the ring.

He eyes her eyeing the ring. "I've opened a safety deposit box. Give me your ring tomorrow and I'll go to the bank."

"It's safe in my jewelry box, Jack."

"No, it's not."

"But what if I want to wear it?" She expects him to return her sly look with one of his own. But all he does is focus back on his magazine, as if he'd found something there in the fine print. Fuddled, Jamie examines his brooding profile. She had never expected him to wear the ring. She'd just assumed neither of them would wear their wedding bands.

"This Thompson guy's really a buffoon," he says.

Sunday morning, Jamie is sitting in the middle of her bed surrounded by interview forms from yesterday and other benchmark data she's collected over the course of the project. She is having difficulty being sympathetic to her peers' complaints, especially the women. Don't they understand what kind of business they've signed up for? The firm can feign a 360 degree review process all it wants, but in the end it will be the revenues a consultant brings in that will count, not all this warm and fuzzy, unquantifiable criteria. Let's face it, if business is going take on a feminine side, they're going to have to blow up the world and start fresh with women running it. Until then, we're all just going to have to keep pretending.

She flings herself back on the bed and sighs. Her report is due next week and she's made little progress, discombobulated as she's been by her new living situation, and now, all this yelling and cursing coming through the wall. Though at the moment it's dead silent; she figures it must be half-time, that Jack's muted the TV and they've gone to his computer to hunt for sports gossip on the Italian websites.

After the game they call their mothers.

Jamie cracks open her door and listens. Gibberish, some yelling, mostly Jack sounding miserable. After he hangs up he and Silvestro argue briefly, then Silvestro goes to church.

"You're not going with him?" Jamie asks, coming out of the room.

Jack doesn't bother responding. He's already given her his lecture on religion. When he left Italy, he left religion.

"What do you want for lunch?"

"A salad?"

"I'm making *pasta aglio e olio*." He seems distracted from the call.

"Why do you put yourself through this?" she says, still fathoming how often Jack calls his mother only to argue, seemingly, for fifteen minutes straight.

"Put myself through what?"

"These calls with your mother every other day."

"It's not every other day."

She holds her tongue, certain it's every other day. "I talk to my mother, at best, once a month."

"That's your problem." He hands her the green card application. Sign here. Okay, and here. Sure. She follows his no-nonsense instructions, banally. He's been thorough and meticulous about the documents and forms, and there will be no holes for the INS to poke through. He has dealt with them before and harbors no trust for them. Jamie has an instinct to review the fine print, but to prove a point, she doesn't. She signs all that needs to be signed and he tucks the paperwork back into his briefcase, reminding her that he's landlocked during the petition period, so he'll be spending a lot of time on the phone with Luca.

"I'm landlocked too," she says. "The Partner called me this morning. Boeing's postponed. I'm doing internal work."

"That's good."

"It actually sucks, but it's necessary to round out my Partner Book, I suppose."

"It's good in the sense that the INS may be stopping by and it's better if you're here." He goes on to say that they must be diligent. They've only been together for five months, after all, and he is currently unemployed. There'll be questions about that.

"Hopefully you'll have an offer before that happens."

"It's enough that I'm interviewing."

"And you're taking Lockheed if they offer."

"No."

She wasn't asking a question.

"I'm not going to go back to work, Jamie."

She tries not to act surprised because she shouldn't be, not entirely anyway, the way he's been feverishly working on those tank designs.

"So it's no longer a hobby," she says, taking a seat at the dining room table.

He takes the chair next to her. "I came here with the anticipation that I'd never have to work for *the man*."

He says the word with such sorrow, such angst. She wonders if by *man* he is referring to America.

"…and yet that is all I've done."

"I understand," she says after a moment, even though she doesn't. She works for the man. She's always preferred working for the man.

"I have enough savings to get me through the next year, and hopefully at some point the vineyard will give me a salary."

She squeezes her palms together on the table.

"What do you think?" he says.

"It sounds like you know what you want," she says.

"I do, Jamie. For once." He is gazing intently at the table. She is gazing at the strong features of his profile. "Then do it," she says.

He looks at her. "Are you sure?"

No, she doesn't say, squeezing his hand. "I'm sure."

"Oh, and by the way," he stands up. "We need to open a joint checking and credit account."

She stares at him for a hard moment. "Are you trying to kill me all at once?"

"It's temporary," he says.

She presses her feet firmly into the hardwood. Acquiescing to the joint phone message was bad enough, but then she reminds herself, this was all her idea. She steadies her voice, "My credit card expenditures are nobody's business."

"Jamie…"

"It's the principle. I've worked my whole life. I merge disparate financial accounts for a living. You know, Jack, it's a mess, a disaster, everything is exposed."

He doesn't disagree.

"It's not that I don't want to share my money with you. I don't want you to share your money with me, either."

"What money?" he sarcastically points out.

"I will not need your money, ever," she assures him.

"What money?" he repeats.

"And when you leave, where will I be then?" Her voice sounds strangled, unrecognizable.

He is staring at her, amused.

She is out of breath. "This is not funny, Giovanni."

"You think I think this is funny?"

"Yes, I do."

He pretends to stop smiling.

She watches him for a moment. "Fine," she says at last. "Merge the accounts, whatever. We can always separate them again."

CHAPTER 11

E Gia', La Juve!

"THE STINKING ROSE!"

"Jill made the reservation. I can't change it."

"Why not?"

"You liked North Beach Pizza."

"My father is from Napoli, Jamie. That was not pizza."

"I've told you a million times you don't have to go to dinner with us." Personally, Jamie is looking forward to some fried calamari and garlic bread (American style, and there is a huge difference), dishes that have disappeared from her life since Giovanni came into it.

According to Giovanni, North Beach, San Francisco's Little Italy, is no destination for Italian food, not to a first-generation Italian anyway. Since Silvestro's arrival they've stopped going out for Thai or Chinese. Even if they go to the Red Door for drinks they are back by nine, the block table already set, the pot of water ready for boil. Each night it's a new kind of pasta, each night a new story from Silvestro about how some beautiful American girl has refused yet another of his aggressive and overt advances, those that Jamie has continually counseled him against. He can't help himself; just to see a blond cross the street makes him burst with joy. Silvestro has moved on from the *la professoressa;* now he's in love with the bartender at the Red Door, whom Jamie has been tipping rather generously. The good news is that his quest for *amore* is forcing him to practice his English, which has improved tremendously. The problem is that it has been four weeks and Silvestro has not had so much as a coffee date, and Jamie is starting to get worried.

"Take Silvestro to that place on Polk with the young crowd. I'll tell Jill you have a friend in town, or you sprained your ankle playing soccer."

"That's a sports bar, Jamie."

She'd forgotten.

"We're not going to sit around and watch baseball with a bunch of obnoxious, drunk Americans."

"What about a dance place?" she says, not looking at him. "Silvestro likes to dance."

"Jamie," he says calmly, sternly. "I'm not taking him to a dance place."

She bites her lip, imagining the look on his face.

"I'm going with you to dinner."

The problem is that she is beginning to love this look of his. In fact, she thinks this look is eating away at her ability to think rationally. "I know," she says, turning at him and releasing a smile. "But what will we do with Silvestro? He can't come. It's enough to manage with just you, but we can't leave him home alone."

"He's twenty-three, he'll be fine."

"He seems so vulnerable."

"He's Italian. He still lives with his parents."

Jamie wonders if she is forming a small crush, and yet her affection for Silvestro is as a big sister, almost maternal. Anyway, the decision is made for them. Friday evening Silvestro bursts through the door having just come from class. He is flushed, wide eyed, out of breath. He's going on about a haircut, new 501s, a Polo shirt, and do they think he needs a shave? They are all standing in the hallway where he has corralled them, Jamie examining his chin for facial hair, and he announces that he has met the love of his life! He puts up a hand before Giovanni can comment and adds, "You think Silvestro is making talk again, I know, but this girl is the most spectacular girl." It's his imploring eyes that Jamie can't resist. His excitement is infectious.

"A Belgian girl. She has joined my class."

Giovanni's face comes to life. "Belgian?"

They exchange something about Belgian women in Italian that Giovanni promises to inform Jamie of later.

The girl speaks no English, and certainly no Italian, Silvestro goes on to explain, but he has managed to communicate his desire to take her to dinner Saturday night and she has accepted! There is a moment of silence, then Jamie makes a high five gesture. They stare at her hand, which she immediately pulls down. "Well, this is exciting, anyway."

"Yes, exciting!" Silvestro exclaims. Then he draws his face into a cool, calm state by pulling imaginary strings down either side of his cheeks. They immediately spring back up. "How can she refuse the charm of Silvestro?"

"Not to mention that face," Jamie adds.

"So tomorrow we can go shopping all together?" He makes a circling gesture with his finger, as if he were spinning a record—the three of them are a circle, a family circle.

"Of course, tomorrow, absolutely," Jamie says.

"It's okay you don't work?"

"Of course," she lies.

"*Grande-Jamie-grande.*"

"Juve's playing tomorrow," Giovanni warns, in no uncertain terms. "And then I've got a meeting with a distributor in Sonoma."

"Certainly a woman is more important than the Juve game," Jamie says.

"*E gia', la Juve!*" Silvestro cheers, running his hand through the waning curls on his head. "Where will I get my fantastic hair cut?"

"You barely have hair," Giovanni reminds him.

"He could use a trim," Jamie says.

"Yes, this is what I think," Silvestro says to Jamie. "We think the same."

They have migrated from the hall into the kitchen without knowing it. Giovanni is pulling things out of the fridge.

"Now, I must tell you." Silvestro pauses to clear his throat. "There is one little problem." He strokes his chin. "One very tiny, tiny, tiny little problem."

"N-O." Giovanni cuts him short.

Silvestro turns to Jamie and continues. "The Belgian girl, she stays with a family in Millbrae and she is very unhappy because there is nothing going on in Millbrae."

"So she can come into the city," Giovanni says.

"Yes. This is what I think. I show her this city. This bee-yoo-tee-ful city. This is not the problem."

"I don't want to hear the problem," Giovanni says.

"She has no car."

"She can take a bus."

"You can take Jack's car and go get her," Jamie, waving off Jack, assures Silvestro. "You drive a stick right?"

Silvestro steps back and gives her the most admonishing look, for it's an insult to even have to say it. "I am from Rome, Jamie; Italy, home of the Ferrari, champions of the Formula One. Of course I drive a stick, of course I am the best driver in the world!"

"You can't drink and drive though," she adds instinctively, awkwardly, thinking of all the times in college that she'd done just that.

"*Assolutamente no,*" Silvestro stands at attention and assures her.

"Then it will be okay," she says, looking at Giovanni, who is looking at her like this is not okay.

"*Scusami,*" Silvestro says to Jamie. "Now I must explain to my cousin in Italian, to make him understand." He does his explaining, which doesn't seem to be doing any good because Jack's dispassionate expression has not wavered. Jamie loads up the shaker with ice and listens impatiently. "Silvestro can practice driving the GTI tomorrow," she says finally, pulling the vodka bottle from the freezer, and Silvestro cups his arm around her, militant style, so that they can face Jack together. Her hand is freezing but she can't feel it. This kid has warmed her blood.

"His father is not just my uncle, Jamie, but my *padrino,* my Godfather. He has trusted me to take care of this little *mascalzone* (scoundrel)!"

Silvestro drops to his knees, his hands in a prayer before his face.

Giovanni flicks his chin, "What happens to me if something happens to you?" He turns and heads for the bedroom.

Silvestro shuffles behind him on his knees, his hands still in prayer.

"For heavens sake, Jack, just say yes," Jamie says, and even Jack can't keep from smiling.

The Juve game is at seven the next morning. Jack still hasn't decided about the car, and Silvestro knows that if Juve loses, all hope is lost. Luckily, today they play Livorno, which Silvestro assures Jamie is the worst team in the league. Still, the scene is utterly tense—Silvestro watches while chain-smoking out the window; Giovanni watches from the edge of the couch, rocking silently back and forth; Jamie watches from a safe distance, on the opposite end of the couch where she is worrying that she's not getting any work done on the ANR Aerospace/Seongsu proposal. The project is in South Korea, of all places, and she's working with a New York Partner who expects a draft by Monday. Even with a Hail Mary pitch, there's little chance they'll win. Still, she needs to prove herself to as many Partners in the firm as possible. If only she would get her ass off this couch, but she's vested too much time in the game now. There are no timeouts or stops, so if you blink and they score you've watched the whole thing for nothing. She has learned not to ask questions, that in fact, it's better not to make any sound at all; until Juve scores and Giovanni gets up and kicks a couch cushion across the floor while Silvestro screams at the top of his lungs. Soon another goal is scored, and she's up and screaming too.

They buy the jeans, a new polo shirt, and then Giovanni takes Silvestro on a practice drive to Sonoma for his meeting with the distributor. "You want my car, you work for it. The distributor is from Rome, so put on that Roman charm of yours." Silvestro does, apparently. He returns from the meeting all puffed up, though not from the meeting per se, as much as because he has mastered driving the GTI. Jack is satisfied because although the distributor was noncommittal about Ruffoli wine, he gave Jack the names of "his guys in New York."

"He was a bit of a *coatto*," Silvestro mumbles in Roman dialect.

"Brute," Jack translates. And then, "This guy here is quite the salesman." He slaps Silvestro on the shoulder, almost knocking him down. "Perhaps there's a future for the *mascalzone* after all."

"Please, I beg you, Giovanni, you must tell this to my father." Silvestro is waving his palms together and going on in Italian now.

"Speak in English!" Jack yells. "And then we'll see."

They send Silvestro off with a map and detailed directions on how to get to the Belgian girl's house and back. Then they take a cab to the Stinking Rose, where they find Jill waiting for them in the crowded bar, sipping a Cosmopolitan. The stiff drink puts Jamie on alert; it means her sister hasn't been out in a while. Jamie and Jill grew up in Southern California, surrounded by beach bums and beer guzzlers. In college it was more of the same. When they went to parties they didn't get drunk, they got trashed. These days though, now with children and working at the Fed, her sister rarely lets loose, and when she does it's with someone she can trust—not her husband Philip, but Jamie, and in desperate moments, their mother. Inevitably, Jamie and Jill will get drunk, talk loud, and then Jill will want to end the night at some dark place with thumping music.

"What's the word," Jill stands up. In a suit she is a tall, striking presence, one you wouldn't know just had twins, in-vitro style. She'd married relatively late, at thirty-four, and wasn't about to waste time trying to conceive naturally. Jill is all about planning and getting things done.

"You don't look Italian," Jill says after Jamie introduces Jack. He is the only man in the touristy bar wearing a blazer and dress shirt with jeans, European style, what he never fails to wear when they go out. "And you don't have an accent," Jill adds when Jack orders drinks; her expression to Jamie saying: *Are you sure this guy's giving you the real scoop?*

Jamie's response: "Next time he'll wear the gold chain."

Their drinks come. They toast and sip, which is when Jamie notices the wedding band on Jack's finger and panics silently for a moment. Jill, who does not miss a thing, has noticed the ring as well. Had he been wearing it earlier? No, he had definitely not been wearing it earlier. She would have seen it and told him to take it off. She wonders if he put it on clandestinely in the cab. Her sister mentions nothing, and they take their drinks to their table.

About that missing accent, Jack explains to Jill that he was educated in private international schools in Italy, where English was the primary language.

"Where did you guys meet again?"

"Norwest bought L-3," Jack says while Jamie is chewing her olive. "I worked at L-3."

Jill looks at Jamie. "Weren't you the consultant on that deal?"

"I'm not there anymore," Jack adds.

"He took the severance package," Jamie says.

"So where are you working now?"

"He's interviewing," Jamie says.

"I'm working on my golf swing."

"He's kidding."

"If I could I'd play golf all day…"

"He's waiting for an offer from Lockheed," Jamie says.

"Actually, I'm getting more involved in my family's vineyard."

"They want to export their wine to the states," Jamie adds.

"Lockheed, you said?"

"It's really good," Jamie says, about the wine.

"One of Congressman Lehman's aides, his wife is a big-wig at Lockheed. I'm sure she'd do me a favor," Jill mentions.

"No favors," Jack says.

"A call wouldn't hurt," Jamie says.

Jack picks up the wine menu. "A bottle?"

Jill mentions a Syrah.

"How about a nice Barbera?"

"Fine," Jill says.

"We can get the Syrah," Jamie says.

"When in Rome," Jill says.

"In which case we'd order the Frascati," Jack says.

The waiter brings the restaurant's signature roasted garlic. Giovanni orders the wine and Jill orders a calamari appetizer for the table. For a main Jill orders the shrimp scampi, Jack gets the sole, and Jamie a Caesar salad because she has seen the size of the portions going by. The place is packed and boisterous, the bar standing room only, and the wait for a table is over an hour.

"Maybe The Stinking Rose will buy your wine," Jill says. "These places make a mint."

"The idea is high end restaurants," Jamie says, regretting it immediately, as if this restaurant Jill selected isn't upscale enough.

"People here won't know what a Barolo is," Jack adds.

Jamie wonders if her sister knows what a Barolo is, for Jamie certainly hadn't until she met Jack. Even though wine is a hobby for Jill and her husband, a real estate developer in

Virginia, a hobby in that they belong to a variety of clubs in California and make biannual excursions to Napa Valley.

The waiter brings their wine, and after a taste Jack nods and the waiter fills their glasses. Meanwhile, the calamari are delivered, along with Jamie's salad. While Jill and Jamie pluck at the calamari with their fingers, Giovanni scoops some onto his plate with the serving spoon and then proceeds to eat, highly civilized, with his fork. When the basket of garlic bread is passed to him, he passes it on as if it were contaminated. Jamie wants to ask him what's wrong with it, but then imagines his answer: *This is not garlic bread, Jamie. There is no garlic on this bread, Jamie. There is no such thing as garlic bread in Italy, Jamie.*

A private smile, and then she picks up her glass. They toast and sip. There is always that initial shock, though each day it's less, at the severe dryness to some of the wines Jack serves her. Jamie can't imagine her sister is pleased by this, although it's impossible to tell what Jill is thinking when her face goes stealth like it has now. Certainly she would never say anything rude. She might be thinking that Jack is being cheap, for the Barbera, after all, is only thirty bucks while the Syrah is forty-two. Or, she might be asking herself why Jamie is living with this guy when she has made it clear to Jill that she is uninterested in long-term relationships. Or, she might still be stuck on why Jamie would risk her reputation by having a relationship with a client. Anyway, whatever Jill is really thinking, she turns to Jack and says, "What's with the wedding ring?"

There is a pause.

Jack glances down at the ring, then at Jill. "Your sister didn't tell you?"

Jamie, who has just sipped her wine, swallows as calmly as she can. "His wife died," she says. "And he still wears the ring."

Jill goes pale. Jack goes pale. A baby wails, and Giovanni crucifies Jamie in Italian. His words hit the air so curtly that Jill is visibly startled. After the echo of his outburst subsides, Jill leans forward and puts her greasy hand on Jack's arm. "Oh my God, I'm so sorry," she says, mortified, sympathy pouring from every fiber of her being because this is the exact kind of pain that terrifies her.

Jamie can't interpret Giovanni's exact words, but she understands what he has said, and so she takes a deep breath and tells her sister that no, actually, that is not true, and she does not know why she just said that.

"Your wife didn't die?" Jill is squeezing his arm now, confused.

"No."

"She's alive?"

"Yes."

Jill turns to Jamie who is now chewing her salad, her face a jumble of fury, disappointment, jealousy, worry.

Jamie's face says that the Caesar dressing on her salad is too goopy, that she should have ordered the balsamic, or creamy Italian, or the Roquefort…

Jill's face says that she sees her little sister is living with a married man, a serious disaster situation, one that will need a serious exit plan.

Jamie is thinking about how in Italy there is only one dressing choice: olive oil, vinegar, salt, and pepper, the ratios of which you adjust yourself.

Jill is still waiting for an explanation.

Jamie, wiping her mouth. "I'm his wife."

A scrutinizing silence.

"You're starting to piss me off."

"It's nothing to get all freaked out over."

The waiter brings the rest of their food. Jill stares at her plate until he leaves, then looks Jack squarely in the eyes. "The two of you are married?"

"He needed his green card."

"And you didn't tell me!"

Jill looks so hurt that Jamie can't look at her, so she turns to Giovanni who is eyeing the shrimp scampi Jill has not touched. He leans back in his chair, "*Ma dai* shrimp scampi. *Scampi* means shrimp in Italian. They should just call it *scampi*."

"Or shrimp shrimp," Jamie smiles. They smile at each other.

"This is not funny," Jill says.

"I was going to tell you."

"Does Mom know?"

Their wine bottle is empty. "He wasn't supposed to wear the ring."

"Why not?" Jill cries in frustration. "Where's yours?"

"They were going to send him back to Italy." Jamie pushes the truth a bit. "We wouldn't have done it if it wasn't necessary."

She feels Jack sit back and go silent upon the words she has just said, and this subtle show of disappointment brings a rush of emotion to her eyes. She knows he doesn't like her to say that, yet she says it anyway. She looks away, but there is no hiding from sleuth Jill, who, seeing the mist in her sister's eyes, orders three glasses of champagne and dessert, then picks up the tab. "We'll have to have a proper celebration," she announces Jill-style, determined to achieve a positive outcome. "A party, something!"

"Nothing," Jamie says, trying desperately to push the tears back. She does not know what has come over her. "I'm serious, Jill."

Jack hails a cab and they drop Jill at her hotel. Jamie gets out to say goodbye and Jill quickly drags her under the awning. They are both wobbling from the wine, but Jill's eyes are dead straight and serious. "This is all going to be fine, Jamie. We'll figure it out. We can work this out. We can make this work out."

"I know," Jamie assures her, thinking: *make what work out?* She gets back in the cab. *Why does everyone have to make such a big deal about marriage?* It has been rather painless up to this point, Jamie thinks, until Giovanni asks her why she had to drink so much, a question she doesn't like, and she remains silent for the rest of the ride home.

CHAPTER 12

Confession

LATE IN THE EVENING they watch Letterman while waiting for Silvestro to return, Jamie on the floor nursing hiccups, Giovanni stretched out on the couch. It is one o'clock by the time they hear the key turn in the lock, the door open, and two voices.

Two voices?

Shuffling, giggling, then footsteps down the hall. Jamie stands up and pretends to be half sober. Silvestro is coming toward them, but the girl has disappeared into his room down the hall. "The date went well, I guess?" says Jamie, looking over his shoulder.

With a smile that will never be forgotten, Silvestro goes on quickly about the beautiful drive he took the Belgian girl on, over Golden Gate Bridge, up to the Marin Headlands, back to Ocean Beach—an impressive tour, and yet not at all what the three of them had mapped out earlier. "Now I am afraid it is too late to drive her back."

"Oh. Okay," Jamie says. She isn't his parent, after all. "Just practice safe sex."

"Jamie," Giovanni snaps.

She turns back to Silvestro. "You don't practice safe sex in Italy?"

Silvestro is looking at her like she is drunk, which she is. He is astonished by her brashness perhaps, but his expression reveals nothing about what he intends to do with the Belgian girl tonight. For all Jamie knows they will just be sleeping together, as in snoring. Perhaps he is a virgin, or perhaps the Belgian girl will do other things to him so that he can remain a virgin. Her mind is spinning these thoughts later, in bed. "Is it the church?" she asks Giovanni, who doesn't look up from what he's reading. "Is he really going to abstain?"

"No."

"So he won't use a condom because of the church?"

He slaps down his magazine. "Of course he'll use a condom."

She waits. "Oh, I see," she says, turning over. "They use birth control. We're just not allowed to talk about it."

"That's right."

She flips onto her back and stares at the ceiling, seized by anger suddenly.

"Is something wrong with that?" he asks.

Is something wrong with that? Of course something's wrong with that! She unclenches her jaw, knowing that part of her reaction is the alcohol doing its work. Giovanni knows this too, which is why he will not engage her in further conversation. He won't even try to humor her. He will read the *Wine*

Spectator, switch off the light, and fall directly asleep, or so she must assume. In the morning, she won't remember.

She wakes with a seed of hypocrisy planted and growing, last night's anger still festering, the fact that her sister knows that they are married a waking, sobering reality. Anyway, it all incents her to stay locked in her room working on her proposal. She emerges at five p.m., just as Silvestro returns from driving the Belgian girl back to Millbrae. She barely gets to glimpse his guilty happiness before he rushes out the door again because the last church service is at six. She stands pondering the door that just closed behind him. The fact that Silvestro is going to church is not what brings her hangover back. Silvestro has gone to church every Sunday since his arrival, and he does not drag himself there, but goes willingly and diligently, religion a living and breathing part of him. Today, though, after last night, Jamie just assumed that out of respect he might skip it.

"Church," Jamie says, standing in the kitchen doorway stifling a wave of nausea.

"Yes, Jamie," Jack says wearily, at the stove cooking a sauce. "He's going to church."

"Will he confess?"

"Yes."

"About the sex?"

"No."

"Isn't that hypocritical?"

He doesn't answer.

"What does he think about you not going to church?"

"He knows to leave it alone."

The mixed scent of tomato, basil, and garlic seeps into her pores, soothing her stomach, and she slumps against the doorway. "I just don't get it."

"There's nothing to get."

"Please, help me get it."

"It's fundamental."

"Will he confess about the birth control?"

He bangs the pot into the sink, which startles her. He never fails to startle her. He fills the pot with water, places it on the burner to boil, pours in an enormous amount of salt.

"You guys looked at me last night like I was an asshole for even bringing it up."

"You said it, not me."

"So I'm the asshole?"

He still won't look at her. She tells herself to go into her bedroom, shut the door and never come out. She tells herself to go pack a bag and leave. She doesn't want their stinking food. She doesn't want to be patronized in her own home. Don't breathe, she tells herself. Don't look, she tells herself. Do not, for Gods sake, sit down on that stool, she tells herself, watching him break off a piece of baguette and drop it into the pot of red sauce. "Oops," he says, fishing back out the soaked bread and slipping it into his mouth. He likes what he tastes. No, he loves what he tastes. He is ecstatic about what he tastes, his expression says, and she cannot take her eyes from him. She falls into a stool, props her chin on her hand. He breaks off another piece of bread, drops it into the sauce. "Oops," he says again, grinning. Then he retrieves the bread from the sauce and holds it out for her. "Blow on it," he says. And she does.

CHAPTER 13

An Nyoung Ha Seh Yo
("Hello" in Korean)

ILVESTRO'S DATE WITH the Belgian girl repeats itself every night for the next two weeks, until the Belgian girl must return to her boyfriend back in Belgium.

Boyfriend?

But Silvestro has exchanged addresses with her. There is hope that one day she will visit him in the great city of Rome.

There is no hope; Jamie doesn't tell him.

"Once she sees my bee-yoo-tee-ful city, what choice will she have then but to fall madly in love with me?"

He seems ecstatic to have loved at all.

How had Jamie let her emotions get caught up in this?

Silvestro returns to Italy two weeks later, and Jamie feels as if she's missing a limb.

"I am waiting for you in Rome, Jamie. And you will see my city, my bee-yoo-tee-ful city."

Silvestro's mantra stays with her all week, as if he'd left his thumping heart behind as a reminder.

Friday night, home from work, she finds Jack slumped on the couch in front of *Seinfeld*. Nothing is sizzling or bubbling on the stove. "Let's go out," he says, and she plops down beside him. "Yeah, okay."

Boeing is back on. Next week Jamie must start traveling back and forth to Seattle. The INS still hasn't come by or called, and Jack is worried about Jamie not being around. She is more numb than worried, what with the Belgian girl leaving for home and Silvestro leaving for home, it has reminded Jamie of the brutal end that comes of things you attach yourself to. Soon Giovanni will leave for home too, won't he? The vineyard, she understands now, is a quest to find his roots after a decade of absence. Jamie is not part of his roots; she will never be part of his roots.

She almost wants the INS to come by and get suspicious that she is only there on weekends. She can decide what she wants the authorities to perceive of this marriage, whether it is real or not. It's all a matter of perception anyway, smoke screens, what her parents did, what every married couple does—believing what they want to believe, and having others believe it too. But the INS doesn't come by, and after three months Giovanni receives notice that his green card has been approved, pending the INS interview, that is. With this pending approval comes a document that allows him to travel outside the U.S. while he waits for the interview, which may not be scheduled for many months.

He books a flight to Italy for the following week.

It is wet and cold in Seattle, where Jamie is when she hears this news. She is supposed to be in San Francisco, but there is a wicked rainstorm and the airport is shut down. It is Friday night and she is absolutely miserable, lying in her Hyatt hotel bed, the phone cradled between her ear and the pillow, the TV muted, making her way through a half bottle of wine and minibar dinner.

"It's perfect timing, Jamie. Luca's about to harvest, and now I can be there for the testing of our new fermentation design. I want this done right. Italians will cut corners."

She can hear the embers burning on the cigar he is puffing. "When will you go?"

"Next week."

A pause.

"You'll be okay, right?"

"You already asked me that."

The line goes silent.

The glass of wine balancing on her hip almost falls over. She grabs it and sits up, "I'll be here, working on my Partner Book." She turns toward the rain-pounded window. "I won't even know you're gone."

And it's true, really. Things she enjoys doing with Giovanni she had already enjoyed doing by herself (herself, not alone, there's a difference)—drinking and eating for instance, the fundamentals, though she reverts to the finger foods she'd grown up on: sliced turkey, crackers, and string cheese. The act of eating still brings pleasure, and she can enjoy nights drinking wine, listening to music, and watching the sunset; she must never allow herself to depend on Jack for that. Plus, she can work late and not feel guilty. She goes out with some friends from business school on a couple of occasions. They go dancing and she gets trashed and comes home and sleeps in the bathroom. It feels good to be unbridled. This is what she had been so petrified of losing, after all—space, time, herself. After weeks pass like this it becomes easier to imagine him not returning. He'd left the ring behind, after all, locked in that safety deposit box, with hers.

Although she speaks with Giovanni on the phone every day, Jamie is no good on the phone. She cannot say *I love you* on a phone. She cannot say *I miss you* on a phone. It feels fake and untrue compared to the real emotion pulsing in her heart. Plus, if Giovanni was unreadable before, on the phone he is tortuous; his tone even-keeled (unless he's lamenting about Luca's stubbornness), his words few. He's no gossip, and if she asks questions about his family, particularly his mother, he will grunt or worse, play ignorant. Jamie needs to see his eyes, his face, to understand what he is saying. She often hangs up with haste and frustration, before he can barely utter his goodbye, then she sits there clenched in angst, tears springing from her eyes.

She does not bother asking if he'll be back for Thanksgiving. She knows what he thinks about turkey and cranberry. They are having problems with the tanks, he tells her, and he'll need to stay longer. When Christmas rolls around she encourages him to extend his stay, as if it is a test of her own will. He tells her to come to Italy, but there is no conviction in his voice, she decides. She tells him she is planning to go to Big Bear and spend Christmas with her Dad. Jill and Philip are bringing the twins and Jamie feels obligated to be there.

As the departure day looms closer, visions of herself there become too painful—Christmas at her father's house is big and boisterous. His second wife already had kids of her own when they married, plus a big extended family, plus the kids they then had together. Carols, gift exchange games, crab dip from bread bowls. Dinner is buffet style, with plates on laps in disparate places of the house, a football game perpetually on. The few times Jamie did go she sat eating with Jill on the carpeted stairs, or alone.

At the last minute Jamie gives Jill a work excuse and does not go to Big Bear. Along with everything else, Jamie does not want to face the wrath of her sister's *I told you so* expression after Jamie tells her that Giovanni has been in Italy for two months.

"He can do what he wants," Jamie says defensively. "This is the kind of relationship we have." She often has conversations like this with her sister, the words encased in bubbles over her head. Besides, Jamie isn't exactly lying; she is busy, in fact, preparing for a review of her preliminary Partner Book with Donald in January. She'll present it to the Board in April. If all goes well, by next June she will have her partnership, and that will bring even more responsibility. She will work even harder.

After a short stay in New York to meet with distributors, Jack is back in San Francisco for New Years. Of course he has to come back, she chides him over the phone, his INS letter has arrived and his interview has been scheduled. They've been apart two months, one week, and four days, is his no-nonsense response—forget the vineyard, forget the INS, he can't take it any longer! He's going nuts. This, a rare show of emotion, throttles her. *Two months, one week, and four days*—did he really count? *Separation is good for us,* was her meek attempt at assuaging him, for she is trying to remain unaffected by his return. In the end, though, she surprises him at the airport, even thinks of buying flowers, but at the last minute backs into a corner because her heart's pounding too hard and she's blushing uncontrollably. This, and it's only the flight monitor she's staring at. "Landed."

It's that corner from which she spots him exiting customs at the same moment he spots her, his hair and face a deeper gold, his look pensive, searching.

Two months, one week, and four days of morbid assumptions, wiped out by one embrace.

The prototype is at last going well. Jack is excited to tell her everything and feed her the cheese he's brought back, have her taste the wine from one of the two-dozen bottles he's flown over in special packing cases for upcoming tastings here in the States. It was important he was at the Villa to ensure the work was done at all, he implores again, slicing a piece of the salami that Luca had made especially for her. They top that off with more wine, and the *torrone* she likes. Giovanni goes on about the ideas they have for distribution and marketing, and Zio Marco helping them negotiate with the Crespi to buy back the three hectares that they sold them during the bankruptcy.

"I thought Zio Marco was against the idea…"

"Simona is designing a new series of labels using Nonno Giacomo's watercolors. Oh, and Antonia is pregnant…" Jamie feels as if she's in a dense, foggy dream, standing on a hillside watching the earth fall through his fingers. She'd left Villa Ruffoli with no intention of returning. Now, with him beside her, it feels like she never left.

"Some mid-size producers are interested in licensing my fermentation technology. There is a lot going on. Our issue now is capitalization. We need money."

"I can loan you money," she says without hesitation.

"Zio Marco is working on some financing options with his bank."

"I will lend you the money if you need it."

He gets lost in a thought, it seems. She wonders if he heard her, or if she even made the offer in earnest.

Their green card interview is scheduled for the first Friday in April, a week before her Board presentation. Jamie flies home on Thursday from Seattle, where the Boeing project looks to be delayed again. She and Jack make plans to meet at the INS at two-thirty. He will come directly from his meeting with a distributor South of Market, and Jamie from her office downtown, where she is meeting with Donald again to go through her Partner Book one last time. She is ready; her numbers look good for the year. Her election to be Partner is all but a formality. This morning, before she even sits down, Donald informs Jamie that they have won the ANR Aerospace/ Seongsu merger project in South Korea, largely as a result of her hard work on the proposal that she'd almost forgotten by now. Chris, the firm's celebrated New York partner, will run the deal. Jamie will be the on site junior partner.

She could be tipping over in her chair right now, she isn't sure. Donald acknowledges that she looks pale, and that she's been working beyond the call of duty, which will not go unnoticed.

"What about Boeing?" she manages to ask finally, with a tremble in her voice that she hopes he cannot detect.

"Boeing's jerking us around; Chris wants you in Korea ASAP and what Chris wants, Chris gets." He waits for the anticipated reaction—being sought after by Chris is an honor— but Jamie can only sit there, motionless. She is wondering why this possibility had not occurred to her before now, as the blood continues to drain from her face. She forces a smile and tells Donald she is thrilled.

"Of course we'll have to bump your presentation to the Board next week, but a commitment to Korea will make their decision on your partnership even easier—next quarter, when we meet again."

She walks out of Donald's office not feeling her body. She can't deny fore-knowing this course of events. This is how partnerships work, by having serious clients with serious revenues. But Korea...she hadn't anticipated that. Her numbers will be astronomical. The Korea job is a fact of her career, period. She has worked hard for this, and in her office now with the door shut, Jamie is willing herself to be thrilled. She should recalculate her year-end bonus, call Chris and get a jump start on the assignment, but all she can do is stare at her watch for long, absent minutes. Then she grabs her briefcase and hurries out of the building.

It's too close to take a cab, so she runs, then walks, then runs again. The sun is blaring, the sky windless and blue, completely incongruous with the San Francisco she knows. She is sweating by the time she gets there at two-thirty, a half hour before the interview yet thirty minutes late by Jack's standards. She must scurry a flock of pigeons to proceed up the wide cement stairs, passing a hefty line of Visa applicants to get through the entrance. Green card applicants are directed to the third floor, which is overflowing with bodies. She deftly scans the benches, which are all taken, then the throngs of people lined up against the walls, and spots Giovanni rather easily. He's a foot taller than everyone else and impressively dressed in a black suit and yellow tie, but it's the irony she can't miss, the way he's glaring at his watch as if she were late—his grandfather's

Rolex, the one he retrieved from the safety deposit box just that morning, along with their rings.

At last, she reaches him.

"Your jaw is twitching," she says.

"It may take a while," he says.

She looks around the room in amazement.

"Two-hundred and fifty thousand each year," he says, answering the question in her mind.

"And some day you'll thank me for this?"

"Or you'll thank me." He pulls the ring from his pocket.

She lifts her left hand and he slides it on, a wry exchange, a melting touch, and then he goes back to studying the documents he's gathered in a manila folder: marriage certificate, green card application, joint bank account statements, apartment lease with both their names on it, wedding photo, Stinking Rose photo. There is a photo of her with Jack's family that she takes from his hand. "I don't remember this being taken."

He takes the picture from her and puts it back in its place.

Everything is in its place. He is ready. He deserves to be here.

She is ready. She deserves to go there.

So why is there a hint of scorn in the air? Is this the groveling, the sucking up that each of them, respectively, have had to do? She could have said no to Seoul. "Should I be nervous?"

"Just be honest."

"Honest."

"And say as little as possible."

"What am I getting in return for this again?"

"No sarcasm, no funny business."

"Isn't it interesting that we got married so you can have the freedom to leave?"

"In fact, let me do the talking."

"Don't you see the irony?"

"And don't ask any questions."

"Just a little bit of irony?"

"I said no questions."

Another thirty minutes pass before Giovanni's name is called. They head down a dreary corridor into a dank, windowless office where they sit in hard chairs and face a desk stacked with paperwork. Behind this desk sits an expressionless man; small, dark skinned, dark haired, wearing a short sleeve dress shirt.

He barely acknowledges them.

Jack hands over his application along with their marriage certificate, keeping the other materials at the ready on his lap.

The man examines the application.

It's quiet for a time.

Jamie tries to catch Giovanni's eyes, but he is staring straight ahead. She doesn't have to touch his hands to know that his palms are sweating. The muscle in his cheek is still doing its thing, and she stays focused on that for a time, until it occurs to her that the man has asked her a question. She uncrosses her legs and moves to the edge of her seat as if she were about to make a presentation to the Board of one of her clients, where she always feels like she's half lying, like she has manipulated the numbers to make them work the way the client wants them to work. Then it occurs to her that she has nothing to say, she can't even remember the man's question. So she says "Um," and pretends to ponder, while Giovanni shifts in his seat.

"I asked how you met Giovanni."

Her heart is beating through her chest. She knows the answer. They met in a bar, where his black-tunneled eyes instantly swallowed her up.

Jack clears his throat.

"I saw him in a bar," releases from her at last. "…well no, actually before that, I think."

The man, who had been staring at her blandly, is now getting interested.

"I was consulting for the company he worked for." Even that didn't sound right. In fact, she couldn't recall how it had actually happened, or if Giovanni would remember a different version of their meeting; if he understood how many times she'd seen him before she approached him, how she'd already fallen for him by the time she…and then it occurs to her that it is time to speak. "A co-worker introduced us."

She detects a hint of amusement in the man's eyes, which linger on hers before he draws his attention back to the application. "And how long have you been together?"

Silence.

He seems afraid to look back up, as if he's embarrassed by something.

"A year and a half," Giovanni says, after the question has lingered. "March 2nd, if you count our first date."

"He's good with dates," Jamie adds. *Why is she so nervous?*

There are a few more banal questions, all of which are a blur, a blip, because before Jamie can shift in her seat the man has stamped and signed Giovanni's green card application. He does not ask for the wedding photos, bank statements, or any of the proof Giovanni so carefully organized and collected. Apparently he needs no proof. He is only human, after all.

Giovanni stands and receives his passport with the new status insertion from the man who seems to be wondering why they are both still standing there. It has only been, maybe, twenty minutes.

"That's it?" she says to Jack as they make their way back down the hall.

Jack refuses to speak until they are out of the building and around the block, at which point he abruptly stops and whips around, "What happened to you in there!?"

She stares back, pale faced, dumb. "Sorry, I don't know. I just…I ran a blank on where we met."

"It's very simple. We met in a bar."

"Did we?" Her eyes are wild. "Or did we meet somewhere else, long before?"

He's looking at her like she's a lunatic.

She feels like a lunatic.

"Never mind," he says finally. "It's over now."

He pulls out the passport. They stand staring at the worn page where the temporary green card has been attached. "It's not even green," she says. He will receive the permanent card in the mail in four weeks. That's not green either, apparently, but it doesn't matter. He is a Permanent Resident. "Conditional Permanent Resident," he reminds her.

They are home now, seated outside on the narrow balcony that hangs off their living room, halfway through a bottle of champagne. It is one of the rare city days, hot and breezeless, the bay tranquil and blue, that they can sit out here without freezing.

"So what happens now?" she says.

"We drink," he says, refilling their glasses.

"I mean what happens in two years, with your green card?"

"We'll apply to have my conditional status removed."

"And that'll be the end of it."

"That'll be the beginning of it."

"That's what I meant."

He lights a Cuban.

"So what will you do with all this freedom America has granted you?" She is trying to sound upbeat, but the sun is now setting, and the reality of Korea is, too.

He puffs languorously, parting his lips to let the smoke out. "Actually, I was thinking about spending some time in New York."

There is a pause.

"I thought you said that distributor was a sleazebag," Jamie stalls, discombobulated, trying to make sense of this and what it could mean in light of Korea.

He turns to face her, and she can tell he has put a lot of thought into this, as he does with everything. "New York is where the market is, Jamie. The Bay Area is all about California wines, and the collectors in Silicon Valley want French. New York has a stronger connection with Italian wines, and a much broader view."

She keeps her gaze forward. The fog is starting to roll in. She knew this weather wouldn't last. Soon the Bay Bridge will be gone. "My partnership is here. I can't go with you."

"So we'll have a cross country relationship for a while."

"Our careers come first," she agrees.

"For however long it takes."

"I suppose they'd transfer me to New York if I asked them to," she says, pulling her wedding band over her knuckle, pushing it back. "But I'd have to give up my partnership bid. It would be like starting over again."

"I'm not asking you to do that."

"I was just saying…"

"You're on the road all the time anyway."

"Do it," she says, pulling and pushing.

"We'll still see each other on weekends. Instead of flying home to San Francisco, you can fly to New York, or I'll come to where you are. It'll be an adventure, something new."

She doesn't respond, and he asks her what's wrong.

She sips her drink. He's as excited and upbeat as she's ever seen him. "I envy your passion." Her lips are trembling.

"What is it?" he demands, turning to her.

She turns to the water. "They want to send me to Seoul for six months."

"Six months?" His voice is thin.

"With a trip home every five weeks."

He clears his throat, shifts, "What's the project?"

She explains it to him, wiggling, tugging, pulling, pushing.

He's listening, intently like he does, but each moment that goes by his face grows a little paler. It's sinking in.

"You've always wanted to go to Asia," he manages finally, trying to sound upbeat.

"I know," she says, contemplating Asia, imagining the shock on her sister's face when Jamie tells her she's going there. This time she pulls so hard that the band actually comes off. She'd bought the more expensive gold for their wedding rings, weightier, with softly rounded edges, and at the last minute, on a whim, she'd let the jeweler inscribe the date on the insides. She squints at it now, at the date she pretends to have forgotten. "It's been how long?"

"Eight months," he says proudly, without hesitation. Then he looks at his watch. "And thirteen days."

"Thirteen days?" She turns and sighs at the fog. "It doesn't feel like we're married."

"Good."

"Is this how married people live?"

"It's how we live."

CHAPTER 14

Auguri! Tanti Auguri!

*T*HEY GET RID OF THE APARTMENT. Jack has taken a cheap sublet in New York and Jamie now resides in the luxurious Grand Hyatt Seoul. "We'll save a boatload of money on rent," she'd insisted. In reality, with Jack thousands of miles away, she'd suddenly felt the need to get rid of everything.

"But how can you leave my bee-yoo-tee-ful city?" Silvestro was aghast when Jack broke the news to him over the phone. *Because we are moving on to other things.* Jamie is thinking now, thousands of miles away from both of them. *It's what Americans do. We go where the work is. We bury ourselves in it. We get ahead.*

We carry on whole relationships through invisible phone networks.

"My cousin, Maria," Giovanni is telling her now through one of them. "She's getting married in Vico Equense."

Jamie can hardly respond; it's two a.m. in Seoul and she's still at the Seongsu offices. She'd stepped into an empty conference room to call, as she has every night, leaving behind a room full of consultants from Singapore and London with their heads together trying to figure out how to change the way Koreans work so that three hundred employees can be "saved" (eliminated) from the merged ANR/Seongsu entity.

"My father's brother's only daughter," Jack goes on.

The line goes silent. She can barely think. Any minute now Chris is going to call, demanding those financial updates. Tomorrow they are presenting preliminary findings to Charles, CEO of ANR's Korean subsidiary, their primary stakeholder and project champion. The following week she goes on her one week leave. She'd been dreaming of the bay window, that spectacular bridge, the sunlight that hits her bed at around three p.m. "How come you didn't mention this before?"

"Because I wasn't sure I was going."

Then it occurs to her that there is no three p.m. sun anymore. There is no apartment anymore. On her last leave they'd met in New York.

"My dad's going to be there and I wasn't sure I was ready..." he pauses, and she's caught off guard. He rarely mentions his dad.

"Ready for what?"

"Forget it," he says, after a pause. "Nothing."

"What was all that about him fleeing south, to Sicily or wherever?"

"Napoli, Jamie," he says. "Papá owns a pharmacy there. Every year he makes the obligatory trip to see me in Vico Equense, where I have always gone each summer to see my grandfather, my father's father, until he died that is, and after that I went to see Zia and Zio."

"Okay, fine, but what does this have to do with me?"

"They want to meet you."

There is a silence.

"Please come."

"Why?"

"What do you mean, why?"

She is in Korea, he is in New York, that is why. She'd just assumed they'd meet in New York again as planned. Her work has been exhausting and she needs detox, peace, Jack. She has no emotional bandwidth for Giovanni right now, to discover more of this Italian man who seems to continually surprise her, who consumes her thoughts from any distance. Does the depth of him never end? Plus, in Italy before his family she will have to be ON, she will have to say the right things and do the right things so as not to look like one of those vulgar Americans; to eat politely even after she's full. She's surprised that he's even asked her to come.

"Where is Vico Equense?" she asks, from somewhere below her belly.

"The Gulf of Napoli, Jamie," as if she should know.

"I thought you spent summers at Villa Ruffoli with Nonno Giacomo."

"*Agosto,* always, in Vico Equense. Have you not been listening?"

"And your mother?" she asks, after some hesitation.

"She doesn't travel south of Rome."

A long, slow sigh. "How do I get there?"

She flies first class to Rome, eight hours from Seoul. Every so often her mind floats outside her window and looks back in at the woman sitting there, working away on her laptop.

She thinks back to the definitive moment in her youth when all whimsical childhood fantasies of herself as an adult were devoured by one vision: she in her twenties and thirties, rootless, flying from one glamorous destination to the other for work and being paid a lot to do it. The vision had come true. The presentation had gone well. The Koreans had bought in. She's exhausted, but it's an exhilarating kind of exhaustion, one that comes from knowing you've worked hard at becoming the person you dreamed you'd be. Chris may be uncompromising, beyond demanding, not to mention eccentric, but he's brilliant. He satiates her thirst for knowledge and experience. Sure, the CEO may be hitting on her, but as far as Jamie's concerned a requisite amount of harassment is part of the job. She is a woman rising in what is still largely a man's corporate world. She'll keep Charles' advances to herself and perhaps even use his weakness to her advantage. She knows where professional lines are drawn vs. blurred. This merger is going to be a huge, career making success; Chris has assured her. It is almost overwhelming, which must be why she starts crying somewhere over Mongolia, and can't stop.

In Rome, she is numb with jetlag.

On the train to Vico Equense, next to Giovanni, she's loopy. They are drinking Italian wine out of thin paper cups. Her legs feel like jelly, and her head has melted into the seat rest. He is explaining, with wild, abandoned eyes, how the European Championship League differs from National Championship League, and then how the World Cup differs from the European Cup. Yesterday she was number crunching "saves" with the team, and a formula pops into her head even now, for precision is the key: keep the "saves" mathematically precise, this way the Koreans can't challenge the results.

"Do they even know I exist?"

She glances at him, disturbed by the question, and then quickly waves it off. "Chris thinks I've got some secret Italian lover."

"I suppose that's true."

"It's just easier." She doesn't say what she really thinks, which is that if the managing partners at the firm know she is married they will not take her partnership seriously. "Junior" will never be removed from her title. They will be calculating when she will become pregnant, and then pregnant again. They will be wondering when the stress will be too much for her, when she will ask to go part time or work from home. They will be wondering when she will quit. "Does it really make a difference if or who we tell?"

"I've told Zia Renata."

Her mouth falls open; it had been a rhetorical question.

"That we're engaged, anyway."

Panic rushes through her. "But we're not engaged. We've never been engaged."

"I'm pretty sure there were a few days there when we were engaged."

She's not paid much attention to the sights streaming by, so lost is she in Jack's voice, his laugh, the way his mouth turns up at the ends; but now she can see that they are bulleting straight for a hole in an oncoming mountain. It's bizarre, dizzying, and she must look away just as everything goes dark and screaming silent. Why did he have to say anything? Especially since they'd agreed to wait until the two-year mark, when Jack could apply for his permanent residency. Why, why, why!? Blinding light again, blue sky and rocky cliffs cresting boundlessly upward. *Where the hell are we?* He keeps mentioning the sea, but she cannot see it. Perhaps this is not the right stop. Perhaps there is farther to go.

She turns around to see what he's looking at. "Is that…?"

"Vesuvius."

A patch of dark cloud hovers over the opening, but otherwise it's lush and green and alive. "It's not going to erupt or anything, is it?"

He shrugs with a look like anything's possible.

They face forward again.

"Jill told me I'm supposed to see Pompeii. I don't think I can leave without seeing Pompeii."

He jumps up suddenly. They are pulling into the station. He retrieves their bags from the overhead rack and hurries her into the vestibule by the exit, as if the train might not actually stop at all, but rather slow to a speed from which they can jump.

There is no one on the platform that Jamie can see. It is a small, sleepy station with one of those bizarre newspaper kiosks that serve as a mini shopping mall. They head for the lone bar and see Zia Renata running toward them, a petite bundle of muted, suffering colors, apologizing profusely for being two minutes late. Zia Renata and Jack argue briefly, about where, exactly, they had agreed to meet. She wears a fitted shirt over leggings, thick black hair braided over one shoulder, a man's Rolex, a gold chain and no makeup. Her eyes are dark like the tunnels they just plummeted through; her English selected carefully and executed perfectly.

She hates to drive, she assures Jamie (pronounced "Jimmy" with Zia's accent) maneuvering her Fiat Stilo with the lurching clutch out of the station, beeping her horn every chance she gets even though there is little traffic and few pedestrians. It is the first of September, summer is officially over, the tourists gone. Zia refers to Jack for conference on which turn to make, as if she'd never driven in this town without him. Perhaps she hasn't. She prefers to travel by bicycle, she tells Jamie, though she directs most of her exchanges to her nephew, brisk and unspoken, as if what they need to say to each other doesn't need to be said. Meanwhile, Jamie gazes out the window at the ghostly maze of streets enfolded into this cliff, the weathered apartments with laundry dangling over the rails of tiny balconies that look out onto other balconies.

They circle through a roundabout of roundabouts, a piazza that seems bland, if bland were a word one could use to describe a piazza, though it is famous for its pizza-by-the-meter, Jack tells her. The Fiat whizzes up a narrow street then down another, taking a harrowing turn along a cliff's edge. Jamie has still not glimpsed the sea, but she has a lofty, weightless feeling.

At last they pull up to a pale pink, three-story apartment complex and Zia cries, somewhat startlingly, "Poor Giorgio," at the man, presumably Giorgio, pacing in the car park with his hands jammed into the pockets of a military vest. He's not frowning, Giovanni assures Jamie. It's just that his lips curve naturally downward like that every time he's forced to resume his position as brother and father. *Poor Giorgio.* He's not dead, clearly, even though he is the man in the photo Jamie had seen in La Mamma's shrine. Even the vest is the same; there is no question. So perhaps he's dying? The way Zia Renata keeps saying "Poor Giorgio," he might as well be. Jamie will have to ask Jack later about his father's health status, and while she's at it she might as well inquire about his own, because if a shrine is for the dead, as Jack had explained it, then along with his father's photo, what was that toddler photo of Jack doing there beside it?

Giorgio, a shorter version of Zia Renata, is dressed in a darker shade of muted colors. Jack stands a foot taller than either of them, though he shares his father's amber eyes, the shimmer of light that touches him as they embrace, the low words exchanged but not translated, the awkwardness as they part and step back from each other.

"*Dottore,*" Jack uses his father's title as way of introduction. Giorgio bows his head, albeit mockingly, with a gleam in his eye. His son is no *Dottore* even though he, too, has an advanced degree. In Italy, anybody with an advanced degree gets the Dr. title.

"*Tanti auguri.*" Giorgio leans in to kiss, barely, each of Jamie's cheeks. The scent of tobacco and soap lingers. Jamie turns to Jack for a translation.

"He's congratulating us," Jack clears his throat and says. "On our engagement."

"Yes, of course," Jamie surrenders. A nervous smile of thanks, then she averts her gaze to the sea—if only she could see it. "Where is the sea?"

A conference takes place. The woman sweeping the balcony above their heads has something to add. Jamie's feet move before she can stop them, for she's spotted a sliver of shimmering blue down one of the narrow streets. Jack says something but she can't hear him. More balconies, more ladies, "*ciao,* Renata," someone calls out from above. "*Tanti auguri,* Giovanni," calls another to Jack, on Jamie's heels now. Their engagement is news, apparently. Past a *campanile* and underneath a pale orange archway, spilling out onto a large terrace, Jamie stops abruptly and gasps, soundlessly, into a silence that feels infinite.

"Not bad, huh?"

Her heart is beating wildly, but she forces herself to step forward, slowly, and peek over the railing down a thousand foot drop. Another gasp. She averts her gaze to the horizon, a blue iridescence stretching on into infinity. "Jesus," she says.

"Madonna," he says, nodding at a statue mounted perilously on the cliff's edge right next to them. Jamie blinks at it, then back at the horizon, at distant islands she should know the names of, "Is that…"

"Yes, Jamie."

"But it's not going to erupt, right?"

He doesn't bother answering.

It is the blue that consumes her; glittering, vast and endless.

"Nonno Carlo loved Vico Equense so much," Jack explains, "that he retired here from Napoli twenty years ago, and bought three apartments in the same complex, one for each of his children. Zio Silvio and Papá each got one on the top floor with sea views. Zia Renata got one on the ground floor with no view, which she is still steaming about because she insists it's infested with mold and cockroaches. While he was alive, Nonno lived in Zio Silvio's apartment, and when he became ill, Zia moved in to care for him until his death. This left Zio Silvio, when he came for summers, stuck staying in Zia's first floor flat. Now, with Nonno dead, Zia's refused to move back to the first floor."

"What about your father's apartment?"

"Papá sold it the first chance he got."

"*E' stupido*," Zia Renata says, finally catching up with them, sweaty and breathless. "*Tuo papá e' stupido!*"

Jack doesn't seem to disagree. "Zia says the value of her apartment has skyrocketed as Vico Equense has become a tourist destination. More hotels are going up even now."

"*Che brutti alberghi.*" They all pivot around so that Zia can point with disgust toward the cliffs scaling up behind them, at the construction going on there, but Jamie can't see what she's talking about. She doesn't see any hotels or tourists, just more apartment complexes poking out here and there haphazardly, as if no thought has been put into the development of this town. It won't be mentioned in any guidebook, she is sure, such as the town her boss, Chris, had gone on about when Jamie had mentioned her trip to southern Italy. A little town called Positano that she absolutely had to see, where pastel-colored houses filled with gardens and bougainvillea burst majestically up the cliffside and shimmer golden in the light of dusk. According to Chris, and no doubt a host of others like Chris, there is no point in going to the Amalfi and not visiting Positano.

Jamie turns back and peeks over the rail again. "How do you get down to the beach?" Orange and green umbrellas dot the thin stretch of shore. "Are there ropes and bungees?"

"You like the beach?" Zia Renata asks.

"I grew up at the beach."

"It's not a beach like you know," Jack says.

"I think I can see that."

"It's rocky and has no waves."

"The water is not so clean," Zia assures them, and Jack rolls his eyes. "There's an elevator," he tells Jamie.

She thinks he's kidding.

CHAPTER 15
Lucrezia

*T*HEY RETURN TO ZIA's apartment to find that Giorgio has lugged all their suitcases up three flights of narrow steps to the fourth floor by himself. This he is proud of, if not burdened to report while lighting his Toscano. They might as well be on the hundredth floor; that's how high up it feels when Jamie steps through the entrance and sees more of that infinite blue out the terrace doors across the room from her. Wafts of sea air mix with the scent of cigar, perhaps something cooking on the stove, and Jamie can feel her muscles relax, a warmth she cannot explain.

Actually, this is Zio Silvio's apartment, Giorgio reminds Jack to remind Jamie, which sends Zia into a tizzy. An argument ensues and at once the airy expanse becomes what it is, tiny and confined. Furniture consumes the one room that serves all living purposes: a quilt-covered couch, an easy chair

161

worn and faded with someone's absence, a dark wood cabinet full of tiny war trinkets, an old TV showing a scantily clad woman conversing with a group of elderly, overly tan men in dark suits. The scratched and nicked wood dining table looks like it's been in the family for generations. And, as if there wasn't enough smoke already, Giovanni pulls out a carton of Duty Free Marlboro Reds from his suitcase and gives it to Zia Renata. To his father goes a 12 year old bottle of scotch, which Giorgio will never drink because it's too expensive. Zia gives Jack two silver coins for his collection, and the two examine them together for a minute. Jamie hadn't even known he had a collection.

Giorgio hands Jack an odd sized envelope that he immediately slips inside the pocket of his blazer. Murmurs ensue over that. Zia looks on with shame, or perhaps pride; it's so hard to tell what's going on. They could be discussing a funeral.

All this and they haven't even moved beyond the entrance doorway.

Giorgio, satisfied and somewhat embarrassed by whatever generosity he has just bestowed upon his son, goes off to hide the scotch from Zio Silvio. Zia Renata gestures for Jamie to gather her suitcase and follow her. She will be sleeping in Nonno's room, a five-foot shuffle from where they all just were. "It's John Wayne's room now.

"*Il gatto*," she explains, getting down on her knees and reaching under the bed. "Nonno loved John Wayne." It's a struggle for her to stand back up with the cat in her arms, a humongous black and white. She holds him out so Jamie can examine his wide girth. "Poor John Wayne."

Meanwhile, Jack is examining the antique prints hanging on the wall—Santa Chiara, Castel Nuovo, Certosa di San Martino. They will be his, Zia Renata tells him, once he is married, per Nonno Carlo's wishes. Jack looks astonished, and very pleased. They are originals, Zia assures Jamie, and very valuable. *More prints? He's already got so many prints.* "They're yours, too," he says.

It takes a moment for what he's said to reach her, for it's odd to think of them owning things jointly. Up until this moment they have owned nothing jointly. In fact, to date Jamie has never owned anything of particular value. Her furniture is handed down from Jill, all of which she'd given to Good Will when they moved out of the San Francisco apartment. All Jamie has left now are clothes and that wedding ring…she gazes at the bed, suddenly sleepy, lulled by thoughts of the sea she cannot see, and yet its presence is overwhelming.

Giovanni blows his nose into the hand sewn handkerchief he keeps tucked inside the front pocket of his jeans, with a startling ferociousness. He is allergic to cats, Zia Renata informs Jamie, which is why he will be sleeping in Zio Silvio's apartment on the ground floor. *You mean your apartment.* Jamie watches Jack fold up the dirty handkerchief and slide it back where it belongs, a disconcerting sight she will never get used to. Allergic? Zia seems very pleased to alert Jamie to this little idiosyncrasy of Jack's, like she had been about his coin collection. Opening the window might help, Jamie suggests selfishly, because it's she who's having difficulty breathing suddenly. She rushes to the window, which sends Zia Renata into distress because Nonno preferred the window closed and certainly the breeze will give Jamie pneumonia. It takes the three of them to get it cracked open, about an inch.

"It'll be fine," Jack assures her after Zia Renata leaves to go prepare the fish for the stray cats that live in the parking garage. Jamie goes and shuts the door. "I'm just curious, why didn't we stay in one of those hotels across the street?"

Jack reopens the door and then wanders around the matchbox-sized space, picking things up and setting them down. "Did you see Zia's Rolex?" He picks up a small Alessi clock from the desk. "It was Nonno's." Sets it down. "It's solid gold."

"I thought he worked for the government."

"In Italy a manager in the government is a prestigious position."

"But how does a government employee afford three seaside apartments?" she says dubiously, a gleam in her eye, which he immediately admonishes.

"Don't automatically assume graft, Jamie," he says. "There are honest people here. It's a socialist system; the government provides a vast safety net especially for its employees, including a nice pension. Plus, my grandfather received a package when he was discharged from the military after the war."

"Okay, okay, I was just asking."

"Southern Italy's not a gangster movie, Jamie."

"I heard you I heard you…anyway," she says, switching subjects. "About that hotel…"

"What hotel?"

"The one down the street."

"There's no need to spend that kind of money, Jamie."

"We have the money."

"That's not the point."

"The point is that you're thirty-three, a grown man. You can do what you want; there's no need for you to sleep on a couch."

"It's just not something you do here." He is angry.

Jamie is confused. She sits on the bed, which collapses around her. "This isn't turning out how I thought."

"You knew we'd tell people eventually."

"No, actually, I didn't."

"You told your sister."

"No, you told her."

"It'll be alright, Jamie."

"You already said that."

He kisses her, one last gaze, and leaves without shutting the door. She goes and closes it after him, staring at it for a good solid minute before turning back around. Sparse, grim, ghostly—she imagines that Zia Renata keeps this room just as it was when Nonno departed it. On the beaten wood desk are old photos in tiny, tarnished frames: Nonno at the dining table, shirtless, a cigarette dangling from his mouth, a platter of seafood before him; Nonno with a plump, scowling boy that Jamie can only presume to be Giovanni. There is a face shot of a bronzed, unsmiling woman in dark glasses gazing off into the windswept distance, Nonna, the mother of this dark brood Jamie presumes, the woman who died long before Giovanni was born.

Her eyes catch something unexpected, a computer printed picture of Giovanni and some girl tucked inside one of the other frames. He's younger, his hair thicker, wavier, and the girl is pretty, perhaps Italian, Jamie wonders, stretching out on the bed with the photo. The afghan is hairy from John Wayne, whose paws she sees now swatting under the doorframe.

She'd once broached the topic of ex-girlfriends with Jack, but he'd recoiled, almost insulted. There's no point in discussing THAT.

She wakes sometime later from an awful dream, disoriented; the air pungent, drool on her pillow. She extracts the picture from her armpit and blinks at the Alessi clock; it's almost one p.m. She flattens the crinkles and puts the photo back where she found it, then stumbles from the room. Rays of sun come at her. She is half dazed and somewhat embarrassed by her dream, where she'd been scouring some campus party for an ex-boyfriend. They'd dated six months before he dumped her, but that was eons ago—she'd long since moved on from him. It feels like someone just took a stab at her scar, though, which makes her wonder if all her scars are at risk. If love could be like that, like being ripped open.

The TV is still on, though the wood table has been moved out of the corner and set for lunch, or dinner, she's not quite sure anymore. Italy is one long, endless meal and perhaps she's still dreaming, but the phrase "sit-down dinner" comes to mind, along with the rarely used dining table of her childhood. It would be a special occasion—a birthday, graduation, Thanksgiving—when her mother would say, "We're going to have a sit-down dinner," as opposed to just "dinner."

Words are tumbling from the kitchen, Giovanni and Zia Renata in discussion. Jamie goes over and peeks into the tiny, closed off space with a porthole for a window. Jack is studying a worn leather book that is open on the counter. Zia is studying him. Her skin is moist and supple, like Jack's. She looks much younger than her fifty-five years, and Jamie wonders if Italians have a claim to beauty. Their movements around each other are organic and graceful while their language remains unbalanced, familial, harsh. Jack moves from the sink to the stove. Zia is beside him, then behind him, then on the other side of him, making her point, something about Lucrezia—an ingredient for the recipe, a ghost from their past, one of the stray cats—Jamie has no idea. Their voices rise and fall, reaching a crescendo with Giovanni yelling, "No!" which is when Jamie backs off, and they finally notice her.

"Zia was wondering why you don't cook," Giovanni says.

This can't possibly be what they were just discussing. Jamie's eyes search his, amused. In her twenties she would have been offended by this question as a stab at her American-born right to success at whatever cost. She does have a CFA/MBA after all, and a variety of other achievements that she can't in this instant remember. She blinks and swallows and gazes into their faces. "Food wasn't a priority."

"She wants to know what your priority was," he says, dousing the squid with wine.

"My ability to support myself," Jamie responds, knowing they can't hear her in the combustion of oil and wine exploding into the air. She makes a point of not blaming her lack of domestic graces on her parents' divorce or her mother's untraditional priorities, because from them Jamie had grown independent and strong. "To not depend on anyone or anything," she says, under the din of their conference about the pasta's *al dente* quality, and at once Jamie becomes incensed with the stubbornness and inertia of their culture. What she has said, "support myself," means absolutely nothing to them. It will never, in a million years, mean something to them. It is yet another American concept lost in translation.

Her frustration has nowhere to go, so she follows John Wayne, who has waddled out onto the balcony; he disappears behind a cluster of spice and herb plants. Laundry is drying on a stand nearby, the image seizing Jamie with a sudden conviction not to see her underwear fluttering there, ever. This she will make clear, she assures herself, going and standing at the railing to let the high sun and pleasant breeze wash over her face. The cloud cluster over Vesuvius has not changed; it remains frozen in time, the sea too, green with shimmering patches of blue, nothing like the ocean of her home. As a kid Jamie had spent summers at the beach just a few blocks from the house she grew up in. Before her parents' divorce, her father would insist on coming with her, sitting fretfully on the shore with her towel at the ready, watching her ride wave after wave on her rubber raft. She loved the bouncing thrill, tumbling in a white wash of oblivion, always surfacing, popping up at the last minute, inconceivably. I'm okay, Dad. I'm okay, I'm okay!

She turns around, startled to find Giorgio there, relighting the same cigar. He puffs until it's lit, half smiling at her through the smoke.

She half smiles back.

"*Renata mi ha detto che vai a Villa Ruffoli?*"

She looks behind her, then back at Giorgio. "I don't…"

"*Scusami,*" Giorgio says, switching to English. "You go to Villa Ruffoli?"

"I have been to Villa Ruffoli."

"*Ti piace?* Do you like Villa Ruffoli?"

She gets the feeling she's not supposed to say yes.

"Villa Ruffoli is no Italy, Jimmy." He pulls from his cigar. "Napoli is Italy, Jimmy. There is no place like Napoli." His eyes are slits. "Napoli is a wounded city, yes. It is the place for wounded people. There are many floors below the sirens…and the sweats of half-drowned people."

Jamie's confused about that last part.

"My son tells you it is Africa?"

Your son has told me nothing, she doesn't say. "Perhaps Jack and I will visit Napoli." She does not know why she says this.

"*Mah,*" he resigns. "My son is an American now." His mouth and shoulders, everything pulls downward. A moment passes. Then Giorgio thrusts his head back up to the sky, startling her. "My son, the *americano!*" His fist is raised in victory.

Or a long lost battle.

Jamie examines him through the smoke an uncomfortable minute longer, trying yet not wanting to see what is boiling there below the surface. She makes some excuse and slips back inside, where Zia Renata is presently lamenting to Giovanni's deaf ears about Lucrezia's health. Apparently, Lucrezia's health problems are Jack's fault for living in America. Her blood pressure is dangerously high, her cholesterol fatal, and Giovanni must convince Giorgio to return with Lucrezia to Vico Equense, to be near the thermal springs and unpolluted air.

Giovanni assures Jamie that Lucrezia's health is fine, and Giorgio will never leave Napoli.

"That's the impression I'm getting," Jamie says. "Please, God, tell me who is this Lucrezia, because I had the impression that she was a cat."

"*Mia sorella*," Zia says. "Sister."

"Adopted sister," Jack adds.

"I didn't know you had a sister."

"My dad's and Zia Renata's sister. Lucrezia is my aunt."

"*La domestica*," Zia Renata clarifies, and no one translates (maid), but maybe that's because Giorgio has entered and silenced the room; you could cut the tension with a knife. They sit for lunch, though Giorgio won't look at Zia Renata now, especially when she speaks. Nor does he speak, for fear she might respond.

The only thing left to do is critique the food. The fried zucchini (a dish very different from American fried zucchini) does not have enough garlic, Giorgio insists while helping himself to more. There is a big wet ball of buffalo mozzarella that Zia bought fresh down the road, but that doesn't quite seem to meet expectations. The eggplants marinated in garlic, oil and spices from Zia's garden are very good; she is willing to agree, but the clams are too salty, Giovanni admits, though only after Zia has harassed him to so that she can go off in a defensive wail because the idea of disappointing Giovanni upsets her so. Zia assures him that this is not her fault, for the fisherman in the green boat retired last month, and now they must go to the fisherman in the blue boat, where the fish is not so good. Giorgio chimes in here: no fish will ever be as good as from Spaccanapoli, where he buys his. This he proclaims while refilling his wine glass from the jug he'd bought from a guy in Posillipo, who gives him the absolute best deal. Jack asks for the winemaker's name, but Giorgio tightens his lips because he's revealed too much already.

"*I vini campani sono i migliori, non come i vini schifosi piemontesi,*" Giorgio says. "*Come quelli dei Ruffoli.*" He opens his hands, squeezes his shoulders together. "Eh Giovanni?"

"My brother says that no grapes can compare with the grapes of Vesuvius," Zia translates for Jamie, and on this one thing Zia and Giorgio agree: Northern Italians know nothing. "*Non capiscono niente!*" Zia and Giorgio go on about it now, not just *il vino,* but *la pasta, la pizza, il pane…* Jack sips from his glass unresponsively. Jamie nudges him to get out the Ruffoli Barolo he brought to set his father straight, but Jack returns her a warning glance, which is when it occurs to Jamie that Jack has not told his father or Zia Renata that he has quit his job to run the Ruffoli vineyard. After all, his dad once fled the place like it was Vesuvius itself, erupting.

CHAPTER 16

Agosto a Vico Equense

*J*ACK WASN'T KIDDING about that elevator. It dropped them right down into a cave that then opened up onto the beach, if you can call it that; more like a rocky inlet at the bottom of a perilous cliff, where colorful row boats speckle the shoreline and locals wade in the sea. There are two cabanas with paved walkways leading out to small clusters of umbrellas, one cluster orange, one cluster green.

Nonno Carlo had belonged to the orange cluster, his position after thirty years prestigious, coveted, closest to the sea. Upon Nonno's death it had been bequeathed to Zio Silvio, and presently it's where Jack and Jamie are lying on lounges that feel practically on top of each other. The umbrellas are almost touching and she can barely see the sky. Where she had grown up you'd just plop your towel down on the sand and still be twenty yards from anyone else. Here, it's like, why ever part?

"I don't understand," she says.

"You can put it down," he says, thinking she's referring to the umbrella.

"What was all that at lunch?"

Jack's straddling his lounge, hunched over his *Corriere*. "They don't print that in American papers," he says, ignoring her question.

"Why do you stay in the States…when you could have all this?"

"I have all this," he says, not looking up from his paper.

"Seriously, Jack. The tension back there was unbearable."

He looks at her—*what tension?*—though she refuses to believe he does not know what she's talking about. At last he does pull his eyes from his paper to say that it wasn't always like this. Staring far out at the horizon, he takes one of those worldly breaths of his, one that reminds her that their relationship is not about what she wants from him, but what he is able to give her; that sudden, playful look in his eyes, the aching memories of when he was a kid.

"I couldn't wait for August to come," he begins, turning to her. "You know in Italy everyone takes the month of August off."

"The whole month?"

"Everything shuts down."

"That doesn't seem very productive."

"Papá still worked for Nonno Giacomo in Torino back then, but in August, he and I always came south. That drive to Vico Equense was the most time I ever spent alone with Papá. Once there, he'd stay for two days max, and then he'd drag Lucrezia off to meet school friends of theirs in Napoli."

"He just left you here?"

"Sometimes he'd leave sooner…depending. He and Nonno Carlo did not get along."

"Why?"

He looks at her, or through her, so it feels. Then he abruptly waves a hand in the air. "Anyway I wasn't alone. I was with Nonno and Zia Renata…though Zia Renata still worked back then. Mostly it was Nonno and me, which meant we were free to eat what we wanted. All Nonno wanted was fish and pasta. If he didn't cook it himself then we would eat at the same fish restaurant he'd been going to for years, until he got into a fight with the owner that is, and then he'd have to find a new fish restaurant, and the cycle continued. He was a tyrant about those meals. God forbid I was a second late for lunch…one o'clock, no exceptions…or if I left a breadcrumb on my plate…'You don't know what hunger is,' he would say, all he would ever say, about his days in the war."

His eyes narrow in on her. "What's so funny?"

"Are you aware that all your memories revolve around food?"

He thinks about it.

She applies more sunscreen.

"There's the sea," he offers, a light in his eyes. "Nonno loved the sea. Every morning he would row his *pattino* for miles along the shore. He'd work out with weights or go to the tanning salon. Then he'd come home and prepare *sogliole* for lunch…"

"Ah, see? Food again!"

"*Ma lasciamo stare.*" Leave me alone.

"I'm kidding. Go on."

"Forget it."

"Come on."

He is back to his paper.

"You never mentioned Lucrezia."

"I did," he says, after some delay.

"No. You didn't."

He puts aside the paper, lies half down on his side. "Nonno adopted Lucrezia from a refugee orphanage in Trieste when she was thirteen, just after he returned from the war to find that his wife had died of pneumonia. He had three young children and needed the help, and though Lucrezia did much of the cooking and cleaning, Nonno treated her like part of the family. She helps Giorgio with the pharmacy in Napoli now."

"Is it really like Africa?"

He looks at her oddly.

"Your father said you would say it's like Africa."

He smirks.

"You haven't told Giorgio about the vineyard, have you?"

"No."

"Why?"

"Because it's none of his fucking business!"

A wave splashes against a rock somewhere.

The couple next to them is staring.

It's an outburst she believes worthy of an apology.

None comes.

She lies back and pulls the attached, adjustable head shade over her face.

"Jamie, my father didn't even go to his own father's funeral."

"He seems so miserable. Like he's been banished to the city of wounded souls or something…"

"He only pretends to be miserable, to hide how guilty he feels." Jack flips onto his back. "And anyway, what's there to be happy about? He's Italian."

She squints at him. His skin seems to be bronzing before her eyes, in fact, everything about him is darker suddenly, or perhaps it's the shadow presently over him, in the shape of a tall, big bellied, Speedo wearing man, perfectly tanned and glistening with oil.

"Ah, here is Zio Silvio!" Giovanni jumps up. "You can ask him about Giorgio's misery." They kiss, embrace. "*Bravo tanti auguri!*" Zio Silvio bellows. A thick gold chain around his neck, Armani sunglasses, a towel in one hand, a pack of cigarettes and his cell phone in the other. His hair is too dark to be its natural color.

Silvio's eyes linger on Jamie's breasts as she stands to greet him. "*Tanti auguri!*" He kisses her cheeks. If she feels exposed in her bikini, then she feels bare naked each time a *tanti aurguri* is directed her way. She is starting to wonder, if not worry, about how this engagement façade will end.

Silvio drops his towel and lights a cigarette. "*Facciamo una passeggiata,* and we can discuss Giorgio, if you wish."

They stroll down to the pebbly shore, but before they discuss Giorgio they must discuss football. Then Giovanni must describe the seafood pasta he made for lunch. Silvio describes his lunch with his daughter's future in-laws with gestures that make Jack laugh. He must make the sign of the cross for his dead wife, may she rest in peace, now that their only child, Maria, is at last getting married at the age of thirty-five. They must exchange gossip with a neighbor while the water laps over their feet. Silvio must check out all the women. By now Jamie's forgotten about Giorgio, her gaze lazily wandering the serene scene—light breeze off the water, the shore oddly pristine, no weird smells or trash, even the people look like they've just stepped out of the shower or had a fresh shave.

"*Allora,* Giorgio," Zio Silvio sighs in honor of his brother, then goes on with Giovanni in Italian. Their discussion grows vibrant; there are some brief, filtered translations: Zio Silvio's apartment in Napoli is not far from Giorgio's. Giorgio is not poor, he just pretends to be poor so that he won't have to send money to La Mamma. He labors all hours of the day and night at the pharmacy and saves every penny he earns. He is happy in Napoli, to be far away from the north, though he will never be free. And then, Jamie is not sure about this last translation. 'We Italians can never be free.'

"It is as I told you," Jack says to her. "In America you are free."

"*L'amore ti libera,*" Silvio adds with a bit of mischief. "Love sets you free," and Jamie finds herself blushing.

"*Hai fatto bene, Giovanni. Il vino e' fantastico!*" Zio Silvio cries out suddenly. Jamie, startled, looks around her, wondering if Vesuvius has suddenly erupted, until the two men fall over laughing, and Jack explains that Papá will find out soon enough about his son's return to Villa Ruffoli, since Zio Silvio is serving the Ruffoli Barolo with the rabbit at Maria's reception.

"A cousin of Zio Silvio's deceased wife will be at their table, an important wine merchant from the Veneto. Zio Silvio and I have it all planned," Jack informs her.

"What will your father do when he sees the Villa Ruffoli Barolo bottle on the table?"

Jack meets Zio's gaze. "It will serve him right." Then they grasp each other's shoulders with such affection that she must avert her eyes. "*Grazie* Silvio, *grazie,*" says Jack. Jamie barely knows what has transpired, it's all so tragic and convoluted, intimate and touching. She peers down each end of the shore. "Is there anywhere I can go for a run around here?"

They look at her.

"Does the beach continue on past that rocky corner?"

Blank looks; Jack translates Jamie's question for Zio Silvio, who looks concerned and calls over the neighbor. The neighbor calls over another neighbor and soon there is a conference going on.

"Run? Run where?" they all must know.

"I mean jog, as in exercise."

"*Ah si, si, ho capito.*" There is more conferencing before they decide that now is not a good time to run; soon it will be high tide. And there is the *malavita* (thieves). It is dangerous. "*Non farla andare a correre,*" the woman says. Please do not let Jamie run.

The next morning Jamie runs anyway, a little jaunt around town. They are right; it is hopeless. Not because of the *malavita* or the cold breeze or steep inclines, but because everyone stares at her. Why are you running? Relax lady. It's only eight a.m. She stops, walks back, and borrows Zia Renata's computer to check e-mail. The connection is surprisingly good, but the keyboard is Italian and it takes Jamie a frustrating thirty minutes to maneuver into her firm's website, at which point her stomach immediately drops. The first e-mail is from Chris, telling her that the client (in other words Charles) wants her back in Seoul right away. There is a problem with the Phase I numbers.

Shit.

Initial panic is followed by a rush of adrenaline; she is indispensable—they can't do this deal without her. She looks at the clock, nine a.m., and then goes to Nonno's room where John Wayne has taken over the bed. She shuts the door and calls Chris in New York on her cell. The Koreans are going to Charles with different numbers, he says, expecting her call even though it's three a.m. his time. John Wayne lumbers into a crouch position while she assures Chris that they'd expected this, they'd expected the Koreans to push back, that it's part of the plan and where her formulas come in. Plus, they've got Charles on their side.

He's counting on her, he warns, hanging up.

Jamie gets out her laptop and starts re-running scenarios. John Wayne stumbles off the bed and paws at the door. She goes to let him out, but hears Zia Renata sweeping on the other side and decides against it. There is no refuting the formulas. She calls the ANR CFO at four p.m. Seoul time. He's Korean, as is everyone who works at ANR's Korean subsidiary, except for Charles and two others who were brought over from the company's headquarters in Chicago to run things. An us-against-them mentality prevails. Korea's not a change culture, the CFO tells her in that thick accent she has not yet been able to tune her ear to. Her eyes roll back, picturing him at his desk, behind a plume of smoke and dripping ash, shaking his head yes when what he really means is no.

"This is not change," she reassures him, bringing her eyes back. "It's a paradigm shift. We were all on the same page when I left. The workers will be re-skilled and re-educated; they'll find better jobs. It is the natural course of things." She gets off the phone and calls her travel agent about flights. The knot has returned to her stomach, which means that her life is back in order. There is no question that she will go back and make right whatever is wrong.

When she finally does emerge from her room she trips over John Wayne who's lying there as if dead. He snarls and darts for the door, which she at last opens so that he can dive behind a plant just around the corner. "Sorry," she follows him out, then crouches down to soothe him, but he bats at her hand. She stumbles backward into a bookshelf, rubbing the scratch he's left on her thumb.

"Do you like Philip Roth?"

Jamie jumps, startled, for Zia is but a breath away from her. Stepping sideways, she says, "I don't read very much fiction."

"Giovanni loves to read. You must read, Jamie."

"The women in my family are all math majors."

Zia pulls down a book by Dorothy Parker. "Take this."

Jamie reads the quote on the back cover. "I like to have a martini, two at the very most, three I'm under the table, four I'm under my host." It's the first time Jamie has smiled that morning. "Do you always read in English?"

Zia shrugs, as if her talent for the English language is natural—until she starts mentioning trips to America she's taken: Orlando for a high school exchange program; subsequent trips to Boston, Ithaca, Chicago, Dallas… In fact, as it turns out, she's tracked Giovanni across the U.S. "Giorgio sends me because he must work and La Mamma is afraid to fly and Lucrezia…" Zia stops herself. She pulls a tiny picture frame off the bookshelf. "Poor Lucrezia." Two, young, mismatched girls, one of whom is clearly not southern—tall, with loose, cascading hair. Her arm is draped around Zia Renata, the tiny one with the braid. "I cannot visit her in Napoli, and Giorgio will not bring her here."

"Why can't you go to Napoli?"

"Napoli is full of disease and trash, Jimmy."

"Why did Lucrezia not come to Vico Equense for the wedding?"

"Lucrezia is the only one Giorgio trusts to run the pharmacy." She contemplates the photo. "*Mah*," she resigns, setting it back down. "You would like Lucrezia. She works hard, like you. She is always working at the pharmacy, always seeing to the girls and helping them with their women problems." She searches Jamie's eyes for understanding. "Lucrezia and Giorgio sell contraception illegally."

"Contraception is illegal?"

"Only certain kinds, like the morning after pill. They believe that if it's available in other countries, it should be available here, too."

Jamie isn't sure what to say.

"I miss Lucrezia," Zia confesses.

Or where this conversation is going.

Zia goes on about Lucrezia's limoncello now, and her fried dough. "*Mamma mia* ask Giovanni about Lucrezia's fried dough." Then, with dire urgency, "You must have Giovanni take you to Napoli, Jimmy! You must meet Lucrezia." Her voice is slurred. "Poor Giovanni," she wails suddenly, startlingly. If Jamie didn't already know the difference between an Italian martini and a Dorothy Parker one, she would think, enviously, that the woman might have already partaken in a few of Dorothy's drinks.

"I plan to visit Giovanni in New York as soon as John Wayne dies," Zia continues. "I have always wanted to visit New York, but I cannot leave John Wayne now. He is very ill, you know. Did I tell you he is very ill? When will you be married?" No pauses, no breaths. John Wayne waddles by then, and they fix their eyes on him.

We are already married, Jamie imagines the words flowing from her lips, but in reality it's Zia who has spoken. "I am afraid I cannot come to your wedding. You see, I hate weddings."

Jamie bites her lip to keep from smiling, or choking, or both. There is no way in hell she is having a wedding.

She finds Jack at a bar in the piazza where Zia informed her the men would be watching a football game. A burst of laughter explodes as she enters; apparently the game is over, because she spots Jack at the bar with Silvio and Giorgio, chatting with the owner. Silvio and Giorgio are bent over. Jack, clutching his stomach, tells her that Zio Silvio is in the middle of a story that they've all heard a million times. The owner mixes Jamie a "congratulatory" aperitif that she sips while Zio Silvio finishes over another burst of laughter.

"*Viva il Duce!*" Giorgio stands at attention and shouts—at her, she gets the feeling, squinting back at him, unsure what exactly is so hysterical, for Giorgio and Silvio have fallen over laughing again, and then they salute their way out of the bar.

"*Viva il Duce?*" she asks.

"It's stupid," Jack says, shaking his head.

"What's stupid?"

"Not worth translating."

"Shouldn't that be my decision?"

Apparently not, for he offers her no response. A feeling of absolute ignorance envelops her, and suddenly she is glad she must leave. She can't wait to fucking leave. This place is ridiculous. These people are ridiculous.

Koreans are ridiculous.

Or maybe it is she who is ridiculous.

They have moved their way into a seat at an outside table, twice as expensive as the counter, which is why they never sit at an outside table—but he has seen the look on her face. A table is in order. *Un caffé americano* is in order. He waits until the waiter has delivered it before asking her, pointedly, what's wrong. He knows by now that it has nothing to do with *il Duce*.

"I don't have an ear for languages, that's what's wrong."

"You're doing fine…You just need to listen."

"Even when they speak English—your father, Zio Silvio—I don't understand them."

"It's not just language and gestures, Jamie; it's culture, too. Italians are heavily tied to our past, to tradition. It's who we are."

"To be an American means you don't have to be tied to anything."

"That's because you go back, what, a few hundred years?"

A notion she'd always been proud of, today sounds like defeat, and she blinks up at him. "I've got to go back to Seoul. There's a problem with the numbers."

He recoils, ever so slightly.

"I spoke with Chris this morning. Charles wants me back."

"The CEO who's trying to hit on you?"

She doesn't respond. They've discussed this. It's a non-issue.

His face is pale, confused, and she sinks into her chair. Whatever rush of adrenaline she felt before is at once gone as though it never existed, as they sit staring into each other's dimming eyes, the reality of their situation hitting them both at once. In the last three months they've seen each other exactly ten days and there is no end in sight to the work still needed to make the Korea project a success; or forget success at this point, just not a failure.

"You can't leave before the wedding."

"This is my job! What do you want me to do?" It comes out sounding desperate and harsh, but it is directed at herself more than anyone else. "Sorry…"

"It's okay."

"It's not okay."

"It'll be fine."

"It won't be fine." She smiles through wet eyes. "Anyway," she sips her coffee, cold now; "the wedding is tomorrow. I won't leave before that."

CHAPTER 17

Frutti di Mare

*I*T'S THE MORNING OF the wedding. Zia Renata is pacing around in her housedress, sweating at the thought of Giovanni and Jamie driving to the church in her Fiat.

"You're not going?" Jamie asks.

"Oh no, Jimmy, I never go to weddings. *Mah, allora* Giovanni, where will you park? And the brake, there is a problem with the brake in the Stilo. Traffic will be a disaster. *Dio mio.*"

She hates weddings. She has made this clear to anyone who will listen, and yet Jack convinces her to come anyway. How he does this, Jamie does not want to fathom, but after some private conference, just like that, Zia changes from her housedress into a dress not much different from her housedress, hops into her car, and speeds them far up into the hills in the little Fiat with the lurching clutch.

"Why must you leave Vico Equense, Jimmy?" Zia Renata asks when they are paused at one of the few traffic lights.

"It's only two days early," Jamie offers, an attempt at nonchalance when in fact she's feeling overwhelmingly guilty, as if she and this woman have just tasted their first martini together; the glass is still tantalizingly, dangerously full, and now Jamie has to go.

"You'll be back next year, yes?"

"Certainly."

"And you like Vico Equense, yes?"

"*Attenzione!*" Jack yells, because the light has turned green.

"I hope you like Vico Equense," Zia says, gunning it.

Jamie, flung back against her seat, is wondering why everyone wants her to like Italy so much. It's always the first question she is asked, like she'd want to be the first person to ever say no.

It is a tiny, crumbling, Romanesque church located on the edge of town in a wooded area shaded by trees. The gray stones sink inward, the brick lay uneven. It is a small wedding, maybe fifty guests, men moving around in dark suits and thin ties, women looking as if they've just emerged from the sea, tanned and glistening, cigarette in hand. No shawls necessary down here.

The church is only a third full and thankfully absent the fear and terror in the proceedings that Jamie remembers from Luca and Antonia's wedding. She and Jack sit behind Giorgio and Zio Silvio who is with his girlfriend, Gabriella, whom no one knew he was bringing. The entire church is buzzing with gossip. "*Puttana*," Zia Renata refers to her, moaning persistently, "Poor Maria," and something about the wedding being ruined.

Jack, meanwhile, goes over and over the reading he must give, intent on not exposing the American accent he may have acquired over the years. When his moment comes he heads up to the podium, and, facing the bride and groom, bestows words upon them that he stopped believing long ago. "His Italian is perfect," Zia leans over and whispers in Jamie's ear, her eyes on Giovanni, not leaving Giovanni. Jamie's eyes don't leave him either. There's a heavy wood carving of Jesus on the cross hanging from a wire just above his head. She's petrified the wire will snap, and the cross will come down and strike him dead.

"I think Zia Renata is in love with you," Jamie says. They are waiting under a shaded vestibule outside after the ceremony.

"Oh please, Jamie, stop it."

"I don't mean it in a negative way. I mean it to say that I think she and I might be connected from some past life or something."

"Oh really."

"Why has she never married?"

"Why don't you ask her?"

"Maybe I will."

"Don't ask her, Jamie. Just stay out of it."

"Out of what?" She nudges him. "Look. The *puttana* is on her way over."

"Don't say that word, Jamie. That's a terrible word."

"But you guys were the ones saying it."

Sultry, forty maybe, DG sunglasses perched on her head, serious cleavage. She reintroduces herself to Giovanni. Besides being Zio Silvio's mistress, she is the daughter of the brother of the owner of the fish restaurant that Nonno Carlo used to take Giovanni to every day. He blushes at something the woman says, then clears his throat, "*Ti presento la mia fidanzata.*"

The woman looks Jamie up and down, takes her hand, "*Piacere.*" Then she says something to Giovanni and leaves.

"What did she say?" Jamie wants to know, watching the woman glide off in her stilettos as if she were walking on water not cobble.

"She said we look good together."

Jamie eyes him skeptically. "Her body language said something different."

"She's just checking you out; what you're wearing, how you look."

"That's what I mean. Who does that?"

"She can't help it, she's Italian."

And that's how that conversation ends.

"By the way," Jamie says. "I looked up the literal meaning of *fidanzata.*"

"You did, did you."

"It means female lover."

"I know."

"But doesn't that imply sexual relations?"

"Your point?"

"Well, that's certainly putting it out there. Especially since the Pope just threatened to excommunicate doctors who prescribe the abortion pill, as well as patients who use it."

Here we go.

"It's been all over the papers." In fact, she'd not read the papers. "Zia told me about the contraception business."

"She must have been drinking," he says. "She only talks about it when she's drinking. What else did she tell you?"

"Oh, just your family's long lost secrets." She was joking, but Giovanni goes pale. "I'm kidding, Jack... Hell, maybe I do need to sit her down and get her drunk."

"Don't kid yourself, Jamie. Whatever Zia Renata told you my father was doing, believe me he's doing it for the money and not for some greater good."

Jack shares a nod with Zio Silvio, who is now fleeing the church. They watch the proceedings for a while. Zio Silvio has gone to fetch his freshly polished black GTI and driven it up an impossible incline to get to the church doors. Dodging the ricocheting rice, he loads Maria and her new husband into the car to take them to the reception at a nearby *agriturismo*.

"Zia also told me that Silvio was with the *puttana* while his wife was ill."

"It's none of my business...or yours."

"In other words, it's true."

He doesn't respond.

"And your father? He must have lovers."

He looks at her sharply. "You're stereotyping again."

"I'm not stereotyping."

"Yes you are...I know it's hard to believe, Jamie, but there are known cases in Italy where married couples actually love each other, have sexual relations only with each other, and use birth control. Silvio has a good heart."

"I'm sure he does."

"He bought Maria and her husband an apartment in Napoli for three-hundred-thousand Euros, his entire savings, as a wedding present."

"Right."

"He'll live off his pension now."

Jamie gives him a second look, because she'd thought he was kidding.

"That's what Italians do for their kids."

It takes her a minute to adjust, and then it still doesn't translate. "I just paid off my student loans. Soon I'll have a mortgage."

"You're planning on buying a house?"

"In theory, you know what I mean."

"I come from a cash society. I have no idea what you mean."

Jamie's still back on that house Zio Silvio bought. "Good thing he's only got one kid."

"There's a reason why Italy has one of the lowest birth rates in the world."

"So when does your father buy us a house?"

"Papá says the pharmacy's not doing well."

"I was being facetious."

"So was I. The pharmacy is never doing well: taxes, corruption, insurance, the list goes on. It's what he says so that La Mamma won't ask him to send more money."

"And that envelope? What was that, condoms?"

For a minute she thinks he might turn and slap her.

"Guilt," he says finally, sounding both defeated and resigned. He turns to watch Silvio's car tear down the hill, gravel spraying everywhere.

They are one of the first to arrive at the *agriturismo*, a quiet, serene location on top of a hill with distant views of the Bay of Naples. The sky is blue and endless; a few small clouds float by with a warm, dry breeze. Jack and Giorgio go off to smoke a Toscano. In fact, they are often going off to smoke a Toscano, an unspoken compromise, their way of existing together, of talking. Everyone else seems to have taken the scenic route in order to be late. Even the staff is missing, and the doors to the main farmhouse are locked, the inside darkened even though tables have been set for lunch.

Zia Renata, now on a desperate and sweaty search for water, leads Jamie to the other side of the farmhouse where through a window they spot a busboy and knock harder. He comes over with the expression, *what are you doing here?* Behind him, a group of waiters is gathered around a TV. The busboy seems confused by what Zia is asking and calls over the manager. More discussion ensues before the busboy walks reluctantly off to find two glasses and a pitcher. At this point Jamie asks for a bathroom, which sets Zia on alarm. Is Jamie ill? Should Zia go with her?

"Please no, I'm fine," is Jamie's response. "*Sinistra, destra, dritto,*" left, right, straight, a stumble down some stairs, past a kitchen where activity is going on, and then through a door where she is presented with a toilet and a pull chain. After she pees she sits down on the lid for a time breathing freely, content to be alone, in the company of herself. She figures she's got about ten minutes before people start looking for her. She rests her eyes shut, imagining Giovanni's family catching sight of her hiding away in here; they'd think her a freak. Anybody, anywhere in the world would think she was a freak. Except Jack maybe. He wouldn't like it but he'd understand it, the way he seems to understand her.

When at last she returns, the glass doors have been cast open onto the garden filling with guests. Tables not there before are now overflowing with antipasti and glasses of prosecco. She grabs two glasses and takes one to where Jack is, by a fountain with his father and some young men who have joined them. After being introduced to a second generation of cousins, Jamie informs them about the game going on inside, and they all rush in that direction.

Jack takes Jamie over to meet the bride—Maria—shy, plain, glasses, hair so thin it can't stay in its bun. Her husband is the son of Zio Silvio's tailor in Napoli. His shop is in the Vomero, a few doors down from the lawyers' office in which Silvio worked for thirty years. The apartment Zio Silvio bought Maria and her new husband is next to his own, which is not far from the tailor shop. Maria hovers close to her groom the entire afternoon, not appearing to know but a few people at the wedding. The guests are mostly Zio Silvio's friends, and then, as is the courteous tradition: the gardener, the janitor, the cabana boy, the guy who works the newspaper kiosk, the café owner's son.

They drink prosecco and eat little balls of buffalo mozzarella and *pomodori*, and *fritto di mare* in sweltering heat for what seems like hours, until finally somebody complains and it occurs to everyone that many of the men are inside watching the end of the game. They hear a big roar. Then the doors are opened and lunch is served.

It's a relief to be inside where it's cool and out of the beating sun. Jamie and Jack sit at a table with Zia Renata, Giorgio, Zio Silvio and his girlfriend, Gabriella *(puttana)*, plus the cousin of Silvio's deceased wife who is the wine merchant from Veneto, and platters of *polpette di riso* and *sfogliatelle*. The men take off their jackets and loosen their ties. The women lean back and fan their chests, including Zia Renata, who now turns and translates a question Gabriella has called across the table at Jamie, which is whether her and Jack's wedding will take place in Italy or America. Thankfully, Gabriella begins flirting with Giorgio and seems uninterested in an answer, so Jamie pretends not to have one. She leans over and says to Jack, low, so no one can hear, "Maybe now's a good time to tell them we're already married."

He squeezes her knee, hard.

"Ouch," she says.

"Shhhh," he says, continuing his conversation with the wine merchant on his left.

Wine flows freely, *Greco di Tufo, Fiano di Avellino* the fruits of Vesuvio in full swing. *Baccala' con peperoni,* then *risotto ai frutti di mare.* Zia Renata has forgotten that she hates weddings, apparently. When she is not wielding a fork she's wielding that fan, breathless. Every so often she will cry out the names of the poor in a pretense of misery, but otherwise, she is having a splendid time translating for Jamie all the treasures being set before them, as well as tidbits of the conversations going on all at once around them, and Jamie is thankful that Zia changed her mind and came, for both Zia's sake and Jamie's. In Zia Jamie can see her own reclusive tendencies, a guardedness toward happiness, the kind that only comes in moments, these moments.

The Ruffoli Barolo is at last poured with the braised rabbit infused with local spices. Zio Silvio is using it to make a toast. Somewhere in his speech the news comes out, as far as Jamie can tell, about Jack's new endeavor. There are some *oohs* and *ahhs* about the wine, not to mention the requisite rousing: so expensive and extravagant are these northerners from Piemonte, but it's all in good fun and Jack doesn't seem to mind. Or this is what Jamie thinks she understands, until Zio sits down and Jack takes out his handkerchief and blows his nose as if something Zio said had touched him very deeply, and she realizes that she's understood nothing, nothing at all. More toasts are made. Jamie's eyes are on Giorgio now, who has yet to touch his wine glass and is staring at the Ruffoli bottle as if it might contaminate him. When the toasts are finished, the party din returns and Jack starts describing some of the things he is doing at the vineyard in response to somebody's question.

"*Buono,*" Zia Renata says, sipping the wine again and again.

"*Molto buono. Vero* Giorgio?" Gabriella agrees, goading Giorgio, for they all know about his tainted Ruffoli past. Giorgio's response is "I pay only five Euros for my demijohn of Taurasi. Why I pay more for a bottle? Why all these bottles? Why wine so big deal suddenly? Wine is wine."

"*Buono il Barolo, che buono…*" the wine merchant on Jack's left says.

"*I Ruffoli non capiscono niente,*" Giorgio assures them, his face exploding red. "*Non. Capiscono. Niente!*"

Further debate ensues.

Giorgio, stewing, says to Jamie, "My son is an engineer. Why?" He glances at Giovanni. "Eh, Giovanni? Because of me, that's why. The Ruffoli send my son to big university in America, and here is the poor Neapolitan who ends up paying the tuition!" He picks up his glass, downs the wine, sets the glass back down, all while Giovanni sits motionless, like he'd expected this, perhaps somehow even wanted this.

Zia Renata, fanning her neck, turns to Jamie. "When will you and Giovanni be moving to Italy?" A deep pleasure is buried in her face. The whole table is waiting for an answer. Jamie turns to Jack, wondering what he might have to say to that, but Jack is not there. She does not know where he has gone, and everyone resumes the meal as if nothing has happened. Even Giorgio is pouring himself another glass of wine.

"Not bad this wine, eh?" He speaks mischievously, to no one in particular because no one is paying him any attention, except Jamie, that is. She's keened her eyes on him, waiting for his gaze to meet hers, which at last it does and for a moment they stay like that, neither flinching. Then he brings a finger under an eye and pulls down on the skin as if he were trying to make his eye bigger. It's an Italian gesture she's seen someone use before. She does not know what it means.

The guests float outside for liquors and biscotti. Jamie takes a limoncello over to Jack, who is seated back by the fountain with his cigar.

"Aren't you glad you're leaving?" he says.

"No," she lies, handing him the glass.

"It's not as good as Lucrezia's," he says, handing it back.

She sits down next to him. "I'm supposed to ask you about her fried dough."

He smiles, far off.

She sips the liquid for the first time, surprised by the thick, icy texture, the gooey sweetness, the tartness of lemon, the faint shock of something burning. "So is this what this is about, Jack? This whole Ruffoli vineyard resurrection, just so you can piss off your father?"

He takes a long puff from his cigar, releases the smoke. "Papá paid off my MIT tuition only on the condition that after graduation I wouldn't return to Italy. He wanted me to live in America." He pauses. "Both my grandparents were dead. Villa Ruffoli was bankrupt. Papá had gone back to Napoli. He said there was nothing to come back to."

"Maybe he was trying to do you a favor..."

"And look where it's gotten me. What have I accomplished in the States?"

"Maybe he was doing us a favor." She squeezes his thigh.

"Villa Ruffoli's mine, Jamie. Nonno entrusted it to me. And yet for all those years after the bankruptcy, in the wake of all the rumors and ugliness, I tried to convince myself that I didn't belong to it."

It's as if she's hearing him for the first time, as if the seed he's planted in her is at last sprouting roots. "Did he really take money from the company?"

"Who told you that?"

"That's what they say, right?"

"No one says anything."

"But it's there, in the rumors you mentioned. It's lurking in peoples' minds."

"You mean like where did he get the money to pay for my college tuition?"

"That might be one question."

For which he apparently has no answer.

"What does he say happened?"

His eyes grow distant.

"Don't tell me you never asked."

"Look, Jamie," he says sharply. "It's just something we don't talk about in my family."

"But this isn't your family, Jack; it's you and me."

His jaw clenches.

"Don't you want to know?"

"No."

"There are ways to know."

"Leave it alone…"

"I'm just saying…"

"You don't know anything, Jamie."

She pulls back. "I know some things."

"There's no point."

There's more to this point, she thinks.

A long silence. The limoncello disappears.

"Why did you bring me here, Jack?"

His eyes remain vacant for an indeterminate amount of time. Then he smiles, his whole face opens up suddenly, as if the question itself is unfathomable, as if to say, my dear poor neglected child, just look out at the gorgeous horizon before you, past the shimmering silver and into the deepest of blues. Taste the fruit on your lips and in the air. Isn't the answer obvious?

CHAPTER 18

Home

*I*T QUICKLY BECOMES CLEAR that the Koreans will never see it their way. Change isn't going to happen, and yet, "Do whatever it takes," Chris keeps saying. Make the "saves" happen.

Charles' wife is back in the States for a few weeks. Can Jamie come over for a quiet dinner? Jamie has been holding off her client's advances with work excuses, assuring Jack on their daily phone calls that the poor man is just lonely. He's sixty, biding his time, waiting to get reassigned, hopefully back to the States. Meanwhile, he won't eat outside the Army PX. His advances are more amusing than anything else.

What she doesn't mention to Jack is that Charles has been putting on the pressure of late, what with his wife gone. Late night phone calls, knocks on her hotel room door that she keeps double locked, gifts; repeated invitations to a "quiet dinner." Jamie needs his leadership to champion scope changes to the project, not to mention keep the Koreans to their promises, so at last she does accept his invitation...*whatever it takes.*

Now they have had their dinner in the dining room of the exquisite teak house in which the bank has housed Charles and his wife. The home is in one of Seoul's most prestigious neighborhoods—complete with servants and drivers, the man is not suffering. They have moved to the formal living room now, where tea, soju, and rice cakes are waiting. Charles sidles up next to her on the couch, sets his hand on her knee. It takes Jamie a moment to realize that this is the part where she is supposed to push his hand away, move to the other side of the couch and redirect the conversation to business.

Apparently, one hesitation is all it takes; he moves in to kiss her. *Oh dear,* though she is not so surprised, she supposes. She scoots backward but he's gripping her shoulders now. In all her worst case scenarios about this dinner, struggling free from Charles had not been one of them. In fact there is a fleeting, horrific moment where Jamie isn't sure she can struggle free—but he does let go eventually, and she springs up from the couch.

SO not wanting this to be a "scene" or a "situation," she smiles as if nothing's happened and asks, as casually as she can manage, if the driver might take her home now. She's got an early meeting in the morning. But thank you Charles. Thank you so much!

Thank you!? Really? Is that what she actually said to him? This horrendous thought awakens Jamie the next morning full of guilt and insecurity about whether she'd led him on just by going. She's tangled in her sheets with empty mini bar bottles and the phone, which has just rung, cradled to her ear.

"Are you crying?"

She doesn't say anything.

"Why are you crying?"

"Can you just please…" she pinches the bridge of her nose. "Can you just take me through your golf round with the distributors and not ask me any questions?"

There is a heavy silence, and then Jack begins, slowly, describing his first drive. It's something she's come to depend on, for he has this way of describing each shot with a sensory detail and emotion that puts her there, not here. It's something to grab onto. It doesn't matter, he is telling her by the fifth hole, where he hooks his drive off the tee. It'll be over soon, he is saying, when a draw with his five-iron lands pin-high, but then he three-putts.

There is a long silence after he birdies eighteen.

"Maybe I'm not cut out for this," she says in a thin, barely audible voice.

"You're cut out for this."

"I think there's something wrong with me."

"There's nothing wrong with you."

"I don't think I can do it."

"Do what?"

"This," she ekes out, and his voice grows heavy and deep.

"You should tell Chris about the CEO."

She leaps off the bed. "I can't tell Chris. Do you know what it would mean if I told Chris!?" Her words pound at her temples, and when she still can't speak he says, "Then just come home." It's just a word. Home. Like love is a word—it means nothing. Until he says it. *Home.*

It is three months more before the Koreans fully win over Charles, the project officially collapses, and Jamie can return home.

Home?

❧

Jack's cheap Manhattan sublet turns out to be a swanky loft on Eighteenth Street. It's cheap only because the owner is Jack's best friend from MIT, a bond trader on temporary assignment in London. Tiberio is also Italian, as is everything in the apartment... Can one call that home?

Nevertheless, it's where Jamie stumbles around in a stupor for two weeks while Chris does the spinning and damage control on ANR Aerospace, who is suing them for failing to achieve the "saves" for which they'd been contracted. Then she gets a call from Donald, her Managing Partner in San Francisco, and just as she's thinking *here it comes, I've been "figured out," everything I've worked so hard for is really going to end like this, just as I'd feared worst,* he tells her congratulations, they're officially promoting her to Junior Partner and they want her in Irvine ASAP to take over the Army Corps of Engineers account.

Dumbfounded, confused, perplexed, relieved, sorry, embarrassed, anxious, and above all, feeling entirely inadequate, she starts to pack a bag. They had failed in Korea. She had failed. And yet, she's been made a partner. Junior Partner.

"Failure in America means only one thing," Jack reminds her from the bedroom doorway. "Opportunity."

She flashes him a tight smile.

"In Italy there is no room for failure. It's why Italians keep their jobs forever, and why each time I quit a job, my father practically has a coronary. But in America, failure is a part of success." He hands her her laptop charger.

"Are you mocking me?"

"No, I'm serious. It's the beauty of this country. You learn from the experience, you try again. It's part of the entrepreneurial spirit."

"I don't want to go," is all she says.

"I don't want you to go."

She travels from New York to Irvine every week, from Irvine to New York every weekend, and depending on how Jamie feels and to whom she is talking at a particular moment, her home is either location. For Jill, that home is Irvine, even though Jamie is presently speaking to her from New York.

"Have you thought about buying a house?"

"I'm looking," Jamie lies. She is standing at the windows of Jack's sublet, staring over the tops of buildings to the Empire State.

"Now that you're a Partner, you're going to need the write off."

"Junior Partner."

"Still."

A siren screams by.

"Are you back in New York?"

Jamie backs away from the window.

"Again? So, what, you're going to fly there every weekend?"

A guilty smile.

"I thought this was a marriage of convenience. It doesn't sound very convenient."

"You're funny," Jamie says.

"When does he get his permanent residency?"

"October." She thinks about October, four months from now.

"What happens then?"

"We get divorced." By now of course she is kidding, sort of, but her sister goes stone cold silent.

"Half of American marriages end in divorce, Jill. There are two of us sisters. You do the math."

After a pause, "Why doesn't he just move to Irvine?"

It would never occur to Jamie to ask Jack to move to Irvine.

"Your partnership is in Irvine."

"Junior partnership." She closes her eyes. "New York is where Jack's business is." There's an urgency in her voice, a desperation that surprises her, as if Jack's success is more imperative than her own suddenly, a preposterous and foreign notion... Her eyes pop open. "How are the twins?"

"Huge." No hesitation. She goes on about the crawling and the teething and the amazing dexterity for a while, albeit longingly, guiltily. She only sees them at night, when she's exhausted, and weekends are a blur. Next week she's off to San Francisco for work again. There's a crack in her voice, followed by the defensive diatribe about her nanny, and why she has to have one. Jamie's heard it all before, because oddly, her sister has been calling more frequently since having the girls, even though one would think, what with motherhood added to a stressful career, she'd have less time to chat.

"I know a good lawyer," says Jill, back on point. "When the time comes. If you need one."

"Right. Got that. Thanks." Jamie hangs up, wondering why she continues to feed Jill this dire expectation about her green card marriage. The disparity between her true feelings regarding her relationship with Jack and what she has led others to believe about their relationship has grown to such a point that even she is becoming confused. It is as if her heart is making its way out onto her sleeve, and Jill is like a hound dog. She sniffs out tragedy. It gives her a purpose, something to fix, something to do, and feeding her this will keep her off the trail of what's really going on with Jamie.

What is really going on with Jamie? Well, Jamie is not sure, but she has this sense that whatever it is needs protecting.

Jack, freshly showered and dressed in a dark suit, comes up to Jamie, still disheveled in a tank and his boxers, from behind and wraps his arms around her. "I smell of you," he says and she sinks her shoulders into his chest. She'd still not managed to look directly into his eyes since they'd been making love earlier and she'd come so hard that she'd broken down in tears because everything with him can feel so raw and ripped open. "When we go to Rome for Tiberio's wedding, I was thinking, I want to take you to Sperlonga." He pauses. "Just you and me."

She gives him a very skeptical, sidelong glance, but then can't help dreaming about this place, Sperlonga, that Jack has reminisced about so often—the quaint, one bedroom villa tucked away in a private alcove on the sand just a few steps from the Mediterranean. The place belongs to Silvestro's mother's family, and when Giovanni was a boy La Mamma would take him there during warmer months to stay sometimes. He and Silvestro would spend all day by the water, erecting sandcastles that Giovanni's Godfather, Zio Lorenzo, La Mamma's brother, would intricately architect. Giovanni would build them, and Silvestro would carry the buckets of water back and forth from the sea. Jack is caught up in the memories now, even though Jamie has not committed to going with him to Rome for Tiberio's wedding. She'd had, at one point, a good reason not to go. She is trying to remember now what that reason was, and why she was so incensed the last time she left Italy. She can't seem to recall, here in his arms, seduced by his memories.

She breaks free of his hold, suddenly, urgently, moving around the room to study its contents for the millionth time. "This place is amazing," she says yet again. His eyes have

followed hers to where her gaze has settled on the Cassina dining table that could double as an ice sculpture. She is standing
with her back to him because she can't bear for him to see her
this vulnerable.

"It's Italian," he says.

"The modern and ancient at once, it doesn't make sense."

"Italy doesn't make sense."

"Speaking of which," she turns around. "Who is this Sal
guy anyway?"

He looks at his watch. *Cazzo.* "He's from Napoli," he says,
hurrying for the door. "That's all you need to know."

He's gone, and Jamie is left to wonder what he meant
by that. Giorgio is from Napoli, all she needs to know about
him too, apparently, according to Jack, and she gets an image
of Giorgio then, the frown, the sea stretching out to infinity
beyond him, that gesture where he pulls his eye down. She
finally asked Jack what it meant. "Exactly that," he'd said.
"Keep. Your. Eye. Open."

Watch out, in other words; what Jamie is presently doing
out the window, watching for suspicious behavior inside apartments across the street. It's not the sea, but the view into other
people's lives is no less mesmerizing. At six she takes a shower,
primps, and changes outfits countless times. She'll be meeting
Jack's MIT friends tonight for the first time, not to mention
this Sal person. "He doesn't just sell wine," Jack had assured
Jamie, let's be clear about that. Sal is the top Italian wine
merchant in New York City. Born in Napoli, raised on Long
Island, Jack had been courting a meeting with Sal for months,
and it's finally paid off. Sal has invited Jack to show his bottles
at his Barolo tasting, a premier event taking place at his flag-
ship store, which happens to be just around the corner. The
location is a lucky break, because it's thirty degrees out, and

Jamie, still a Southern California girl at heart, hadn't thought to bring a hat or scarf.

She is shivering by the time she pushes open the wine shop's heavy door, standing still after it slows to a quiet shut behind her, because something feels off. She'd been expecting rustic charm, flamboyant chaos, sounds of Pavarotti, but it's as if she's just entered a Prada store—hushed, sterile, intimidating, a gorgeous blond behind the counter eyeing Jamie with intense interest. Men in dark suits are conferring with other men in dark suits. There is one coming for Jamie now. She wonders if he is going to ask her to leave.

"Can I help you find something?"

"No, thank you. I'm just looking."

"If you need anything…"

"Certainly."

He stands hovering behind her.

The bottles are individually displayed on shelves with dim lighting, as if they are precious artifacts. After a quick perusal, no bottle appears to cost less than sixty dollars.

A hand squeezes her shoulder and she jumps. Not the man, thankfully, but Jack, who proceeds to pull her over to meet Sal, the brainchild behind this uncomfortably exclusive establishment, a man she can identify before they even get to him. Gelled, jet-black hair that is probably a toupee, he's groomed and manicured to the hilt, and certainly too tan for this weather.

Jamie has an almost compulsive need to give the person to whom she's speaking her undivided attention. She attributes this trait to her father, who when she was young so often disparaged about no one listening to him when he spoke. Not on her watch. When her father spoke, Jamie listened, and to listen meant direct eye contact. As a result, it became rote, and after years it became such that looking someone in the eye could often tell her instantly what she needed to know about the other person. It does so now, when Sal's eyes fleet away from hers. He then proceeds to say something to Jack in Italian, as if he suddenly doesn't speak English, when he'd just been speaking it with an American man, quite fluently in fact, as Jamie walked up a moment ago. For *le donne,* apparently, Sal reserves only his most languorous glances, those given to the lady's backside as she glides away. Jamie feels one on her now, or imagines it there, as Jack takes her over to meet his friends.

A Spaniard, a Turk, a Persian, a Singaporean—all dressed in Wall Street attire, all swirling, smelling, and sipping, all members of Jack's foreigners-preferred fraternity at MIT.

"Is that jasmine or cherry?" Jamie offers after introductions, smelling her glass. "I'm kidding," she adds quickly, nervously, when they start to shoot off answers. Silly answers, and she soon realizes that they are kidding, too.

"In fact, I'm a martini drinker."

"Vodka or gin?" the Persian wants to know, and Jamie, who is thinking "right question," says. "Vodka."

"Twist or olive?"

"Olive."

"I'm a beer drinker," says the Sing.

"So why are we all here again?" says the Turk.

"Because wine is a hot investment," says the Spaniard.

"An asset," says the Persian.

"Asset?"

"Age it, sell it."

"What about drinking it."

"French wine sure, but Italian?"

"The cheese is good," says the Sing.

Jamie turns to the Spaniard and asks him what kind of finance he works in. "Goldman," is his rather confused, cryptic response. Apparently, Jamie just crossed some line—we can talk about wine, we can talk about cheese, but we can't talk about work. She has to remember that these men, while they've done well in America, or better perhaps to say that America has done well for them, aren't Americans. They live here, yes, like Jack, to suck America of what it has to offer them, but it will never be their country. In their countries, business and pleasure do not go hand in hand.

The Spaniard doesn't return her ill-fated question, thankfully, because suddenly Jamie has no interest in talking about jobs, particularly her own. She works on the corporate side of finance, more of a bean counter role, something these men might yawn at, not to mention that they'd laugh at her "huge" bonus, on a completely different stratosphere than theirs. It no longer matters though, because they've moved on to discussing vacations in the Maldives or the South of France, and Jamie wanders off looking for the cheese plate. *Vacations? Who takes vacations?*

She returns with a plate of cheese in time to hear the Persian bet the Singaporean how long Jack will last at the vineyard; an inside joke, one she gets being herself so intimately familiar with Jack's reputation for changing jobs. Plus, it's Italy, so go the murmurs now, the raised brows, "What can one possibly get done in Italy?" Hell, Europe for that matter. Asia is where it's at, someone says, and Jamie almost spits out her wine. She tells them that she just spent eight months in Korea, and they look at her like she's nuts. Why would you ever want to go to Seoul? It's all Koreans in Seoul. It was a great experience, she says, rather desperately. It was, it really was! And then a demoralizing feeling takes over. Perhaps Asia is only where it's at if you are Asian.

There is brotherly caution in their tones regarding Ruffoli wine; they are both protective and skeptical of Jack and his venture. Jamie's eyes narrow in defense, even though they are only voicing her own initial thoughts—that this venture of Jack's would be another passing fling, but now... She spots Jack across the room, holding up his glass so a customer can examine the wine. His gaze, both soft and intense, is reflected in the ruby-orange liquid, and her knees buckle. Something stirs inside her, some kind of knowledge or acceptance about the fact that Jack is long past doing what he's been trained to do, he's doing the only thing he can do. He'll be off to Italy again next week, to work with Luca on operations and meet with more distributors and merchants. There is no longer any question about giving up. For better or worse, the vineyard is his future; but what will that mean for her in four months?

She gazes at him longer, unable to pull her eyes away. The only choice she has now is to do everything she can to help him. She tells his friends, casually, about the investors currently courting Jack, which is of course not true. This is a whole new kind of wine making, she assures them, in that there's nothing new about it at all. "You'll see, let the bottles age for ten years and watch the value skyrocket." They each walk away with a case for their impressive cellars, though it's hard to tell if they even liked the wine, or what they thought of Jamie.

Transplants, immigrants, foreigners—bonded forever, a sacred club.

The tasting is over. Jack is saying goodbye to one last customer, and Sal is going over some things on his computer with the gorgeous blond, pausing every few moments to glance down at her breasts. Jamie wanders over when the blond steps away. Ever so casually, so as not to scare him off, she says, "I'm curious about why you had Jack pour his '92 when the Mascarelli's poured their '96?" She's learned a little something about Barolo by now, like that '96 was a great year, and '92 a notoriously bad year.

Sal glances at her a moment longer than he might normally, then goes back to what he's doing. "The '92s go for half the price," he says, not taking his eyes from the computer screen. He seems almost nervous. Jamie's not blond, and she wonders if this is the problem. He continues, "Restaurateurs and sommeliers are always looking for well priced, artisan wines to balance out their menus. It's a way to draw attention to an unknown as well as demonstrate Villa Ruffoli's ability to turn sub par growing conditions into favorable vintages."

Okay that's not a bad answer, asshole. "How do you think buyers will respond to Villa Ruffoli's home grown, eco-friendly methods?"

"It's fine marketing, but there's a balance missing when it comes to production. The overhead for eco-friendly status presents costs and challenges that compromise any long term profit formula."

Jack steps up just then, and Sal practically leaps out of his chair so that the two of them can take relief in their own language; lots of gesticulating. Sal's guttural dialect grates on Jamie's nerves, and she wanders off. The cheese is all gone. She reads a brochure from a stack lying on a table.

"I can't figure out if that guy's a misogynist, or simply an asshole. Is it really that difficult to look at me when he's talking?" They've just left the store, headed toward Union Square to grab a bite. Jack has paused and is frowning at her head. "Where's your hat?"

"And what was all that gesticulating about?"

"You can't go out in this weather without a hat and scarf." He takes off his scarf and wraps it around her neck, making sure her ears are covered. "We were talking about Napoli."

She assumes he's talking about the city.

"They have a new coach. He's a total idiot. It's going to be a disaster. The whole city is in an uproar."

"The soccer team? That's what you were discussing?"

He nudges her playfully.

She is not finding this funny, she tells him.

"Sal is a big Napoli fan, Jamie. There is nothing funny about that."

They start walking again.

"At least give me a read. I can never tell. How did the tasting go?"

"We sold out of the '92 too fast, Sal says."

"Ship him more."

"We don't have anymore."

"You don't have anymore?"

"It was a small vintage. Luca won't compromise on quality."

This was the balance Sal was talking about.

"Sal wants to make a site visit, see our production process, meet Luca, and understand our capacity before he commits to a shipment."

"Wow, that's awesome, Jack."

He shrugs, a gleam in his eye. "I guess he likes me."

"He does know what he's talking about, I'll give him that..."

"He's got a trip planned next July."

"In six months? Are you kidding? Fly him out now." Jamie's wheels are churning. "I read his brochure. He consults. Hire him as a consultant."

"We don't need a consultant," he shakes his head. "You Americans and your consultants."

"Thanks."

"I didn't mean you."

"Sure."

"Look, we know what we're doing. We've created our own taste and fuck anybody who doesn't like it."

"That attitude's going to get you nowhere."

"Anyway, I know what he's going to say. He's going to say we need more hectares."

"I thought you were buying back the Crespi hectares?"

"Zio Marco is still negotiating the price, not to mention doing a lot of ass kissing after Luca's grand performance at the wedding."

"I've got money to invest, Jack."

He looks at her.

"I saved a shitload when I was in Korea. Plus there's my bonus, and my other savings. I've told you this before."

He doesn't say anything.

"It's like you don't want my help."

"I want your help."

"Then what about that bank loan?"

"Zio Marco's submitting the paperwork."

"But why is it taking so long!? Does he know what he's doing?"

"I trust Zio Marco, Jamie. He's been dealing with the finances for a decade, no issues."

"What's the financial model look like?"

"He's a banker, not an analyst."

"I'm not asking him. I'm asking you. Which bottles make you money and which ones don't? If Barolo has the big margins, why are you still producing Barbarescos and Nebbiolos?"

"Why are you attacking me?"

"I'm not attacking you."

They've stopped walking again.

"Look, Jamie," he says, forcing calm. "I'm an engineer. I understand process and technology. I understand how to leverage the sun, moon, and earth in order to optimize that technology. This is what I'm good at."

Which is why you need to hire Sal as a consultant, she thinks. She has a life plan, and living by the earth and the moon and the sun is not part of it.

"I also understand Italians," he continues, "how they think, how they eat, which translates to how they drink."

"That's not good enough," she says. "Your gut is all well and good, but it isn't a business model."

His face goes hard as he turns and walks off.

"There's a saying in America," she calls after him. "Go big or go home." Then she stands there, catching up with the woman who just said that, the same woman who just tried to ramrod American changes into a Korean culture, the same woman who almost compromised herself as a woman because she'd been blinded by that "big" payoff, the same woman who knows what she needs to do now, which is to go to Villa Ruffoli and get a look into their finances, meet with the bankers, get the process moving. *Are three more hectares enough?*

Let it go, she begs herself. Don't be that woman. Don't push him. Let things unfold. Besides, she is terrified of what getting involved with the vineyard might mean, getting entangled in ways that are difficult to untangle.

Her feet are moving now as if they are somebody else's feet, running to catch up with him.

"I'm sorry," she says, grabbing his arm on a busy corner and making him stop. "I don't know what's wrong with me."

They stand there, staring at each other.

"It takes time, Jamie."

"I'm thirty-four. Soon I'll be forty. I don't have much more time."

"I know what I'm doing, Jamie."

This incessant need to make a difference, to prove her worth, where does it come from? Is it because of her Dad, because she couldn't be the daughter he wanted? She adored him when she was a child. He had been a caregiver, a listener for her woes, as she was to him about the hurried, modern world that continually baffled him. He couldn't keep up and eventually became bitter, especially when his younger child, his last hope, ultimately chose a most-traveled path. Jamie had followed in the super-efficient superstar Jill's footsteps—and looking at it now, on this street corner in the present moment, staring at this man who makes her stomach flutter and her heart ache—where has her path led her, exactly?

"I'll take care of it," Giovanni says.

"I know you will. I believe in you." A taxi whooshes by. The earth shifts slightly. Dust and stray trash resettle around them. "I just want to help, that's all."

CHAPTER 19

U.S. vs. Brazil

MARCH BRINGS SPRING RAINS and a visit from Simona. She has finished her Paris internship and has no plans for what comes next. She is in love, after all, with Gabir, an Algerian she met in Paris.

"Only Simona," was Jack's comment upon seeing the two lovebirds—one golden, one black, equally handsome, a striking couple. Simona is full of life, laughter, and style. Her hair is cut short, curls all over the place. Gabir is six-foot-five-inches tall, his body languid, graceful. He is elegant in both dress and speech, but more importantly he works for FIFA, the International Football Federation, and Jack is beside himself with this good fortune. Gabir is in town because FIFA is hosting a friendly game between the U.S. and Brazil. The idea is to start getting U.S. fans excited about next year's World Cup. "Only in the U.S. does one need to get fans excited about a World Cup," Jack says to her, admonishingly, as if it were Jamie's fault.

The flight from Irvine was late getting in. Jamie is harried and exhausted but excited, if not slightly nervous, to see the passionate, free thinking cousin of Jack's that she met over two years ago at Villa Ruffoli. The four of them are eating at Delhi Palace. "It's our favorite restaurant," Jamie tells them over her menu. Giovanni, however, feigns indifference, which irritates her. It's too high end, he'd warned her earlier that week when she was making the reservation. "So we'll treat," she'd said. "We'll split the tab," he'd said. "They can't afford to split the tab," she'd said. "Let's go somewhere else," he'd said, and she'd thought, *why are we fighting about this?*

Anyway, here they are having a great time at Delhi Palace, just as she'd anticipated. Their speech is a chaotic mix of French, Italian, and English. Then there's The World Cup, its own language, and Giovanni has much to discuss with Gabir about strategy surrounding the groupings and coaches and players, not to mention how he can get tickets to the games in Germany next year. Gabir will root for France if Algeria does not qualify. France and Italy are bitter rivals, of course, but you wouldn't know it the way the two of them are getting along now.

It's as if, stranded here in this football-ignorant country, Gabir and Jack have become of one nation, the football nation. They are instantly brothers, but even Gabir is no match for Giovanni in World Cup trivia. Giovanni can recite every goal going back to 1930, and seems to be doing so now, which is when Jamie and Simona step outside because Simona is in dire need of a cigarette. She has not told her parents about Gabir, she admits to Jamie. If her mother knew Gabir was Algerian... she makes a praying hand gesture. *Mamma mia.* She giggles and laughs.

"Are you guys serious?"

"Gabir is moving to Berlin to prepare for *Il Mondiale*. He asks me to go with him."

"Really."

"But I do not know for sure…" she takes a drag. "There is nothing for me to do in Berlin."

"What about your art?"

"I must find a job that pays me money."

"I suppose."

"And my sculptures are no good. Everyone says this."

"And you believe them?"

"I should not?"

Jamie must take a serious pause here, for her instinct is to cheer Simona on. *You are talented. Keep at it. Go after your dream!* The equivalent of Kool Aid, the stuff we Americans pass around like a drug: anything's possible; if you work hard enough you can achieve what you want. Basically, it means telling people what they want to hear. Should Simona listen to these people who are telling her her art is no good? Is there something to say for simply *giving up?*

"Ah, but Jamie, I am so sad. I have just arrived and you are leaving."

"Not until Sunday."

"But why must you leave on Sunday? You must stay and help me figure out what I will do." She stamps out her cigarette. Giovanni is at the window waving at them to come back in.

Small plates of *sooley, poori, kabab,* and *dahl* have filled their table, plus the bottle of Jordan Cabernet that Jamie had ordered. Delhi Palace is the only restaurant she and Jack frequent that serves no Italian wine. The bottle is seventy bucks, but Jamie thinks of it as her little indulgence—wine from her side of the world. Simona makes a toast to Jack and Jamie's engagement, their façade having traveled north, apparently. Simona had heard about it from Zia Claudia, who was told by La Mamma, who got the news from Zia Renata before Jack had the chance to tell his mother himself. "Should be a fun phone call," Jamie chides Jack, sipping her wine.

She frowns. The wine tastes thicker and sweeter than she remembers.

"Fourteen-and-a-half percent," Jack reminds her, reading from the label "You know it's a California wine when the alcohol content is fourteen-and-a-half percent."

"What is it for Italian wines?" Simona asks.

"Thirteen-and-a-half, maybe fourteen," Jack answers, glaring playfully at Jamie.

"It's not my fault," she says back.

When they finish the bottle Jamie orders another, but it tastes even sweeter this time, which confuses her. Could her palate be changing? She is staring into her glass contemplating this idea and doesn't see the check arrive until it is in Gabir's hand. Jack, who's hand was one moment too late, offers to take the check, but Gabir insists. *Don't take no for an answer!* Jamie's eyes scream, but that's exactly what Jack does, and Jamie is beside herself with mortification.

"How could you not insist on at least splitting the check?" she demands to know later. They are in bed, whisper shouting, because Gabir and Simona are sleeping on the other side of the wall and this loft has little soundproofing.

"Did you want me to arm wrestle him for it?"

"The wine I ordered was so expensive. That check had to be at least three hundred dollars."

He opens his magazine. "I told you we shouldn't have gone there."

She flips over, infuriated by the look in his eyes, in all their eyes. She is a frivolous American money waster. They could have simply gone to Curry Hill for cheap, greasy Indian; or they could have cooked a simple meal of pasta at home. Jamie, who'd been looking forward to this night and enamored all through dinner, feels jealous now—a strange, new, terrifying emotion. It isn't even a human being she's jealous about. It's more elusive than that.

After tossing and turning for some time trying to sleep, she rolls onto her side and watches him read, which he does calmly, contently, no thought of tomorrow, next year, no thought of the past, of dinner. No regrets. "I think I'm going to stay the week in New York," she says.

He lowers his magazine. "I thought you were sleeping."

She averts her gaze. "What I need to accomplish this week I can do by phone and e-mail." She is speaking to herself more than to him. Chris is traveling, no doubt. She can use his office. Anybody worth anything at the firm is traveling. "It would be fun to spend more time with Simona," she says.

"You could use a break," he says.

She rolls onto her back and sighs at the ceiling.

"Close your eyes," he says softly, and she does.

He rubs her head until she falls asleep.

As it turns out, Chris is in town. Jamie runs into him in the Midtown office on his way to catch a meeting downtown; he practically bowls her over in the hall. "You," he says, that gleam in his eye, like *you and I have been through Asia together and we can speak with grunts now*. "Lunch tomorrow," he says. She really hadn't expected that.

She waits for Chris at his table at Cipriani. Of all places, it's the one restaurant Giovanni has vowed never to enter in his lifetime. To enter is to be raped, according to Sal. There are no prices on the menu. The space is stuffy, formal, packed with suits and models; but this is not what's making Jamie nervous. She doesn't know why she is so nervous. Korea was six months ago, the lawsuits have been settled and paid. There is no need to be nervous, she assures herself while watching the waiter set a diet coke in Chris's place just in time for his arrival.

"ANR just paid the last invoice," he says, heaving his hefty frame into a chair. He sends back the coke for more ice, orders appetizers with the wave of a hand, and then gives her a hard, alarming stare. "That little fucker." There is no need to name names. Jamie knows who the little fucker is, the little fucker who has double crossed them in the end by refusing to sign off on their invoices, and it's important she not cave.

Chris relaxes his gaze. "We got him in the end."

"Where is he now?"

"He's been transferred to Taiwan."

"He'll be miserable in Taiwan."

"He deserves to be miserable in Taiwan."

There is a pause here for her to admit what Chris seems to suspect, but she admits nothing. She will take what happened with Charles to her grave.

No worries, because Chris has already moved on, seemingly, scouring his blackberry for that revised proposal someone was supposed to send him. His phone rings when the appetizers come. "Where the fuck is it?" he says into the phone. "…It better be." He clicks off and looks at her. "Do you want to go to Hong Kong?"

"Sure," she says without blinking.

He sits back, examines her.

She sits back, examines him. "If I didn't have the Corps."

"Fuck the Corps. The Corps is a dead end client. I don't know why Donald's got you out there."

"We just won two more projects at $250k each."

"I'm talking about five million over three years, Jamie. Asia is where it's at."

There it is again. "I've always wanted to go to Hong Kong," she says, thinking of Korea, of how quickly she'd said yes to that too, how blindly one's will adjusts, adapts, pulses forward.

"Do you want me to talk to Donald?"

She freezes, mentally screams *No!* Only she cannot say it; it won't come out.

Chris goes on cryptically about Hong Kong while scanning his Blackberry, and Jamie leaves lunch with an ache in her stomach. She'd forgotten to eat, or been afraid to, for fear that it might come back up. At the loft she runs into Simona, just back from a *passeggiata* around the East Village. Gabir has taken Giovanni to a practice session at the stadium, and they won't be back until dinner. "Let's go to the Guggenheim," Jamie says. "A Broadway musical, anything!" She is desperate for big, American-style entertainment, anything to distract her from the fact that she might have just sent herself to Hong Kong.

Simona smiles excitedly at all these suggestions, and yet somehow they end up footing it toward no known destination. They pause briefly at Madison Square Park to snap a photo of a squirrel (apparently they don't have squirrels in Italy), before continuing up Fifth Avenue. As they approach the Empire State Building Jamie looks up and asks, "Do you want to go to the top?" Jamie's never been to the top, she's always wanted to go to the top, and certainly it will be exciting, to be at the top—but Simona has no desire to go up. She'd much rather step inside a souvenir shop right there on the main level. She buys a purse that says I Love NY, a tiny replica of the Statue of Liberty, a Flatiron key chain, a fake Swatch, and still no dent has been made in the list of things she must buy for her family back home.

Farther up Fifth, the tourist population now massing around them, they hit H&M. Simona spends a good hour in the store, then again in Brooks Brothers, and of course they don't miss MACY's on their way back. Jamie's feet are killing her and yet Simona is barely fatigued. She remains enamored, full of energy and life. MACY's is packed but Simona is unruffled. Jamie, on the other hand, is confused, exhausted, and deflated. *Shopping? Is this really going to be it?*

Jamie suggests a taxi home, but Simona seems embarrassed to even consider such an extravagance. Plus, they have passed by a McDonalds and her eyes are lit up. Jamie thinks that certainly the girl must be kidding, but the girl is not kidding. After Delhi Palace, Jamie is afraid to suggest an alternative because any alternative will be more expensive than McDonald's. Jamie hasn't been into a McDonald's since she can remember, but she buys a Big Mac anyway and wonders if hamburgers, Levis, Timberland, MACY's, and Brooks Brothers are the only things Italians value about the U.S.

They are seated at a formica table; Simona is slicing her burger in half with a plastic knife. "I think I must go back to Italy and get a job," she says, "but it is so difficult to find a job in Italy, especially for women." They'd been discussing her going off with Gabir to Berlin. Simona isn't sure what to do. Meanwhile, Jamie has noticed two other groups of Italians sitting nearby. The place is packed with tourists.

"Surely things are changing," Jamie says. It's hard to imagine in this day and age that there are no jobs for women in Italy.

"Did you know that women make up a smaller portion of the workforce in Italy than any other country in the European Union?"

Jamie flashes her a skeptical look; Simona must have her numbers wrong. That can't be possible.

"Besides Malta, that is."

Is it possible? Jamie thinks for a moment. "How about getting an MFA? A Masters of Fine Arts," Jamie explains, after seeing Simona's depleted expression. "There are so many things you could do with a higher education, like teaching art or running a gallery."

Simona nods intently, drawn into Jamie's passion. "Yes, I would like to do this."

"Good!" Jamie sits back, feeling charged and useful.

"But there is no such program in Italy."

"Come to the States."

"Ah, but of course, *sarebbe bello*. Mah, alas, I am afraid I would miss Mamma and Papá and my cousin Caterina, who is like a little sister to me."

"But you live in Paris…"

"My parents will be very sad if I do not come back, Jamie. This is my problem."

Jamie's mind is still stuck on the word miss. It's not resonating. At least not in the way Simona is using the word, as in missing family enough to pass up on a chance at personal advancement or growth. Is Simona saying she needs them? That she can't live without them? Jamie is truly stumped. Sure, she misses her family sometimes, but *needing?* She stopped needing her father a long time ago, and her mother raised Jamie to never need her for anything. Their lives are disparate. Isn't that how they're supposed to be? Jamie gets stuck pondering this until an image comes to mind. Far back in time, at her first and highly coveted slumber party, Jamie had had to wake her friend's dad in the middle of the night to take her home, for no other reason than that she was homesick.

Simona is saying something, but Jamie is preoccupied with the image of herself on that walk of shame with that father to her home, which was just across the street. Where does that ache for home go? What happens to it in America? How is it that people from Italy never lose it? Her legs are throbbing so hard that she can't hear, but she forces herself to tune back in. Simona is asking where she and Giovanni will be married, America or Italy?

"We are already married."

There is a pause.

"Jack needed his green card," and then, regretting it, "don't tell anyone."

Simona's eyes widen, but for only a moment. Then she smiles, mischievously. *"Mamma mia..."* She makes the praying hand gesture. "Only in America can you live in this way!"

"I suppose."

"I think it would be hard to live in this way. I do not have the courage you do."

Jamie wonders if courage means the same thing in both languages. Courage is not what's driving her. As usual, when she considers her identity and strength, her thoughts go straight to her work. If she really had courage, she would stand up for her fellow career women and rat out Charles.

"It's the intellectual challenge of my job, the feeling of being fulfilled that keeps me going." She contemplates this a moment. "In America we must be fulfilled!" There is pure mockery in her tone. Recently at the Corps, her job has lacked any intellectual challenge. Certainly in Hong Kong there will be intellectual challenge. She must not stop searching for it. Mustn't she?

A pang of guilt hits Jamie then, for starting this fulfillment business with Simona. A woman in Italy could hardly change jobs simply because she was not "fulfilled." Jamie takes a bite out of her Big Mac, and it occurs to her that along the road to all this fulfillment and achievement, she's managed to become a food snob. This fact stays with her as she chews the lifeless, dry meat, staring with irony at the woman across from her. *I'm a food snob because of you Italians, and yet you're the one sitting here making me eat poison.* Jamie sets her burger down, unable to finish. When Simona is done they pick up their trays and dump their contents in the garbage.

On Friday Jack makes pasta for dinner. Afterward, he and Gabir discuss Zidane's departure from Juventus for Real Madrid a few years back, something Giovanni is still thankful for apparently, and Simona writes postcards home. No music is playing, no TV. Jamie is cleaning the dishes, signing each postcard Simona hands her, ready to crawl out of her skin because it's Friday night and she's craving an adrenaline rush, a stiff drink, or perhaps just a heavier wine than Nebbiolo. That Jordan cabernet comes tantalizingly to mind. She is feeling anti-establishment, and apparently her taste for wine is a prisoner of her emotion.

Chris has not called. She has not called Chris. Hong Kong was apparently just a game he was playing with her, and she with him. Still, in the back of her mind, thoughts of places where no one knows her remain. Oblivion is what she needs right now, but everyone else seems happy to be nestled here at home, in close proximity of each other, with good food, good conversation, and no need for entertainment of any kind—no movie or Broadway show, not the night club that Jamie has suggested five times, no need for the excess so essential to an American, or at least this American.

For Simona, it's enough to be in the captivated presence of the cousin she was so close to when growing up. Gabir is French, after all, and while he and Simona are clearly in love, Jamie can sense the cavern between them as if she is staring in a mirror. Each time Jack and Simona reminisce about their childhood summers at Villa Ruffoli, which is often if not constant, it's the two of them and no one else. Even presently, they are bursting out in laughter about La Mamma's *arrosto farcito,* the recipe that has been passed down through generations of Ruffoli women, the meat that is always dry and tasteless. Their eyes are watering they are laughing so hard. Apparently, they now announce to Jamie and Gabir as if their lives, too, are at stake, the *arrosto* tradition ends with them.

"I know of a nice bar," Jamie suggests, joining Simona at the window for a cigarette. A bar is the only tradition Jamie knows, passed down to her from Jill, her Partners, peers, and in desperate cases, her mother. After a serious day at work, you meet at the nearest bar for a serious drink.

"Ah, *si,* we take a coffee, yes?"

"Sure," Jamie says, after some delay.

The men join them for their *passeggiata* to Washington Square Park. It's no piazza, but the Washington Arch is respectable by any standards and at least New York is a walking city, because these people like to walk. Giovanni and Gabir remain engrossed in their discussion, lagging behind.

"...and so I ask myself, what would my friend Jamie do?" Simona is clearly continuing a chat that Jamie is supposed to be a part of. She smiles as if she's been listening.

"I'm going to Berlin," Simona announces, wide-eyed and staring at Jamie like she is the Statue of Liberty.

Jamie's eyes go wide back.

"In America you are so free. I want to be free too. I must travel and see the world before I go home to Italy for good."

Jamie almost feels guilty.

At this point Jack grabs her hand to keep her from crossing the street she hadn't known she'd been crossing. There was a break in the traffic and she'd just gone, like she always did, even though the light was red. She yanks her hand from his and runs across anyway, then stands waving at them from the other side. This is her, being free—because she is free, isn't she?

The next day, Jack tells her the great news! He has finagled extra tickets to the Brazil-Italy friendly game. "You have to go, Jamie," he insists upon seeing her unenthusiastic response. He's got that possessed look on his face, and she knows that he is, in part, trying to get her out of the funk she's been in for the past few days. "You have not lived until you see Brazilian fans dancing in the stands."

So instead of being on a plane to Hong Kong, or even back to her non-intellectually challenging client in Irvine, she is on a bus heading to Giants Stadium with a bunch of hooligans, wondering if she hasn't accidentally entered some alternate universe, because she is, in fact, curious about this game they are going to see.

Giovanni also invited Sal and his son, and forced them all to take the early bus. (Simona opted out of the game to spend her last day shopping.) The first to arrive in their section of the stadium, Jamie's immediate instinct is to go get beer and popcorn, but every time she mentions this to Jack he nods his head at the field, "Just wait." His eyes are glued on the players warming up while Jamie's are on the spectators filling the stands. They are mostly foreigners with only pockets of Americans, plus the Brazilian section Jack had been all excited about; with yellow and green painted flesh swaying to the beat of samba drums.

Unfortunately, she "just waited" too long. Now the game has started and she's at the beer stand; the ONLY soul at the beer stand, the only one in the entire concessions area, for that matter. She might be the only one out of her seat, it occurs to her. She makes her way back under the annoying glare from some of the patrons.

She offers Jack some beer as she sits down, but at this point she might as well not exist.

He curses in Italian at some shirtless Americans standing in his way.

Jamie sets the beer down and gets focused on the action.

Five minutes go by. "We're not so bad," she says.

Ten minutes.

"We're really holding our own," she tells him.

He nods, not taking his eyes off the field.

Another five minutes go by. She's actually really impressed with the American players, and is about to tell him so when he leans in and says low, "You know, the U.S. can't win," as if he's letting her in on a little secret.

She frowns at him, then narrows her eyes back on the field, a fire lit within. "Don't take us for granted. We never give up, you know."

She isn't sure how many minutes pass before the U.S. scores the first goal, only that she is up and cheering before anyone else. Giovanni is up and cheering too.

"See, I told you!"

The rest of the half plays on, scoreless. Giovanni rocks back and forth in his seat. Sal wrings his hands while his son sits next to him waving an Italian flag in one hand and a U.S. flag in the other. When the half closes, Jamie goes to the bathroom. If the place was a ghost town before, it's packed now, and yet when the whistle blows, everyone is at once back in their seat, including Jamie this time. Her beer, still full, is long forgotten. This sport is not about beer.

Twenty minutes into the second half and still no spectacular Brazil goal. Hope seeps into her veins.

Another ten minutes and she is imagining the victory. Certainly, it was only a matter of time before the U.S. would dominate this sport like they have every other sport—this is the thought that runs through her head. The anticipation is unbearable as the last minutes play out. The U.S. is going to beat the best team ever. Yes, this is going to happen...

"Goooooooaaaaaaallllll!" The scream almost knocks Jamie out of her seat. It is Giovanni, on his feet before Jamie even knows what has happened, which is that Brazil just scored in the last two minutes of the game. Everyone who isn't American, which is almost the entire stadium, is up on feet and chairs. It is this that stuns her, even destroys her a little—not the fact that Brazil then scores another quick goal to win the game, not that the U.S. loses, but that everyone wants the U.S. to lose, that Giovanni and Sal are reaching five rows over to slap hands with a group of Italians. When at last he sits back down, she stares at him in disbelief. "You were rooting for them all along?"

He looks at her, then back at the field.

"I'd understand if the U.S. was playing Italy."

He remains expressionless.

"How could you not root for the U.S.?" She won't let up. "You live here. They've given you a green card..."

"Jamie," he says abruptly, in the din of beating drums and jiggling bodies. He looks directly at her. "It's Brazil." His tone indicates that there is no point in him saying anything more than that. She will never understand football. She will never understand him. Petty and childish, yes, but this is a moment of serious reckoning.

CHAPTER 20

Pasta Asciutta

*I*T IS FRIDAY, DUSK. She just watched the sun burn through the ocean while driving along PCH to her mom's house, where she plans to spend the weekend. She explained to Giovanni that she needed to work and couldn't make it back to New York. In reality, after her time with Simona, she's feeling moody and distant. The Corps is a stable client, a sure thing in terms of revenue, but she keeps hearing Chris's words, "dead-end," and then her own voice pontificating to Simona about the intellectual challenge of her job. What does that actually mean? Traffic is slow, and along this stretch of beach it grows particularly monotonous. Who are these surfers? What do they do for a living? Are they intellectually challenged? Are they fulfilled?

Her mother is fulfilled, with her business, her charitable work, her boards, so fulfilled that they've met for drinks only

231

once in the four months since Jamie's been on assignment in Irvine. Although her mother had left a variety of messages for Jamie, admittedly; it was Jamie who couldn't figure out her schedule, what with all the flying back and forth to New York. But alas, she needed to get something off her chest. After that dinner at Delhi Palace with Simona, Jack told Jamie in no uncertain terms that he was telling his mother the truth about their green card marriage. He seemed surprised when she put up no fight, and then told him that she wanted to do the same with hers.

At a bar near LAX over gin and tonics, her mother was pragmatic, if not impressed by the boldness of Jamie's decision. She took a languorous sip of her drink, while Jamie, with an airplane roaring over her head, asked her mother if she didn't think her daughter had gone nuts. "Nonsense," said her mother. "You girls know what you want. I've always said that. I never have to worry about you girls."

And it was true. She never had to worry about her daughters. She was a hands-off, trusting mother who left her children alone with their decisions. It's what Jamie has always loved about her. No doting, no fawning, no second guessing. Sink or swim, swim or sink, either way the sun always rose, and when it did she'd be up and dressed and off to work. What started out as a typing service run out of their home to help put their father through grad school, grew into a full blown temp agency now worth somewhere in the millions. She's not rich by any means and lives mostly off her income, which is generous. She's never been a saver, always a spender, and so, like many Americans, she spends a lot on interest fees; but she gets to do what she wants, her decisions are hers alone to make. Jamie and Jill managed themselves through meals, puberty, heartbreaks, and hangovers, while her mother focused on instilling in her daughters the things that mattered. Education, and self-sustainability. A savings account and part-time job at her temp agency were Jamie's thirteenth birthday presents. Her mother would match half of what Jamie put away each month toward a car. It was a used Toyota, but her mother paid the insurance and had it polished and wrapped in a big bow. She wanted Jamie to have her freedom and space as much as Jamie did.

As Jamie enters her mother's home now, space is the first thing that comes to her mind. Clean lines, hushed tones, walled windows—nothing extravagant, nothing nostalgic but for a gorgeous expanse of ocean to stare at. Jamie's plans are to spend the weekend lounging on the sundrenched patio doing just that, pretending not to miss Giovanni terribly and forcing herself to get some perspective, distance, space. She drops her bag in the guest bedroom, for the first time wondering why she wasn't, in fact, simply staying at her mother's while on assignment here, as say, a normal daughter might, like Simona for instance. In fact, when Simona had asked after Jamie's mother, mentioning how nice it must be to spend all this time with her, Jamie was too embarrassed to tell her otherwise. It simply didn't occur to Jamie to stay an hour's drive away from her client, especially when she can stay in a paid-for fancy hotel just steps away from work, with all the amenities she might need right there at her fingertips.

She heads to the kitchen to unload the groceries she bought on the way over. She hears a car pulling into the garage, a trunk opening and closing, heels clicking on the tiles—the familiar sounds of her mother returning home from work. "What's all this?" The back kitchen door closes behind her.

"I was going to make some pasta," Jamie says, dumping the last contents of the bag.

Her mother frowns. "But that's so much trouble, dear. I made reservations at Micks."

"It's no trouble." On the counter are large cans of imported San Marzano tomatoes that Jamie had to hunt through two stores to find, a box of Barilla penne pasta, the kind with the ridges Jack insists are critical to hold the sauce, a chunk of Parmigiano Reggiano cheese, extra-virgin olive oil, whole garlic, fresh basil.

Her mom is staring at what only minutes ago was a pristine, empty countertop. "I'm not sure I have a pan for all that."

Jamie is on her knees, rummaging through a low cupboard. She pulls out the soup pot her mom uses to heat Campbell's. There's no free cutting board, just that piece of wood jammed into a slot above the silverware drawer. She starts by attacking the garlic bulb. In fact, this is the first time Jamie has peeled a piece of garlic on her own, so she is taken aback when it sits before her, peeled, unsure how she did it, though her mother has gone and changed and come back in the amount of time it took Jamie to do so.

"What's this your sister tells me about a divorce?"

Jamie stops what she's doing because slicing a garlic bulb requires complete and undivided attention, and her attention is now on the fact that it is unlike her mother to inquire so directly about her life. That's Jill's job. "Did Jill put you up to this?"

"She's worried about you."

"I simply told her what she wanted to hear."

"She wanted to hear that you're getting a divorce?"

"Doesn't everyone? Don't we all want everyone else's relationship to end so ours won't have to?"

Her mother is staring at her. "Is something wrong, Jamie?"

"Probably."

"So you're not getting a divorce?"

"How does one ever know the answer to that question, Mom?" The garlic sizzles and spurts, and Jamie drops her shoulders. "Sorry, Mom. What I mean is, well, sometimes it's just easier for me to imagine Jack already gone."

"Where is he going?"

"Because this way I won't be blindsided."

"Oh. You mean, like I was?"

"I guess, maybe. No. Not necessarily."

"Then what is it, Jamie?"

NON BRUCIARE L'AGLIO, don't burn the garlic, the phrase pops startlingly into Jamie's head and she glances behind her at the burner, which she turns down quickly!

"Are you pregnant?"

"You're not helping me focus here, Mom."

"So you're not pregnant?"

"No, Mom."

"Well that's a relief," her mother says, falling into a stool at the counter.

"What's that supposed to mean?"

"Oh nothing." Her mother pauses in thought. When she speaks again, her voice has changed. "It's just that I always thought you'd do something different."

Jamie pours the tomatoes into the sizzling garlic, adds the basil. "Like what?" she wants to know. "Exactly."

"Oh, I don't know." Her mom's tone is unusually dreamy. Perhaps it's the garlic wafting through the air. "Like the theater. Remember how your father used to direct you in those plays?"

"That was high school, Mom."

The sauce comes to a boil. A tomato bursts and splatters on Jamie's blouse. She stares at it, stunned.

"That does smell good," her mother says, as if seeing with a knew eye the scene unfolding before her—mother and daughter, in the kitchen, cooking together. Well sort of. "Tell me all about Italy," she says suddenly. "About his family."

"It's not all it's cracked up to be."

"I'm sure it's wonderful."

"So says you and everyone else."

"How do you pronounce his name again? In Italian?"

"Giovanni," Jamie says, sconce the Italian flamboyance. It sounds so silly when she says it the way they say it, the way her mother is trying to say it now. "If Giovanni were listening to you he'd be having a coronary, Mom," Jamie says, back on her knees now digging out an old crockpot, which will have to do for boiling the pasta.

Chuckling at her attempts at Italian, then at the crockpot, her mom resigns and gets the gin. "You like yours up, right?"

It's not vodka, but her mother knows how her daughter likes her drink.

The sauce is simmering as the pasta water works its way to a boil. Jamie's got some gin in her now. "The Italy I see isn't the one you see in guidebooks, Mom."

"But isn't that what makes it so special?"

"I'm sure I should feel lucky; his family is very warm and kind, but they can also be intensely quiet and brooding and..." Her voice tapers off into blankness. She takes another sip of her drink. "I'm supposed to meet Jack in Rome in two weeks, but I just can't imagine it."

"Why?"

"I don't know, exactly. Each time I go it feels as if something is being taken away from me."

"Jack?"

Jamie wonders. Is it Jack? Herself? Them? She doesn't know. "I think there's some kind of metamorphosis going on inside me, and it hurts."

"It's called learning to be married, dear," her mother says after a delay. "I fought it every step of the way without even knowing it."

"Fought for it, or against it?"

Her mother's expression darkens. So does her tone. "I know you don't believe this, Jamie, but I did want it badly with your father. The problem is I wanted it too badly. I wanted it perfect. The perfect husband, the perfect marriage, the perfect family. I couldn't compromise. And in the end, I couldn't live with what would ultimately be *imperfect*. So I ran to my career. I put my career first…in all my relationships." She pauses. "Which is why I am here in this big, beautiful house, alone."

Jamie goes still; the world goes still. She never thought of her mother as alone. She's so busy, has so many friends and people who care about her, financially safe and secure, dependent upon nobody. "But you're not alone, Mom," Jamie manages. "I mean alone, alone."

Her mother doesn't seem so sure. Neither does Jamie, and they fall silent now, each in their own thoughts.

"I wished I had had the courage to give it all up for a man," her mother says finally. Jamie, who'd been getting down plates, almost drops them. It's a statement that goes against everything her mother has ever taught her. "You don't mean that, Mom."

"Passion and love—that's what a woman needs." Her gaze is pointed.

"Why are you looking at me like that, Mom?"

"Like what?"

"I haven't given it all up for a man, Mom."

Her lips curve upward ever so slightly. "I didn't say you did."

NON SCUOCERE LA PASTA! "Oh shit," Jamie gasps, and runs over to check the pasta. Just in time, barely in time; well, it might be a touch overcooked—how the hell is she supposed to know? Her mother's got her all flustered. She drains the water. Her mother is up and standing behind her, both of them getting steam facials. She dumps the pasta into a big bowl that her mother had to hunt down. She seems entirely delighted, suddenly, by all this activity going on in her kitchen. Jamie mixes the sauce in with the pasta, and then her mother, in the spirit of things, goes and gets the green can of Kraft Parmesan cheese from the fridge.

"MA NO! CHE SCHIFO!" Oh no, gross!

Her mother freezes.

Jamie bites her lip. Did she really just say that? "Sorry, Mom. That was Giovanni talking." Apparently, he's a living, breathing force inside her now, whether she wants him there or not. The knowledge brings tears to her eyes, and laughter, for her mother is still standing there holding the can, staring at her daughter with the most alarmed of expressions.

Jamie, dabbing her eyes with the back of her hand, takes the can from her mother and returns it back to the fridge.

Her mom makes them another round of drinks. Jamie serves their plates, then takes the hunk of parmigiano she'd bought and grates it directly on the pasta. Her mother takes a long, contemplative bite, and then her face opens up like she's going to die, it's so good. "I think I need to get to know this Giovanni person."

"Me too," Jamie says dully. She takes her own bite, the flavors dig and tug. "Sometimes I feel like *I* barely know him. In Italy he literally turns into another person with another name." Her heart starts beating faster, along with her thoughts, as if her mother had opened up a floodgate. "You know, this may sound stupid, but our countries are our blood. I'm beginning to really understand this. He and I, we don't have the same blood. We may as well have been raised on different planets.

"For example," Jamie goes on, barely able to pause. But then she remembers something and jumps up. Fresh basil, that last touch she'd forgotten. "He took me to a soccer game in New York two weeks ago. U.S. was playing Brazil." Her hands tremble as she rips off a few leaves and throws them on each of their portions, which confuses her mother to no end, like what are you doing throwing weeds onto my food? "So here I am rooting for my country, thinking that I've never been more in sync with this person next to me, never more connected, especially when the U.S. scored that impossible goal and the two of us shot up from our seats and cheered at the top of our lungs as if our internal fires were lit by the same flame." She sits back down, slumping. "And then I find out that he was rooting for Brazil all along."

Her mother is gazing at her plate, "You've got to tell me how you made this, dear."

Jamie jumps up again. L'OLIO! Olive oil! "It may need some drizzled on top. You can do that. He does it all the time." She sits back down with the bottle and continues. "It wasn't like we were playing against Italy. I would understand if he wanted Italy to beat the U.S. I'm fine with that, but it wasn't Italy. It was Brazil! In fact, it was almost as if he wasn't rooting for Brazil so much as rooting against the U.S." She pauses to take another bite. "I married the man to help him get a green card and he roots against America in a game against Brazil?! Do you see what I mean?" Her mouth is full. "He's a closet U.S. hater. That's what he is. He hates the U.S.!" She contemplates this anew while continuing to eat. "This is pretty good," it occurs to her. "Well, not as good as his, but not bad at all, for me." She looks up at her mother here, startled to find her staring back at her with an expression of complete and utter bemusement. "What? What's so funny?"

Her mother can't seem to let the moment go, as if she were recalculating something, plugging in new assumptions to some equation with no solution.

"Mom."

"Jamie dear, have you been listening to yourself?"

Jamie glances behind her, looking for the person to whom her mother might be speaking. Alas, there is no one else, only Jamie. She slumps in her seat and sighs, because she knows what her mother is going to say next.

"I mean, who wouldn't want to go to Rome?"

CHAPTER 21

Viva gli Sposi!

*S*ILVESTRO MEETS THEM at the airport in Rome, looking the same as he did when they'd waved him off at SFO two years ago: big, hopeful eyes, mischievous grin, strong hands and nose. Now he's dressed in a uniform, in the final three months of the one year compulsory military service required of all Italians. Jack had managed to skirt this law by living in the U.S. for the past decade (a law now eradicated).

"Ancora tre mesi," Silvestro drones now, counting the days until his freedom. He is maneuvering them through the terminal, tossing Jamie forlorn, apologetic looks every so often because, "My English may be...how do you say?"

"Rusty?"

"Ah yes, rusty. But perhaps no. Perhaps..." He slices his neck with an index finger.

"I see."

"You understand?"

"It will be okay."

"Okay," and they have once again reached their universal language.

They fold into Silvestro's parents' Lancia Thema because his Ford Ka is impossibly small. He drives like a maniac, darting in and out of speeding traffic that comes to a standstill once they enter the city center. It is rush hour. There are no lanes, and traffic lights seem to be optional, not to mention the free for all of Vespas. The sidewalk is simply a passing lane.

Roman ruins infiltrate their surroundings, almost randomly. A crumbling column is a lamppost; the remains of a triumphal arch a turn lane. Giovanni keeps his foot pressed against the passenger side floorboard. They cram their way through a dizzying amount of back streets and roundabouts until finally Silvestro pulls up short, double parks, and they get out in the middle of the street. This is where the true Romans live, he announces. Yes, he is just going to leave the car there for now.

It's a relatively quiet street along the Tiber River, opposite the ancient, historic center. They duck through a wood door cut out of a larger wood door, pass through a courtyard with a trickling fountain, enter a lobby veiled in early morning haze where the attendant is asleep at a desk. The elevator is an iron cage and fits only Jamie with Giovanni and their luggage. They watch Silvestro wind up the stairs around them as they rattle in ascent. They hear water leaking somewhere. The stop at the top is jolting. Silvestro slides open the elevator gate for them, out of breath.

He calls out *O-oh* to his parents as he unlatches the front door, sets down their luggage, and waits. *O-oh, O-oh,* they call back in succession, an Italian version of "yoo hoo." There is a minute of shuffling before Giovanni's godparents come careening around a corner and into the entranceway wearing house slippers, wool sweaters, and warm smiles. In fact, they are beaming with warmth, aglow of it, not to mention the curiosity sparkling in their eyes after kisses and hugs are exchanged and everyone is left standing there staring at each other.

How does one start when one can't communicate?

One starts as Jack's Godfather—doughy, scruffy and bashful—does, by apologizing profusely to Jamie (through Jack) for not speaking her language. Jamie assures him, through Jack, that it is she who should speak Italian. In fact, she goes so far as to promise, "Next time!" even though it has never occurred to her to learn Italian—at least not until this very moment.

"*Allora.*" (Well then.) Silvestro picks up their bags and as one little family unit they all move into the first bedroom off the entrance. Jack and Jamie will be sleeping in the same silky, hunter green décor, apparently. No separate bedrooms? She eyes Jack. His lips are turned down at the ends, which means he's smiling with the irony she has failed to get until this moment, the reason for all their sparkling gazes. Jamie and Jack are "newlyweds." Jack smiles and translates what Godmother has just said.

"*Viva gli sposi!*" Hurray for the newlyweds!

Jamie swallows and takes a breath, waiting for panic to flood her veins as she realizes that the fiction she's created, more and more, is turning into some kind of reality. Once Jack had told his mother, he'd wanted to tell everybody. Two years or not, he was done with the façade, he had told her.

Now, standing here on the precipice of this bedroom blessed by God and laden with his artifacts, Jamie is waiting for something to happen, for perhaps fear to strike her dead. Oddly, nothing strikes her dead. In fact, she is swept up by something else. A breeze from the room's tall windows that have been cast open. She rushes over and sticks her head out into the rising sun. *Newlyweds?* Ah, so be it, she thinks, for the first time feeling like one.

Silvestro and Jack squeeze in on either side of her, taking turns pointing out The Vatican and St. Peter's sprawled on her right, the dome of the Pantheon bubbling out of the ancient center, the Tiber snaking all around them. It's hard to find a response. Amazing, is what she comes up with, and Silvestro, who has been watching her intently, agrees, and they laugh. Of course it's amazing.

She pulls her head back inside, accidentally bumping into Godparents who are hovering there with a long plastic tube that they push into Giovanni's hands. He stares at it quietly for a minute, then extracts what's inside with trembling hands. A wedding present, he murmurs to Jamie, who unconsciously steps back because gifts make her uncomfortable. It is a rebellious reaction of her own upbringing, as gifts from her side of the world are always ceremonious and built up to great expectation—dinner, a speech, perhaps a slide presentation, certainly a cake, would all preamble any gift that sat wrapped and bowed on the living room coffee table. At Christmas they'd always opened presents one by one, each item spotlighted, the boxes big and many. It was their mother's ritual, one Jill and Jamie turned into a competition about who could give the biggest, and largest number of, gifts. Until their father left, and the ritual died, at least for Jamie, because it said everything about them that he hated.

It's the opposite here. In Italy there is no grandiosity. Gifts, little and singular, are exchanged in one chaotic barrage upon entry through the front door, before one has even sat down and caught their breath. Jack seems to have lost his breath now, holding open the tube's contents—a set of large blueprints that are stained, faded and worn at the edges. No less than awed, he exchanges a deep look of gratitude with Godfather, and soon their little family unit is on the move again, into the dining room this time, to spread the prints out on the gilded marble dining table.

These are not picture prints like the ones Jack has back in New York, but architectural drawings, designs, the original specifications for Villa Ruffoli, Jack tells her. Bisnonno gave them to Nonno Giacomo who, just before he died, passed them on to Zio Lorenzo as an offer of reconciliation because the two had not spoken in twenty years. Zio Lorenzo, Nonno Giacomo's only son, had refused to go into the family steel business. His passion was history and design, and on a mission to pursue his dream, he went to Rome and became an architect. The designs belong to Giovanni now, who remains speechless as Godfather points out items of interest on the pages. Jack nods and traces along with his fingers until he comes across something that confuses him. Their talk turns low and subdued and then finally dissolves into silence as Jack re-rolls the drawings ever so carefully and reinserts them into the tube. He and Godfather will go through the designs in detail later, when they have more time.

Now it is time to take a coffee, yes?

They continue down a long hall with different doors leading into the parlor, library, and living area. The ceilings are vaulted and frescoed. The ceramic floors are painted with intricate patterns. Each room has an expansive view of Rome and is adorned with antiques, paintings, and sculptures from the nineteenth century. There is a veil of dust in the air and over the ornate furniture and heavy tapestries. The only exception is the kitchen, which is a tiny hole somewhere in back. They are all crowded there now, watching Godmother heat the tiny espresso maker on the ancient stove that she must ignite with a pilot light. She will make two batches of coffee to get everyone served.

"We must not sleep," Jack says, already strategizing their jetlag. "We must try to stay up as long as possible." The four of them speak in Italian while Jamie contemplates the word sleep. This is not a dream, she assures herself, catching the flicker of gold on Jack's left hand as he downs his coffee. He's wearing his wedding band and she's not hyperventilating. No one has asked where her ring is, but then, Jamie notices, not even Godmother wears a wedding ring. Her hands are plain except for a tiny sliver of gold on her wrist to tell time. In fact, most of the women Jamie has encountered here wear only simple gold weddings bands, if anything. Except La Mamma… and thinking of jewels, a vision of Jack's mother flashes in Jamie's mind, engulfed in tears at the thought of Jack's wedding ring unsanctioned by God. Jack never actually described her reaction to the news. "She'll get over it," was all he'd said.

"Where is La Mamma?" it occurs to Jamie to ask. Her brain is half asleep. Her eyes have drifted closed. She is sleep-standing. A walk would be good, someone says. "Jamie?" another person says, and she opens her eyes. Yes, she agrees, fresh air would be good.

A stroll over Ponte Cavour, a hazardous street crossing at Via Ripetta, and they are in Piazza Navona. It is easily the size of a football field, lined with cafes around the perimeter, windows above overflowing with flower boxes, three massive fountains along the center. Godfather and Giovanni walk with linked arms as if it were the most natural of things. Godfather is pointing out intricacies of the architecture around them, Borromini and Bernini, the Fontana dei Quattro Fiumi, the overwrought façade on Sant'Agnese. It is June, and for whatever reason, perhaps the early hour, not crowded. Jamie is wandering sleepily along, but when they get to the Pantheon a hunger pain sends an alarm off inside her: she is in Italy, it is ten a.m. and lunch is not until one. She won't survive. Her eyes reflexively search out Jack, still huddled with Godfather just outside the wondrous structure as if they are about to enter for the first time, even though Jack has told her that he and Godfather have taken this *passeggiata* many times.

Inside, the two men's voices are hushed as they wander around together, absorbed in their engineering worlds, an unspoken bond. Jamie is staring up at that unfathomable hole in the center of the dome, the one that keeps this whole thing standing, apparently. Sunlight is pouring through it. She's dying to go and stand in the spot where it shines, but for some reason it's roped off. Anyway, she can't move now, sequestered as she suddenly is by Godmother on one side and Silvestro on the other, the three of them standing there staring up at it together. The hole of hunger in Jamie's stomach is gone, satiated by the quiet warmth of these people who never cease crossing the barrier of her private space.

It is Silvestro who finally breaks the silence. "I am afraid that we must…" he inserts a hand gesture here in place of the English he cannot find, like he's scooping at the air with his palm, "or Papá and Giovanni will never leave this place." He and his mother share a knowing smile. Then together they tell Jamie, via Silvestro's rusty translations, about the day of Silvestro's birth. La Mamma was with Godmother in the labor room, but Godfather was so nervous that he brought Giovanni, six-years-old at the time, here, to the Pantheon, then to the Vatican, then the Basilica. It was a long labor, apparently, and Giovanni has shared Godfather's passion for history and design ever since.

They float out of the Pantheon, past cafes and pushcarts just opening for business, under an archway, around a narrow bend, off the beaten path. Their procession lazes on, stopping every so often for Jack to translate Godfather's insight into a particular ruin or building, like this fountain they all stand before now, a gold lion's head low to the ground, stained and unkempt. Godmother's great-grandfather designed it to pipe all the way down into the system of Roman aqueducts.

Impressive, Jamie is thinking.

"*Che brutta*," Godfather says.

"It's ugly," Jack translates, and she laughs, unexpectedly.

After lunch, Jamie and Jack, unable to keep their eyes open any longer, retire to their room and get busy pushing the two beds together so that they can take a nap. "I thought your mother always came to Rome when you did," Jamie finally has the opportunity to ask.

"She's helping Antonia with the baby."

"It's me, right? She didn't come because of me."

"Ha!"

"What do you mean, Ha!?"

He's shaking his head.

"Why are you shaking your head?"

"Don't kid yourself, Jamie. No woman—American or otherwise—is going to deter an Italian mother from being with her son if that is what she wants."

"Then why isn't she here?"

"I told her not to come."

"Why?"

"Because I'll see her at the villa next week when I go to meet Sal..." he hesitates. "And because it's just easier."

She should be thrilled.

"I thought you'd be thrilled."

She goes to the window, looks out for a time. "I like your Godparents," she says, turning back.

"I knew you would."

"There's something about them..." she pauses. She hadn't expected to feel so much a part of things. "They're very warm."

"They're good people."

"I would have thought La Mamma would have turned them against me."

"It's not a conspiracy, Jamie."

She feels like an eight year old.

"And anyway I don't know what you're talking about. My mother likes you."

She looks at him like he's crazy.

"You're just not what she expected."

"What about that girl in the picture? Is she what your mother expected?"

"What girl in what picture?" She proceeds to remind him about the digital printout she'd found in Nonno Carlo's room, back in Vico Equense. When she'd mentioned it to him the first time, he'd brushed it off. "You never told me. Was she Italian?"

"No."

"American?"

His silence means yes.

"And you brought her here?"

He hesitates, and then casually says that he took her to Vico Equense, once.

"Oh."

"Does it matter?"

It shouldn't matter.

"It was a long time ago, Jamie. I met her in college. We broke up after two years."

Two years? She and Jack have just passed their two years. "No, it doesn't matter," she lies, mortified by her own naïve thoughts, for thinking that she was the first girl he'd ever brought home.

He's stripped down to his boxers and crawled into bed.

She remains by the window, fondling the velvet curtains.

"Jamie, come to bed."

She runs her finger along the gold veins in the antique desk right there; she eyes the crystal chandelier. "You would never know," she says finally. "The way they dress, their demeanor…"

"Never know what?" he yawns, stretches an arm behind his head.

"This place is a palace."

He looks around, as if he'd never really thought about it.

"Except for that kitchen anyway."

"In Italy kitchens aren't for show, they're for cooking."

"It's almost as if they're ashamed of their wealth."

"Catholics are supposed to suffer in piousness and guilt," he says, noticing the Prada sandals she is now slipping off her feet. "And if we're not suffering, certainly we're guilty about it."

"Tiberio's Italian." She's thinking of his chef's kitchen back in New York.

"Not really. Not anymore."

Then what are you? But she has no chance to ask, because he's already drifted off to sleep, or pretended to anyway.

CHAPTER 22

Forza Napoli!

𝒜FTER DINNER, Jamie, Jack, and Silvestro go to meet Tiberio and his friends at a wine bar in Piazza Sant'Eustachio. "So Italians do go out drinking," Jamie says, surprised by the crowd. It's rare to see an Italian standing up holding a glass of wine, especially one with a stem on it. "Of course Italians go out drinking," Jack responds. "They just won't get trashed."

The bar is crowded and it takes Silvestro's Roman dialect to get the bartender's attention long enough to bring them the wine list. The concept of a wine bar in Italy is new and rather American, Silvestro and Jack admit. "You can thank Thompson for this."

"Or Starbucks," she says. "We did the same with coffee. Is there a Starbucks in Rome?"

They flash her disgusted looks.

"Calm down, I was just asking. It's not like I want to go or anything." Another lie, how she wouldn't love a voluminous amount of scalding coffee served in a paper cup with a lid on it instead of the tiny thimbleful she can expect to get every morning.

The list is mostly Piedmont, Tuscan, and Roman wines. Jack orders two different Barberas and a Nebbiolo and they take their glasses to a table out on the piazza. The Barolo selection is awful, Jack disparages, and way overpriced. Silvestro leans forward in his seat, "Ah yes, but this is my brilliant idea." If only his hands could speak for him. "We make the selection better. We sell our wine in these places."

Jack sits back. "My cousin is brilliant."

"This is what I know."

They must converse in Italian now, they inform her apologetically. She pretends she is not relieved and sits back, thankful for the freedom to take in her surroundings. She's not sure she could find this place, even with a map. Locals mostly, quiet, peaceful, water splashing in a fountain somewhere. The sky is a purplish gray. She assumes they are discussing Sal's visit to Villa Ruffoli next week and the responsibilities Silvestro will assume at the vineyard when he is free from the *sti cazzi* (what a pain) military, a stint that began when Silvestro quit university last year. It was not long after returning from San Francisco that he went to his parents and announced that he didn't want to be an architect.

Jamie was speechless when she'd first heard the news. "So no degree at all?"

"There's no point in starting over."

"But that's four years, just wasted."

"It's Italy, Jamie," one shrug of Jack's shoulders, an *e'cosi'*, and this is the way it is.

"What did his parents say?"

"They are resigned," he'd told her, and that, "Godfather only wants his son to be happy, to find something about which he can be passionate. He did this himself, after all."

Jamie's thoughts are interrupted by a sudden shift in Jack's tone as he and Silvestro discuss the best route for Jack to take in the morning on his drive to Firenze. It's a drive Jack is infuriated about, she is painfully aware. Tiberio had graciously ordered ten cases of Ruffoli Barolo for his wedding reception being held tomorrow night at the prestigious Villa Miani. Jack was furious to discover upon his arrival that the cases had still not arrived from Villa Ruffoli. Apparently, Luca's truck had broken down and the transport service he uses does not work on weekends, so now Jack must leave at six a.m. tomorrow to meet Luca in Firenze, halfway to Alba, to transfer the wine. The Ford Ka is faster but won't fit the cases, so Jack will have to take the Thema… better to leave at five then.

"I'll go with you," Jamie says.

"You'll stay here," he says.

"*Non ti preoccupare Giovanni,*" Silvestro says. Don't worry, Giovanni.

Jack says, "It's only the premier caterer in Italy. No big deal."

Apparently Villa Miani's wine list is usually closed, and Tiberio had to pull some serious strings to get Ruffoli wine on it.

Jack pounds on the table, startling them both. "We've got to get our shit together." There is a pause while the vibration settles. "Luca's going to have to accept serious changes, and my cousin here," Jack waves pinched fingers at Silvestro, "is going to have to step up to the plate."

Silvestro looks at Jamie. "Plate?"

"You're going to have to get serious."

"I am only serious," he says, shakily lighting his cigarette.

Jack pulls the cigarette out of Silvestro's mouth. "You've gotta stop chasing girls and dicking around."

Silvestro looks at Jamie. "*Che e'* 'dicking around'?"

It's at this moment that Tiberio shows up with his friends. Two hours late, they come by twos and threes on Vespas; dark, mostly thin, wild-haired people clutching cell phones and not wearing helmets. They descend on the square as if they own the place, and then sit shoulder to shoulder around a far off table.

Jamie, Jack, and Silvestro are about to head over and join them when Jack's cell phone rings. He looks at the number and picks up, "*Forza Napoli!*" It's how he answers calls from the south, which sends Jamie on alert. He rarely gets calls from the south. They only call when something is wrong. He marches off to the far end of the piazza, the phone crammed to his ear, while Jamie and Silvestro sit back down where they are. "*Fanno i fighetti,*" Silvestro says, nodding disparagingly over to Tiberio and his friends. He can say this about them because his mother is a friend of Tiberio's mother, and Silvestro has been to their house many times for dinner and has met many of Tiberio's friends. "How do you say...I cannot translate *pariolini?*"

Jamie looks over at their table, littered with cigarette packs, ashtrays, and cell phones. "In the U.S. we call them Eurotrash."

"Ah yes, this word I know." He waves his hands together in prayer. "*Ma dai* must I go to this Eurotrash wedding? This wedding will be very boring, and my parents will be at this wedding. I cannot be Silvestro with my parents. *Hai capito?*"

"*Ho capito.*"

He smiles. They understand each other.

Jack is back. He falls into the chair as if the wind has been knocked out of him.

"Was that your father?"

He looks past her, stone faced, and throws his phone on the table.

Jamie and Silvestro share a quick glance, but whatever it is will have to wait, as Jack abruptly stands to greet Tiberio, who is on his way over.

At last, Jamie thinks upon sight of Jack's best friend, an overweight Italian, but then he's been living in the States for over a decade, she reminds herself. He's got the tan, though, and the pinstriped dress shirt hanging out over designer jeans, leather loafers, no socks. Still Italian.

Vespas are charging up. "My friends already want to leave," Tiberio tells them, greeting Jamie with kisses that feel airy. "They don't like these wine bars."

Silvestro looks around. "*Boh.*"

Tiberio says, "They're like Starbucks, eh?"

"That's what I said," Jamie says to Giovanni. "See. I'm not stupid."

She's trying to be funny, but he's not laughing.

"I'm going to meet them in Piazza Navona. You guys should come," Tiberio says, though his offer lacks enthusiasm. He seems antsy, distracted, and Jamie expects him to leave right then, but then he falls into a seat next to Jack, orders a Campari, and doesn't seem to want to go anywhere. Perhaps his lack of enthusiasm is directed at himself and not them. He sips and sighs and looks around as if he doesn't belong here either, not the wine bar, but Rome, Italy. He is marrying a Swede, lives in London, works for an American company. He is also an only child, like Silvestro and Giovanni. His duty is to his mother; otherwise, he'd probably not come back to Italy that often. This is disclosed by the intimate conversation he and Jack have naturally fallen into, as if they'd just seen each other yesterday when in fact it's been over a year. The way it is with good friends.

"Once you've lived outside Italy," Tiberio continues, "and for this long, it's almost impossible to come back. You want so much to come back, but you simply can't live in a cluster fuck anymore."

Jamie glances at Silvestro, who is glancing at Jack, who is staring into his glass.

"Don't get me wrong," Tiberio continues, both pragmatic and resigned. "I love Italy. And I admire what you are doing, Jack, being your own boss. But I can't do what you do. I'll never be my own boss because once you trade bonds that's all you can do, trade bonds, or run departments that trade bonds. If I lose my job, I'll have to find another firm where I can trade bonds. I'll always have to work for a firm."

Silvestro exhales smoke. "I say why make money for somebody else when you can make it for yourself?"

"Trust me," Tiberio says. "I make money for myself, and that's part of the problem. You get chained to the lifestyle, and the only thing left to do is make more money."

They fall silent, especially Jamie, for Tiberio has just put into words what Jamie could never.

"What about you, Silvestro?" Tiberio pivots toward him and says. "Would you ever leave Italy?"

Silvestro sits back, and after a long sigh says that his dream is to live in San Francisco.

"You should," Jamie says urgently, a reflex. One she immediately regrets when Silvestro says, "This is not so simple."

"Of course," she says apologetically, wondering when it's going to get through her thick scull that American mottos like "Go" and "Do" don't resonate here. She glances at Giovanni because normally he's the first to remind her of this, but his gaze is fixed far off down the piazza. It's not clear that he's even listening to their conversation.

"Giovanni?"

"Silvestro is right," he says, turning back, though something about him remains absent. "It's not easy to leave Italy. I would not have gone to the States if Nonno Giacomo had not insisted."

"My father was a visiting professor at MIT," Tiberio adds. "There was no question I would go to MIT."

"But you see, Tiberio and I are rare exceptions," Jack explains.

"Don't Italian kids want to go away to college?"

"It is hard to leave Italy," Silvestro says.

"Simona has left Italy," Jamie says.

Silvestro sits forward abruptly here. "*Ma che cosa ha fatto Simona?*" he says to Jack, then again, louder, "*Ma che cazzo ha fatto?*"

Jack responds in Italian, and they digress into a debate about Simona and Gabir. Silvestro seems against the relationship, though Jamie is afraid to ask why. She's afraid she'll learn why. "*Scusami,*" Silvestro apologizes, after Jack insists they drop the subject.

"We were talking about you going to San Francisco," Jamie reminds them.

"*Mah,*" Silvestro resigns. "For me…I could never live that far from my parents."

Jamie's conversation with Simona, who had essentially said the same thing, comes reeling back. These are words Jamie would never hear from the mouth of a twenty-six-year old American male (even if he thought it he'd never admit it), but there is no shame in Silvestro's eyes.

"It is true," he assures Jamie, acknowledging the astonishment on her face. "My parents do not know about the real Silvestro. That I smoke, for instance. That I go out with girls or what I do with my friends. It is true that I am very different from my parents who are very conservative; but we are very close. Especially my father, I think, would be very sad if I left."

They go quiet for a moment. Then Tiberio hooks his arm around Silvestro's neck and starts going on about how much of a *mammone* (mama's boy) he is. This digresses into a Roman dialect-fueled discussion about football, Roma, Formula One, Ferrari. Even Jack can't understand much of what they are saying, their dialect his excuse, though Jamie is sure the reason is that phone call.

At some point it's one a.m., time to go home—or so she thinks when Tiberio and Silvestro simultaneously jump up out of their chairs and motion for Jack and Jamie to follow. At last, the two Romans have agreed on something, but it's not about going home. What they've agreed upon is the best bakery in Rome. It will open in one hour and they must be there at exactly that time to get the first pastries out of the oven. You've never tasted anything like this in your life, they assure Jamie, all of them hurrying to Silvestro's car, as if she were going to say no. This, the night before Tiberio's wedding, is his parting bachelor wish; no shots or strippers or dancing, he wants *cornetti* fresh out of the oven.

Silvestro races them there in the Ka, leaving in the dust all the reasons one CANNOT live in Italy for the sake of this one reason one should and MUST live in Italy, this warm pastry folding over Tiberio's hand presently as he tries to get the *cornetto* into his mouth. They are standing outside the bakery in the dark empty street, sucking them down.

"I love Italy," Tiberio moans.

"Why would you live anywhere else?" Silvestro agrees.

Jamie is asking herself the same question. This *cornetto* is like a drug.

A minute later, wiping her face with a napkin, she finally notices Jack. He's seated on the bumper, rubbing his head in his hands.

CHAPTER 23

A Man is Human

"IT'S LIKE I'M moving backward, and everyone else is moving forward," he says at about four a.m. as they lie together, sleepless.

It takes a minute for what he has said to reach her. Her first day in Rome had been so unexpectedly perfect. She wants to linger in the sweetness of that *cornetto* a while longer, in the soft blue light of the moon on their bare bodies. She wants to bask in their love making, and the heat of this tender night.

Only now this dark cloud, this feeling of dread. "It's going to take time," she says finally. "You said that."

"I'm running out of time. You said that."

She searches her memory.

"Tiberio is right," he says. "Having worked in America now, I expect things done a certain way, a different way."

"Weren't you the guy who just told me, yesterday I think it was, how much progress the vineyard is making? The farmers are interested in your tank design, the new bottle manufacturer, signing on three more restaurants, not to mention Villa Miani, not to mention Sal's visit next week... You've got so many great things going right now."

"Maybe what I'm trying to do is impossible. Do you know what it's taken just to get a new electrical line run?"

She can't understand this sudden change of certainty, the darkness and doubt coming from him where before there was determination and enthusiasm. Her heart begins to pound—what uncertainty does to her. "I don't understand the sudden switch."

"It's impossible."

She lets out a sigh that seems to go on forever. "Then why are you doing it?"

He stares at the ceiling, in some kind of agony, she can tell. Then he looks at her and says, "I don't think I've ever not been miserable."

This is quite a statement. She can't fathom a response.

"Professionally I mean."

It's as if the wind has been knocked out of her.

There is a whiff of mist in his eyes, a look of loss that frightens her, and she can't help thinking of what Simona had said about Jack being the "Chosen One." Why was Jack chosen? What was Jack chosen for? In America we are not chosen. We choose ourselves. Our burdens are self imposed, not part of some bigger obligation. We, the individual, are the bigger obligation, we are the biggest.

So what do you do when a man lays bare for you his demons and fears, his weaknesses and insecurities?

"Jack, please, what the hell was that call about?"

He looks past her.

"Your father never calls you, Jack. Why did he call now?"

He seems locked up, and it occurs to her that she might never be able to get in. It's the first time she's seen him like this. He's always been a decisive guy, certain to the point of adamant. It's that confidence that had drawn her to him in the first place. Even taking this big risk, leaving engineering for the vineyard, he'd been sure. She can't deny that inkling of relief she always feels to hear him say, "I'll take care of it."

"Lucrezia is dead."

There is a moment where everything skips a beat. Then she sits up on one elbow and stares down at him.

He's got his forearm covering his eyes. "A stroke."

"Lucrezia," she says, hesitating. "As in, your father's sister."

"Adopted sister."

"But you said her health was fine…"

"Please, Jamie. Please do me this favor and don't ask me any more about it now. I can't talk now. I'm exhausted, and I have to get up in a few hours. I need to sleep."

"I'm supposed to sleep?"

"Don't say anything to Godparents or Silvestro until after the wedding. La Mamma will know soon enough…"

"But how is he?"

"Who?"

"Your father, who else?"

"It was Zio Silvio who called. I have not spoken to Papá." On his side, facing her, his hands make a pillow. "I'll deal with it after the wedding." He shuts his eyes and the door, the Jack door. Subject closed.

She lay her head in close to his, and with their foreheads almost touching, their concaving frames form an odd shaped heart within which she's left to feel the beat of him, the soft pulse of his breath; neither of which reveal what's going on inside him in this moment, other than that he seems to be shouldering some burden for her, for all of them, and she thinks how unfair it must be, to be a man.

"I'll be fine," he whispers into her ear; a dream perhaps, for it is still dark outside. She'd dozed off, finally. In the dream he is dressed and ready to go, hesitant to go, studying her face and not wanting to go. She wants to tell him she loves him, that she'll drive with him to Firenze, that she never wants to be apart from him again, but the words won't come. And then, dream or not, he is gone.

CHAPTER 24

Chi Va Piano,
Va Sano e Va Lontano

*F*OUR HUNDRED GUESTS stand to watch Tiberio's bride make her entrance. Catherine, a freelance writer for a British paper, is from a wealthy Swedish family who has spared no expense for this event. The church, situated in Piazza del Popolo, is so immense and fantastical that the bride looks mostly inconsequential coming down the aisle. Even the dreaded organ music feels hollow, swallowed up by the towering, cave-like walls. Jamie, for her part, is melting. Her phone is hot in her hand, as she wills it to vibrate. At last it does, and she shows the text to Silvestro seated next to her. *Made it, going straight to Villa Miani with wine.* Jamie looks up at the ceiling and thanks whatever God or Saint is there floating in the frescoes. Silvestro wipes his beaded head.

The ceremony commences in English, and continues in Swedish and Italian. It took Tiberio forever to find a Roman Catholic priest who speaks all three languages. Jamie wonders if it was worth it, because each language sounds the same, droning and dire, like it's all just so fucking inevitable. The elder Italians sit huddled together with grieved looks on their faces. The younger Italians, Silvestro included, sit as they might every Sunday, imagining their confessions with wandering eyes. The cosmopolite contingent, those who flew in from London, Tokyo, America, Sweden and elsewhere, fidget and whisper in each other's ears.

Jamie, feeling horribly transparent in these holy settings, is sitting still as a Roman statue when all of a sudden she feels Silvestro's body lock and freeze next to her. He's latched onto something, or someone, so says the eye-popping look he is presently giving Jamie: over there, his eyes say. She looks over there. It's a girl of course, seven pews up and to the left, shimmering under a hue of golden light. Jamie lifts an eyebrow at Silvestro who returns the gesture, a moment's exchange, and then he sets his gaze on the yellow-haired girl for the remainder of the three-hour ceremony.

"Perhaps this wedding will not be so boring after all," he says, as they attempt to follow the girl out of the church after the ceremony is over. They immediately lose her in the procession, and then cannot find her outside amidst the rice throwing chaos on the church steps, nor amongst the hoards of guests peeling off in Alphas or Themas to the reception. They follow his parents back to the Ford Ka, Silvestro already lamenting about how slow his father will drive.

"*Chi va piano, va sano e va lontano,*" Godfather offers his impatient son. It takes Silvestro a minute to get it translated right: *he who goes slow remains safe and goes far.* "Ah, yes," Jamie pretends to agree, then leans over and whispers, "Don't worry, we'll find her."

Villa Miani, built by some Count in the eighteen hundreds, is set high up on the slope of Monte Mario. They park in a lot at the bottom and take a shuttle up the private drive through a vast park and gardens. They are greeted at the top with a glass of champagne (not prosecco?) and advised to stroll along the hillside path to the entrance, to watch the sun set over St. Peters on their way. She pauses upon sight of Giovanni, already there at the railing with his glass, looking out at a sky full of color. It's stunning. He's stunning, and her lips part, the sight of him there momentarily taking her breath away.

"Is the wedding in Italy very different from America?" Godmother wants to know. She has sidled up to Jamie suddenly, startling her once again with proximity, so much so that Jamie has a hard time interpreting the question even though it was asked in English. Long moments pass as she searches for words to relate how she feels about the Italian wedding, the words she's never been able to find. Until now. "It's so serious," the full realization hitting her at once. "So desperate and serious."

"But marriage is serious, no?"

Jamie, who has suddenly stopped walking, blinks at the horizon. Is marriage serious? Her focus falls on Jack, whose gaze is now upon her, the look of deep loss still there as it had been early that morning. She feels his loss all the way to her core, as she does Godmother's examining eyes, her curious gaze. It's as if Jamie's been caught, seen through, and though their bodies walk on now, Jamie's mind stays back in that moment, *But marriage is serious, no?* She is trying to grapple with the feeling that she's made some grave mistake, some serious omission, like the fact that the day would come when she would need to be there for Jack, the human not the God, that she would want to be there for him, in sickness, in health, and ultimately, yes, in grief, but not in any way know how. She didn't think she'd want to become part of his life.

Yes Godmother, forgive me my sins. Green card or not, marriage is serious. It was always serious.

Jamie turns to the woman prepared to admit this for the first time, but just as she does a friend of Godmother's interrupts them, and Jamie politely excuses herself. She makes a beeline for Jack, who searches her face as she approaches. I'm all right, she says without words. I may have been missing before but I'm here now. His hand finds hers; she wants to ask about news, if he's spoken to his father and if there is anything she can do, but alas there is a more pressing presence calling. They turn and look out at it together. The Eternal City, shimmering in a rose colored dusk.

"*Bello 'sto matrimonio!*" Beautiful wedding! Silvestro has popped his head between theirs.

Jamie steps back. "Silvestro spotted an Angel."

"*Una cerimonia stupenda…*"

The eternal moment folds back up as Jack checks his watch and instructs Silvestro to meet him in the kitchen in exactly one hour to open the bottles.

"*E' una grande serata per il vino Ruffoli.* It is a great night for Ruffoli wine. *Mah,* the best. This, I know."

"Not one minute more, or less."

Silvestro glances around for his Angel, but abruptly closes his expression with those imaginary strings upon sight of his parents coming toward them. More smiles, that infectious warmth. Godfather takes Giovanni's arm, and their heads fall together in that thoughtful bow. Their voices blend into a murmur. There is something almost spiritual about the man, an aura of gentle peace, and Jamie listens as if she understands.

She feels like she understands, as Godfather points out certain intricacies of Villa Miani's design that are similar to the original Villa Ruffoli. He turns and does the same about the various domed and steepled structures poking out here and there on the horizon. Then even he is stunned into silence, all of them quiet now, each lost inside his or her own thoughts.

Stone columns flank the entrance to the reception hall. They head toward one of the many grand parlor rooms where appetizers are being served. Silvestro is at once beside her, panting with news that he must share about the Angel. "Principessa Isabella Savelli," he announces, and then waits for her reaction, which is to grab a glass of champagne from a passing waiter.

Seriously, a princess? He assures her that this is true, that he has learned this directly from Tiberio's mother. He nods in the direction of where the Angel stands closely guarded by her parents, and explains that his efforts to get near her have so far been thwarted. Jamie looks over at the girl and finds herself squinting as if into a brilliant light. She actually looks like a princess, a fact one might think Silvestro would be deterred by.

He is not.

All during dinner he remains preoccupied with thoughts of meeting her. Long tables frame a flamboyant Bernini sculpture on an outdoor terrace overlooking the vast gardens and lake. Rome at night sets the background. New age music is playing and candles flutter from every crevice. White-gloved waiters are serving the first course. "You're going to die," Giovanni says, in some desperate quest to lavish in the fruits of this evening. This, his last supper.

"I already know that."

"It's stuffed with *foie gras*."

"What is stuffed?" (A zucchini flower.)

Giovanni switches his plate with Silvestro's, which is still untouched because he is presently making his second tour around the tables. Each time he passes behind the Principessa he slows, as if he might have the fantastic luck of her falling back in her chair just in time for him to catch her.

Zucchinis have flowers?

The second course is white truffle risotto. It is served with a Brunello wine that Giovanni lingers in thought over. When he's finished his glass he picks up Silvestro's, who has just returned. "*Ma dai* Silvestro, sit down," Giovanni says. "*Mangia.*"

"*Non ho fame,*" Silvestro cannot eat, he insists, staring forlornly at his plate.

When Villa Ruffoli's Barolo is served with the leg of lamb, Jack and Silvestro move around the tables making sure people are enjoying the wine. When they opened the bottles earlier to breathe, they discovered three bad corks and subsequently tasted each bottle to make sure there were no irregularities. Jack is back now with another bottle for their table. He pours glasses for the Spaniard, Turk, and Persian, here with their once-working wives. "Now this is a wine," he slaps his hand down and says, already looped.

With the wedding cake come doves and fireworks and a dessert wine. Then everyone moves down the hill to a grassy area where a sultry Egyptian tent has been erected for dancing and after-partying. The older guests leave, including Godparents, who seem rather confused by the extravagance. Silvestro lights his first cigarette of the night now that they are gone, at once despairing about the Principessa's departure. "I will be right back," he says after a moment, and goes to hunt for her.

Jack steps up holding a Scotch, this, their first moment alone together since meeting at the railing. "Did you speak with your father yet?"

"No."

"What about Zia Renata?"

"I told you, Jamie, I'm going to deal with it tomorrow, after the wedding."

"Will you go to Napoli for the funeral?"

"She'll be buried in Vico Equense, next to Nonno."

The Spaniard comes over to inform them that the Turk is ordering shots of Grappa. "Who drinks shots of Grappa?" she asks.

"The Turk," they say in unison.

She looks around, "Don't you and Tiberio have American friends from MIT?"

"They're here," Jack says, then proceeds to count off two.

She looks at him skeptically.

"At least I have friends," he says.

The Spaniard says, "Ouch."

The Turk comes back with shot glasses for everyone but Jamie.

"I'll get you one," Giovanni offers quickly, apologetically. She waves him off and leaves, sensing his need to be with his friends. If it's space he wants, this she can give him. She is all about space. She is an expert on space. She could use some space herself right now, taking a random path leading to yet another lookout point where yet another gorgeous view of Rome sparkles before her in the night.

The words, *marriage is serious,* form above Jamie's head in a charcoal cloud. Smoke, floating up from two women with cigarettes nearby. Jamie watches them for a moment. They are conversing in that gesticulating language; so close, so intimate. Actually, Jamie does have friends, she reminds herself, going back to Jack's comment. There's her roommate from college whom she's out of touch with; a friend from business school who works for a bank in Asia now. Then there's Jill, of course, with whom Jamie struggles to identify, for with age comes self-involvement, a burrowing down, the beginning of that great disappearing act.

When she returns to the tent, the Turk is flirting with a young woman while his pregnant wife slouches in a nearby chair, exhausted. The Persian's wife is dancing with the Spaniard and Jack is bobbing up and down in the middle of the packed dance floor. He's got that goofy smile on his face that means he's drunk. "I am making progress," someone says in her ear. It is Silvestro, and as always, she is relieved to see him.

"She is still here?"

"It is a miracle."

"Have you met her?"

"Not just yet." But soon, the twinkle in his eye says.

Jamie grabs Tiberio just then as he is passing by, and asks him for some scoop on the Principessa. "She's got a boyfriend," is his response.

"Let me guess, he's a prince."

There is a gleam in Tibero's eye as the crowd enfolds him again.

That wasn't so helpful, Jamie frowns; then tells Silvestro (who did not hear the boyfriend remark) to go over to the Principessa and introduce himself. He does so without hesitation, which upsets her because she wasn't really serious. She'd thought they would at least discuss it for a while. She has to remember that to an Italian, at least the ones she's met, what you say is what you mean. They are very literal people, and it drives her nuts. She hates the thought of Silvestro being rejected, again. Where does he get this infinite stream of faith? And then she looks up at the Godly Roman sky and thinks, *what a stupid question.*

She watches him hover outside the circle of girls surrounding the Principessa. When the circle starts dancing, Silvestro starts dancing. It is unclear from where Jamie is standing what happens after that, until Silvestro returns not ten minutes later to inform Jamie that he has just kissed her hand, and he will not wash his lips for a thousand days. "Well, there you have it," she says, to no one really, because he is off again.

Jamie makes her way onto the dance floor to join Jack, who looks like he needs joining. In his inebriated state this may be her only chance to actually dance with him, their first dance. She takes his hands in hers and tries to lead, but he in no way wants to be led, nor can he lead, so they just hold each other and sway.

They are still swaying when someone taps her shoulder. She looks but there is no one. She looks the other way and there is Silvestro, smiling widely. "Ah, she is amazing," he says, his eyes on his Angel. Then he bops across the dance floor and is gone again. The next time she sees him he is dancing with the Principessa. Jamie is not amazed by this exactly; Silvestro does not take no for an answer. After the dance is over the Principessa smiles politely and returns to her friends. Jamie is sure by the girl's expression that she's not interested.

She loses track of Silvestro after that, and must presume he's been dejected, that the Principessa has told him about the boyfriend and so he's gone home. It is four a.m. and Giovanni is arm-and-arm with Tiberio and the Spaniard on the dance floor, swaying to the beat of some rap song. They are the final few guests to leave, riding the last shuttle down with a group of drunken Brits who proceed to goad Giovanni about the fact that Ferrari would be nothing if not for a German, that it was Schumacher who brought order to the dysfunctional Italian team.

"It's unlike you not to have a comeback," she says, when the shuttle drops them in the parking lot.

"They're right," is his only response, looking around to get his bearings.

It's a beautiful night, the apartment is not far, and they decide to walk.

"Where does all this money come from anyway?" she says, glancing back at the moonlit Villa.

"Trading bonds."

"Why don't you trade bonds?"

"You want me to trade bonds?"

"I was kidding, Jack."

He stumbles on a cobblestone. She grabs his hand. There will be no conversing with him tonight.

They head toward the path that snakes along the silky black river, but after just one block they spot Silvestro across the street, on his knees before the Principessa who is standing by an open car door. They stop still in their tracks. In a moment the princess will get in that car, drive away and be gone, perhaps forever, or so say Silvestro's hands, which are together in prayer, begging her to stay. She is smiling down at him; amused, bewildered. It's a private moment, one Jamie can't take her eyes from. Even Jack, in his drunken state, is captivated. How often do you see someone fall in love so openly, so boldly? What man has the courage? What woman?

Time passes. Then Jack tugs at Jamie's hand and they hurry past, unnoticed.

They continue along the river in silence, sweating under the starry Roman sky. The lights from the bridge illuminate the water.

CHAPTER 25

Sperlonga

$\mathcal{T}$HE NEXT MORNING, Giovanni is horribly hung over. Normally the *americana* is the one with her head in the toilet and the Italian is the one with no sympathy. Anyway, this morning she is too busy for sympathy. She is trying to save Silvestro from certain death. With his parents already gone to the mountains for the weekend, the lovesick creature has decided, sometime during his sleepless night, to take the one o'clock train to Siena this day so that he can take a coffee with the Principessa this evening. Jamie is at first speechless, especially when he tells her it's a three to four hour train ride. Then he jokes about how the train schedules in Italy depend upon what kind of pasta the conductor ate that day… "Does she even know you're coming?"

"No. Not exactly."

"Do you know where she lives?"

"She has given me her telephone number. You see, it is here, on my hand that I will never wash."

"*Ma dai*," Giovanni groans, sheet white, entering the room and falling onto Silvestro's bed.

"But what if she's not there?"

Giovanni repeats her question to Silvestro in Italian and then translates back the answer, "Then he will take the train back."

There is nothing more to say. He has showered, changed, used Giovanni's cologne and now they have only to decide on what shirt he will wear—a dress shirt, certainly, no jacket, just a red sweater around his neck.

After he leaves, the apartment is filled with his absence. Jack throws up a few times in the toilet. It's rather violent.

His cell rings incessantly. He finally turns it off and lies in bed all day.

They were supposed to leave for Sperlonga tomorrow, but Jamie assumes that is canceled. All other details regarding Lucrezia's death will have to wait until Jack resurrects himself from the dead. This takes place around eight p.m., when suddenly and all at once he decides he wants a pizza. Not just any pizza, he assures her, but the best pizza in Rome.

They head out with the map Silvestro had drawn before leaving. After spending the day in a dank haze, the fresh night air feels, even in Jack's mood, perhaps because of Jack's mood, majestic. The bustling cafes and city lights are like stars all around her. A kinetic, strange giddiness takes hold of Jamie as they cross the bridge, maneuver through the intersection at Via Ripetta, and get immediately lost in a maze of cobbled streets. And while she is lost, Jack insists he knows where he's going, and how wonderful it feels to let go and follow him blindly, to trust so inherently. She could live like this, she thinks, barely aware that they have searched every side street between the Spanish Steps and the Pantheon and have yet to find The Best Pizza in Rome. Ah, but who cares.

They have circled back, once again, into Piazza Navona. "That restaurant looks nice," she offers causally, eyeing a quaint outside table that he turns away from. They are off again, this time down a narrow, winding passageway. Determination bores from his eyes. He knows where it is. The moon disappears behind clouds. After some turns they land in a vacant, darkened piazza. As Jack steps under a dim church lamp to examine the map, his cell goes off, piercing the silence and her nerves. "Just answer it, Jack!"

He marches off, telling her to hurry. It's not safe. She watches him go, determined to be patient, to not bitch or complain because she gets the idea that he is waiting for her to complain just so that he can yell at her for complaining, or so that he can just yell... but she doesn't feel like complaining. She will scour the ends of this earth for The Best Pizza in Rome. She will search with him until he finds what he is so desperately looking for.

This can't be right.

Something is not right.

They are back at the Pantheon now. A huge clap of thunder sends their gazes to the sky, at the rain suddenly coming down in sheets. She puts out her hands, stunned, immediately soaked. She thinks it might be a sign, or at least a reason to look at each other and laugh, but when she turns to him he's not there. He has ducked under an awning right next to a quaint little café that everybody is rushing into for cover. She runs over to him, puts her back up against the wall next to his. He looks left, right, then directly into the rain, as if he could make it stop.

"It'll stop," she says, and they wait a little longer.

Five minutes go by and it doesn't stop and she is getting cold. He has not looked at her, not once.

"What is wrong with you?"

He refuses to speak.

"Giovanni, come on," she says. "This has been going on for two days."

His jaw is clenched.

"Have you at least spoken to your father? I presume that's him calling? Why won't you answer?"

Still nothing.

She waits a little longer. "I'll go with you to the funeral," she says, as if it were the answer to all his problems. "I know you've got Sal coming next week. I could…"

"No!" He yells it so loud that even in the rain, people turn.

Her eyes narrow, ever so slowly. "It's not like they were blood related," she says, finally guessing what he is struggling with.

There is a delay, the kind that happens after thunder.

"They were lovers, right? Your father and Lucrezia."

He looks at her sharply. "What did Zia Renata tell you?"

"She told me nothing, Jack, but I'm not stupid." (His reaction confirmed her guess, but she can't tell him that now.) "It's okay, Jack…"

"No…it's not okay."

"Why can't you at least talk about it?"

Silence.

"You've got to talk to someone."

"No," he says, not looking at her. "I don't."

More silence.

"Look," he says. "I'm going to deal with things here. You should just go back to New York."

Perhaps it's the way he won't look at her. "Fuck off," she says.

"What did you say?"

She holds her tongue to keep from saying it again.

"Let's just go back," he says, walking off.

She watches him go, thinking, *if that man does not turn around and come back for me, this will be it.*

Precious seconds pass. He doesn't turn. He doesn't come back. So then, this is it.

Humiliation is all it takes, apparently, for the love that has stretched so deep to turn into fury. Burning fury. How could he leave her here, stranded? No matter his agony, his grief, there's this thing called human decency, respect, which is when it occurs to her that she'll be lost if she doesn't follow him. So much for respect. Now she has to trail him like a wet dog, but only close enough to make out his form in the torrential downpour. Her pride won't let her get closer. She even tries to smile, to regain the complacency she enjoyed only minutes ago, or at least some semblance of control as the rain slides down her face, back, and arms. The tears of this Eternal City beating down upon her.

Two men take up pace behind her. "*Che figa,*" one says. "*Bonazza,*" the other says. She quickens her pace. They quicken theirs. By now Jack is out of sight and she is sure she has made a wrong turn. Her heart starts racing. More uncertain turns. The men stay close behind. A Vespa whizzes by, the driver flicks her hair with his hand and she gasps, stumbles backward into the two men. Flailing now, she frees herself and marches off, still too pissed to run. The men, amused, stay where they are.

A bridge appears in the distance. Whether it's the right bridge she's unsure; they all look spectacularly the same. It may even be drowning, or perhaps it is she who is drowning, going over her alternatives, like checking into a hotel or hailing a taxi to the airport. If only she had her passport and some money, but alas, her pockets are bare, not even a purse. She's come to entrust everything to Giovanni on these trips. *What's happening to me?*

It turns out to be the right bridge, because there is Via Ripetta and its slew of Vespas and cars careening through the traffic light that might as well not be there. She doesn't hesitate. The drivers honk, curse, throw hand gestures her way as she stumbles through them. Bumpers rub against her thighs as they maneuver around her, though she doesn't feel them until she's halfway across the bridge, grasping the ledge and watching the rain pour down into the river.

She finds the door in the door, climbs through it, and takes the stairs up to the fourth floor. He has left the front door open for her. She steps inside, dripping wet but not cold; nor is she hungry or thirsty or angry. She is hollowed out. She'd not expected to want to be there for him, the deep sense of peace that feeling would bring her, and now she finds out that there is no "there" for her to be. It's what she had feared all along. That place, truly beside him, doesn't exist. She's fallen into the ultimate trap, the deepest pit from which it may be impossible to escape. She quietly takes off her shoes, pads to the bathroom and dries off. Then she goes to their room where he is lying face down on the two beds they have pushed together to make one, his head resting on his forearms. Weightless, making no sound, she lies down on her back, pulls the thin sheet over her body, crosses her arms over her chest, a dead man's pose. At sometime in the night, she falls asleep.

Silvestro returns relatively early the next morning, having spent half the night on the train from Siena. He makes them coffee in the kitchen and the three of them sit around the tiny formica table so that Silvestro can smoke out the small window and tell them about his time with the Principessa. Jamie still cannot form words. When she looks at Jack she sees only Giovanni—unmoving, hard as stone, infuriatingly unapologetic. They still have not spoken, nor mentioned anything to Silvestro about canceling Sperlonga, their Italian getaway that will remain a ridiculous idea.

So she stares out the window where Silvestro's smoke is floating and focuses on his pain, not her own. He is pacing around, unable to sit down, encouraged, confused, at a loss, his body language says.

"I am a very funny guy, yes?" he stops and asks finally. "People say I always make them laugh, that I am Silvestro, funny guy."

"Yes," Jamie says. "You're a funny guy."

"But here is the strange thing." He pauses. "She does not laugh at my jokes. There is not this…" he waves either hand back and forth to indicate a direct connection "…like with us."

"I see."

"You see?"

"Yes, I see."

"But ah, she is so bee-yoo-tee-ful. And she is so kind. And my heart is exploding!" He jolts up from his chair, paces around, sits back down. "So, then you see my dilemma."

Jamie feels Giovanni's eyes on hers, which are on Silvestro. "It takes a long time," she says, pausing. "And then you still don't know." Without looking at Jack, she asks him to translate, LITERALLY, emphasizing WORD-FOR-WORD, because who knows what the hell he's really telling people when he translates for her.

"When Giovanni and I went out alone for the first time, I had the same feeling as you do now. I wasn't sure we were connecting. With me, I either connect or I don't. It's very simple to know whom I can be with and whom I cannot."

"Yes. This is me. You and me, we are alike in this way."

"In fact, in those first few moments my gut told me that Jack and I might be fundamentally wrong for each other, other than the intense physical energy we both felt. He seemed too real, too heartfelt in the few words he did say. My irony seemed to bounce off him. Oh, I don't know how to explain it, just that there were a lot of awkward pauses. When he dropped me off he kissed me goodbye on the cheek for heavens sake. I figured I'd never hear from him again. When he called the next morning, I was shocked. There was a simple, naked honesty in his voice that took my breath away. We saw each other that night, and the next…" She stops herself, out of breath, out of mind, and unsure what Giovanni has translated, just that he is staring at her now.

She is staring at the table.

Silvestro takes her hand. "You are my friend," he says.

She lifts her head. "You will get to know her better," she lies, desperately. "This is what I'm saying." What she does not say is that you don't get to know someone better, only deeper. The incompatible things you sense about them in those first few moments remain real and alive. Do not ever forget them. They do not go away.

"Ah! This is what I think." Silvestro stands up, excited. Then he glances at his watch. "And now you must go to the beach! You must leave for Sperlonga before there is traffic."

Jamie remains seated.

Jack remains seated.

"*Siete pronti?*" Are you ready?

CHAPTER 26

Freedom

N O, FOR THE FIRST TIME, Jamie is not ready.

She is not ready to leave Italy, but she does, and early per Jack's request, laying over in New York on her way back to California because after two years Jack is expecting his Permanent Residency Application to be amongst his held mail. Jamie must find it, sign it, and leave it in a safe place.

She does find it, but she doesn't sign it. She lets it sit there all weekend, unopened. She waters Tiberio's plants, goes on long, jetlagged walks in the early dawn; it had once been so fateful a milestone, she recalls. With his permanent residency status they can divorce and Jack can keep his green card. Freedom. It was her mission to give him this all along, a dare she had with herself to let him go easily when this time came, so intent was she on proving something about marriage, what that something is she can't even define any more. All she knows now is that neither of them are free any longer, not really.

"What happens if I don't sign it?" she asks facetiously on the phone the night before her flight to LAX.

A long sigh on the other end.

Or perhaps that's the sea she hears, or the lofty breeze sifting through Nonno's room, where Jack has told her he is staying, because apparently, John Wayne has died too. A lump hits Jamie's throat when he tells her that, but she forces herself not to care, not to ask how Zia Renata is doing. After Rome, Jamie made a vow to herself not to inquire with Giovanni about his father or Lucrezia, the funeral, or any of his family for that matter. She is not going to fall back into that trap, to set herself up for that kind of humiliation again.

"I can't apply for my U.S. Citizenship if you don't sign the application, Jamie."

She'd been staring out the window onto the street, at people heading off in this or that direction, on their way to meaningful places, presumably. "You're applying for U.S. Citizenship?"

"If I spend longer than six months of the year abroad, married or not, I'll lose my green card."

"Is that what it's been? More than six months?"

"It will be this year, with everything we've got going on."

The vision of him blurs and pulls away—will it soon be gone altogether? "You left me, Jack."

There is a pause.

"What are you talking about?"

"Rome, Jack. I'm talking about Rome! YOU LEFT ME IN THE MIDDLE OF ROME." She had tried to forget it, tried to white the pain out in her mind, like he and every other man apparently can do. "I know you were hurting, Jack,

but I can't forget it. I can't just move past it like you can."
She waits breathlessly to see if he might have something to
say, even now.

"What does this have to do with signing the application?"
He is trying to be playful.

She is not feeling playful. "I thought it was over, Jack."

"What was over?"

Her eyes close. "Us."

His silence feels different this time.

"You haven't even said you're sorry."

Like gravity pulling him downward.

"See, you still can't."

Why can't he?

"You've got to give me something here, Jack. Please, or I
don't think…"

"I'm sorry," he says, barely a whisper, and it throws her.

Some time passes before he can speak again. "I miss you,"
he says.

She sighs.

"I wish you were here."

"I wanted to be there. You told me to go home."

"I know, I know. It's my fault…I made a mistake. I…" He
pauses. She waits for him to go on. But deep down she knows
that he will not be able to go on, and the silence becomes
deafening. It's as if she'd forced open a wound, and now he's
bleeding, his agony pulsing through the phone wire, and she
can't bear it. She's got to make it stop. "I'm sorry, Jack. It's not
all your fault. I know I push, that I have expectations…"

"Jamie."

"What?"

"I love you."

A long moment passes. "I love you."

There it is, the first time she's ever said it over the phone. And she'd been right. It doesn't sound the way it feels. The words aren't enough.

🐌

She signs the application just before hurrying out the door to catch her flight to L.A. It's as if everything about today has washed away everything about yesterday, and the same with yesterday, and the day before that.

Now she is gripping the plane seat rests, holding on for dear life. Turbulence never used to bother her.

Is this how change happens? She likes herself. She has no desire to change. She has not made a conscious decision to change, and yet by the time she lands in L.A. she is on the phone doing just that, changing. She makes an appointment to meet with Donald, the Managing Partner, in San Francisco the following day. She takes the first shuttle out the next morning.

Jamie does not use marriage or family as an excuse for resigning. She does not want to be a cliché. *I am a cliché.* No, I am not a cliché. Donald is stunned, disappointed, put off. Few women would turn down a partnership, junior or otherwise. She has a duty, an obligation to her gender. The firm has invested in her. She is moving to New York, she says. He insists on a transfer, or that she take time to think about this decision. She tells him she wants to "do something different." In fact, the point is very simple. There is no such thing as a balanced life or going part-time with this kind of job. Nor would she want there to be. For Jamie, work is commitment, inflexible, uncompromising. For her it's all or nothing, a trait she used to think worked to her advantage, but now she has changed; everything has changed.

"I quit my job," she says to Jack when he calls. Her voice is flat and emotionless, but inside her nerves are quivering desperately. She needs a sign from him, something to tell her that she is doing the right thing, that she will still be herself. "I want you to be happy," he says, after a painfully long pause. "You need to do what makes you happy." His voice is absolute, certain—as she had known in the deepest part of her heart that it would be. The hole in her self-worth has been plugged for now. But in reality, after they hang up, the relief grows bittersweet, for he has told her nothing, reassured her about nothing. Everything is up to her, as it always has been; the way it should be, the way she had always wanted it, or thought she did.

CHAPTER 27

Italian for Beginners

*I*T FEELS ODD to be there just waiting when Jack returns from Italy two weeks later.

She's unpacked some of her clothes, but most things are still in boxes she's afraid to open, which is a good thing, because the first thing Jack tells her upon his return is that they have to move out. Tiberio will be spending more time in New York for work, and he and Catherine will need the loft.

"Of course," she says, taking a look around the open, sparsely furnished space. This is when it hits her, and she spins around to tell him that this is what she wants, space with nothing in it. Let's start with space. "We'll buy a space and go from there," she says, following him to the kitchen. He's going through the pots and pans, figuring out which ones are his. "We should have a mortgage," she adds. "So we can write off the debt."

He continues foraging.

"We need to start building equity, Jack."

"Debt, equity, how can you say those two things together?"

She tells him about her mother forcing her father to buy a house when they were first married, and it's what saved them financially later, when things got rough.

"Things aren't going to get rough."

"How do you know?"

He stands up and starts going through the knives. "I won't let them get rough."

She examines his cool confidence. It's as if he'd never voiced those dark thoughts to her in Rome. "Nothing is certain. How are you always so certain?"

"I'm certain because it's a choice; one I will make when the time comes."

"When what time comes?"

"I'll go back to engineering before I let things get rough."

"It's not always a choice."

"Yes, Jamie, it is." He is looking at her like how dare she say he can't provide for her.

She has no intention of having him provide for her.

"Be a little sensitive, Jamie."

She thought she was being sensitive.

"Have a little faith in me."

Is this what couples talk about when they talk about the future? Is this where everything goes wrong?

For three Sundays in a row, she drags him to open houses.

"Is it the apartment you want, or the write-off?" he asks on the fourth Sunday. They have just seen a one-bedroom in the East Village with good light that he seems to like.

"The price is a little high, but I really like it," she says. "Don't you?" They are at a nearby café, at a table by the window.

He is thinking about it.

"The apartment will be gone," she says.

"You're impetuous."

"You're too analytical."

"We can't afford it."

She shows him her spreadsheet.

He stares at the numbers. She's left no dispute. "I can manage the downpayment, but since I don't currently have a H-2, you're going to need to show an income from Villa Ruffoli." She looks up at him. "You guys have tax returns, right?" She doesn't wait for a response. "I know you don't take a salary, per se, but we'll work it out on paper for the banks." She is shifted all the way forward. "Don't worry," she adds, when he doesn't respond. "Soon I'll have a job.'"

It seems like he's thinking about it.

"Well?" She fully expects him to say yes, for his mind to naturally sync with hers and vice versa.

"I think we should wait," he says, setting down the paper.

Oh, love's ruse. She sets her gaze west out the window, vowing to hold it there until California comes into view. This excel spreadsheet is the culmination of her worth up to this point, her entire self, exposed, all the way down to that last zero in her monthly income column. Here she is. *But where is he?* It's like their relationship is a circle; they keep circling around the same place. Who is he?

She has no insight into his finances. Those joint checking and savings accounts they'd opened for his green card went defunct after their interview. He'd maintained a separate business account all along and now uses it solely. He has a credit card, but refrains from using it and always pays it off immediately when he does, as if he doesn't want anyone tracking his purchases. He glances over his shoulder when he uses an ATM.

She turns and faces him directly. "I assume your resistance to invest in real estate is just another example of your inability to trust."

"Look who's talking? And actually, my reasons are much simpler. In Italy we don't buy something unless we have the money to pay for it."

"What is that supposed to mean?"

"In Italy debt is not an asset. Even my college was paid for in cash. I brought it over with me in a suitcase." There is a serious pause. "Okay," he says, "that part I was kidding about."

She is not finding this funny.

"I just think we should wait, Jamie." His voice thins, "… with all that's going on."

He's told her nothing of what's going on. "You must know, Jack, that you've told me nothing of what's going on. Nothing about Lucrezia's death, her and your father's relationship, why he left Villa Ruffoli all those years ago, his morbid ascent into bitterness and misery…"

"You told me you didn't want to know."

She sits back with dead eyes and crosses her arms over her chest.

"Okay, fine." He slams down his hand on the table. "You really want to know why I won't talk about it?"

Not sure any more.

"It's very simple, Jamie. I don't want to fucking deal with it!"

"Deal with what?"

"My father, my mother; Jesus, Jamie, all of it!" The words echo and then settle around them. Jack slumps back in his chair, one shoulder lower than the other. "I'll tell you what's going on," he says. "Papá won't eat. He won't leave the house, not even to take a coffee or get the paper. He paces about the apartment, nervous, waiting to die. He has lost weight. The doctor has put him on anti-depressants, but someone must be there to make sure he takes them, and eats properly. Zia Renata is there now, but she wants me to convince Papá to move into her apartment in Vico Equense, because Zia Renata hates Napoli. She says Napoli is full of thieves and garbage. Papá will be happier in Vico Equense, she says, also because Zio Silvio is there.

"La Mamma, on the other hand, is even more convinced, with Lucrezia now gone, that Papá will return to Villa Ruffoli, where the air is dryer and cooler and better for his health. He will get well in Alba. Zia Renata thinks it is La Mamma's duty to come south and care for her husband. Zia Renata says that La Mamma is selfish, that she has always been very selfish. She never took care of her own husband, and that is why Papá ran back to Lucrezia. Zio Marco insists that Papá married La Mamma for her money, and when there was no more money, there was no more Papá. Papá says Zio Marco is a crook and Zia Maddalena is a whore and Villa Ruffoli is too cold. He will never go back to Villa Ruffoli." With this, Jack downs his water and slams down the glass.

Jamie is biting her lip, startled, in disbelief; and yet it's all she can do to not burst out in laughter.

"Now do you see why I despise talking about it?"

For God's sake don't laugh.

He shakes his head no… as in, you better not laugh.

It's not funny, she agrees.

No, you're right it's funny, he resigns finally, releasing the laugh he himself had been holding in—months, years, a lifetime—as does she, though they are hollow laughs, with no sound.

They let the apartment go and find a rental on the lower east side, a third floor walk-up. It has one bedroom with a shoebox-sized kitchen that Jack bumps around in when he cooks. He makes two trips to Italy in the next three months. Despite all the misery surrounding Lucrezia's death, Sal's visit to Villa Ruffoli was a success. He and Luca hit it off once two bottles of Bisnonno's '68 were opened. The first tasted like vinegar and Sal laughed; the second tasted like home, and Luca cried. Sal went wild over Jack's fermentation device. They've hired lawyers to patent the design. Luca has even caved and made peace with the Crespi, finally, and they've come to an agreement on a price for the hectares.

Giovanni has just returned from a trip and is already talking about going back… September, harvest, a plethora of wine events in which they'll participate. Tastings in La Morra and Alba, a food pairing in Torino. "You're coming, aren't you?"

She stares at him blankly. "I've just moved my life to New York, Jack. Can I at least settle in?"

"You can't miss harvest."

Rome comes screaming back. Will she ever be able to forget it? "I'm not ready for Italy."

"It's the best time of year."

"But I just agreed to do some accounting for Sal's friend."

"Why?"

"What do you mean, 'why?'"

"I thought you wanted to try something different."

"Right. A theater actress, at forty."

"You're thirty-five."

"Close enough."

"You should give yourself some time."

She sighs herself onto a stool at the high table they've got positioned just outside the kitchen, and pretends to examine the delicacies before her. In anticipation of his return she'd gone to the farmers market for fresh tomatoes and basil, then twenty blocks to the fancy deli for imported prosciutto and mozzarella. It's all spread out on the table now as Jack hands her a glass of wine and tells her that she doesn't need to work, because soon, hopefully, Villa Ruffoli will be in the black.

"Of course I'll work." She sips her wine. "My savings aren't going to last forever. Sal says that he can refer me more clients. Hell, I could start a consulting company for that matter—outsourced finances for the restaurant community..."

"You mean Sal, the misogynist?"

She smiles meekly. "Okay, maybe I read him wrong."

He waits for her to say more.

"I seem to be reading everybody wrong these days." *Including myself,* she doesn't add. She'd been trying to sound passionate about the finance work, but her tone nevertheless remained flat and bland. She has no desire to build her own consulting business. It's just something to say so she doesn't sound like a lost and wandering underachiever. This accounting gig with Sal's friend is only a few hours a day and even that feels like too much. She'd be happy to spend the time sniffing around open-air markets, seeing strange movies and off-Broadway shows, or simply wandering the streets of this incredible city.

It's strange, and a bit scary, for her mind to have all this free space. When she'd been consumed by work, moving from project to project, she'd no time for reflection. Instead, she'd become an expert at detachment, at compartmentalization. When Jack was in Italy, it meant he wasn't with her, and if he wasn't with her, if they weren't talking on the phone, did he exist? It was just easier that way. There was no time for thoughts of Jill, and wondering why they'd grown distant. Or the friends she'd let fall from her life, and with such ease, it seemed. There was no time for visions of childhood, of her father, the ones consuming her now.

Jamie had been fifteen when her father came home and told her that he'd fallen in love with another woman, before he'd even told her mother. Jamie was his closest confidant, and he'd asked what she thought he should do. She was stunned by how vivid the memory still was, the sight of her father's face as he'd let her know that the life he wanted was no longer with them.

After the divorce, her father's life existed apart from hers, and not until they'd visit or speak by phone did the relationship re-exist—the nostalgia, the guilt, love, and pain. The emotion was contained. But now, all these questions: Had she forgiven him? Could she? Could she forgive herself for letting him go so easily? For only wanting him to be happy? Did she blame him more now that she was grown and could judge as an adult the burden he'd placed on her then?

More recently, when Jack's been in Italy, she sometimes thinks she can feel his soul trying to surface itself. An ache, usually at night when she's lying alone in bed, turns into an image of them together, entwined, she telling him from her depths how much she loves him. It's all so desperately dramatic. So much so that when she does see him at last face to face, she goes stoic, almost inert in order to counterbalance that desperation. Her first words will be sarcasm, words she can hide behind because he will let her. Because he will see right through those words, like today, when he returns from Italy and he asks her if she missed him and she shrugs, "Were you gone?" He will take her in his arms and hold her tightly, until the ache she'd been denying herself is gone. Until the irony is gone. Until all that's left is them. It can take hours, and in the end they'll vow never to be apart this long again, until they are, like they will be next month when Jack is in La Morra, Alba, and Torino. Why can't she just go with him? Why is it so complicated for her?

"Jamie?" he says, startling her back to the present. "The tastings? Are you coming?"

She thinks for a moment. "Where is La Morra again?"

"The next hill over from ours."

She was hoping for the next country over.

"You can't avoid my mother forever, Jamie."

She hates the fact that he can see right through her. "I was hoping we could resurrect the idea of Sperlonga—that cottage on the private alcove of that tranquil little bay…"

"I'll be busy," he stops her, his mind at once ruminating on all that needs to be done with the vineyard.

"I could work for you," she says offhandedly, then when he doesn't respond, more passionately. "Seriously, Jack. It makes the most prudent sense if you think about it."

He's wrapping his prosciutto around a grissini (bread stick) and doesn't respond.

"You know you need the help. You've been working on that loan forever. I could help you with that."

"You have no idea. You'd go nuts."

"We'd work well together," she says, ironically, apologetically, for not ten minutes earlier they'd argued because they weren't working well together. Jack had been unpacking his suitcase when she decided to get a head start on dinner. When he came into the kitchen and saw what she was doing, he rushed to the sink, washed his hands, and quickly took the knife from her. "You'll hurt yourself," he'd said, staring with horror at the beautiful tomato she'd just mangled.

"I thought it would be fun to try and cook together." She pulled Lucrezia's cookbook from the shelf and started sifting through it. "This is what couples do, you know."

"Not in Italy," he'd said, reaching for the book. "We're not in Italy, Jack," she'd responded, holding onto it. They tugged at the same time, which caused the ancient spine to crack and a few crusted pages to flutter their way to the floor. She gasped and dropped down on her knees to gather them, apologizing profusely, but he'd ordered her out! "Get out!" In a tone that only she could possibly find endearing. She'd backed up against the doorway while he put the pages back. In her hand was a picture that had fallen to the floor, and when she handed it to Jack he went still, gazing at it. A grown Giovanni standing next to his dad, only they appeared to be the same height. Giovanni has on a big, glowing smile, while Giorgio's eyes speak nothing but mischief. They seem to be sharing some internal joke. "I was crouching down," Jack said, clearing a knot in his throat. "So we'd be the same height for the picture.

"It's very cute."

"My dad was always self conscious that I was so much taller than him."

She watched him gaze wistfully at the photo a moment longer, disarmed, yet again, by the intensity of his nostalgia, how quickly it could rise to the surface and how quickly he could bury it, as he did then, when he slipped the photo back inside the pages and went to hide the book away.

While he was gone, Jamie stood there remembering a time when she'd been just as happy to stand in the kitchen doorway, when she'd had no desire to enter his domain; but she's been starting to see this kitchen as a tiny porthole to all the kitchens of his homeland. Each time she gets sucked into its vortex, something goes wrong.

Up until she'd quit her job three months ago, their relationship had consisted of mostly weekends—three years of them. She used to think that was part of their relationship's enamor: absence makes the heart grow fonder, etc. Now Jamie's beginning to realize that absence is simply what it is, absence.

Now they are together day in and day out for chunks of time, and it seems natural to want to help, to be present in his life, in their life. Even now, after his outburst, she still can't stop herself from trying. He could use her help with the vineyard's finances, she's certain of this. "You've got to get some visibility into those numbers, Jack."

"Zio Marco's been doing things his way for a long time."

"All I'm saying is that I'm a good resource, and I've got to invest myself somewhere. I may not be a specialist in the kitchen, but number crunching is my specialty. Let me be useful. I want to be a part of this."

I want to be a part of you.

He pours more wine. "What's that saying in America? About the eggs?"

"Don't put all your eggs in one basket," she responds, and then narrows her eyes at him. "So, what, you're the basket in this scenario?"

"I'm just saying…"

"And I'm the egg?"

He's got that silly grin on his face.

"Are you saying we should diversify?"

"I'm saying I want to take care of you."

"I don't need protecting, Jack." Though deep down she wonders if she does, for she'd gone from not wanting to need him at all to wanting to tie herself to him in more ways than one. He's protecting her from herself, to be sure, and yet…

"If you don't want my help in the kitchen, or at the Villa, then what am I supposed to give you?"

He reaches over, caresses her face, and looks into her eyes. "You're already giving it to me."

❧

The next day while Jack is out, Jamie hunts down Lucrezia's cookbook. After her funeral, Zia Renata retrieved the book from Napoli at Jack's request. It's the only possession of hers he has, and Jamie knows how much it means to him. Not even Giorgio knows Jack has it. Anyway, something about those recipes had gnawed at Jamie all night, making her toss and turn. By morning she'd barely slept. She'd found the book rather easily in his sacred underwear drawer, this time opening it slowly so as not to wear the spine further or leave any smudges or fingerprints, because she is sure he would detect them. The handwriting is craggily and scribbled; in the margins there are doodles and little Fellini-like drawings. She stares at each recipe for long moments before turning the page to the next, letting each one sink in, finally seeing what had been bothering her because suddenly it's so obvious.

She can't read them.

Of course she knows this, consciously: Giovanni and his family speak a different language. It's been recognized and considered in her consciousness countless times, but never has it been a hard, cold truth like the one hitting her now. Three years after knowing her husband as intimately as she could possibly know anyone, they still speak a different language! *How is she supposed to understand him if she doesn't understand his native tongue?*

That evening she stops at a bookstore on her way back from her part-time work for Sal's friend, and buys Italian language tapes with an accompanying workbook.

"Don't laugh," she says, showing him the tapes that night when he gets home.

"I'm not laughing."

"I thought you could teach me."

He comes over and kisses her hard on the mouth. "*Dimmi qualcosa?*"

She blushes. She has no idea what he is saying.

Say something in Italian, is what he was saying.

"*Cosa ha mangiare?*" she manages.

"*Cosa HAI mangiato!*" He wastes no time correcting her.

Another night, along with her lesson book she has a bowl of beans marinated in olive oil, leeks, hot pepper, and garlic on the table. He gives the bowl a good stare from a few feet back, as if avoiding contamination. Then he moves forward, slowly, to taste it. "*Buono,*" he says.

She eyes him suspiciously.

"*Molto buono.*" He tastes more, looking entirely pleased, and it occurs to her that he really is pleased. Maybe relationships just take time. "Yours is better," she assures him.

"*Parlami in italiano!*" Speak to me in Italian!

They'd agreed on twenty minutes of Italian each day. He was making her stick to it the way they'd made Silvestro stick to English when he'd come to visit them in San Francisco, what seemed like a lifetime ago.

She tries to think of what to say. Nothing comes.

You have to think in Italian.

She tells him that it might help if he asks her a question, to which he responds, "*Fammi una domanda,*" which in English means, ask me a question.

"No, I meant ask me a question."

"Oh." He thinks of one. "*Cos' hai imparato oggi?*" What did you learn today?

Minutes go by before she answers back, "*Ho imparato che l' italiano non e' facile.*" Today I learned that Italian is not easy.

He repeats the phrase, accentuating the rolled "r," then asks her, "*Cos' hai mangiato per pranzo?*" What did you eat for lunch?

"*Insalata*," she manages to answer after a good minute.

"Open your mouth," he says. "Italians pronounce every letter. "*I-n-s-a-l-a-t-a*."

"*Scusi.*"

"*Scusami*," he corrects her.

"I feel like a three year old."

"You sound like one."

"You're not really helping."

"I'm helping."

"Forget it."

"Come on."

As the week progresses, twenty minutes turn into ten, five, then zero. He insists on correcting her pronunciation too vehemently for her tastes.

"Forget about the pronunciation," she keeps telling him. "Am I saying it right?"

"You've got to pronounce it correctly, otherwise you aren't saying it right, and then what's the point?"

They get nowhere.

"You're a terrible teacher."

"You're not listening."

"You're infuriating." She gets up and leaves the table. If relationships take time, and time has passed, then why are they back at the beginning? A minute later she returns. "We need to talk about something other than weather and food."

"Simona *e' incinta!*"

"English, please, can we speak in English?"

"Pregnant." It comes out flat in English. "Simona's pregnant."

"Simona's pregnant?"

"That's what I said."

"So she and Gabir…"

"…She and Michele, from Torino; they'll be married next month."

He gives her a minute to process this information.

"Michele is the son of Zio Marco's business partner. The baby will be born in the fall."

"The baby's Gabir's," she says definitively.

"It's not Gabir's."

"Of course it's Gabir's."

"Jamie, the baby is not Gabir's."

She decides not to fight him on this. The idea of Simona pregnant is still not reality.

"It's disappointing, I know," he offers. "Where will I get my World Cup tickets?"

"Did you speak to Simona?"

"She and Gabir are still friends, tickets shouldn't be a problem."

"Not about the stupid tickets," she gasps. "She's in love with Gabir. She told me."

"Look, Jamie," he says pointedly. "I like Gabir too…" A long sigh. "…but maybe it's better for everyone this way."

"Are all Italians this racist?"

"Probably."

"And are we living in the dark ages? No abortion?"

"It's none of my business."

"It's what I would do."

He doesn't seem to know how to respond to this.

"It'll be pretty obvious once it's born."

"Why are you being so vicious?"

"I don't know," she sighs, in search of an answer. She is in latent shock, perhaps, at the state of her life.

She gives up on Italian language home schooling and joins a class. The class is small; six people around a table. Everyone is a beginner, more or less. Within just a few sessions she is the most advanced of the group. She studies, yes; ever the overachiever; but it's more than that. It almost feels as if she's absorbed the words and dictum via osmosis, from sitting around all those overcrowded tables with his family. Plus, there is no pressure or embarrassment in the sessions, just some nervous giggles and silly bursts of laughter.

Jamie finds her time with these strangers a release, an enjoyment that she had not expected. This is her little piece of Italy without him. In fact, she wishes she could see the country on her own, to form her own identification with it. Perhaps then she could at last love it the way every other person in her class seems to love it, not to mention every other person in the world. Three of her classmates are going back for second or third visits. The other two are already in love with the country from books and movies; no need to visit, the language will do.

All of them stare at Jamie, wantonly. They gaze at her with sparkling eyes, as if she is the luckiest person on the face of the earth to be married to an Italian. She smiles and pretends that she is. "It must be wonderful," they say, beaming. "It is," she says, beaming back.

CHAPTER 28

Pizza Hut

SAL SENT OUT A PRESS RELEASE announcing to his wine club members about the hot new biodynamic Barolo vintner he's signed on from Alba. Above the description of the wine is a picture of Luca and Jack next to their new fermentation device. A piece of the crumbling villa can be seen in the background. Since then their weekends have been filled with wine events via Sal's connections. He seems to have taken Jack on as a kind of project, while Jack has taken Sal on as a surrogate elder. He confers with Sal on most things about the vineyard, and since Luca likes Sal, it works to Jack's advantage to have Sal confirming for Luca Jack's proposals for improvements.

Jamie has warmed to Sal, obviously, and he keeps referring her clients for some reason, though he still mostly communicates to her through his blond secretary or Jack, but she's trying to let go of her strict paradigms on what is polite and what is not when dealing with other cultures. This is Sal's style, and he probably doesn't mean her ill will. Plus, she is glad that Jack has someone unbiased with whom he can consult on matters regarding the vineyard, especially since he doesn't seem to take Jamie's advice. It had been Jamie's suggestion to cease production of the Nebbiolos and Barbarescos in order to concentrate solely on Barolos, but Jack didn't actually implement the change until Sal recommended it many months later.

One weekend, while Jack and Sal head off to a wine event upstate, Jamie heads off to Virginia to resurrect her own relationship with a surrogate elder. She's been avoiding Jill's calls since her rather abrupt career change, now almost a year ago, and she's overdue for a visit to see her nieces. She rents a car and drives the four hours to Jill and Philip's new home in the countryside. The last mile stretch of road narrows and winds around horse ranches, farms, and vineyards, at the end of which is a cul-de-sac of private, elaborate homes, her sister's the one perched at the crest of the hill overlooking a valley, a sprawling villa treated to look centuries old.

Jamie is stunned. Jill and Philip had been working on the construction for years, but she had no idea.

"Philip gets all the credit," Jill says later, taking Jamie on the tour. They are standing in the great room, a massive kitchen and living area stretched under cathedral ceilings and façade candelabras. "He worked tirelessly with designers and architects and blah, blah, blah…" Jill waves a careless hand in the air.

"I suppose we could have just bought a place in Tuscany," Philip says, hurrying into the room and giving Jamie a big hug. "It would have been cheaper." He's holding a digital camera with a foot-long lens, and as he's talking he's darting about looking for the instructions that came with it. Everything Philip does is in warp speed. "I figured that with both of our jobs and the kids, realistically Jill and I won't be getting to Tuscany any time soon. So what the hell, I thought I'd bring Tuscany here."

"It's beautiful," Jamie says, admittingly envious, but at the same time unsettled by a thought that might not have struck her three years ago: *over the top*. Philip and Jill have always operated at one hundred and twenty percent. To stroll is to sprint. To drive is to race. To be is to be, well, the best. Something that hits Jamie only now, how hard she had tried to keep up with them.

"We flew everything in; the stones, the oak, the tapestries." Philip pauses to check a setting on his camera. Meanwhile, Jill is standing there looking if not guilty, then embarrassed. Neither Philip nor she come from money. Philip holds up the camera and takes a shot of Jamie and Jill together, before they have a chance to protest. "Where did you say Giovanni is from?"

"Piemonte," Jamie responds.

Philip pulls the camera from his eye.

"Near Alba," she adds.

Still nothing.

"In the North, near Turin."

He shrugs and puts the camera back to his eye. So goes Jack's monologue: "American tourists don't come to Piemonte, they don't buy vacation villas in Piemonte, and few go wine tasting in Piemonte. Piemonte was born of farmers; Tuscany was born of kings." *This home could be for a king*, Jamie thinks. There are six bathrooms, five bedrooms, a game room, a theater, a pool room, a wine cellar, and his and her offices; not to mention a small vineyard out back. Flat screens and computers are everywhere.

"The house is so technology-driven that no one knows how to work anything," Jill says dully, giving Philip a sidelong glance. Neither of them cook, yet the kitchen has two of everything:

dishwashers, sinks, refrigerators, pantries, stoves. The kitchen island is the size of a queen bed. They are in the living room now, where the antique wood dining table seats twenty, so a conversation from one end to the other means yelling, and yet both Philip and Jill live far from extended family, or even have time to sit and eat around a table.

They finish the tour and return to the great room. Philip disappears with the camera, and Jill looks tired, Jamie notices, but also full of strength and drive. She would never admit to fatigue or even a slight ache in her back from toting Kim around on one hip. The girl hasn't allowed her mother to set her down once since Jamie arrived. The other one, Katie, has been clinging onto Jamie's leg. She must have embedded in her memory Jamie's last visit, where she spent hours on the floor seesawing the girl up and down in such a fashion. Jamie had been so sore the next day she could barely walk.

Jill, on the other hand, is not even breaking a sweat. Her arms are solid muscle, her sweatshirt has a big wet stain on it, her shorts have a tear in them, her sandals are worn, and she could give a rat's ass about any of it. She's more concerned about the magician and the clown and the kids having the best time imaginable. The girls' two-year birthday party is set to begin in an hour, and if the entertainment doesn't show all hell will break loose. There is a large pile of presents already on the kitchen table, even though the guests have yet to arrive. A humongous bowl of pretzels sits nearby, along with potato chips and onion dip, Doritos, salsa and guacamole, M&Ms and cashews, all from Costco. "I know it's all too much," Jill says, attempting to set down Kim, who begins to scream. "… but we have a ball." She picks Kim back up and sits down with her on the couch. Katie, meanwhile, is at the Doritos bowl shoveling chips into her mouth and crumbs are falling all over the place.

Gift boxes and wrapping paper are strewn about as the girls couldn't wait and had to open at least a few gifts.

"Do you have scissors?" Jamie asks, eyeing the price tag still hanging from Kim's new dress.

Jill rips the tag off with one hand. "You know me," she says. "I don't have a moment to even brush my teeth."

Katie comes and takes Jamie's hand and leads her to the windows that look out onto a reflecting pool, honey colored pastures, amber and green hills beyond. Nothing but clear blue sky, the Capitol dome far off in the distance, supposedly, though the big red contraption Katie is excitedly showing Jamie at present blocks it from view... "Don't worry, it's not here permanently," Jill says about the bouncy machine.

"It looks like fun," Jamie says to Katie, succumbing to the sticky warmth of her little fingers.

"I can teach you," the girl says. "We hold hands and jump."

"It's my specialty."

Katie runs off for more chips.

Jamie wipes the Dorito residue onto her pants thinking, *when in Rome,* and goes over and sits down beside Jill on the couch.

"I want to hear about this new job of yours," Jill says, pulling something out from under her butt.

"In fact why don't you just bring the bowl over here," Jamie calls to Katie.

"You're working for whom now?"

Jamie, glancing anywhere but at Jill, "A restaurant supply company, helping out a friend, mostly. It fell into my lap." As does the bowl that Katie just delivered, the one Jamie caught just before it tumbled over. "They're considering some acquisitions," Jamie continues, flashing Katie a cross-eyed look. "They want to grow. Anyway, it's temporary, until I hear back from some larger firms." She doesn't know why she's said any of that. It's not true.

"I imagine the head hunters are after you."

She shoves a Dorito in her mouth. "Mmmm." Not true either. She'd blown them off.

"I don't get why the firm wouldn't transfer you to New York. It's ridiculous."

It's a wonder. Jamie shrugs.

"Did they say why?" That's Jill. Relentless.

"Not really."

"You got married. You needed to move. They can't fire you for that. You should sue."

"Sue?"

"It's discrimination!"

"Are those lemon trees?" Jamie says, pointing out the window.

Jill glances indifferently over her shoulder. "I guess. Philip's got the landscapers planting a ton of stuff out there.

Jamie sets the bowl aside and goes over to look.

"I have no idea what any of it is."

Ever since that day when Jamie drove with Jack to that tasting upstate and he'd swerved off the road suddenly because he'd spotted a patch of lemon trees tucked away in the brush, (those he'd proceeded to poach so that he could come home and spend the entire next day making Lucrezia's limoncello), Jamie can't see a lemon tree without blushing. She's blushing now, thinking about their freezer stuffed with frosted bottles of the stuff you can only sip in thimblefuls, how in their lifetime they'll never be able to drink it all. Minutes pass before she can feel Jill's gaze boring into her back. "So it's the vineyard," her sister says in resignation.

"It's going really well!" Jamie says too loudly, stepping back from the window. "We're going to Italy next month for the harvest. Jack's got a ton of events lined up." Until this moment, Jamie did not know she was going to harvest, that the reasons she'd been taking all those language classes was just for that purpose. "La Morra, Alba, Torino." She hadn't realized until now that she wanted to go, that she'd come here to say goodbye.

"La Morra? Is that near The Lakes?" Jill goes on about Lake Como for some time, where she and Philip spent their honeymoon.

"Then there's Vinitaly next year in Verona."

"What about the restaurant supply company?"

Jamie, keeping her distance by the window, says that the company is pretty flexible, which is a lie, for she'd already helped the company find a permanent, full-time CFO and was no longer working there.

A hard, scrutinizing moment passes between them.

"What did Jack say about your leaving the firm?"

"Do what you want," Jamie responds, coming closer now, for she'd been prepared for this question—these questions—and there was no more point in avoiding them.

"That's what he said?"

"He wants me to be happy."

After a pause, "Seriously?"

"Seriously."

"Philip wouldn't put up with it for one minute."

"Put up with what?"

"If I quit my job."

"You want to quit your job?"

"No!" She lowers her voice. "No."

"And why wouldn't he go for it?"

Jill shrugs, thinking about it. "The truth is, he makes enough money now. We don't need my salary, which is laughable compared to his; but it's not about the money. It's the intellectual thing. He likes the fact that I work. He always has. We're in similar professions, and we like to discuss the economy, the markets. He respects what I do. I respect what I do. It makes me feel good, like I'm contributing. I couldn't imagine what I would do if..." She pauses.

Are we really defined only by what we do in our work lives? Does it honestly end there?

"I'm not saying you're not contributing, Jamie. It's tough, doing both: the personal, the professional. I've got Genevieve now to help with the kids during the week. Thank God for her. She's great with the girls, but the guilt is awful. I'm not complaining of course. I love being a mother, and I love my job, but the guilt is exhausting."

How about defining ourselves by how we love? "It was my decision," Jamie blurts out. "They would have transferred me, even offered to, but I wanted out."

There is a moment of silence. Jill had had her suspicions, this is no shocking surprise, and yet her face is pale, nevertheless. "You quit your partnership," she says, repeating the phrase.

"Should I get you some water?"

Jill flashes her a stony smile.

"Look, Jill, I'm sorry I didn't tell you the truth before. Maybe I wasn't ready to believe it myself."

"It's okay, you don't have to..."

"It's not okay, nothing is okay."

She doesn't know how to respond to that.

"I had a combination of reasons, Jill. While I thrived on the challenge of solving intellectual problems, corporate business is still mostly a man's world, or at least the part of it that I trained my whole life to do. For a while I was a perfect fit, with my detachment skills, my blind drive, my affinity to brilliance, eccentricity all the better—even if it meant turning a blind eye sometimes to behavior that I knew was just wrong." Jamie pauses here to close her eyes on that awful vision. When she opens them, Jill is motionless. "There's a lot of shit that I've never called people on because I don't believe they will change, not without a fight anyway, and I'm not interested in being a fighter. Korea was a living, breathing example of that. I just don't have the energy, will, or desire to lead the current battle for social justice and gender equality. Call me a quitter, but I don't see the point. I convinced myself and everyone around me for years that my work was fulfilling, but really it was just draining me, and I was ready to give it up. I'm proud of everything I've accomplished, and no one can ever take that from me, but I'm ready for a new chapter, to try something different."

Jill sits still for another moment. Then, quietly, she says, "You say people don't change, and yet you seem to be changing before my eyes."

"Am I really changing? Or just finally giving in to who I've been all along?" Jamie releases a long, slow breath. "To be honest, Jill, I don't know what I want to do next."

"But you're so good at what you do."

Jamie stares out the window. "I'm not even sure what it is I do...anymore." Seconds pass before she hears from behind her a surprising and barely audible, "Me either." Jamie turns around to meet her sister's gaze. A moment passes before Jill breaks the spell and says, "The problem is that once you quit..."

"I know..."

"...it's hard to go back."

"There is no going back, Jill. I realize that."

❦

That night, as she lies in the monstrous guest bed with the thousand count sheets, stuffed and comatose from the Pizza Hut Jill had delivered for the party and the syrupy California wine, Jamie can't sleep. She keeps seeing Jill in her slobbered shirt, torn shorts and worn shoes. She's always preferred to shop at Target and Costco. That has not changed. She hasn't changed. All this other stuff—the imported house, the foreign cars and fine art—it's at such odds with her sister's personality, even Philip's. Philip's got an enormous cellar under the house with cases and cases of wine, and yet he'd had beer with dinner. In fact, he doesn't really like wine, he'd told her. So why the cellar? Are we programmed to want these things? Is it America that sets these expectations? Is this the American dream? Is this why Jamie whines to Jack about not yet having seen Tuscany or Venice or the Italian Riviera, of not staying in chateaus or having rooms with perfect views, when she's never even stayed in a chateau or a room with a perfect view?

She calls Jack, unable to sleep.

"When are you coming home?" starts the conversation.

"When are you?" For a while they just lie there listening to each other breathe. Then Jamie gives Jack a quick picture of her sister's life, the incongruence, her voice fading off at the end, "I think I'm having a little revelation."

"I understand."

"How could you possibly?"

"I think I get it."

"Then explain it to me, because I don't get it."

"You need to be broken down and built back up."

"That's not funny."

"I wasn't being funny."

They hang up. She lies awake a bit longer, reassuring herself that without Giovanni other events would have led her here, to this same place, this purgatory, this hyperspace. He is enabling her to become herself; her self is not disappearing.

CHAPTER 29
Blind Faith

*I*T'S EARLY SEPTEMBER, the edge of fall. The trees have turned red and gold, but clouds hover low and a little ominous. "Rains this early won't be good for the harvest," Giovanni says. He is taking Jamie on a tour of the property, three and a half years since her first visit, three and a half years of being 'buried in work'. Like a parallel universe, so much has happened here, and Jack is excited to show her the changes that have been made—the new fermentation technology that they've refined and now patented. They already have orders for three licenses. They've purchased new oak barrels and are renovating the cellar to accommodate twenty thousand bottles. A *cantina* has been set up for tastings just off the courtyard.

They go down into the cellar and stop briefly in the office so he can show Jamie the new computer. "See," he says, "I listen." She'd been bugging him about getting his accounts into the twenty-first century.

Caterina is at the desk, texting on her phone.

"*Vai a lavorare, Caterina,*" Giovanni says, imploring the girl to get to work.

"*Giovanni e' un dittatore,*" Caterina says, setting down her phone and frowning at the screen. "*Che rottura 'sto Quickbooks.*" Quickbooks, what a pain.

Part of Jack's new strategy is putting Caterina in charge of the accounts. The poor girl's been working all morning trying to get Quickbooks set up.

"She's all of what? Fifteen?" Jamie says, after they leave.

"Seventeen," he responds. "She's smart, and better than Luca, whom I've banned from the office. Plus, Zio Marco seems to cooperate more with her than he does Luca or me. She just needs a little motivation, and some guidance, which I'm too busy to give." He clears his throat and Jamie waits, wondering why it's impossible for him to ask her for help, if it's a man thing, an Italian thing, or something else. "We need those reports completed for our meeting with the bankers next week."

"I thought you already had that meeting."

"Zio Marco had to postpone it, but more importantly…" He spreads some blueprints out on an old wood table that backs up against some large, new, stainless steel apparatus. "Check out Godfather's designs for the redevelopment."

"He finished them?"

Jack points to the western side of the villa's structure that is now closed off. "These will be our rooms."

She stares at the drawings, tempering her excitement.

"I'll need to register you as my wife."

She's pointing at what looks like a balcony. "Overlooking the vineyard, it's beautiful."

"Then you can get your Italian Citizenship."

She flashes him an examining look. Jack's U.S. Citizenship application was approved last month. He's just waiting now for the letter announcing the date of his swearing in ceremony, which he's required to attend. Hand over heart, he'll repeat the vow and have his dual citizenship, but she'd never considered Italian citizenship a necessity for herself. Looking back at the plans, she says, "Our own bathroom would be nice."

"Privacy would be nice."

"Privacy?" she says, playfully. "And how exactly is that word translated in Italian?"

He thinks about it. No, he admits finally, there isn't a direct translation.

"What I thought."

"Trust me. I'm taking care of it."

He has her try the 2000 and 2001s they will be introducing at the tastings this year. Then they take a walk through the vineyards that cascade down the lazy hill she remembers, only now the air is sweet, the peaches ripe, and the leaves on the vines ablaze of vermillion and gold. They walk farther down the slope this time to where their vineyard butts up against the Crespi's. The nearest hectares have the look and feel of Ruffoli vines, but according to Luca they've been ravaged since the Crespi took ownership of them fifteen years ago. He has been working on their resuscitation even though the return of them won't be finalized until the loan comes through.

Meanwhile, the Crespi have graciously agreed to let Luca harvest the grapes off the hectares this season anyway, for a percentage of the profits of course. This way Villa Ruffoli can meet its growing capacity needs, as wine sales have doubled since the ever-charming and clever Silvestro came on board as a salesman. This is to be the first year they will need to produce twenty thousand bottles.

Giovanni stops walking abruptly and narrows his gaze down the hillside, where clusters of pickers are sifting their way through the Crespi vines, their bins overflowing with luscious purple grapes. He takes out his cell and calls Luca, who's phone proceeds to ring just down the hill. They follow the sound and find him pulling dead leaves off a low cluster. "The Crespi are picking," Jack tells him. "It's only September 15th. The grapes can't be ready this early, can they?"

"They aren't."

"Then why are they picking?"

"They are afraid of the rains. I am not afraid of the rains."

Jamie sits down next to Luca's son, Giacomo, under a nearby tree. His face is sticky and purple, and he's playing with the toy taxi car Jamie brought for him from New York. He offers her a grape from the stash surrounding him and she slips it into her mouth, surprised to find the skin so thick and chewy; she must spit part of it out into her hand.

Luca tells Jack, "The spring was cool, the summer hot and dry, and my grapes need more sugar."

"Are you sure?"

"Of course not."

"What's the measure?"

"Eighteen."

"Did you use that refractometer I bought you?"

"I use my tongue," Luca says, "I use my eyes, my nose." He takes the pulp covered grape seed from Jamie's hand. See how they are tan," he shows her. "That is no good. They must be brown."

Jack stands and looks up at the heavy, clouded sky. "Rain is coming, Luca. The rain comes and you are fucked."

"You not trust me now?"

"I trust you, but you better be right."

"Have a little faith, cousin."

"So this is it." Jamie blinks up at them. "All the sweat and tears and hard work, all those commitments and obligations, this is what it comes down to, weather?"

They are staring at her with two half smiles—Jack's resigned, Luca's resolved—that don't quite form a whole.

"Ah, but Jamie this is the point," Luca bellows, jumping up and scooping up a giggling Giacomo. "Grapes are unsure for their lifetime. It makes the wine special, *complicato*, like *una bella donna*. Like *amore*, love, one wine is like no other wine. The troubles make it yours. Beauty is not in what others say we should be or how we should look, smell, and taste. Our wine is of us. Each year we bring something new... I especially look forward to this year's harvest, to see what it holds."

Jack assures Jamie that his cousin is high on sugar.

"Ah, but I am so happy you are here, that we are all together."

"Get some sleep, Luca."

Jamie and Jack ascend farther up the hill where the vineyard turns into dense woods that they cut through to get to the road. It's steep, but they are still musing on Luca's words, perhaps even floating, and so the effort feels weightless. Jack takes her by the hand and tells her that when he was a boy, a grass path led from the villa through the pastures and orchards to the church. Every Sunday all the families would parade up along the path, Giovanni and Luca taking up the back, usually running, always late.

The road they take now is paved and they must press their backs against the stoned wall when cars pass every so often. It's a steep, final ascent and then they are standing before a faded orange façade with three arches, a bell tower, rectory, and cemetery to one side. No other souls but theirs, no other sounds but the breath of the wind and a few birds. It is a small, simple church, and yet it is Jamie who feels small, for it had been right here all along, the Chiesa Ruffoli, so close, and yet he'd not brought her here before. Perhaps he'd known she was not ready to come.

He leads her through a side gate, past a sleepy attendant and down a wall of graves toward a mammoth iron cross sitting on top of a marble pedestal. Beyond this cross she can see a succession of churches on distant hills, their crosses glinting, calling to each other like beacons. They walk down another wall of graves, past small glass rooms with flower-decked tombs inside. The back of the cemetery looks out over the valley. It is here where Giovanni steps up onto a low, twelve-foot square slab of dark marble with the Ruffoli emblem carved into its center. "It's for the whole clan," he says, staring down at it.

Jamie, who had stepped up onto the platform with him, now steps down off it.

"It's Godfather's design. Nice, no?"

Her first thought, one she immediately represses, is to wonder whether the bodies are buried in separate casings or simply thrown into a pile on top of each other. "Does this include you?"

"This includes me."

A light breeze blows through the tops of the trees, and then through her, as she turns to face the lush, golden valley. "I suppose it's peaceful here."

"There's even a spot for my wife."

She turns back and stares at him. He is crouched down now, reading on an adjacent wall the engravings of those already buried. "I want my ashes spread in the ocean, Jack."

He brushes some dirt off a tiny wall plaque.

"That's important to me," she adds, contemplating some realization, an end, one that includes him. It's an impossible conclusion and yet somehow she knows this is how it will be. "Are you going to be buried in that thing?"

"My brother is buried here."

There is a moment's pause…

"Maurizio Juliano."

…Maybe a gust of wind, a ghost of confusion passing through her.

"Meningitis, at two. Before I was born."

The image of La Mamma's shrine tucked away in that decaying alcove flashes before Jamie's mind, and how jealous she had been thinking that the central attraction on it, that elaborately decked toddler photo, was Jack. *A shrine, Jamie, is for the dead.*

She moves around the platform closer to him. "You should have told me Jack," she says, in a voice of quiet urgency.

He stands and stretches. "There's more."

She's afraid to ask.

"Apparently she was pregnant at the time, three months, and lost the baby."

"Apparently?"

He looks past her. "No one talks about it. Even the miscarriage is a rumor. My father certainly won't discuss it. Mamma says a lot of things when she's upset or depressed. I never know what's true."

"What things?"

"Oh, that God was punishing her."

"For what?"

He hesitates. He seems almost embarrassed.

"For what, Jack?"

"For getting pregnant with Maurizio out of wedlock."

She lets out a little gasp of disbelief, almost like laughter, until she sees his face and her voice drops to stone. "You're not serious."

He gives her a moment.

More moments.

At last she exhales deeply, at the world, at herself, for how naïve she'd been about his mother and the meaning of this place: about many things. "That's a heavy burden, Jack."

"She's never gotten over it."

"I meant for you."

He steps down off the platform. "We should go."

She hesitates, wanting to ask more, wanting him to say more. He takes her hand and holds it tightly. Then he leads her away in silence. His way of telling her there isn't always *more*. Some things just are.

Love. Marriage. This church, for instance, it is just here and there is no need to discuss their mutual disbeliefs.

They enter through a side door, he ahead of her because she has hesitated, if only perhaps to see if he might come back for her. He does. Down the aisle is a beam of warm, hazy light. He leads her there, then into one of the few pews that feels like it might topple over. Wood, frescoes, and darkness—the church was built in the year fourteen-hundred-thirty-two, a sign says. They stare at the gilded altar; behind it, Jesus nailed to the cross.

"It won't be so bad," he says, and she knows what he is asking.

"We should talk about children," she says.

"Yes," he says.

"I don't know that I…"

He squeezes her hand.

He is asking for blind faith.

CHAPTER 30

Harvest

*I*T RAINS DURING THE NIGHT. Jamie lies listening to the patter on the roof, and Giovanni can't sleep from worry over the harvest. They toss and turn and get up at dawn. It was almost easier sleeping in Jack's childhood bed (since upgraded to a king by way of joining two single mattresses), when tossing and turning and falling through the crack wasn't an option. Three days go by like this, anxiously waiting for the rains to stop. Even the discussion of food is drowned out by their obsession with the rains and when it will be time to harvest the grapes.

Antonia's brothers are standing by with their trucks and buckets, waiting for Luca's call. The equipment, tanks, and barrels have all been cleaned, then cleaned again. Now the sun is here, and Jamie thinks that for sure it must be time to pick, but it is not. "We must be patient," Luca says. "We must let the vines absorb the rain," he says as they watch the Crespi haul in their last load, their truck decked in celebratory flowers, family and friends parading behind it. The dinner they have continues loudly on the Crespi property throughout the night.

Two sun-filled days later, Jack is loading up the van for the Alba tasting, a week-long extravaganza of wine and food pairings that can't be missed. Jamie is sitting in the garden waiting for...

"Always late!" Giovanni calls out from some unseen location upon sight of Silvestro making his way up the path.

"I am on time," Silvestro calls back, all beams and smiles, heading toward Jamie to steal a moment with her before they leave. She rushes to greet him. They have not seen each other since Rome, and she always wonders what he will be like, if the passing of time and the trials of life will have dulled his enthusiasm and yearning. "*Mah*, Jamie," he says low. "Please don't tell Giovanni that I have come just now from Siena where I have seen my Principessa. She is so beautiful. She makes me so happy. Ah, but it is like a dream, as I knew it would be."

Thankfully, he's exactly the same, and Jamie smiles. She's in the dream now, too.

"Ah, you are the only person I can say this to who will believe me," he says, and now she desperately wants a mirror. She wants to hold it up to her face and see this person, this person now in this dream.

"You must meet her, Jamie. We must plan a meeting. I have told her all about you. Of course you will not be able to speak to her because she knows not one word of English, but just to be with her and you will see..."

"Silvesssstttrrroo!"

"*Calma*, Giovanni! It is only nine o'clock. We have plenty of time."

"*Il vino in macchina, dai!*"

Jamie helps them load the last of the wine. After the van is packed and they are just about to drive off, La Mamma rushes up to the car with a care package overflowing with meats and cheeses and bread, as if Jack and Silvestro are traveling half a day and not an hour. It had been Jamie's idea to stay behind. Sal and his exclusive entourage will be at the Alba event, but that is not the reason. She isn't exactly sure of the reason. "You'll be alright here," he assures her one last time, as if he, too, is wondering.

The next day Jamie wanders around the property. Everyone seems to have vanished suddenly. It's peaceful, and she's enjoying her solitary exploration of the upgrades, the flourishing gardens and paths, the little makeshift *cantina* with its ad hoc collection of antique wood furnishings, those that sit in strange contrast to the shiny silver devices tucked here and there. She is quite startled to come upon a strange man meandering around the tanks in the fermentation garage. Forties, lanky, wiry glasses, not unattractive, though the sneakers are a dead give away.

"You're American," he says when he turns and sees her, what she was just thinking about him.

"Is it that obvious?"

They share a look of mutual understanding.

"Peter Thompson," he says by way of introduction. There is an anticipatory pause, as if she might already know his name.

"I'm surprised to see that you are not picking yet."

She shrugs, "Join the club." Then, on further examination. "Do you have an appointment? Giovanni's in Alba, but I can go get Luca from the vineyard."

"I don't have an appointment. I was simply here, and thought I'd stop by and see some wine."

Zia Claudia normally does the tastings, and Jamie considers going to get her now, but then what the hell, this is, after all, why she'd stayed behind, to try this life without Jack as her buffer. She leads the guest to the *cantina*, goes behind the counter, and grabs a bottle from the cooler. "Here," she says, opening it clumsily. She puts out a glass and pours him a taste. "People like this."

He brings the glass to his nose for a lingering moment, sets it down. "How long have you lived in Italy?"

She hesitates, playing with the idea. "Not long."

"My wife loves Italy."

"Most people do." And then, facetiously, "What is it about Italy?"

He shrugs, "And she's French."

Ha! Jamie smiles, and he laughs. If there's one thing Jamie's learned, it's that the French and Italians make a pastime of looking down on each other.

"So you live in France, then?"

"Ten years now."

"And you like living there?"

"Je l'aime très beaucoup."

"Sorry, but I can barely speak Italian."

"I said I like it very much."

"Will you ever move back to the States?"

"Does one move back?"

"That's what I'm asking."

He thinks for a moment. "Eventually, yes, I will go back."

Not "we," Jamie notes, along with the distant look in his eyes.

Some silence.

"What do you think…" he asks finally, staring into the glass again. "…about the wine?"

Surprised by the question, embarrassed, she hadn't thought to contemplate the wine, now a living, breathing part of her. Luca's speech comes to mind, the one about the singularity of wines, like love, every sip is different, every moment is different. It's the culmination of those moments that makes an impression, an attachment or feeling. She's beginning to understand this now. "I've been drinking these wines for four years now and I still can't describe them. I know that I like them, now. I didn't used to like them. I preferred less dry wines before."

"This is where you've planted roots, then."

She refocuses her gaze on him. "I've come to realize that wine is a reflection of one's environment and emotions. My taste for wine changes with my mood. When I'm mad at Giovanni, I crave something thick and creamy."

"Ah, California! This must be where you are from."

She laughs. "Yes, of all places for a redhead. I grew up at the beach."

"Do you miss it?"

She thinks of the beach, her father watching her bounce and tumble in the surf…

"What did you do there before you came here?" He puts the glass to his nose again.

"I was a financial consultant."

"I was guessing an artist."

"Really?"

"Don't worry, I used to be a banker," he muses, putting his glass up to the light. "Thin," he says. "Clean."

"Thin, clean," she repeats the words, hoping to store them for future use.

"The color is complex."

"Amber," Jamie offers.

"Orange," he says, and she thinks back to her first brush with a Barolo.

"Why are you laughing?"

"No reason," she smiles, pouring a glass and taking a sip.

"I think the wine will be interesting," he says.

"But you haven't even tasted it."

"I don't have to."

Early that evening, Jamie is lying on her marital bed trying to ignore the guilt she feels, as if it's seeping through the mattress. She will hardly sleep tonight knowing that La Mamma is downstairs, propped on her knees at that altar of hers, praying for Jack's salvation because, according to her, until God sanctions their union, they are sleeping together in sin. Something Jamie would have scoffed at before, now makes her feel nauseous.

There is a tap at the door, which pushes open before Jamie can say, "I'm not dressed." Barely having time to pull a shirt over herself, La Mamma, as if hearing Jamie's thoughts, has dragged into the room a mound of white silk and broken lace—her mother's wedding dress.

Jamie stares at the dress.

La Mamma is going on about something. *Alta*, tall. *Magra*, thin. Her mother was tall and thin, Jamie deciphers, and the dress will need to be taken out, of course, so there is no time to waste. Jamie must try it on now.

Now?

Yes, now.

She is hoping the woman might at least step out of the room, but no chance. Jamie removes her shirt and steps into the dress that La Mamma is holding out for her. Painful minutes go by while La Mamma fastens the tiny hooks that go up the back. She pinches the shoulders, tugs at the pearl-trimmed hems. She will need to take out the sleeves, but otherwise, the woman's eyes fill with tears; the dress fits. Neither of them can pretend otherwise, and La Mamma almost looks disappointed.

There are no mirrors in any of the rooms, so Jamie goes into the bathroom and stands on the bidet. The dress is simple, thank God, and yes, she had agreed to this: a church wedding. She steps down off the bidet. There is some commotion going on outside in the hall; a baby is crying. Jamie does not want anyone to see her dressed like this so she stays in the bathroom, hoping they'll go away; but it's only a few seconds before La Mamma knocks, and then Luca pops a grape into Jamie's mouth when she opens the door.

She chews and swallows.

"We harvest," Luca announces.

"Now?"

"Now." Then Luca sees her dress and pushes the door open fully. "*Che bella!*" Antonia is right behind him, holding the crying baby.

Jamie's face turns red. All this fabric and she's never felt so naked.

"You will watch the baby?" La Mamma says.

"Me?"

"Antonia is our best picker," Luca says.

"But certainly I can help too…"

Antonia is already shaking her head, *assolutamente no*, Jamie is too precious and delicate for such manual labor.

Anyway, Antonia's brothers are on their way, and Luca has called Giovanni to come back from Alba early. "It will be better if Jamie will help La Mamma watch the baby."

At dusk Antonia's brothers arrive and the picking, hauling, and crushing begin. It's easier on the grapes to process them at night when it is cool, Luca insists. The best thing Jamie can do is stay out of the way. La Mamma tells her this again that evening, after Jamie comes downstairs dressed in shorts and an oversized blouse tied at her waist, still insisting she can pick. Zia Claudia, covered from head to toe in baggy clothes and wearing picking gloves, has just dropped off the sleeping baby and is headed out the door with two-year-old Giacomo.

"If Giacomo can pick…"

"*Ma no,* Jamie," La Mamma says.

"I've got to do something."

"But I do this so many times," Zia Claudia says, Jamie on her heels as she heads outside. "For me it is no problem."

From the edge of the courtyard, Jamie watches Claudia and Giacomo disappear down the hillside into the vines that have been strung with paper lanterns. There is faint laughter; otherwise the work is done quietly under the full moon, in an ambience of peace. Back inside the baby is still asleep, and La Mamma and Zia Maddalena are preparing a late supper for all the workers. Jamie helps set the table, feeling out of sorts and out of place. She'd stayed behind because she wanted to try Italy without Jack, but she hadn't realized until now how protected and cocooned he'd kept her. She's barely tried but a few words of the Italian she'd learned. Every time she starts to speak it, Jack steps in and says the words for her, and she's been just as happy to let him.

She stares down at the baby, wishing it would wake up. Jamie is not great with babies, but at least it would give her

something to do. "*Ti piacciono i bambini?*" (Do you like babies?)
La Mamma is next to Jamie now, wanting to know. After a
slight pause, Jamie breathes in a dose of courage and says,
in Italian, "*Ho due nipoti.*" (I have two nieces.) It takes a few
moments for these new words to break through the barrier
that separates them, and another minute for both of them to
realize that they have communicated without assistance for
the first time. La Mamma clasps her hands together in glee.
Jamie, her Italian fueled, tells La Mamma, in Italian, that she
also has three half-brothers from her father's second marriage,
though she rarely sees them. La Mamma's face holds an even
wider fascination now, for this is the most they've ever said to
each other. La Mamma responds then, but at a pace too fast
for Jamie to interpret; something about dates for the church
wedding. Will Jamie's family be flying out? If so, La Mamma
will need to call the hotel in town and make a reservation, since
none of Villa Ruffoli's rooms will yet be ready.

"They can't make it!"

La Mamma's excitement wanes. Certainly your father will
be here, she admonishes.

Jamie's heart is pounding. It had been a knee jerk reaction.
Why had she responded so harshly?

He will want to walk you down the aisle and give you
away. The woman's face is desperate now, as Jamie's must be,
because she's trying to figure out why it is her father can't walk
her down the aisle? He can walk, certainly. But no, she knows
why; the painful vision is coming back to her now, her father
walking Jill down the aisle of a church that no one in their
family, all atheists, had ever patronized. It had been selected
for its pristine location close to the cliffs. Her father's teenage
sons were the ushers, and he himself cried the whole way to
the altar. Jamie always assumed that those tears meant he was

happy in his new life. Now she wonders if maybe he wasn't just a little sad, too. If being around his daughters was as painful for him as it was for them.

He'll cry for Jamie, too, that's why she can't have him here. She won't be able to suffer it.

Eight the next morning, Jamie heads downstairs to the kitchen where La Mamma is feeding and singing to the giggling and cooing baby. The only other time Jamie has seen La Mamma this happy is, well, never. The closest would be when she took communion at Luca's wedding, but that was more about peace than happiness. La Mamma settles the baby into Jamie's arms to see if she, too, could be so happy, but the baby starts to wail. Jamie gently bounces the baby up and down. She sways, paces. Jamie is nothing if not perseverant; she is prepared to do this all night, but La Mamma quickly steps in and takes the baby back. Jill had done the same, Jamie recalls, those times she'd held either Katie or Kim (or both) while they were crying, wanting to give Jill a much-needed break but ultimately unable to. A few minutes of watching Jamie struggle, is it too much for people to bear?

"You must go to Caterina," La Mamma insists with a sudden urgency. Caterina had come looking for Jamie earlier, apparently. "*Vai, vai da Caterina,* Jamie." Jamie rushes out the door.

There is a flurry of activity in the covered courtyard just above the cellar. The bins that were empty yesterday are now filled with purple grape sludge. A brother-in-law is inside one of the bins, delicately shoveling the grapes through a filter.

Farther on, in large steel tanks, the sludge is fermenting into must. Over one of them stands Luca, hands on hips.

"*Fermentare*," he says, perplexed by his uselessness. He used to have to stand here with a hose for three hours twice a day in order to push down the sludge, he explains to her. Now all he does is clean the pump and flip a switch. "*Tuo marito e' una testa di cazzo ma e' anche un genio!*" (Your husband is a pain in the ass, but also a genius.)

She can't tell if Luca is happy or disappointed about the device, even though it was a compliment, of sorts, that he just gave Jack. *Genio* means genius, but it's the word *marito* on which Jamie is now stuck. *Marito,* husband, she wonders if she'll ever get used to this word, assigned to the man that she loves. Perhaps, she muses, the gap between herself and the rest of the married world will close once she walks down that aisle before God and Giovanni slips that ring on her finger. This, the missing puzzle piece, only once it's found and snapped into place will the picture of her marriage at last be completed. It's not something she believes logically, of course, but in her heart... She might even be looking forward to it.

Jamie leaves Luca still shaking his head over the device and follows the path down to the workshop. She finds the cellar door in the ivy wall and manages to push her way through. She can't find the light switch that was there before, but a soft orange glow is leaking from somewhere and she makes her way down the stairs heading toward it—past the barrels, through a tunnel of brick to an office more like a cold, damp closet. Caterina sits before a computer, frowning.

"I'm a wiz at Quickbooks," Jamie says.

Caterina looks up. "*E' vero?*"

"*E' vero.*"

A sigh escapes the girl, who has changed in the nearly four years since Jamie last saw her. Her blond hair is now died black, she's wearing a super short miniskirt, and her breasts are practically falling out of her top. Jamie remembers her as bookish and aloof, superior in that Italian, self-loving way. She is not so aloof now. She hops up and encourages Jamie to take her place. "I wish to be in the vineyards with my brother, but Giovanni has tied me to this chair."

"He can be sort of a tyrant."

"Tyrant?"

"Dictator."

"Ah, this word I know."

Up until recently, Luca had paid all the bills with cash and handshakes, Caterina explains. Every few months he and Zio Marco would "add things up." Accounts were kept by hand; she points to a stack of files on the desk. Jamie opens one, a mess, closes it. Sometimes Luca paid bills with pig parts or even chickens.

Jamie says that it might be better to start with last year's tax returns. Caterina tells Jamie that this is the problem, or one of the problems anyway. They don't have the tax return copies.

"Zio Marco, as your banker, should have copies," Jamie says.

"Yes, and this is the problem. There was a fire at the Bank of Torino, and the copies are gone."

Jamie examines Caterina for seriousness. The girl is serious.

"Bank Statements?"

"Ah, these I have."

"Good."

And the term document for the loan, where's that?

Caterina hunts through the folders.

Jamie begins fiddling with the chart of accounts up on the screen. We'll need to create categories to really understand cash flow. We'll go through each line item. She tries to manipulate the data on the screen, but immediately gets tangled up in the keys. "*Porca miseria.*" It's an Italian keyboard. QuickBooks is in Italian, too. She stands up and lets Caterina sit back down.

They are in the cellar most of the day.

And the next day.

And the day after that.

Shoveling, crushing, and pumping go on above their heads.

Now Jamie is examining a report she's at last managed to generate from all this incomprehensible data. She is confused by what she sees in the cash accounts, for there's no reason, certainly, with the uptick in receivables from the bump in sales, that the villa shouldn't be making a profit.

Then there is an account labeled, "*Affitto*" that she doesn't understand, and another with no label. Both have large monthly cash outlays with no supporting documentation, and the fact that Caterina is ignorant about them puts Jamie on alert.

"*Affitto* means rent." Caterina shrugs and says.

Jamie frowns. "Are you leasing back the property?"

"It's like paying rent," Jamie adds, at Caterina's blank expression.

"Why would we pay rent? It's our property."

At this point Luca comes bursting in, his shirt stained purple, exhausted, animated. "Giovanni will not be disappointed," he announces, and Jamie, incapable of putting things off, does not waste time asking him about the unknown accounts. Luca goes still and his eyes recede. He scratches his head and says that he thinks those accounts have to do with taxes, and that she should ask Zio Marco about that. Then he lights a cigarette and leans back against the brick wall. "We do all the hard work." He makes a wild hand gesture. "And where is The Chosen One?"

For the first time, Jamie searches Luca's banter for deeper meaning, like resentment, the kind that makes people do stupid things. After all, Nonno Giacomo had left the villa and vineyard to Jack, not Luca, or anybody else for that matter. Jamie reaches for the cigarette Luca offers her. He lights it, and then watches her pretend it's a relief to smoke.

"Where is the deed to Villa Ruffoli?" she asks, exhaling. Hers is an awful hunch.

Luca looks at Caterina, who looks back at him and shrugs. Luca shrugs, then heads off again, saying, "Zio Marco should know, but he's hunting for mushrooms in France and won't be back until Sunday."

Jamie puts out her cigarette and gets Caterina going on a deed search on the Internet, but there is no way to search for a deed on the Internet in Italy, apparently. She has Caterina call the records office at the City of Torino, prompting her on what to say. They are asking for simple information, what is readily available in the States, what should take one call, but what seems like a thousand redirected calls later, Jamie, without thought, picks up the phone and calls Jill at the Federal Reserve. Actually, she's at home. Eight a.m. her time, trying to rush off to work with the twins screaming in the background, her nanny sick and trying to find a sitter, all of which falls silent the minute Jamie explains her situation and Jill fully consumes the problem, what takes about thirty seconds before she's working toward a solution—in this case, a classmate of hers from Stanford who now works as a magistrate in Rome. She'll make some calls and get back. Click.

Simona comes into the office as Jamie hangs up the phone. Just in from Torino to help celebrate the harvest, Simona looks gorgeous, full breasted, her skin flushed and glowing. "I shouldn't be smoking she says," lighting up. You could never tell by her figure that she's five months pregnant, except for a little, perfect bulge. "Can you believe I will be a mother?"

"In fact, no," Jamie says, and Simona laughs.

A noise from the *cantina* sends Simona to the open door. "If Mamma comes, I will hide. Please do not tell Mamma I am here. She will want me to take a rest, to eat, to sleep. I must be healthy for my baby, always the baby..." She waves her cigarette in the air and laughs. "It is so wonderful that you have finally come back to Villa Ruffoli, Jamie, but why you stay down here all day?"

"Caterina is teaching me Italian accounting."

"It is most interesting, no?"

Jamie raises an eyebrow.

"How is Caterina? *Intelligente,* no?"

"She will be a shrewd businesswoman."

"Like the famous Jamie; *grande,* Caterina, *grande.*" Simona goes over and wraps her arms around her cousin presently trading text messages with someone on her cell phone. "If she wasn't so, how do you say, *matta per i ragazzi.*"

"Boy crazy."

"Ah yes, boy crazy."

Caterina snorts at an incoming text, her fingers at work, already responding.

"And you have moved to New York?" Simona says. "You no longer travel, I hear."

E' vero.

"And I work at the antique store now, with Michele."

"I heard," Jamie says, searching the woman's eyes for that connection they'd once had. It's still there, but alas, perhaps they have both disappointed. "You can still sculpt for pleasure, no?"

"*Mah*," she says, gazing off. "You must ask yourself," a wry smile, "why does Simona marry Michele from Torino when she talks so much about seeing the world?"

Before I might have asked myself, but not today, Jamie thinks, staying silent.

"I am marrying Michele because I have known him all my life and I am almost thirty and this is my father's wish." Her shoulders, chest, and arms fall into motion. "Michele is older. He restores antiques and makes a good living. He is a good, decent man who loves my parents. My father has bought us an apartment next to his in *Via della Rocca* because my baby will need grandparents, and I will need Mamma and Papá." She pauses. Takes a drag. "I choose my husband."

"I think I understand," Jamie says, but in reality she is lost. Her mind is back on those unclaimed accounts. Why was her immediate reaction to call Jill? What a silly thing to do.

A motorbike pulls up outside, suspending Jamie's thoughts as Caterina wastes no time packing up her purse and bolting. Jamie pictures the girl riding sidesaddle behind however many boys are on that bike, as she's seen them do, none of them wearing helmets.

She closes her file. "*Allora. Per oggi abbiamo finito.*" We are finished for the day.

"*Brava,*" Simona says. "*Il tuo italiano e' ottimo, Jamie.*" Your Italian is very good, Jamie.

Jamie was unaware she was even speaking Italian. "*Lo so,*" I know, she shrugs, and they laugh at each other, though nothing is really funny about marrying someone because you feel you have no other choice.

CHAPTER 31

Minestra

"HE CHOSEN ONE has made his way back from Alba just in time to bring in the last loads of grapes!" Luca is pretending to lament, but his voice is pure excitement and relief: his closest cousin is by his side, an intimate part of his life. They are off together in a matter of minutes, leaving Jamie little chance to broach Jack about the estate's finances. He and Luca and the others work late into the night and Jack does not fall into bed beside her until two a.m. By seven a.m. he is gone again, when Jamie is woken by her cell phone ringing.

"Have you put money into this thing?" her sister is asking, after confirming Jamie's suspicion that there's a lien on the estate, that those "rent" payments are interest on the debt.

Jamie is sitting up in bed now, in the shirt she'd slept in, grasping this reality.

"I'm having the documents e-mailed to you." She hesitates. "It's not small Jamie."

Up and out of bed now, pacing at the window. "How much?"

"Five hundred thousand Euros."

The pacing stops. "Jesus fucking Christ."

"What are you going to do?"

She thinks about it. "Tell him," Jamie says finally. "We'll have to figure it out."

"I said, what are YOU going to do?"

"Me?"

"You. Where are you in all this?"

Silence.

"Is your name on anything?"

"No."

"Good."

Her body starts to tremble.

"Jamie…"

"Jill, please DON'T!" There is a heavy, harsh after-silence.

"It's just that…"

"Please stop. Please don't say another word."

"You're so talented."

Those words.

"Your skills could really be put to use. You could really be doing something, Jamie."

Hours have passed. Jamie is back down in the office, printing out the e-mailed deed that just came through from Jill, whose words still echo. Jamie, with the deed, heads numbly back to the villa, pausing just outside the angled wooden door that leads down the arched hall and into the kitchen, where she can hear the women bustling about, preparing a big feast. The harvest is in. Lunch will be a big celebration. Everyone will get drunk.

A force pulls Jamie backward, away from the villa and the impending celebration, down the paved road until she finds herself in that tunnel of stone, the town where she's rarely ventured because why venture anywhere in Italy? Like now, for instance, approaching one o'clock, the streets are bare. She should be at home where everyone else is, eating with family.

An empty restaurant. A table by the window. A woman with a pad and pencil is there at once, ready to take Jamie's order because there will be no choices for Jamie to mull over, a menu, for instance. What they have to offer is what they have to offer—*tagliatelle con porcini*. Jamie agrees to take the dish even though she's not hungry, a small contribution to the woman's survival, for certainly she's making no profit. House wine comes in a carafe with a tiny glass from which Jamie sips and stares out, wondering how the woman stays in business, and why. Every so often a vehicle roars by and shakes the windows. The woman cleans the espresso machine, nonplussed. At some point her husband brings the pasta, the steam from which brings water to Jamie's eyes, a delayed reaction to what Jill had said just before hanging up. Jamie pinches the bridge of her nose, recalling the silence that had lingered on the line after, how awful it was because it made everything so obvious.

"I'm just worried about you," Jill had said. "It seems like, I don't know, like you're disappearing."

Jamie looks down. Her pasta has disappeared too, though she doesn't remember eating it. She feels detached from everything suddenly, deceived by herself and no one else. Jill is right. Jamie is good at business, at finance, and so this is what she should be doing. Do what you are good at—a formula for existing that's been tried and tested, a formula that works. Her instincts were right four years ago. Jack should have sold the Villa and set his mother up with a proper trust. Instead, Jamie let herself get caught up in their emotion, and now peoples' lives are at stake.

After leaving the restaurant, Jamie wanders around the narrow streets of the village for a good hour before making her way back up the hill. She buzzes at the gate, which opens, igniting the setters on a barking tirade. Zio Marco is back from mushroom hunting, apparently, though even the dogs don't seem real anymore. None of this seems real. Even that wedding dress is a fantasy.

Giovanni is waiting for her on the terrace, smoking a Toscano. "I've been looking all over for you." He is pretending to be calm, she can tell, if only to stabilize his mother seated next to him, she who is anything but calm. One does not just disappear in Italy. "I was worried," he says.

"I went for a walk," she says, bracing herself for a scolding, for La Mamma has a shawl wrapped tightly about her shoulders and she's clutching something in her hands. Jamie presumes it's her rosary. She says something in Italian to Jack, who then says to Jamie, "La Mamma has something for you." Suddenly there is an irresistible twinkle in his eye—of all things, of all times—and La Mamma is smiling. This is not the reception Jamie had been expecting.

La Mamma begins carefully laying out a very old and delicate piece of lace onto her lap. From a velvet pouch, she pours onto the lace a glittering array of diamonds, rubies, sapphires, different sized gold pendants, rings, and chains, heirlooms passed down to her by her mother and grandmother, a spectacle almost as dazzling as the blue dancing in her eyes as she gazes down at them with no small amount of pride.

"She wants you to select a piece for our wedding," Jack says, with equal pride.

Jamie steps backward. "Oh no, please, I couldn't."

"You have to."

"But Giovanni…"

"Just pick one."

La Mamma is waiting.

Jamie is barely surviving an emotional attachment to humans, but heirlooms? Must she place emotional value on metal and stone too? A ring, say, one you cherish. Your wedding ring perhaps, or your father's wedding ring even better, one he lets you play with as a little girl. You sit on his lap and slide it off his finger and onto your thumb, the only finger it fits, and dream of what it might be like one day to meet your prince. It's a ring that stays with you, one you feel even though it's not there. And then he gives it to you after his divorce for whatever reason that escapes you now. It sits in your jewelry box. Sometimes, when no one is around, you slide the ring back onto your thumb, but it is just a ring now. Metal.

Jack holds in his palm two very large sapphires. Jamie is wondering how much they might be worth, if they might in fact cover some of the debt. "Thank you," she says, grabbing a tiny gold broach.

Satisfied, La Mamma packs up her loot, insisting that Jamie eat, that there is much food left.

"*No, grazie.* I'm just tired. Perhaps later."

"We take a rest," Jack says, putting out his cigar.

Jamie follows him up the stairs. He's weaving slightly, but it's Luca who is skunk drunk, he assures her. Everyone else has fallen into beds anywhere they can find, exhausted. He shuts the door behind them, pulls her into his arms. "I've missed you," he says. She breathes in his freshly showered scent, the sweet smell of his hair, the tobacco on his lips, and she must force herself to pull back, to move to the other side of the room where it is safe.

He falls down on the bed with a drunken sigh and pulls off a shoe.

When a minute goes by and she still hasn't spoken, he focuses his eyes on her and asks what's wrong.

"How do you automatically know something's wrong?"

He pulls off the other shoe. It hits the floor and sounds like "duh."

She paces, from a distance. "I guess I'm wondering why you never asked me to look at the accounts, Jack."

"Ah yes, the accounts."

"I offered a million times, Jack. You know this is what I do."

"I know this is what you do."

"Well, then, answer my question!" It comes out impatient, accusing, and he looks at her, "Why are you attacking me?"

"I'm not attacking you!" She can no longer contain her frustration, confusion, fear about her sister's words: *You are disappearing.*

He stands, abruptly. "Because I knew you'd find something wrong," he says matter of factly, fumbling to unbutton his shirt. "Because I knew that whatever you looked at wouldn't be GOOD ENOUGH. Nothing is ever GOOD ENOUGH for you, Jamie...my job, my mother, our apartment, this villa, ITALY." He goes on, but blood is rushing to her head now and she can't hear. She is too stunned to hear.

There is a long silence in which Rome comes harrowingly back to mind.

He sighs, deeply, as if it had come back to his mind, too. "Don't listen to me, Jamie." He tries to bring her into his arms again.

She steps back. *Four years and this is what he thinks of me?*

"I'm tired, Jamie. I've got fifteen thousand bottles of wine fermenting out there and commitments for twenty, and Luca's still insisting that half is no good."

Her back is at the wall now. "Is that me, Jack? Do I always find something wrong? Am I that person?"

He lifts her chin to meet his. "Jamie," he says in a whisper.

"I don't want to be that person, Jack."

He examines her a moment. "What is it, Jamie?"

If only she could tell him. She doesn't want to know what part he had to play, even if it was simply ignorance.

"What did you find?"

If only she didn't have to say it out loud.

"Jamie." His voice now has a quiet urgency.

She breaks away and moves to the opposite side of the room again. It is safer where she can't feel him physically near her. "There's a lien on the property, Jack."

Silence ensues, a loud and spiraling silence.

"Five hundred thousand Euros, placed on the deed four years ago."

"That's not possible."

She nods her head in the direction of the bed, the deed lying there that he immediately goes and examines. Meanwhile, she's inching her way along the wall and over to the door. She knows it might be some time before what she has said gets through. The property is in serious debt. Their loan will never be approved.

"He can't do this without my co-signature," Jack assures her minutes later, referring to Zio Marco, who signed the lien as trustee.

"Your mother served as your proxy."

He re-scours the document, sees the signature, seethes. A slew of curse words follow, what slowly rises into a crescendo that ends with a hard kick to the bed frame with his foot, and still, it's possibly not registering. She's trying to find his eyes but he won't look at her. "I'm sure La Mamma didn't know what she was doing," Jamie offers, as Jack, of stone now, a wall she'll not get through, sits down on the edge of the bed. "It's probably why Zio Marco suggested you sell the vineyard four years ago, back when you were deciding what to do."

His head falls into his hands.

"What I don't understand is where the five hundred thousand Euros went."

Up again, suddenly, one last kick to the bed frame and he stomps out of the room. She hears him skip steps down to the kitchen, where harsh words are exchanged with La Mamma. Her cries, a door slamming, the kick and crunch of gravel.

Hours later, dusk, Jamie is lying on the bed examining a crack in the ceiling while fingering the gold broach in her hand. She can't stop rubbing her thumb along its softly worn edges, as if it did, in fact, hold meaning, deep meaning, all the world's meaning, not to mention knowledge; *what a fucking mess*. The villa is creepily silent, everyone still sleeping, presumably, or passed out, except for La Mamma, now knocking on Jamie's door. She has fixed a light supper for the three of them. She wants to eat in the garden and has prepared the minestrone soup for Giovanni because Giovanni always wants her minestrone when he is not feeling well.

They are in the kitchen now. Jamie is setting up the little wheeled cart that she's become an expert at maneuvering. La Mamma is at the stove, humming some tune, leaving Jamie both impressed and confused by her stoicism. She wonders what Giovanni said to La Mamma before stomping out, and if the woman has even registered what's coming.

It's eight-thirty. They are seated at the garden table waiting for Jack to arrive before eating. Jamie keeps pouring drops of wine into her glass, drinking them, pouring more drops. We should go ahead and eat, she delicately suggests to La Mamma at one point, but the woman is horrified by even the idea. "*Aspettiamo Giovanni.*" Words released from the depths of her soul. We will wait for my son. Giovanni will be here. We Italians do not miss meals. But Jamie, if she knows Giovanni at all, has the idea that he's not going to be here for this meal, a message she tries to relay to the woman in her own cryptic Italian.

"But why!?" La Mamma demands to know. "Giovanni tells me that the wedding is canceled, and that I have done something wrong. But what have I done wrong, Jamie?"

"There are problems with the villa's finances, but I'll let Jack explain…"

"I do not understand my son. Why must he be so mean to me?" La Mamma gulps some wine for courage. "I am not educated like you," she says rather accusingly, in the Italian that Jamie is struggling desperately to understand. "Perhaps for this reason I've always been a cursed mother. No matter how hard I pray. After the car accident, when Giovanni was left miraculously unhurt, I began to see Maurizio's spirit everywhere. He was calling for me to come and help him, and yet I couldn't seem to… I became very depressed. I prayed and prayed because I did not know what else to do. Giovanni has always been jealous of Maurizio's spirit. He is afraid, like Giorgio, who went back to Napoli when his father died. You see, Jamie, Lucrezia is an evil siren, and Neapolitans are petrified of death."

Silence.

Jamie is wondering if she interpreted correctly.

La Mamma shrugs, "*e' cosi*," as if none of it matters.

Jack sits down between them, startlingly, and reaches for the bread.

Jamie turns to him and blinks. Perhaps she's not interpreting anything right, for she was certain Giovanni wouldn't show. She thought she knew him at least that well, but alas, La Mamma still knows him better; so says her satisfied grin as she runs off to the kitchen and returns with the steaming tureen. She ladles soup into three bowls. Jack grates cheese into his and eats without looking at either of them. Jamie is still waiting for him to give her a sign about what he might have found out. If nothing else to make a joke about the soup, for how many times had he complained to her about *la minestra,* the watery, tasteless soup his mother persistently makes and he persistently detests ever since he was a child? Now he's soaking up the dregs with his bread, which La Mamma presently chastises him for, a watchful eye over his every move.

"*Allora,*" she says, removing the soup and reaching down onto the wheeled cart for the platter of *prosciutto* and *formaggio.*

Jamie pours more wine.

Giovanni, who still hasn't spoken, grabs a piece of prosciutto with his hand and drops it on his plate.

La Mamma stares from his hand to his plate in horror. "What have I done wrong, Giovanni!?" Her cry pierces the night. "I have already invited all the people to the wedding. We cannot cancel now. You must tell me what I have done wrong!"

Jamie puts down the bottle and stands to go. "I'll give you two some privacy to talk."

La Mamma grasps her forearm, "*Stai qui. Mangia il prosciutto e formaggio,* Jamie." Her voice is hoarse, disarming, and in her eyes is the most desperate of looks. "Stay and eat, Jamie," Giovanni agrees, and she looks from La Mamma to him and back again, at a complete loss. The villa is about to go bankrupt. The wedding is certainly off. Giovanni might be about to disown his mother. And yet, what must be done? One must eat the *prosciutto* and *formaggio*… And that's just it, as La Mamma's eyes fill with tears, Jamie at last sees the truth of the woman's desperation, what she means every time she says the word, *mangia*. She doesn't mean, "eat." Not really, anyway. What she means is *stay longer at this table with me. Please. Don't leave me.*

Jamie helps La Mamma with the dishes and then slips outside into a veil of fog and cloud. A barren space where the moon once was. She can barely see the path and must follow the scent of his tobacco down the hill to the hole in the hedge. From there she spots the orange light of his cigar, on the tennis court where they had agreed to meet, far away from La Mamma, from everyone.

"So, what did she say?" Jamie immediately asks, not willing to wait the painful hours it might take him to begin.

He releases smoke from his mouth. "She says that Zio Marco often makes her sign things and she pays no attention. That she trusts Zio Marco. That they have been friends since they were children. That Zio Marco would never do anything to hurt us."

"So she's got no idea where the money went?"

He shakes his head. He is still steaming and mentally poring over the information he gathered when he'd stomped off earlier, before coming back for the minestrone that apparently he doesn't hate.

"And Luca?"

"Luca's drunk, not to mention enraged now, after this news. He told me that work was done on the villa some years back. The support structure running down the hill was about to cave in. Zio Marco came up with the funds."

"But there is no sign of these improvements in any of the books, nothing for contractors or materials."

"That's not how things are done here a lot of the time, Jamie. I told you this was a Mickey Mouse country. They hired Croatians, but the work was fifty thousand Euros, not five hundred thousand. *Ma che cazzo...*"

"And what about Zio Marco?"

Jack's head looks about to explode. It takes a moment for him to compose his words. "He says that La Mamma came to him for the money a long time ago. She was frantic, apparently." He glances at Jamie. "The *testa di cazzo* (shithead) said that La Mamma needed the money for me, that she borrowed the money against the villa for me! Zio Marco claims he thought I knew; 'after all,' he said, 'it is your vineyard.' I thought to myself, he's trying to pin this on me! I told him I had no idea about the lien, and then demanded to know where the money was. He continued to play innocent."

Jack goes dark here for a moment. "He had the gall to then suggest that I consult Giorgio, that maybe Giorgio knows where the money is. I demanded to know what he thinks my father has to do with this, but he just made some smug gesture."

The words came out strangled. "The bankruptcy, now this. It's like I'm cursed."

"Jack stop. You sound like your mother."

"Well?"

"We'll sue. That money's not his."

"It's my fault. I washed my hands of it all, and then even when I returned, I didn't pay attention."

"You trusted Zio Marco. There was no reason not to trust him."

"My father didn't trust him. That could have been a reason."

"What about your father Jack? You don't think…"

"Zio Marco is lying, Jamie. I know this in my gut."

There it is again—his gut. What about facts? "Call your father, Jack. Maybe he'll finally talk about what happened with the bankruptcy."

"I did. After I spoke to Zio Marco."

A moment of silence, for Jack has not spoken to his father in two years, since Lucrezia's funeral. She's almost afraid to ask. "And?"

"I told him about the lien, La Mamma signing as proxy, about Zio Marco accusing me, and making snide inferences about him."

"What did he say?"

"I shouldn't have called him. It was a mistake."

"Jack, what did your father say?"

"What he always says. Nothing. He refuses to defend himself or his actions."

"He must have said something."

He looks at her with darkened eyes. "He laughed. My father laughed. That's what he did. Then he said, '*te l'avevo detto*,' which is when I hung up.

"*Te l'avevo detto?*"

"I told you so."

Jamie starts rubbing her temples. Giorgio is making that gesture with his eye in her mind: watch out. "There's that apartment Zio Marco bought Simona and Michele."

"I know," he says, grabbing her arm. "Come on, let's go."

"Where? What are you going to do?"

He puts out his cigar. "Luca's looking for a baseball bat... and then he and I are going to have another conversation with Zio."

She looks at him, puzzled.

"Do you know what it's like to get hit in the kneecaps with a baseball bat?" His eyes are fixed on hers, ablaze.

She shakes her head no.

"It makes you want to fucking die."

CHAPTER 32

Gooooaallllll!

ACK IN NEW YORK, three months later, the alarm goes off at seven a.m. Jack switches it off, and Jamie rolls over and goes back to sleep.

"You can come if you want." Apparently time has passed, for he's now sitting on the bed beside her, dressed and ready to go.

"I thought you didn't want me to come."

He brushes the hair off her face. "You can come."

She'd only asked him a million times if she should go. He'd insisted a million times that it was just a swearing in ceremony and that she didn't need to go.

She examines his tie.

"*Fer-ra-ga-mo*," he says. Tiny green soccer balls are etched into the red silk. "In honor of the occasion." He speaks face-tiously about his U.S. Citizenship; it's a business transaction, certainly nothing to celebrate.

"I'm coming," she says, no longer believing him.

"Then hurry."

She hops out of bed. They've had so little to celebrate lately.

Jeans, UGGs, a gray sweater, water over her face, a brush to her teeth, no time to putter or think because he is at the door, waiting. Her coat and, on a whim, the digital, just before he pulls her into the elevator.

The N to Herald Square, maneuvering through rush hour, holding hands when possible, surfacing on 34th Street. Early January, the air is cool, crisp, and surprisingly mild; a bold sun and strong wind propel movement forward; even the cars look like they're hydroplaning, she and Jack along with them, their expectant mood a nice reprieve after spending the past three plus months slogging over the Ruffoli trust with bankers and lawyers. Records of the five hundred thousand Euros are nonexistent, and Jack refuses to pursue an expensive lawsuit against Zio Marco, who continues to insist that La Mamma came to him for the money for Jack. La Mamma has for the most part denied this, though she can't seem to remember what she signed when and for what, and it's impossible to have a logical conversation with her about it. Jack fired Zio Marco from the board of trustees and removed all his signing authority. He never got his knees bashed in, but the setters were mysteriously poisoned. He's not shown his face at Villa Ruffoli since.

She stops walking. How long before he notices?

Seconds. He stops and turns. "Sorry, I'll go slower."

All that rushing and they are practically the first ones there, the first of three thousand that is, and that's just for the eight a.m. ceremony. In fact, there will be four ceremonies held that day, and every Wednesday and Friday going on into eternity. A welcoming staffer greets them at the entrance and directs them down an escalator two floors and into a cavernous space of white marble and glass. A long line of registration tables await them; as of yet, no lines. Jack, in his serious face and serious suit, goes to his section and unfolds his paperwork before the man, who appears to be Indian, sitting there.

After a few minutes reviewing Jack's paperwork, the man begins checking off lists of boxes with a red pen on a form. Lines begin to form behind them and all around them as this goes on for a while, the din growing louder. Jamie peers over Jack's shoulder to see what is taking so long. She can't help feeling that something momentous is about to happen, but not this… She freezes, watching the man's pen pause on a box. Something has caught his attention. He refers back to Jack's paperwork and says, "I see you went to Switzerland a few months back."

Jack goes stiff.

Jamie says, "Switzerland?"

"Yes," Jack says, clearing his throat.

The man looks at Jack pointedly for the first time. "You didn't get a divorce while you were over there did you?"

A moment goes by. Jack seems stumped by the question.

"I hope not," Jamie blurts out, half joking, half alarmed.

"In fact, my wife is right here." Jack nudges Jamie in front of him. For the first time, it seems, he needs her help.

"I'm right here," she says, stepping in.

The man peers at Jamie, then Jack, then back at Jamie, unconvinced. The fact that he might doubt their marriage's authenticity for even a second hits Jamie somewhere dark and deep. She holds up her left hand now, to display the ring that even Jack had failed to notice her slip on that morning. She bears her eyes down on the man's. There will be no more uncertainty. She is unsure how much time passes before the man finally pulls his eyes from hers and checks the box. Giovanni is allowed to sign the form, and they are sent through security and into the main hall. Once through, they take a moment to share the same feeling, like they've entered a new dimension, and maybe they have.

"Switzerland?" she asks imploringly.

"Later," he says. "I'll tell you later."

A helper directs Giovanni through a series of entrance doors. Jamie lingers in the lobby for a while, before finally heading up to the balcony where family members are allowed to watch.

There is not much room in the balcony, already full with respectfully dressed people: wives, children, brothers, husbands, excited but weary, like they've moved heaven and earth to be here, and yet have still managed to dress properly, not to mention bring flowers and balloons. Jamie sits down on a carpeted step, undeserving of a seat. She's mocked this whole process to Jack, first him getting his green card, now his Citizenship: you're using us; we're all using each other; you don't deserve to be a citizen. But look at him now. She can already spot him in the crowd of three thousand, there in the front row because he'd made a point of getting here early. He has perfected the English language. He studies American history as if it were his duty. He gets pissed off when she doesn't vote. He dresses for occasions such as this one "out of respect." Jamie hadn't even worn a dress.

A wave of emotion rushes through her. She'll go to Philip and Jill for the money, that's what she'll do. The groveling involved will kill what's left of her, but never mind that, she will do this, for him.

Because he is more deserving than she is.

She snaps a shot of him sitting there; poised, stoic. It might be impossible for anyone but her to know what's going on inside him. He has worked hard to be the man he wants to be, not the man she or anyone else wants him to be.

The moment is thunderous, three thousand people coming to a stand, raising their right hands. Words are recited, repeated. She thinks she may even hear Jack's voice, if only in her mind. And then it is done. His hand is down. "Now it is your opportunity to appreciate what many people born here have taken for granted," the man at the podium says.

The wind has died. The sun feels warm on their backs, and they decide to walk home from the ceremony, for a while staying silent in their own thoughts. She keeps seeing all those people singing the Star Spangled Banner, and then herself struggling to remember the words, she confesses to him now, and that she'd found it hard not to cry.

For a moment she thinks he hasn't heard her. But then he hooks an arm around her neck and whispers into her ear, "I cried too."

The sun ricochets off a building; a flash of blinding white. Who are you? What is that glint in the dark of your eyes? For again, he has surprised her. She has surprised herself.

They walk on silently, her head resting on his shoulder, her emotion building, her thoughts gaining momentum. She could be this person, this person who borrows money from family, this person who asks for help… "I'm going to go to Philip and Jill for the money," she blurts out nervously. "I'll put up my two hundred, and we'll go to them for the rest."

"Jamie."

"It's okay Jack, I can do this."

He sighs. "What I mean is that I don't know anymore, Jamie."

"You don't know what?"

"Maybe the past is the past. Maybe those vines should be dead and buried, the villa sold, once and for all. Maybe it's what I should have done years ago."

She blinks into the sun, trying to process what he's saying.

"Italy's a disaster, Luca's always going to be a pain in the ass, Silvestro is never going to be reliable. And God forbid we get too much rain. We're always going to be just getting by. Is that how we want to live?"

"You can't give up!" She has stopped abruptly at the corner of some street. She doesn't know why she says this, and with such desperation. It would be easier to give up, as she had thought she would do back when she'd discovered the lien, when her first thought had been to call Chris or Donald and ask for her job back. Then she and Jack had returned to New York and she never made those calls. What she had told Jill in Virginia was right—there is no going back, and now it feels as if giving up the vines means giving up everything that they have been about since the beginning, their beginning. "What about Luca and his family?" She pauses. "And Silvestro—you would not have done so well at VinItaly if not for Silvestro. YOU told me that."

He's staring off now.

She's not getting through. "You're really going to let them all down? You're just going to quit?"

"Why do I have to be responsible for everyone?"

She knows where this is coming from. Zia Renata had called that morning on Skype. His father's depression is worse; he's been selling some of his possessions. She wants Jack to come to Napoli, but Jack refuses to come. He thinks his father is bluffing. He thinks there is nothing more to say after, "I told you so."

"Because you are the Chosen One," Jamie finally responds, but to no one, for The Chosen One has escaped into a magazine shop right there as if he already knew the answer to his own question. She follows him inside, where he goes straight to the back and grabs what he needs, what he always needs no matter what, *La Gazzetta Dello Sport*. He's at the counter paying when Jamie, behind him now, spots on the turnstile *Thompson's Wine Buyer's Guide*. She remembers the time, so long ago it seems now, back in San Francisco, when Jack had brought the guide home and then ripped it up and used it as kindling. But the name strikes a different chord now... She picks up one of the guides and searches the introductory pages. We just got the new editions in, the man tells her, as Jamie sees the first name, Peter, and puts the two together: *Peter Thompson*.

"He was there, Jack."

He eyes the guide in her hand.

"This guy, Peter Thompson. He came to the villa."

"When?" he asks, after some delay.

"You were in Alba and I was in the *cantina*, and suddenly, there he was. I showed him some wine."

"You?"

"No one else was around."

"Oh God, which ones?"

She tries to remember.

"Why didn't you tell me!?"

"I don't know," she gasps. "I thought he was just one of those American tourists you're always ragging on."

Jack strips the guide from her hand and begins flipping through it. "Sal kept asking me if Thompson had made a visit. I kept saying no."

"Sal got him to come?"

"Of course, Jamie, who else?"

"He didn't even taste the wine," Jamie recalls now, peering over Jack's shoulder. "He just looked at it and smelled it."

"*Cazzo!*"

The woman behind them is growing impatient.

"A 94," Jamie says, reading over his shoulder. "Is that good?"

"*Porcaccia la miseria!*"

"Jack…"

He buys a half a dozen guides and tells her that it's fucking fantastic.

Her whole body feels like it's smiling, though she's biting her lip so he won't notice. "You have no choice now," she says, as they lug home the guides, pretending they're not impossibly heavy. "The vineyard is a force of its own now. We can't stop it even if we wanted to."

He gets out his key and unlocks the lobby door.

What she doesn't tell him is that it's a sign. The vineyard must keep going, just like she and Giovanni must keep going, if for no other reason than she can't imagine it otherwise. It's like the more her life goes on, the more it becomes the life she is meant to live, not the life she had wanted to live. She thinks of Simona, marrying Michele from Torino. Maybe this will be true for Simona as well. Maybe this is true for every person. "I'll call Jill tomorrow."

"No," he says. "Don't call Jill." He gets on the phone and dials Sal. "I know where to get the money."

"You do?"

"It's the reason I was in Switzerland. Hans Friedrich. Sal contacted him as a favor, back when we discovered the lien. It was just an idea then. He's the heir to one of the world's largest chocolate and coffee distributors."

"And?"

"Hans is friends with Schumacher, Jamie," as if that should tell her everything. "Buddies with Alonso. He has his cigarettes custom made by Davidoff in Zurich."

"Get to the point."

"He's a collector of fine things, including vintage Barolo wine."

"I'm still not getting it."

"Three months ago, per Sal's instruction, I took two of Bisnonno's bottles across the border to Hans' chateau in Verbier. Unfortunately, Hans had already jet-setted off due to a sudden change of plans, so I left the wine with an assistant and didn't expect to hear back. Then, two weeks ago, Hans' assistant called and said that Hans was intrigued by the wine and wanted to make a visit. I stalled. I wasn't sure anymore."

"Sure about what?"

"Selling Bisnonno's wines."

"You're going to sell Bisnonno's wines!"

"That's what I said."

"After he risked his life to save them from the Germans?"

"You have any better ideas?"

CHAPTER 33

Coppa del Mondo

I T TAKES SAL SIX MONTHS to finally get Hans scheduled
to come to the Villa for a tasting. Meanwhile, they've
stopped all capital improvements and slowed down their sales
efforts for the coming year, which is almost impossible given
Thompson's 94 rating, which is how they've managed to stay
afloat; that plus an infusion of capital from Jamie's savings, what
was once going to be a downpayment on a home—equity, debt,
a write-off, security, their future… The cash will take them
through year-end, but at that point…

Jamie's thoughts get interrupted. The speedometer of the
rental car Jack's driving is edging up to 150 kilometers per hour.

"Did someone die?"

He's gripping the steering wheel with white knuckles. Jack
received a text from Luca when their plane landed at Malpensa,
and now Jamie's wondering if perhaps Luca's changed his

mind about selling Bisnonno's wines; or Hans Friedrich has changed his mind about the tasting. Jamie looks at Jack, then the speedometer again, afraid to ask.

It's not until they arrive at Villa Ruffoli that she gets her answer. Forget about the loan, the tasting, the pending bankruptcy, or preparing the *cantina* for the influx of visitors passing through ever since the Thompson rating. Forget that La Mamma's got that wedding dress out again, even though they'd pretty much canceled all plans of a ceremony until they knew what the villa's future would hold. Forget all that.

Everyone is crowded around the TV, watching Italy play Ghana in the World Cup: Caterina with her boyfriend, Luca, Silvestro, Zia Claudia, Giacomo, who is three now, and Antonia with the baby who is now officially the biggest baby Jamie's ever seen. They are all squeezed in on the tiny couch. Giovanni stares at the screen, instantly immersed. It's only after a minute passes that he can manage a glance at Jamie—stoic, pale, panicked—because it's almost the end of the first half and Italy hasn't scored. You can cut the tension in the room with a knife.

"This is the tragedy?"

His eyes are dead set on the action. "We can't lose to Ghana."

Ghana?

"It's impossible for Italy to lose to a second rate team like Ghana." This, at the same moment everyone jumps up and screams Gooooaaaalllllll!

A minute later they're still screaming Gooooaaaalllll!

Jack, a foot from the TV now, "Watch this Jamie!" The station is replaying Pirlo's goal frame by frame, backward and forward, from every angle.

"*Che bello,*" Jamie says, about Pirlo, and Antonia giggles.

"*Allora,* and now we must prepare the antipasti," Zia Claudia gets up and says. She and Antonia head toward the kitchen, "Always the antipasti. Always the people coming to see our Luca's beautiful vines." But Jamie doesn't hear them. She takes the vacant seat they have left, having watched enough soccer with Jack at this point to be, if not hooked, then intrigued, captivated, caught up in the raw emotion, his or hers, it's becoming hard to tell. The tension ensues until Italy scores again, Iaquinta this time, and then the game is over.

"Isn't there anything else we can do?" La Mamma pleads with Jack for the umpteenth time. "You can't sell Bisnonno's wine, Jack. I won't let you."

Jack, immersed in the post-game wrap up, says, "Fine, then. We will sell the villa and you can be out on the street."

La Mamma leaves the room with a big huff.

"Oh Jack," Jamie moans. "Can't you be..." she stops, for Jack won't hear anything anyone says until the show, some bizarre Italian variety show of post-game analysis, is over. Jamie goes to unpack, but then, purposefully or not, she takes a wrong turn down a wrong hall where she finds La Mamma at her altar, praying. Jamie watches her for a moment. When she starts tip toeing backward, La Mamma turns and grabs her hand, and soon Jamie is on her knees too. For Maurizio, for Giorgio, for Nonno, for Nonna, the Villa, for Jack... alas, they pray together. It is Giorgio in the picture; Jamie takes a peek and confirms, something she has been wanting to confirm, and which now makes her wonder if La Mamma knows something about Giorgio that Jack and Jamie don't.

Afterward, Jamie stumbles upstairs with a sadness crushing her chest, a feeling of deep loss for all the dead people she never knew in her family, not to mention those still alive. Perhaps that's why she's still here, unfathomably still here, when she'd always been so desperate to keep family at a distance. Could it be true that, in fact, she had never wanted them at a distance, only she didn't know how to have them close?

These are not my people, these are not my people—or so Jamie had convinced herself about her father's new family, and, unnerved by this thought, she bolts out of her room and out of the villa in search of a distraction. Cash flow statements. Work! And then she remembers that Caterina left some invoices for her to approve in the cellar office, which is where she finds herself now, trying to concentrate over the din of Jack, Silvestro, and Luca's incessant arguing. They are selecting wines for the tasting with Hans, their voices echoing all around her. At some point Jack sticks his head in, and motions for her to come see something.

She'd forgotten about the low ceilings and lack of air as she crawls through a fresh hole Luca has torn out of the wall. A maze of damp, musty passageways presents itself, where boards have been laid over the earth and temporary lighting strung. They had never before done an inventory of Bisnonno's wine beyond what was stored in the hidden vault Luca had shown them four years ago. This new, extended search (thanks to one of the original designs Godfather bestowed upon Jack back in Rome) led them farther and deeper inside the veins and vessels of the villa's underlying organs. Each time they found a new nook, it led them to another cranny. They even found a tunnel leading all the way up to the church. There'd been rumors of it, when Giovanni was a kid.

The bottles have been stacked into pyramids and organized by date and category, indicated by the labels posted on the brick wall. When Jack stops before the '54s, Jamie almost topples over Silvestro, who has bumped into Jack. "*Cazzo.*"

"*Calma.*"

"These are the reserves," Giovanni says. "Eight cases."

Jamie's chest tightens.

He has stopped before another pyramid.

No, literally, she is claustrophobic.

"The '42s," he says. "Twelve cases."

"How many altogether?"

"Two hundred and thirteen."

"Cases?"

Silence.

"Jesus."

Luca has a bottle to his ear now, listening.

"Don't screw around, Luca," Jack says. "Pick those you think have the least chance of being rotten."

Luca sets the bottle down, picks up another one.

"Luca's going to do something stupid," Silvestro assures Jamie.

"Luca understands what's at stake," Giovanni says.

"I am right here," Luca says. "Luca will tell you what Luca understands. If Luca must choose between Bisnonno's wines and his vines, then the choice is no choice at all."

Jamie needs air. Seriously.

"But you've got to see this, Jamie," Jack says, about the magnums with the hand drawn labels; Nonno Giacomo's work as a boy, apparently.

"I'll take your word for it." She manages to find her way back to the opening, crawls out, up the stairs and out the door, gasping, into a thicket of hydrangeas and blinding light.

"I am so glad that we are finally alone!"

She spins around.

It's Silvestro, lighting a cigarette. He'd followed her out. He takes a long, shaky drag. "Jamie," he exhales. "I must tell you what I have not told anyone." His smile is full of mischief, the kind he seems to reserve only for her. "Today I will drive to Santa Margherita to see the Principessa where she has been staying with her parents by the sea. I must convince her to marry me, Jamie."

She squints through the smoke, pretends to make out something in the distance, for she does not want to see his eyes. She does not need to see his eyes. She knows that he is serious.

"Now, you may say, 'but Silvestro, why so soon?' This will be the way of my parents, but I say to myself, look at my friend Jamie and my cousin, the Chosen One, married after only three months."

"Well yes, but…"

"I see this with my very eyes."

She goes quiet. She really does not know what to say anymore, about love.

"And you might say that, perhaps, now is not the best time." He is referring to the villa's dogged situation, she assumes. "But I must go now, today, because she will soon be leaving for Spain with her family for one month."

He lights Jamie's cigarette with his.

"You must go then," she says, and, just like that, he drops his cigarette and leaves. She watches him go, left to smoke alone in his absence, boding him a silent, "*buona fortuna,*" because he will need luck. More often she thinks that being lucky is much of what she and Giovanni are, not because they have found each other, or loved each other, but to be so continually surprised by each other the way they are.

Four o'clock. They are expecting Hans Friedrich at seven. Sal too, though he will arrive separately, coming from a tasting in the Veneto. No matter about that, more importantly, Brazil is playing Croatia in the World Cup, and the men are convened around the TV even though they pretend not to care about Brazil. The Brazilians are lazy and arrogant, they say, riveted by their play.

Zia Claudia is preparing a platter of cheese, Antonia the *agnolotti;* Jamie can't pull herself away from the game, and La Mamma is nowhere to be found. Jack had told her to make herself scarce for the tasting, fearing that she might fall into a blubbering fit. No one has heard from Silvestro, who is still in Santa Margherita but has promised to be back in plenty of time. It is only five, after all, which is when the buzzer to the front gate goes off. *Turisti americani, merde,* Giovanni says, and neither he nor Luca budge from their positions on the couch. Jamie knows what that means. It means who dares visit the villa during a World Cup match but an American?

Or a Swiss. It's Hans Friedrich, and he's early. "*E 'sti svizzeri, sempre in anticipo.*"

Giovanni and Jamie hurry outside to greet the Mercedes, Luca to the cellar to retrieve the wines. An unsmiling, imposing driver opens the car door and out slides Hans, presumably, in a tieless, elegant suit. He is accompanied by a gorgeous brunette, French, his designer, immediately charmed, gazing around as if taking measurements in her head. She should be charmed. It's been a mild June with enough rain, and the cypress are still green and luscious, the roses flush, the thyme pungent.

"We were hoping Croatia would pull an upset," Jack starts the conversation as they head into the *cantina.* "Against Brazil," he adds.

"*Ah si, il Mondiale.*" Hans says, and then, with a touch of arrogance, that he doesn't follow the World Cup.

"But you do follow Formula One," Jack counters.

"Intimately," Hans says, pulling two cigarettes from a gold case, one for him, one for the beauty.

Jack shows them to seats at the long wood table with the mismatched chairs. "I thought Alonso was unstoppable last weekend at Silverstone."

After a drag, "He told me he can't lose this year. Renault is too well organized, and Schumacher's head is already in retirement."

Luca appears with a magnum in each hand.

Jamie wonders why the wine has not been decanted. Luca explains, while opening the bottles and reading her mind, that to appreciate a wine you must take in its first breath, and then each breath thereafter until you've reached the *scolatura*, the last drop.

"The wine will grow and change and one must be committed," the brunette agrees, taking a piece of cheese from the platter Zia Claudia has just set before them.

Luca continues. "Bisnonno always insisted that wine was a living being, that you can't separate it from its surrounding natural elements."

Hans sits back, breathing out smoke.

"Bisnonno was an early adopter of biodynamism," Jack adds. His eyes drift momentarily to Hans' enormous watch. Then he goes on to explain about his great-grandfather's obsession with wine. The brunette seems intrigued, though with Hans it's still hard to tell, especially for Jamie, because now, along with Italian and English, which they all seem to speak fluently, French has been added to the mix, and Jamie is officially lost. She must prepare for a long night, she reminds herself, when Luca pours the '51, swirls, smells, but does not taste. It will be another twenty minutes before he tastes. Only then will it be appropriate for everyone else to taste. When that finally happens still no one speaks; rather, they contemplate. It is too early to speak.

"I'm surprised at all the life left in it," Jack offers about the wine a good forty-five minutes later.

"There's richness and sensuality in the fruit, but it's measured by a mineral acidity," the brunette says, gazing into her glass.

Luca opens the '45, continuing the cycle of letting the wine breathe, tasting it, letting it breathe again.

Two hours later, Jamie is getting sleepy, not to mention hungry. Zia Claudia brings out the *agnolotti* and everyone gets lively again, especially and suddenly Hans, who admits that his mother was part Italian, his first show of animation. She too used to make *agnolotti*, but with rabbit instead of pork, he says, taking a delicate bite and then setting his fork down. They are due for a late supper in Milan. A helicopter is standing by in Cuneo, but before they go the beauty is insisting on a tour. Jack nods at Jamie, who's thinking *why me?*

"We've got lots of plans," Jamie explains as she takes the beauty to see the fermentation tanks, then the cellar where she shows her the villa's original designs, now framed and hung, and then back outside to the lookout point. The sun has just fallen, the sky is ribbons of orange. Soon the valley will be shades of purple. It is rather gorgeous, Jamie agrees, as they take in the view.

"I'd love to see the villa."

Jamie hesitates, she's not sure why, but the woman persists and so Jamie leads her back up the gravel path and through the crooked archway entrance. At the end of the long, vaulted corridor the woman stops, as everyone does, before Nonno Giacomo's watercolors. "They are quite exquisite," she informs Jamie. And then La Mamma is suddenly there, out of nowhere, in all her pride and jewels, carrying a tray of hand baked *amaretti*.

She directs the woman into the living room, a room Jamie has barely entered but once, briefly. Today La Mamma has taken the sheets off the furniture, dusted, put out fresh flowers, perhaps even rearranged the dark paintings on the wall. To the beauty goes the high backed chair while La Mamma assumes it's child sized duplicate next to her. Jamie sits across from them on the tapestry couch. The *amaretti* are her grandmother's recipe, she tells the beauty, who reaches out and takes one. La Mamma pours the woman a glass of Luca's anise liquor and begins to explain about the paintings in the room, those that go back to the eighteen hundreds, the ones Jamie had thought morbid, families foraging through dark and dreary landscapes. She'd never actually looked up at the ceiling before, which she does now as La Mamma indicates the fresco painted there, where plump, naked babies with angel's wings are flying around in a sky of water-stained blue, white puffy clouds, flowers in their hair, reaching out for each other, as if each other were all they had.

The woman looks stunned.

Jamie is stunned, then startled, at La Mamma's sudden declaration, "I was born in this house!" And oh, how her childhood was bursting of fruit and life, never less than twenty people at their dinner table. She goes on about the cooks and the maids and the farmers and the chickens, how she and her friend Marco would steal away into the orchards and eat berries until they were sick. This is where her children were born, where poor Maurizio died and left his ghost to roam the empty rooms. Her story goes on, only now it is Jack's story, soon to be someone else's story, and tears float in La Mamma's eyes at the thought of this house living on without her. She will die in this house, and only now does Jamie understand why Jack had so illogically refused to buy that apartment in the East Village with the tall windows and eastern sun, the one that Jamie had said could be an "investment," or, their "starter house." In Italy there is no such thing as a starter house. There's the house you are born in, the one your children are born in, the one you die in.

In America, you have as many houses as it takes you to get it right.

In America there are two words, house and home. They can hold different meanings. In Italy, there is only one word. *Casa*.

And now Jamie's lost the thread of the conversation. She tries to regain it, but can't seem to. There is mist in the beauty's eyes as she, too, goes on now, in Italian, about her own *casa*. Apparently she grew up in a house like this in France, but an older cousin inherited it a few years ago and the beauty is very sad because she can go very seldom now, and when she does go she feels like an intruder in her own home! La Mamma's got the woman's hand in hers now, and Jamie has the idea that it's time to get the beauty out of here before La Mamma leads her over to the shrine for a prayer session. She is about to say something, but is just then distracted by someone waving at her through the window. She excuses herself and goes outside where she finds Silvestro, out of breath, trembling with the most amazing news. He has asked the Principessa to marry him, and she has said yes!

"Your tie is crooked," Jamie says. "And Giovanni's going to crucify you for being late." It's all she can manage because she can't believe that this girl has said yes.

"But Jamie, you must tell me what you think of my news." He says this while gazing curiously at the brunette sitting in the parlor with La Mamma.

Jamie waits for his eyes to settle back on hers, and then stares deep into them. "I think this girl is very lucky."

"This is what I think! You and I, we think alike."

Jamie laughs. One cannot help but laugh. Otherwise one will be worried out of their minds.

"Ah, but I am so happy!" he says, bounding down the hill like a gazelle while Jamie stands there watching him, in a fog of wine and illogical endings.

The Mercedes peals off an hour later. The gravel hasn't even settled, and Jack and Luca are already back at the villa, arguing. "Forget whether or not Hans liked the wine, he showed no passion for food!" Luca cries, pinching his fingers together before his own chin.

"Not to mention football." Jack mocks a Hans' expression, "A mere peasant sport."

"How can you sell him one single bottle?!"

Jack shakes his head, unsure. "*Svizzeri di merda.*"

Silvestro, who has been trying to keep the peace and, of course, that starry eyed look off his face, now puts his hands together, "*e' cosi'*, Giovanni. It's the way it is, we have no choice."

"Bisnonno would turn over in his grave at the thought of his wine in the hands of a Swiss," Luca says bitterly.

"What's wrong with the Swiss?" Jamie needs to know, and Jack fixes his eyes on hers, piercingly and to make no mistake. "In their entire history they've contributed one thing to the world, Jamie. Do you know what that is?"

She does not.

"The cuckoo clock." His eyes darken but do not flinch. "In Italy, Jamie, for thirty years under the Borgias they had warfare, terror, murder and bloodshed, but they produced Michelangelo, Leonardo da Vinci and the Renaissance. In Switzerland, they had brotherly love and five hundred years of democracy and peace, and what did that produce?"

"The cuckoo clock," she says, dull with the recognition of Orson Welles in the *Third Man*, that movie he'd made her watch for the sole purpose, no doubt, of making this point.

Sal comes running through the door just then. "Am I late? Where are they? Has Hans arrived?"

"You are early," Luca says, "and they have already left."

"*E 'sti Svizzeri, sempre in anticipo.*"

"See," Jack looks at Jamie. "It's not just me. Everybody says that about the Swiss."

"Did he like the wine?" Sal wants to know.

"*Boh,*" is their communal response. It means they have no idea. With the Swiss it is hard to tell.

He said he would call.

He does call, the next day, Sal reports from somewhere in the Abruzzi, after Jamie and Silvestro have managed to convince Luca and Jack that now is not the time to hold grudges or prejudices. "He doesn't want the cases."

Jamie and Jack are in the office. Jack's got Sal on speaker. "He wants the whole estate."

They're confused.

"The vineyard, the villa, everything."

"Seriously?"

He wouldn't kid about something like that.

"Oh my God," Jamie says, after Sal's words catch up with her.

"He won't buy the cases on their own?" Jack wants to know.

"All or nothing."

"The beauty," Jamie mumbles. "I knew I shouldn't have left her alone with La Mamma."

Jack sits back and sighs, vigorously rubbing his eyes. Then he looks at Jamie, who nods in agreement.

"Tell him to go fuck himself," he says.

CHAPTER 34

Gli Azzurri

J AMIE AND GIOVANNI are lying in bed, listening to the church bells go off every thirty minutes. The heat feels like it's beating off the roof as they contemplate Italy facing Ukraine in the Quarterfinals in a few days. Certainly Italy will beat Ukraine, and yet Giovanni must consider all the reasons why they might not. He said that about the Czechs, and then Italy won 2-0. He said that about the Australians in the round of 16, and then Italy beat them 1-0. Every Italian she's met assures her that Italy will lose the next match, and then they win. They keep winning, and now they win again. Italy beats Ukraine 3-0, and Sal calls to say that he's looking for another buyer, and that he'll do what he can but he needs to get back to Hans with an answer. Sal had talked Jack out of telling Hans to go fuck himself, and instead told Hans that

377

Jack would think about his offer, considering that come year-end they may not have a choice.

Meanwhile, Jamie has been drafting a deal with Philip and Jill. Her sister's interest had at first been cool, not to mention guarded, when Jamie approached her about the loan, until she'd mentioned Thompson's 94, and then Jill's ears had perked. She hung up and called Jamie back after talking to Philip. "Show me the numbers for an investment, not a loan," she'd said, "then we'll talk."

Thompson, Jamie is shaking her head, what's not to love about him? She is joking to Jack, trying to lighten his mood in order to get his input on the equity numbers she's since sketched out, but once again he has looked past her, confused and pale, as if he's just seen a ghost. "Oh God, not the Germans."

She spins around at the TV. The game ended minutes ago—Germany destroying Argentina in the Quarterfinals.

"Never underestimate the Germans."

Everyone had predicted Argentina to win, everyone except Jack. Now Italy will face Germany in the Semis and Jack looks seriously concerned. Germany must not win, Jack insists. They don't deserve to win!

Why?

His face is on fire. Because they stole the World Cup in '54, Jamie! And don't let anyone tell you they didn't take the Cup away from us in '90. They simply must, not, win.

"About these equity numbers, Jack…"

"The problem," Giovanni continues, not hearing her, "is that we're playing in Dortmund, and Germany has never lost a game in Dortmund." He grows despondent by this fact, or perhaps some realization has at last sunk in about this deal with Philip and Jill, what it would mean, becoming a minority stakeholder. She's about to bring it up again, but he interrupts her with this one last bastion of hope...

"Don't forget, Jamie, Italy has never lost to Germany in a World Cup game." As if this was a fact she had once known.

Two days later, the fateful game with Germany about to begin, Jamie is down in the cellar reworking the numbers yet again, when Caterina hurries in holding out a cell phone for Jamie to take. It's their new banker from Milan; he had asked for Jack but Jamie will do. After all, she has full authority on all accounts. When Jack restructured the trust and removed Zio Marco, he'd added her as a co-signer on everything. "You're my wife," is all he had said. She'd blinked back at him sitting there not looking at her, remembering a time long ago when she had insisted with so much pride that she would never want his money, or need it. *Everything that once was, seems to be melting into what is,* she thinks, after hanging up with the banker entirely dumbfounded and confused. She's unsure how long she sits there like that, until Caterina informs her that the game is about to start.

At the villa she finds Jack in his game position, seated on the edge of the couch, rocking back and forth, pensive, jaw grindingly silent. Silvestro is chain smoking next to him. Luca is pacing around, yelling at the players even though the game hasn't started. The women are moving about nervously indifferent in the background.

Jamie stands between Jack and the screen.

"You might want to move," he says.

"That was the bank," she says.

The whistle blows behind her.

"There's been a wire transfer of five hundred thousand Euros into the account, Jack."

He waves frantically at her to step aside. She does, saying, "It's from the Bank of Napoli, Jack. And there's only one person we know who lives in Napoli."

Luca groans at a bad pass.

No one has their English turned on apparently, what happens when they watch football. Even Jack, she doesn't think, understood what she has just said.

"Vuol dire che il matrimonio si fa?"

Jamie spins around. La Mamma is standing in the corridor, asking Jamie if this means that the wedding is back on, when there is no way in hell she could have understood what Jamie said.

"Zia Claudia just called me with the news!"

Ah, but of course. Jamie shoots Caterina an evil stare, for she had explicitly told the girl not to say a word to anyone until Jamie had had a chance to discuss it with Jack.

"At last, Papá is returning," La Mamma assures them, which sends Jack into a prayer waving fit. *"Lascia mamma dai, lascia.* I beg you, please, I'm watching the game, *ma dai…"*

La Mamma clamps her mouth shut, resigns herself to a chair, hands wringing, prepared to wait. Jamie does the same in another chair, deciding to lose herself in the match because it's easier than trying to figure out what force of nature—Giorgio, presumably it's Giorgio—propelled money into their account, and then why; she must force herself not to contemplate why, to not let old rumors and suspicions get the better of her.

One hundred and eighteen excruciating minutes later, Italy at last scores—not one, but two goals to beat Germany and win the match. Jack and Silvestro yell for a good ten minutes out the window to everyone in the whole world, who is also yelling. La Mamma is looking at Jamie like she is crazy, which she possibly is, having stepped out of herself in this moment to see that her body has joined Luca on his knees before the TV, arms in the air, both of them screaming at the top of their lungs.

She's unsure whether she'll ever recover from seeing herself like that.

Upstairs with Giovanni now, she is watching him lay his clothes out on the bed, silently, intently. "That's a lot of money, Jack."

"I know, Jamie."

"You realize it's the same amount as the lien."

"I realize that, Jamie."

"You don't think he…"

"Let's not make assumptions, Jamie."

"But you've always said the pharmacy was struggling, Jack. Maybe he needed the money."

"The pharmacy was never struggling, Jamie. Have you not learned anything? My father made a shitload of money selling those black market contraceptives."

"What about a different motive?" She pauses to think. "Your father got your mother pregnant. And if he hadn't, let's say, for instance, if they had had ready access to birth control, he might not have had to marry your mother and could have been with the woman he loved. He and Lucrezia were looking out for other couples."

"So you're saying my father stole to be altruistic?"

"Yes. This is what I'm saying."

He laughs. "Have you completely lost your mind?"

"Probably."

"And when did you become such a romantic?"

"Do you really need to ask that question?"

He gives her a sidelong glance. "I've said it before and I'll say it again, Jamie. My father was in that business purely for the money. And that's what he did: make money." He marches over to his dresser drawer. "But while he's selfish, he's no criminal." He grabs some underwear and socks and brings them back to the bed, looking up at her, briefly. "And you need to understand something about my father's motives, Jamie." He shoves some t-shirts into a canvas bag.

"When Nonno first found out about my father and Lucrezia, he kicked my father out of the house. Papá went north to Torino, as far away as he possibly could, but it wasn't far enough, apparently. My mother, her money, their vows, the church, forget all of that—my father didn't stay with us for any of that. He stayed with us because Nonno wouldn't let him return. He couldn't stand for their relationship. He never could, and Lucrezia loved Nonno too much to defy him. Twenty years later when Nonno finally died was the day my father became free. Two days later he was gone from Alba forever. It didn't take a genius to figure out where he went."

"Oh come on Jack, you don't think he stayed for you? His only son? I've seen the way he looks at you, with such pride and devotion in those dark, brooding eyes of his. I can feel it like the blood running through my veins, there's something deep and unspoken between the two of you." She looks down, feeling it even now. "I used to have that with my father," she says. "Then he left." What had always been an abstract thought is now closing in on her. "I told him to go. Be happy, I said. I couldn't bear to see him suffer. And yet the thing is, Jack, he suffered anyway. I told him that I would be okay if he left. That nothing would ever come between us. But I was never okay. And now everything is between us."

He fumbles with a dress shirt; the rest of him is still.

"At least you never walked away from your father, Jack." She takes the shirt from his hands. "Look at you; even now, after everything, you defend him." She begins to fold the shirt, carefully, in that particular way he likes it folded. And for a while it is like that, the heat of his gaze upon her.

"I don't know, Jamie," he says at last. "I guess deep down I've always felt…" He hesitates. Their eyes meet. "I've always felt that something wasn't right."

Silence consumes them. A long, pensive quiet.

"Jack," she says finally, softly. "We need to know where this money came from."

He comes to life again, tosses her a shoulder bag. "Why do you think I'm packing?"

She hadn't realized he'd been packing.

"You might want to start packing too."

She doesn't ask where they are going. She knows where they are going.

The door bursts open, as if La Mamma knows too, and will hear nothing of it. Giovanni must bring the space heater up to the attic because Papá must not be cold when he returns, and Papá is always cold in the north. She goes on now about what chores must be done and what things they will need to purchase, not to mention the preparations for the church wedding, which, with Giorgio's return, will be an even bigger celebration…

Jack goes over and positions himself squarely in front of her, facing her directly for what might be the first time since Jamie has known him. "Papá is never coming back, Mamma. You must listen to me and understand this."

The words, a lifetime's worth, hang heavy in the air.

Her head starts trembling. "But this is not true, Giovanni, why must you say this!?"

He grasps onto her shoulders. "It is true, Mamma."

She is shaking violently now. "Maurizio would never have been so cruel." And then all at once, she crumbles into his arms.

For a moment, Jack looks stunned. Then slowly, softly, he lays her head on his chest and begins to soothe her with a stirring tenderness, an unspeakable love. They've been through so much together. There are things about him that only she will ever know. He lets her hold him for as long as she needs to—minutes, hours, a lifetime—until her pride returns and at last she releases him. She gets out her lace handkerchief and blows her nose into it. Then she turns, soberly, and insists to Jamie that Maurizio was always so happy a child, always smiling and giggling and so different from Giovanni, always brooding and frowning and worrying. Her eyes smile at the memories. Then she turns back to Giovanni, and with the light of the world in her eyes, she reaches up and touches his face.

CHAPTER 35
Land of Dead Souls

*T*HE EIGHT HOUR TRAIN RIDE is like a gift, a repose in which Jamie gazes out the window and Giovanni scours the four newspapers he bought at the station kiosk. Devouring every last scrap of analysis about the sports and politics of his homeland has always been his way of detaching himself from whatever particular drama surrounds them, that last scene with his mother, for instance, in tears once again as they left, warning them of all the dangers they will face in the south.

They pass through Genova, then along the Riviera, where she sees signs for Bogliasco, Recco… When they pass by Santa Margherita, a smile comes to her eyes. It's where Silvestro proposed to Isabella, and Jamie's mind gets lost inside a castle perched high above the cliffs. She wanders through its maze of medieval walls, through its tall rooms and velvet chambers, where, in one of them, she stumbles upon a golden haired princess leaning out her bedroom window. She is calling down to her forbidden lover who stands on one knee with the sea thrashing behind him.

"Do you think it's really possible?" It's the first time Jamie has spoken since their train departed.

It's the first time Jack has lowered his *Gazzetta*.

"Can love really conquer all?"

"Of course not," might have been the right answer five years ago. But now, neither of them speaks, and the question lingers.

Hours later the question still lingers, as they watch the rocky cliffs flatten along the Tuscan seaside. It lies down with them while they sleep, and wakes with them hours later as they tunnel through luscious mountains. Emerging upon verdant, green hills, Jack points toward some invisible coast and murmurs, "Sperlonga," what has long ceased being a real destination and become a symbol of something else, something enduring and unattainable. Eternal. The color of shimmering rose. Ancient ruins emblazoned on the mind—Piazza Navona, Villa Miani, and then the Pantheon, where they'd gotten into that fight.

"Remember when we got into that awful fight?"

He looks at her. "What fight?"

At last, they reach Campania. Napoli sprawls into view, and Jack admits that he's only been to his father's apartment there once, on a visit in his late twenties. All those summers he spent in Vico Equense with Nonno, the city was just a twenty minute drive away, but he'd never gone. He didn't want to be part of his father's life there…or it wasn't an option for him to be. He doesn't remember exactly why now. Gray shimmers, the sea, they are getting close and she is getting nervous. The last time she saw Jack's father he was giving her that gesture with the eye, "watch out."

She'd not heeded his advice. In fact, she'd done the opposite. She'd quit her job. She'd become dependent, entangled,
involved. She'd become blind like all the rest of them.

And what will Giorgio think of her now?

A cab from the station in the gritty and overwhelmingly
tourist-packed Piazza Garibaldi drives them to some address
Jack has in his Blackberry. Somewhere in the Toledo, a tiny,
dilapidated square where all the apartments are stacked on
top of each other. They ring the buzzer of Giorgio's flat, but
nobody answers. They ring his cousin Maria's flat, but no one
answers there either. Jack inquires with a nearby *sfogliatelle*
vendor who tells them that Giorgio has sold his apartment and
moved away. Jack, whose eyes have fixated for some reason on
the man's hat, goes still with this news.

Blocks later, he stops and stares off, perplexed. He scans
the map on his Blackberry again. They find the pharmacy on
Via Toledo, a busy, traffic jammed thoroughfare that they risk
death trying to cross. The manager tells them that his father
bought Giorgio out two months ago. Jack does not spend time
probing the man; in fact, he doesn't seem terribly surprised or
stunned by this news, only numb.

They exit the store and find the nearest café so Jamie can
use the restroom. When she is done she finds Jack at an outside
table, slunk into a chair before bottled water and coffees. They
sit and drink, speechless, blinking into the glare of the missing
sun. Vesuvius sits in the background, eternal and imposing.
Black soot shrouds the air from the scooters zooming all around
them. As if the day weren't already gray and muggy enough.

"The hat that man was wearing," he says finally, with dead
eyes. "It was Nonno Carlo's beret."

Which man? Which hat?

Minutes pass.

"Giovanni."

He looks at her, startled.

"Are you're telling me that your father sold everything he owns, sent you the money, gave away Nonno Carlo's hat, and left?"

There is no emotion on his face whatsoever.

A ball hits the statue of Dante. Adjacent to them is his piazza, where a group of teenagers is playing soccer around his looming figure; ominous, and yet forgotten even by the elders who sit on benches surrounding it, cigarettes dangling absently from their mouths.

"He could never face me."

"I'm sorry, Jack."

"If he'd been open about Lucrezia, made sense of it to me in some way. If we'd talked about anything openly in my family for that matter, about Maurizio, Mamma's depression, Nonno…"

Jamie sits back.

They fall quiet for a time.

"Who is Dante, anyway?" she says finally.

He wakes from his spell to stare at her, incredulous.

"Well, of course I've heard of him, I'm just not sure of his exact contribution."

"Uh, let's see. To brutally simplify it, he is the Father of the Italian language."

"One might never know it with all the graffiti and pigeon shit all over him."

Jack gets out his cell and calls Zio Silvio, who is immediately disparaged by the fact that Jack had not called to tell him that he was coming to Napoli, for he would have met them at the station, as one does. Jack hadn't wanted to call anyone before coming; he wanted to face his father alone. Only his father is not here, and Jack's first assumption is that he's moved in with Zia Renata in Vico Equense as they all had wanted him to after Lucrezia's death. But Giorgio is not in Vico Equense, Zio informs Jack now, who goes cold with this news. There is a long silence on his end, and then he hangs up.

Caffe' Gambrinus, where Jamie and Jack have moved to now, is bustling and lively. On the corner of the pedestrian drenched Via Toledo, just off the incongruously empty Piazza del Plebiscito, is where thirty minutes later Zio Silvio pulls up on his Ducati, which he parks right there in the pedestrian clogged street. In a moment he's at their table, decked in heavy leather, sweating. Papá has gone to live in Puglia, he tells them, sitting down and lighting a cigarette.

Where the hell is Puglia, she doesn't ask.

Silvio orders them grappa. Jack drinks his in one gulp.

"He didn't want you to know until it was done."

"What's done?" Jamie asks.

"He doesn't want to be a burden. He wants to be in peace."

"Zia Renata must be out of her mind."

"She does not know yet. I was waiting for you to come."

Jack and Zio continue on in Italian while Jamie lets her gaze wander across the street, where a group of teenagers straddle Vespas in front of a store with a sign that says, "The World's Best Pizza." Her mind drifts back to Rome, remembering how she and Jack had searched and searched for such a place. She can't zone out for long though. Jack and Zio Silvio's words keep jarring her back to the reality of this moment. Whether she wants to or not, she is understanding what they are saying, and it's odd to think that there was a time when she hadn't wanted to understand, preferred not to because it was easier that way. A part of her wishes she could go back to that time now, but knows that it is far too late.

Zio Silvio is telling Giovanni that it was better for Giorgio to sell the pharmacy and move away. Jack must take the money and not worry about Giorgio. Giorgio will be well in Puglia. It will be better for Giorgio to live in this way. There is more to understand, presumably, but Jamie is left to read only Jack's expression as it morphs from frustration to anger to pity to some kind of vacant emptiness, especially after Zio Silvio confirms that his father got rid of most of his possessions, including that painting by Palizzi that Jack had admired ever since he was a boy. Not to mention that precious hat, and Jamie has a sudden vision of herself scouring through all the vendors on the Via Toledo in order to retrieve it.

Three espressos and many cigarettes later, Zio Silvio hands Jack a tiny key. Jamie recognizes it as the same one Jack has back home, what opens his father's safety deposit box. Jack explains to her now that he'd gone to Napoli some years back at the request of his father, who took Giovanni to his bank and had him sign for joint access to the box, in case something ever happened to him. Now Zio is telling Jack that the last of his father's things is in that box, things he no longer needs and wants Jack to have.

"But how will he survive?" Jamie wants to know. It's finally sinking in that Jack had been right all along to trust his father, irrespective of how angry he was at him. He never took any money. Giorgio's only crime was love, something Jack knew all along.

"Ah, but do not worry about Giorgio, he who has saved every penny under his mattress since he was three years old. He has enough for himself. Remember, Jamie, what we have said about Giorgio, that he only pretends to be miserable to hide how guilty he feels." A wink, a hug, those double-cheek kisses, and then Zio Silvio zooms off on his Ducati, into a sea of human flesh.

Jamie sits there, stunned.

Jack is still staring at the key in his hand. If he had anticipated anything, money aside, this was not it—to be abandoned
by his father, once again.

At last his gaze leaves the key and stretches far off into
Piazza del Plebiscito—massive, gray, overlooked, unnoticed.
"This is where all the city's grandest festivities used to take place,"
Jack informs her in the dullest, direst of tones. She lets her gaze
settle on it. More pigeon shit, more graffiti, the bay is a moody
shimmer on its left. Drawn, they go and stand like tiny statues
in its nexus, before the colossal semicircular façade of the church
of San Francesco di Paola, which they stare at for a time.

She looks around, as if something is missing. "Where is
everybody?"

He thinks for a moment, then tells her: Rome.

Florence, he says next.

Venice.

The church looks closed, its massive entrance doors hacked
and vandalized, though a tiny side door has been propped open
with a plastic chair. The interior is rich with marble, but the
feeling is cool and funereal, out of harmony with the blood
that Jamie feels surging through her body. Perhaps it's this city
of sirens, or the Kings staring down at her from every direction, but she feels a force alive beyond her, and she can't help
believing that it's those vines. Deeper and deeper they stretch
and sprawl, across worlds and beneath oceans, awakening the
long lost origins of even the deadest souls.

In one of the vestibules, Jack presses a button and a fake
candle lights up. Jamie slips a Euro into the slot—an offering.
She wonders if it's enough.

They decide to walk to the Bank of Napoli. Along the *lungo-
mare,* through narrow alleys, they catch glimpses of generations

of families living cramped in one room. They tunnel through more alleys and streets that turn out to be stairs, down or up, and if they go up they usually keep going up, unfathomably, endlessly, past living room doors and gardens locked behind spiked iron gates, people talking behind windows, silverware clinking, and then up yet again, until the bay of Naples is on their horizon, sparkling in the purple light of dusk. Back down again, he consults the map. They argue about where they are. *How did we manage to get lost in the mafia district?!* Unsmiling men with bandaged appendages and patched eyes play cards in garage-like shops. Jamie and Jack breeze by, nonchalant, unhurried, and utterly unnoticed amongst these Neapolitans, so self-absorbed are they in their Neapolitan lives.

It's as if Jamie and Giovanni don't exist here, and yet here is where they are, in the world they've created. And what a strange and beautiful world it is—the thought hits her with full force while standing in Piazza Matteotti, where Jack has been staring too long at the Fascist-era buildings before them now, as stark and foreboding as the look on his face. They seem misplaced, and suddenly her feet feel like they're exploding through her sandals, the straps cutting at her ankles, every muscle pounding. I'm not crying, she insists, as tears pour down her cheeks. He takes her hand and finds a bench and deposits her there, tells her that it will be okay. Then he orders her not to talk to anyone, go anywhere, or do anything because it is not safe. She watches him enter the building across the street, thinking, and perhaps this was the reason for her tears, *I've never felt so safe.*

Still across from the Bank of Napoli, thirty minutes later Jamie watches Jack stride back out while glancing over his shoulder, a bag tucked tightly under his arm. He comes and sits beside her on the bench and for a while they are quiet.

They consider taking the train back.

No, he is not ready to leave.

Neither is she.

They check into a hotel with bread, wine, mozzarella, and salami that they purchased from a stumbled-upon butcher in some piazza left for dead. Jack proceeds to dump the contents of that safety deposit box out from the bag onto the sagging bed. Jamie is at the window, trying to see what all the commotion is about—but there is no specific commotion, just usual life on this narrow, ascending street that no car could ever fit through, and yet one has done just that, at alarming speed.

At last, her room with a view.

She gets the plastic water cups. Jack pours.

She breathes in.

He breathes out.

For a time they stay like that, taking turns breathing, until slowly Jack begins to sift through the contents: tiny fascist-era trinkets and pins, gold coins, legal documents, velvet pouches— though she soon gets the feeling that it's none of these items he's after. It's the pictures he's after; black and white and faded. She picks up one of a young man in a dark uniform. Jack ponders it, stone faced. "Captured Italians had few options," is all he says, and she sets the picture down.

He sifts through more photos, as if he's searching for something, and then his hand freezes. For a while he just sits there, staring at what he sees in the picture beneath his fingers, though he won't pick it up. His eyes haven't blinked, and now Jamie is afraid to look.

After a while, though, it becomes apparent that he's waiting for her to look. To pick up the picture for him and she does. A young woman standing in front of a hospital cradling a baby. Lucrezia, Jamie can see, based on the picture in Zia Renata's apartment, and Jamie pulls her head back to look at him.

He nods ever so faintly, as if settling something within himself. "Lucrezia had a baby."

She waits for him to go on.

"No one actually told me this. But this is what I know."

Her heart starts beating faster.

"She gave it up for adoption."

There's a buzzing between her ears. She examines the picture more closely. Questions are forming though she refrains from speaking. She's not sure he wants her to speak. So she waits. Waits for him to take the picture from her at last, turn it over, and read the handwritten date there on the other side. It's a date Jamie must absorb for a minute. She's not good with dates, which is odd because she's good with numbers, but when it comes to remembering birthdays, she's terrible. Her sister's, her mother's, she knows the general time frame… This date, however…this birth date might as well be her own.

Calmly, ever so softly. "Did you know it was you?"

He doesn't respond. She doesn't expect him to.

Another silent minute passes. Giovanni can't seem to put the photo down, and she knows now that this is what he'd been after all along, since the beginning.

"The Chosen One," is all he says after some rumination, and Jamie knows what he is saying. What he won't say. Nor will she. There is no Ruffoli in his blood. Nonno Giacomo must have known this, and yet he left the vines and villa to Jack anyway.

They lie down on the bed. He stares at the ceiling; she, with her head on his chest, out the darkened window.

Time evaporates. His breath softens after a while. Something is releasing. In him, in her, it's as if he's breathing into her mind, her thoughts, her questions. No, no questions. She is tired of questions.

He rolls over onto his side, facing her, and pours out the contents of one of the velvet pouches between them. Two gold bands, a thick gold chain, a rosary, and a diamond ring.

He picks up the diamond ring and slips it onto her finger.

"Giorgio was with her in the end. There's comfort in that," she says quietly, staring at the ring on her finger. "They loved each other. You were born out of the most desperate of loves."

A flood to his eyes. He falls over in heaves. The sight is as shocking as it is natural. A heart ripped open, exposed. A warmth inside her. *At last.*

The heaves subside. He is lying on his side and she has wiped his tears away. The ring catches his eye again, and she holds out her hand so they can look at it together.

"May I keep it?" she asks, and he says, after a moment, that he's pretty certain that was his father's intention.

Hunger, deep and aching, overcomes them. They spend some time devouring the cheese and salami. They finish the bottle, try to sleep, unable to sleep, holding on to each other.

"Where is Puglia, anyway?" she asks sometime later into the space just below his ear.

"The heel," he says to the ceiling.

"The heel?"

He turns toward her with distant eyes, "The fucking end, Jamie."

Fireworks sound like a gang shooting. A woman paces around on the floor above them in stilettos. It's three a.m., and even with the window shut and the A/C rattling, they might as well be sleeping in the street.

"Will you go?" she whispers into the darkness, thinking of the end, of how far south one could go, would go. "To Puglia?" she adds, when he doesn't immediately answer. She assumes that, after what they have just discovered, Jack would want to go search for his father; that he would want to know the whole truth. If there was such a thing as whole truth, a reality Giovanni reminds her of now, when he digs his eyes into her soul and says from that deep, dark place of his, "This is as far south as I go."

She wakes with the sun on her back, and for a moment she's not sure where she is. All she knows is that she is alive, breathing air not ocean, for she'd spent her few sleeping hours fleeing a tidal wave, her dad with her towel somewhere, yelling I'm okay, I'm okay, I'm okay. Her eyes fixate on the light pouring through the window, until the pounding in her heart subsides. "You looked so peaceful," Jack says, bent over her now, dressed in the same shirt he'd worn when Italy beat Germany in the Semis. "I didn't want to wake you."

A ball whacks against the wall, then bounces down the street with tiny feet chasing after it. Ah, she blinks back sleepily into his eyes, but if you only knew my dreams.

She, too, slips on the shirt she'd worn when Italy beat Germany (for the odds are against them, he has warned her, and a little luck can't hurt). They go take a coffee in the hotel's postage-sized inner courtyard, fraught with all the pre-game atmosphere and hoopla. Today is THE FINAL. France. Italy. It all ends today, and she is watching him load packs of sugar into his tiny cup as if this might be the end of sugar, too. "What will we do, Jack?" She is feeling rather abstract.

He looks at her. "Pray."

"Pray for what, exactly?"

"For Italy, of course."

"Jack..."

"If Italy wins, anything's possible."

She narrows her eyes at him. "I don't think you've ever said what I've wanted you to say."

He seems pleased by this.

"It's never going to change, is it?"

He looks up at her, searching. "What's never going to change?"

"This," she responds, waving her arms around in the chasm between them.

"You're all I have." He reaches out his hand.

She takes it.

The streets are rivers of red and green flesh. They get swept up in them, downstream to Piazza del Plebicito, where all rivers converge, where she and Jack take up positions with thousands of other chain-smoking Neapolitans before a humongous screen hanging from the Palazzo Reale. Jamie isn't sure why Jack has chosen this spot to watch The Final. It is not like him to fight crowds or risk asphyxiation or not have easy access to a bathroom, but here is where they are, and it's not so bad; the crowd is dense but the people are harmless, paralyzed as they are into one collective state of silent suffering.

The game starts. If it was silent before, you can hear a pin drop now. Jamie glances at Jack, as strange to her as he's ever been, as she is to him, for while he has brought her here, it is up to her to find her way. The quiet is unbearable, until France scores, then Italy scores, and the first half ends agonizingly tied at 1-1. During the break everyone sucks desperately on cigarettes. Then the second half starts, more pin dropping silence, a communal groan or moan here and there, and after all that the half remains scoreless and the game is sent into overtime, which means thirty more minutes of hell. If it remains tied after overtime, they head into the dreaded penalty kicks for which Jack has already threatened he will leave, because he can't watch penalties. If the game was agonizing, penalties are excruciating.

The game goes into penalties.

He doesn't leave. He's in agony, but he doesn't leave.

The penalties happen fast. Then, a pause, followed by a roar so loud it makes no sound. Like a steep descent on a rollercoaster, Jamie's arms shoot up in wild abandon. On screen the players are running around the field with Italian flags draped across their gorgeous, glistening bodies. Plumes of smoke and sprays of liquid cloud the air from the popping of firecrackers and bottles of prosecco. Hands slap hands and bodies bop to the beat of Love Generation. Fireworks pour down, lighting up the bay and everyone all around them, and Giovanni, who is standing there with his head in his hands. It takes Jamie a moment to grapple with the sight, the enormity of it, and her inability to reach him as she becomes sucked farther into the sea of human bodies that has decided to move onward.

She flows with them for a little while, knowing the futility, not to mention dangers of attempting to turn around and fight the tide back to him. It has been a long journey and she is suddenly tired; she wants to sit down. She isn't sure how far she is from him now.

At some point she manages to stumble into a café, surprised and relieved to find it empty, for every last creature is outside rejoicing in this wild, infinite moment. At a table in the far back she falls into a seat, where at last she can hear the beat of her own heart, pounding from the win, the loss, all of it. Why did she let go of him? He's going to be angry that she let go, that she let herself get lost. He's going to be worried out of his mind.

She takes out her cell phone and checks the time. Counts back the hours in her head.

Her chest swells as she touches the numbers. Waiting. It's a minute before he answers. A din of people in the background, the TV, a different kind of football.

"Dad?"

FINE

Thanks to F, as always. To Mom, my reader, enthusiast, friend. And to all the Italian *cugini, zie, zii, genitori, nonni, e amici,* who always so warmly and graciously welcome me into their homes.

NY, 2013

About the Author

*J*ACKIE TOWNSEND is the author of *Reel Life,* a novel. A native of Southern California, she spends a lot of time in places not her own and blogs about belonging (or not belonging), loss, and love at jackietownsend.com.

She lives in New York City with her husband.

Made in the USA
Lexington, KY
24 March 2014